DAY ONE

ALSO BY ABIGAIL DEAN

Girl A

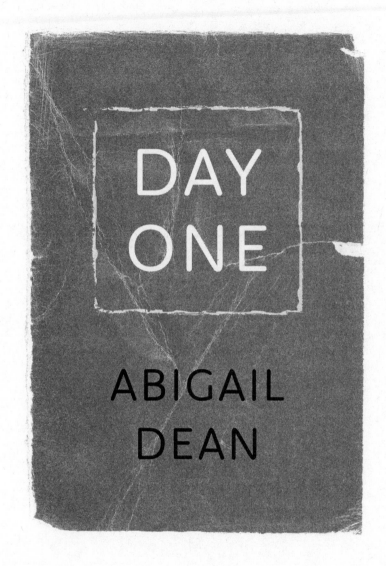

DAY ONE

ABIGAIL DEAN

VIKING

VIKING
An imprint of Penguin Random House LLC
penguinrandomhouse.com

LIBRARY OF CONGRESS CATALOGING-IN-PUBLICATION DATA
Names: Dean, Abigail, author.
Title: Day One: a novel / Abigail Dean.
Description: First edition. | New York: Viking, 2024.
Identifiers: LCCN 2023021455 (print) | LCCN 2023021456 (ebook) |
ISBN 9780593295878 (hardcover) | ISBN 9780593295885 (ebook)
Subjects: LCSH: Suburban life—Fiction. | School shootings—Fiction. |
Conspiracy theories—Fiction. | LCGFT: Thrillers (Fiction) | Novels.
Classification: LCC PR6104.E2347 D39 2024 (print) |
LCC PR6104.E2347 (ebook) | DDC 823/.92—dc23/eng/20230605
LC record available at https://lccn.loc.gov/2023021455
LC ebook record available at https://lccn.loc.gov/2023021456

Printed in the United States of America
1st Printing

Book design by Daniel Lagin

For Josh

DAY ONE

DAY ONE

AVA

She had been teaching at Stonesmere Primary School for twenty years—the headmaster had held a small, excruciating tea party in her honor—and though she would admit it only to Justin and Martha, they were her favorite class yet. They came to Ava at nine years old, with a warning from Mrs. Hutchinson, who had taught them the year before. Some of them were difficult, and some of them—and Mrs. Hutchinson leaned closer to her over the sports day scorecards and touched a finger to her lips—were a few peas short of a casserole. But Mrs. Hutchinson mixed up the children's names into spring term. She kept a Tupperware box of celery on her desk, to crunch between lessons. Ava's last class referred to her as the BUG; it was only on the last day of term that they would admit this stood for Big Unfriendly Giant.

But there had been times, in the first few months, when she wondered if Mrs. Hutchinson was right. The children arrived in her classroom in post-summer gloom, carrying the previous year's grudges. In the second week of term, Charlie Malone broke Oliver Whitfield's nose in a dispute over the under-10s football captaincy. Kit Larkin's mother had died the year before, but he talked about her all the time: every day, without fail, he raised his hand to provide his mother's view on volcanoes, long division, the Trojan War. Alicia Morden, the cleverest kid in the class, refused to raise her hand, and Ava didn't blame her; the children were ruthless. When she, Ava, had worn a multicolored dress one Monday, one of the girls on Table Windermere recoiled and said, "You look like a clown."

All autumn, it rained. They sat at their tables, half interested, smelling of wet dogs. Their anoraks left puddles on the cloakroom floor.

Well. She would not be defeated. It was Justin who suggested it, in that way he had. He would spend a whole conversation distracted by a loose tile or the Gentlemen of Stonesmere WhatsApp group, only to offer her a solution at the end of it.

Give them a little responsibility.

Her first small triumph was a Christmas play. It wasn't standard procedure. Year 5 didn't get a Christmas performance. Stonesmere Primary saved the stage for the children who were cute enough to occupy the stable, or else dependable enough to narrate. Ava overheard Mrs. Hutchinson in the staff room, commenting that some people seemed incapable of waiting their turn. They performed, stubbornly, in their own classroom, with the chairs rammed into rows and a sheet draped over the whiteboard. The windows were dark, which gave the children the thrill of knowing they should be at home. There were two shepherds, a handful of monarchs, a Wise Woman, seven angels, assorted farmyard animals, and Spider-Man. Their part: an extended rendition of "Deck the Halls." At "boughs of holly," they threw paper branches at the audience. They had glasses to clink at "fill the mead cup," and they followed one another in "merry measure" in a conga line out into the hallway, with Kit Larkin at the front, dusted in glitter, laughing so hard he could barely sing. She watched the standing ovation from her desk, her eyes blurred, her fists bunched in triumph.

———

Kit Larkin. All year, she worried about him. There had been the business with the guinea pig, of course (the less said about that, the better). But it was more than that. Each lunchtime, he hovered at the edge of the playground, his hands twitching, as if they longed for a ball to catch. When she took the class on a fishing trip to the river Eden, he was the only kid who didn't catch anything. She had given him her own trout, just so he had something in his bucket.

In January, Kit's father had come to speak to her. Sergeant Larkin appeared at the classroom door just as she was sinking into the pleasure of Friday evening. Larkin had always been kind to her; kinder than most people in town, when it came to non-natives. He had spoken to her on the sidelines of sports pitches, at the lakeside in summer; in places where she did not know how to stand or what to say. She mustered the last smile of the day and waved him in. "Make yourself at home," she said. She realized that the only adult-size chair was her own, so she ushered him to Table Bassenthwaite, to two of the little plastic seats. He was still in uniform. He wore black boots, big as skulls, and she imagined for a moment that his chair would break. The indignity of Larkin, looking up at her from the floor.

"Now, then," she said. "How can I help?"

Justin had been at school with Larkin. He remembered a loner, thin to the sinews, who spent every weekend climbing. He was the last person, Justin said, to become a policeman. Larkin was more likely to shake the criminals' hands and give them directions for the best route around the lake.

A policeman in Stonesmere, though, she said. It's mostly tourists and cows.

Larkin married the first girl who had shown him any interest, as far as Justin knew. She was in the year below at school, and barely five feet tall. She had worked at the supermarket checkout for as long as Ava could remember, perched on a cushion that she brought in from home. Larkin spent fewer weekends at Borrowdale Valley and more weekends renovating a derelict cottage, abandoned on Old Oaks Road. Ava used to see Larkin collecting his wife from the supermarket car park some evenings, his hat brushing the roof of the car and hers hidden below the headrest, so that the passenger seat appeared to be empty. Ava heard they were called Little and Large, around town. There was speculation about the mechanics of their relationship; jokes that Justin didn't laugh at, but didn't challenge, either. Once Little fell ill, the jokes stopped. At the checkout, Little was replaced by a furious woman who quashed any attempt to make conversation and threw customers' items down the conveyor belt. The cushion was gone.

Even on a Friday evening, then, Ava would listen. She would do what she could. But Larkin only held out a bunch of skew-whiff flowers and nodded.

"I wanted to thank you," he said, "for Christmas."

After Kit's mother died, the holidays had become a difficult time of year. The previous Christmas, Larkin said, there had been a conflation. The way he said *conflation*, as if he wasn't sure he had the right word, made her suspect it had come from somebody else. A psychologist, perhaps, or a counselor. Kit had become convinced that his mother was going to deliver the presents. He had addressed his Christmas wish list to her and insisted on buying a box of Ferrero Rocher, his mother's staple, to leave by the stockings.

"It isn't much stranger than the traditional version," Ava said.

"The thought of her," Larkin said, "on the sled."

He looked out over the school fields. A few errant sheep grazed beneath the football posts. Dusk had drawn over the lake. The hills were textureless and dark. When he looked back, she was braced for tears, but instead he was smiling. The smile populated the lines of his face, completing it.

"But this year . . ." he said.

This year, Kit had been occupied with rehearsals for "Deck the Halls." Whole weekends had been spent decorating his crown. He had repeated the performance, verbatim, on Christmas Day.

"He was an excellent king," Ava said.

"I was hoping there may be similar things," Larkin said, "later in the year. Similar opportunities. Theater. Stuff like that."

"Let me give it a think. We could do something at Easter, perhaps. And there'll be Day One, of course."

"Day One," Larkin said. He nodded slowly, remembering, Ava supposed, whatever his own role might have been. "Of course."

She had known of Day One from her very first year in Stonesmere. Each July, at the end of term, the eldest children in the primary school delivered a play to the four-year-olds who would join in September. This way, the headmaster explained, their first real day in school was in fact their second, and all the less frightening for that. Ava had watched her own daughter, Martha, participate in the Day One performance; and Marty, being Marty, had been placed right in the center, with several lines to roar. Justin had found a photograph of his own starring role, austere with exposure, where he staked out a similar position. You see, kid? We're the same.

Ava had not participated in Day One. Twenty-five years in town, and she was still a foreigner, exotic enough that Katie Malone had once asked about her lineage. Her lineage was Dorking and a mother she despised. She had disembarked from a bus with a backpack and half a teaching degree, and never left. She got a tip-off about a classroom assistant job from somebody leaving the YMCA, and she dropped her bag on a bunk and ambled for the school. Two months in, a carpenter was summoned to refurbish the school library, and Ava was appointed to sort through the books. She spent the week lying on the library floor in warm, dusty light, listening to Justin talk of a childhood in Stonesmere, reading to him from the same books he had read as a child. She did her very best voices.

The usual Day One fare was a performance about the town. The children would dress as mountain sprites, or lake-dwelling birds, or, reliably, tourist guides, and would lead the audience on a tour of the local landmarks. The alleys leading down to the lakeside, huddled by galleries and coffee shops. The rugby club—the reigning champions of the North West Second Division, yet again—and the civil green of the bowling lawn. Around the lake: hotels, inlets, farms, walkers descended from Old Man's Edge. Here was the crooked spire of St. Oswald's, and here were the long gardens of Lake View, Crag Brow, gardens kept by people who lived elsewhere.

Not this year.

In May, she carried one of Marty's bobble hats between the desks with twenty-one slips of paper inside it, the name of a country written on each one. The students would research their selected nation, including the capital city, population, and GDP per capita, and collect a few fascinating facts to report. Charlie traded Iceland for Alicia's China, because his dad had once flown there for work. And—when the last slip was gone, she paused, waiting for the clamor to die down—you'll have to learn how to say Welcome to Stonesmere in the local language. Charlie buried his head in his hands. We'll be presenting the results at Day One, live onstage. That was the killer. A chorus of disbelief.

They gathered around the class globe, and she let them find their countries, provided (a) one at a time, and (b) slow spinning; there was no need, Ned, to replicate the earth's actual rotation.

Kit came to her, touching her sleeve. He beckoned her down to him, secret-serious, and flashed the name of the country, hidden between his hands.

"I went there," he whispered, "with my mum."

"In that case," she said, "you'll already be an expert." And he nodded solemnly and took his seat.

On Day One, it was Kit's turn Ava was least looking forward to. She had put him in the middle of the billing. Enough time for them to get into the swing of things, but not enough time for him to lose his nerve. On the morning of the performance, the classroom was a flurry of face paint, mislaid props, costumes starting to molt. She noticed Kit for his stillness. She went to him.

"Butterflies?" she said.

He pondered. "More like caterpillars?"

"That's a much better way of putting it. They're not the most fun. But here's a secret: You should welcome them. They mean that you care."

Ten minutes before they were due to go on, she lined them up in the classroom. Composed them. They walked across the playground to the hall. Huge childish clouds passed across the sun, changing the color of the ground. They followed her up the aisle of plastic chairs, looking at their plimsolls. Once they reached the stage, their eyes roved for their parents. Even the bold—even the Charlie Malones of this world— were trembling. She had warned them that this could happen: That nerves could make a room change its size. That the hall where they gathered for PE and prizes could expand in each direction.

"By the time it's your turn," she had said, "it may be the size of a stadium."

"Old Trafford?" Kit said.

"Maybe," she said, "even bigger."

In the seconds before the performance, a jittering silence settled across the hall. There were grandmothers fumbling for tissues. There were parents squinting at digital cameras. There were siblings standing on laps, or else in high school uniform, radiating boredom and looking at their phones. And here, in front of them all, was her class, wide-eyed and gnawing at their fingers, waiting for her to speak.

She knelt down in front of them and skimmed twenty-one pairs of eyes. Ready? she said, mouthing it, her face saying: Sure you are.

The high school had donated a sixth-form student to operate the stage lights. Samuel Malone, another of the Malone dynasty, whom Ava had taught nearly a decade before. At nine, he had sat in the front row, wearing a supercilious smile and new trainers, asking questions he already knew the answers to. Now he perched over the stage, sunglasses on his head, diminished by puberty.

She nodded to Samuel. The class was lit.

On her fingers, she counted three, two, one.

Alicia Morden was up first. Alicia had no real gift for expression, but she spoke with a loud, clear voice, intended to stir the grandparents at the back of the hall.

"Bonne journée!" Alicia shouted, and that was it, they were off.

There was standing room only, now. She glanced back at the audience. She saw parents mouthing along, the lines rehearsed to memory. Even the teenagers—even the teenagers were smiling. No sign of Marty, though. Not yet. She had not expected Justin to come, of course. There was a new job—there was always a new job—requiring his attention. Mr. Stonesmere knew that you didn't turn down work; not in such a small town.

But Marty—

There was still time.

Up until a year ago, Ava would have had no doubt that Marty would be there. Had known her to the bones. She would still wake up, every now and then, and know that Marty was awake, too. She would turn on the hall light as a kind of signal and wait for Marty to join her in the kitchen. She had been the kind of mother who said things like: We don't have secrets in this family.

And for a long time, she had been right.

There was sweat in the creases of her knees and in the folds under her breasts. The fire door to the left of the stage was closed. She'd been sure—sure that was open. She waved to Mr. Heron at the end of the front row. She pointed to the escape and fanned herself, and he nodded and crept to the door.

Jules got Germany. She carried a pretzel. Ava had spent a month imploring Jules to speak louder, slower; to pretend she was delivering her lines back to shore from a boat in the middle of the lake. "Willkommen in Stonesmere," Jules bellowed, and Ava covered her smile. She would miss them. She usually did. Another little band of humans, marching from her classroom. She had seen them five days a week for the last year. That had to count for something. Didn't it? Or maybe Ava was becoming old and sentimental, just as Marty said she was. She looked down the row of children, each of them ten years old—they had celebrated every birthday with a cake bought by Ava, so there could be no cake hierarchy; she still remembered, with some sadness, the day Leah Perry had brought in an out-of-date Victoria Sponge—and thought of them in a decade's time, older and smarter, smarmier and sadder. Giving their parents hell. There were days when she hated Stonesmere, but she liked that it was small enough to run into her students years—Christ, decades—later. She would see them a foot taller, trailing their parents around the supermarket; or else working their first jobs, saving to Interrail the summer they left high school. They would stop and say hello, and although she would feign irritation—it would be nice to make it out and back without hearing "Mrs. Ward"—she left the conversations burning with a fierce pride.

China, now. They were on a roll. She saw Kit's hands starting to twist. Nearly up. She tried to catch his eye, to pull a stupid face, but he was looking at the ground. From the doors there was the sound of metal on stone, loud enough that a few of the students onstage glanced that way. Mr. Heron was wrestling with the fire escape, red-faced and baffled.

She heard something behind her then, a stirring, and glanced down the aisle. A man stood at the threshold of the hall doors, at the very back of the room, with a tripod in his hands. There was something over his face, a hat of some sorts. She gave Charlie Malone a thumbs-up, a Keep Going, despite the distraction. If this is the photographer, she thought, then we won't be using him again.

She thought: What a dick.

Charlie gave a flourish of a bow, and Ava rolled her eyes. There was one in every class, and it was usually the parents' fault. Kit stepped forward.

He did not speak. His composure was replaced by confusion. He stared past her, to the back of the hall.

She followed his eyes, craning back past lenses and smiles, assembling a scowl. What was it? Some overzealous grandparent, bursting from their seat. That photographer, still fumbling in the aisle. As she turned there was the noise of it, a crack to the eardrum, and when she looked back to the stage, the children's faces were changed.

The man she had thought was the photographer still stood at the back of the hall. But the object in his hands was not a tripod. It was held to his shoulder, and he stared down its barrel. He aimed over the audience, at the stage. He wore a helmet with the visor pulled down over his eyes. He reloaded, turned to his left, and fired across the audience members in the aisle seats, some of them still sitting, some of them just beginning to stand.

Her knees buckled. She looked around to find Marty. Marty, who had promised to come. Marty, who had sat at the kitchen table and said: Sure. Instead, she was confronted with a wall of faces, wide-eyed and desperate, all civility gone. She tried to move against them, and then she was on the floor, beneath shoes. People lay in the aisle, unmoving or scrambling. Others gathered chairs around them, as if they would build a fort. Deep from the chaos came the sound of the gun, too loud to place. The noise reverberated in the pit of her, shaking her organs.

From between chairs she saw the children, cluttered in terror on the stage.

Well, then.

Get up.

YEAR EIGHT

MARTY

ong after I left Stonesmere, people asked about the Stonesmere Massacre, and if they didn't ask, they wanted to. I would hand over my passport or fill in my hometown on some form or other. There—there it was. A solemn double take, as if the town might have left something on my face. At a hotel reception desk, a woman laid her hand over mine and said just how sorry she was. At some miserable team-building day, silence rippled across the circle of chairs. At an empty bar, the tender squinted at my ID and let out a long, low whistle. "Did you know anyone?" he said, and I shook my head and ordered another round.

It still surprised me: not just that he was disappointed, but that he didn't try to hide it.

So I should have been ready. It was only a matter of time. In truth, I had become complacent. After the inquest, I bought a new phone. I no longer searched for my name online. I kept my hair short and blunt. I moved about the confines of a small, predictable life. The flat, hemmed in by identical other flats. The bar, squint-dark, where I wore the same black uniform as all the other girls. The company of my radios, beside the bed and at the kitchen window. The rocking of the Underground carriage, where it was neither day nor night, but always bright and loud: where few people looked up from their phones.

The night it happened, there were delays.

I was in a taxi, somewhere in the bowels of the city, at the end of a late shift. I watched the lights of the buildings, the names of the streets, one postcode flitting to the next. The driver watched me. He was talking about the state of the roads, about traffic and apps, but all the while he watched. In the mirror, his face was curious, then triumphant. Stopped at lights, he turned in his seat.

"I feel," he said, "like I know you."

There was a time when I smiled easily, and this was the smile I delivered. The stuff of winning goals and school tours. My manager had long advised me that I should smile more. It might never happen, he said.

"One of those faces," I said.

"Did you grow up here?" the driver said. He gestured to a concrete slab, ragged with scaffolding. I was tired, I suppose. Tired and proud. I wanted to hear how beautiful it was. How wonderful it must have been—to grow up somewhere like that.

"No," I said. I closed my eyes and waded into the cool of the lake. I did this, sometimes. I had not been back to Stonesmere for several years, but I revisited the place all the time. I would climb into bed anticipating it, savoring the arrival of its colors. Today, I would decide, it will be winter: and there were the Christmas windows, dusted in snow spray, enclosing angels and stables. There were the tourists, lifting baubles or candles, as if they could take a little of our warmth home with them.

"I grew up in the north," I said. "The Lakes."

"The Lakes. Whereabouts?"

"Stonesmere," I said.

"Stonesmere."

"Yes."

The lights had changed, but there was nobody behind us. The driver's face squeezed between the seats, bulging with interest.

"I hear," he said, "that it didn't happen the way they said it did."

And my face was still pleasant enough, I knew, although inside was the old terror, a long-dormant organ beginning to churn.

"I don't know about that," I said.

"The shooter was framed," the driver said. "That's what I hear."

I said nothing.

"If it even happened," the driver said. "Who knows?"

He turned back to the road.

"They just released that kid," the driver said. "That's what I read. The kid who exposed them." He paused triumphantly and drummed his palm on the wheel. "About time."

When I clambered from the taxi I could feel his eyes still on me, impaled in my back. I climbed the shabby staircase and walked along the terrace, past the doors of strangers. Lights were coming on across the building, and within them, people moved hesitantly into the day.

I didn't sleep much at night. I was allocated the latest shift, cash-up and clean-up, and I returned home on the first tube. It mattered little if the bar was busy or quiet. The sign outside said that we closed at four a.m., and that was what I did. The manager called me a glutton for punishment, but I enjoyed the little tasks. Polishing glasses, counting notes. The manager trusted me, he said, because I was unremarkable. He said this on the phone to his girlfriend, who was also a bartender; who was, in comparison, extremely remarkable. This, he explained to her, was why I was better suited to lates. Early in the morning, I would return to the little flat and settle at the table to eat breakfast. I would fall asleep to the noises of footsteps outside the door, traffic slow on the road beneath the building.

That morning, I prepared toast and tea and sat with my phone face down on the kitchen table. When I had seen the flat, the estate agent had explained that the table could be folded out for hosting. For hosting: I enjoyed that.

I took the tea to bed and set my phone on the stool I used as a bedside table, and I tried to summon Stonesmere. The lake, Crag Brow—any of it. But the town was elusive. The streets were incomplete. The mattress came with me, embedded in my spine. After half an hour, I picked my phone back up. I had to brace myself before I entered his name, knowing that his face would appear many times over. There were still people who believed him to be a martyr for the truth. The poor bastard. The taxi driver's hero: the kid who exposed them. I would have liked to read the letters he received. I could imagine the exact satisfaction of his face, sitting on the terrible bed, opening them. When he was sentenced, I spent a lot of time reading about the prison. I read abandoned blogs and advice for visitors. I searched for photographs of the rooms. I liked to picture him, I suppose. I read that he spent twenty-two and a half hours a day in the cell, and that internet access was limited.

The driver was right. There was a news story at the top of the search page, a new addition, and the blood paused in my veins.

They had included a photograph I had never seen. He stood holding a scrap of paper and a prison official's hand. He had pioneered a prison newspaper. His smile was perfectly timid. He wore a suit that made him look like a child at a wedding. He had behaved himself.

As of last week, he was a free man.

It was another thing I should really have been ready for.

Outside, the traffic was moving. Rush hour almost done. The engines roared into rotor blades. The town emerged through summer haze. Not here, I thought. Not this. But it was too late. The bedroom was falling away. The shift smells subsided, unsettled by the wind from the lake. I was already back in the playground, and running.

DAY ONE

MARTY

passed the hopscotch, climbing frame, goalposts chalked on the wall. I passed the first huddles of police, gathered helmeted and armed in the shadow of the school. They gestured to me to move, move, to get out of the way. The hall was long behind me, looking as it always did, still and placid, a place for hymns, exams, gym. "Are you hurt?" somebody said, and I shook my head and kept running. In the car park there were others, cowered behind tires, fled from the hall. They clutched at their bodies, shrinking against the rubber. I stopped at the first vehicle and held to the bonnet. I could see myself in the windscreen, and I checked my face, peering for the features, expecting to find the morning engraved on my face. Instead, I looked ordinary, vacant. I adjusted my ponytail, collar, scraped makeup from below my eyes. The school gates were open. I walked through them and out onto Old School Road.

Drive Slowly for Our Children.

It was still early, and where the trees shaded the road, the air was cool. Police cars were abandoned at angles, like toys left by a child. I was already seen. The people of Stonesmere were gathering halfway down the road, pressed back behind police tape like runners at the beginning of some ragged, desperate race. My skirt had stuck to my thighs, and I plastered it back down and walked toward them, one of the last stragglers, staggering from the school.

If you grew up in Stonesmere, you went to Stonesmere Primary School. I knew it better than most: had spent seven years careening through the bright corridors, and seven more sitting under the Star Board in the foyer, waiting for my mother to finish work. She was always late. There was always a painting to Blu Tack, a parent to appease. Whenever the headmaster saw me, he stopped to talk. He asked about this friend or that; he asked how football was going. More recently, he asked about my plans. He was sure—quite sure—that I was destined for great things. On his more sentimental days, he pointed to the cabinet outside his office and gave me a knowing smile. He'd had lighting installed beneath the trophies, and I could make out several bearing my name.

There was a line of police officers quelling the crowd. Somebody pointed to me, and a policeman turned to watch me come, waiting with his arms spread and his face contorted with pity.

"Were you in there?" he said. "My God. She was in there."

I couldn't speak. There was a commotion at the front of the crowd, a woman on her knees and howling. She was older than my mother, with beige tights and a brooch pinned to her dress. Katie Malone. She had three sons; she would tell you that before she told you her name. I ducked beneath the cordon and into the crowd. "Wait," the policeman said, but his voice was lost beneath the wailing, the noises of sirens and children. The tarmac had torn bloody ladders into Katie Malone's stockings, and the policeman went to lift her.

Like the rest of us, she had dressed that morning for a different occasion.

I couldn't recall my mother's outfit, and I assumed that was why it was so difficult to find her. The details were flustered by panic. She would be wearing something beautiful: this, I knew. Her wardrobe was a bazaar, spilling with silks and lace. There was always a ruffle or a feather peeking between the doors. And so it was strange, because she should—

She should have been easy to find.

She would be at the heart of things. Calming her class or else cradling a stranger. She would be holding a small child in her arms, telling a tall story.

Instead, I saw Mrs. Hutchinson, her head above the crowd, her hands pressed like delicacies against her lips. I saw my dad's school friends— men who had bought me early drinks; men who had sought me out after football games and congratulated me with fond hands—gathering their families in their arms, and turning, sheepish, away. I saw Leah Perry's mother in Lakeview Hotel uniform, the white apron and the embarrassment of frills, standing with her troupe of children. Recognition eased her face. I hadn't seen her in years, and I was surprised she still knew me. She would have last seen me standing at her door, ten or eleven, hoping to avoid her cramped little lounge.

"My mum," I said. "Have you—"

"Not yet, Martha," Leah's mother said. "Not yet."

She pointed to the police hats, bobbing over the crowd.

"We're all still waiting," she said, which wasn't true, because Leah's mother was surrounded by children. Because Leah had been working the breakfast shift at the Boaters. Because her whole family was accounted for.

I was so cold. I wore a tennis skirt and a thin T-shirt. In some other life, I was on the courts, lining up the eleven-year-olds, reminding them how to hold their racquets. A policewoman offered me a silver blanket, something from a spacecraft, and I wrapped it around my shoulders and continued to walk. People were moving in the opposite direction, hurrying, all of them going toward the school. Their faces were stunned and unspeakable. They wore the vestiges of ordinary mornings, Lycra and dressing gowns, cheeks still imprinted with bedsheets. A man clipped me as he went, and I ended up on the ground. I caught a flash of his panic, eyes wild. Other than the trees, the footsteps, there was a terrible silence. I sat on the road and watched the people pass, heading to where I'd come from. I didn't think I could get back up again.

Two students from the high school trotted past, wet-eyed with the thrill of it. "It was a bomb," one of them said.

"If it was a bomb, why are we going closer?"

They clutched at each other, pleasure in their hysteria. They spared me a glance. It was a sight to behold, I guess. Martha Ward, prostrate on the concrete, tangled in a space blanket. If I could have stood, I would have mutilated them. Would have stamped their jaws to the curb. I reached a hand to the road and tried to get up, but my body was trembling, disobedient. Another of the runners stumbled over me, caught my shin with his shoe. He righted himself and continued down the road, and I sat back down.

"Darling," somebody said, just above me. "Oh, darling. Are you all right?"

A shadow fell over my face. There were two of them, a woman and a man, and a great rectangular eye poised between them.

"That's her," the man said. "That's her. She came from the hall."

"Here," the woman said. "Let me help."

She was smiling. She had too many teeth. She reached for my elbow and helped me to my feet, and it was only when I was standing that I understood they had a camera, tilted expectantly over the man's shoulder, waiting for me to talk.

"Now, tell me," the woman said. "Tell me. We saw you. You came from the hall."

The whole town had seen me running from the scene. That was where I had come from. Wasn't it? The school hall.

I was nodding. In my head there was a void of panic.

"Are you able to tell us," the woman said, "what happened?"

From the past hour there came scraps of light and noise. The movement of the doors, swinging in the wind. The things in the aisle. Legs of chairs, bodies. Small shoes. The stealthy movement of liquid on wood. A cheerful, expectant humming, which I realized—in time—to be the ringing of mobile phones.

"What happened," the woman said, "in that hall?"

My memories trembled. I reassembled the room, just as it should have been. Gathered the children back to the stage. Put the chairs back in place. Dried the floor. Tucked phones back into pockets, handbags, palms. There I was, in the heart of the audience, with my mother's hand in mine.

"It was Day One," I said. "It's an annual thing. At the primary school."

The woman looked at me the way everybody likes to be looked at: as if all she wanted to do was listen to me talk. She touched my shoulder, ever so gentle, and held her microphone to my mouth.

If you had asked me, the day after it happened, I wouldn't have been able to recall what I said. The journalist thanked me. She wished me well. She left me standing embarrassingly alone, the blanket tangled around my shins. I don't remember how long I stood there. Nobody was running by then. Stillness stretched from the school and down the road. The police lights were still turning, but there was no need for sirens.

That was where my father found me. He ran differently from the rest of them; ran, as he always did, as if he was in the midst of a race. He already knew some of it. I could tell that right away. There was no discernible line or expression, but his face had changed. The blanket crunched between us. He lifted me into his arms, and my trainers left the ground.

"Were you there?" he said. "God, Marty. Are you OK?"

I nodded.

"Where is she, then?" he said. "Where is she?"

"I didn't—I didn't see—"

"You didn't see if she got out?"

And when I said nothing: "Let's go find her."

We walked back toward the school with our arms locked around each other, like we were running the three-legged dads-and-daughters race. Like we were winning. People greeted my dad as we came. Even then, they liked him to notice them. He offered a series of solemn smiles. He parted the crowd with his height. When I was seven years old, in Mrs. Hutchinson's class, we had to write a piece about My Hero, and among the Ronaldos and the Mandelas, I wrote about him. That's embarrassing enough, I suppose, but what's worse is that even then, at nineteen, crushed to his chest, I was sure nothing bad could happen if he was there.

Later, we were gathered outside a white tent, assembled by the police in the school car park. I had seen other tents, closer to the hall, and the people entering those tents wore strange plastic suits and avoided our eyes. I didn't know what time it was, only that the crowd had thinned. Children had emerged throughout the day, led by police officers and reclaimed fiercely by their families. I wore my dad's coat, and he held me against his body. He held me a little tighter whenever the tent flap moved. A tired man emerged at irregular intervals and said a family name each time. Larkin. Whitfield. I was thinking of reality television, of groups summoned into different rooms to hear their fate. Their fate was that they would sing for another week, perhaps, or be flown to Spain to cook an elaborate six-course meal.

Once a family was inside the tent, they did not emerge again.

"It's OK," my dad said, every now and then. "It's OK."

Somebody had scraped Katie Malone from the tarmac, and she was waiting, too. I focused on not crying. I hadn't cried, at that time, for a good few months, not since everything that happened back in the spring. I had started to consider it something of a record.

When there were very few people left, the tired man drew back the tarpaulin and called for "Ward."

"It's OK," my dad said.

He took my shoulder. He walked us forward. The stupid tears were already here, muddling my way. I saw the officer's face as the curtain fell behind him, and I knew. This was the elimination room. We would not fly to Spain. We would not last the week. A gunman had attacked Stonesmere Primary School that morning, the officer said, and Ava Ward was believed to be one of the victims.

"I'm so very sorry," the officer said. He must have said the line many times that day, and still he played his part well, with grace.

"Can we see her?" my dad said. "In the hospital?"

My dad: this wasn't a role he knew. For fifty-one years he had been cast as the winner. He'd established a carpentry business the same year Stonesmere was named the UK's Prettiest Town by VisitBritain. Five years later, he'd won a contract to install oak flooring at a development of twenty-two luxury second homes just off Lake View. Famously, he scored the last-minute winning try for Stonesmere's First XV in the Northern Combined Divisions Charity Cup. And now—now he was here, in the losers' tent, with Larkin and the Malones.

The officer gave me a quick look, as if I might be the one to do it. I was looking at my dad: saw the exact moment his life changed. Whenever I think about Day One, this is the worst part. I'd remember it at first because I couldn't remember anything else; and later I'd remember to try to dull it, as if in practicing the remembering, I could deprive it of its importance and stop thinking about it altogether.

It never worked. When I remembered this part, it always hurt. It wasn't the mortification of my own sadness, but bearing witness to his.

DAY ONE

TRENT

When Stonesmere happened, he was living at Tim's house. He was sitting on the guest bed with his back to the wall. He was the first awake, and he had made it to the kitchen and back without having to talk to anybody. There was a plate of toast on the duvet, teetering next to his laptop, his phone, a book of local photography.

Trent was working on his latest article, which was entitled "The Dead Sea." "The Dead Sea" described the decline of the UK's seaside towns over the past forty years. Trent had spoken to the men straggled along the seafront, had visited their stained mattresses and shopping trolleys. He had interviewed an arcade manager and the owner of Smugglers World. He had quoted his mother, incensed by second homes and their architectural mishaps, as an anonymous source. Before Tim, he and his mother had lived over in Fairlight Cove, in a bungalow outnumbered by solar-paneled boxes. She was Trent's first and most loyal reader.

Trent had submitted the article to twenty online papers, and now he was incorporating early feedback. The feedback tended to focus on the article's length, which, at fifteen thousand words, had been described by editors, in turn, as ambitious, challenging, and unpalatable.

"I don't know about that," his mother said. "I think it's wonderful." She touched his laptop screen with a glossy nail, where he had recorded her words. There were many things his mother could do—charm a teacher, hold court at the golf club, remove a stain from just about anything—but her writing was slow and labored, and in Christmas cards, beneath the printed greeting, she wrote only her own name. "I sound terrifying," she said. "Don't I?"

Ever since he could remember, Trent had wanted to be a journalist. When he was sixteen, he created a school newspaper, the *Daily Stun*. He was assisted by the Head of English, who had some long-standing grudge with the headmistress, some business about a book banned from the library many years before, and was overjoyed at the opportunity to cause a little disruption.

Against all odds—the headmistress's extensive censorship program, the abominable school printers—the *Daily Stun* had a successful two-year circulation. Trent was polite and inconspicuous enough to get away with articles that might, under another editor, have been construed as rebellion. He had arrived at that particular school at thirteen, halfway through the spring term, and his backstory preceded him. The period before he was introduced, his form teacher informed the class that Trent's father had died, abroad and in service, so everybody needed to be extra, especially nice to him. It was his fourth school. He knew what to do. He walked down the corridors with a nonchalant face and his shoulders back. When people asked about his dad, he told variations of what his mother had said to him, with fewer tears and more guns.

The *Daily Stun*'s greatest scoop was the discovery that school lunch was provided by a disgraced contractor that had once been found to add horsemeat to hamburgers. It was a discovery made by Trent himself, who noticed the branded truck parked outside the cafeteria early one morning. The *Sussex Express* picked up the story, and Trent spoke on the phone to its editor, Arthur Manning, who congratulated him on his audacity. Trent could hear Arthur smoking between sentences, imagined him sitting in a wood-paneled study, encased by books and liquor. When the *Express* was printed, Trent's mother bought five copies. At the end of the article: *This story was first broken by Trent Casey of the* Daily Stun.

He had been early at school because his mother had started dating Tim, who would sometimes materialize at their breakfast table wearing a terrible dressing gown. The *Daily Stun* was a refuge of sorts. Trent had wrangled an old broom cupboard in the English block for the newspaper office, and sometimes he worked there long before the first bell and after the last, until the corridor light beneath the door had slipped away.

At Tim's house, Trent lived in a cream room, with fat pillows and towels of different sizes. Other than the bath towel, he didn't know what anybody would do with them. Trent's mother liked to use this room as evidence Tim liked him, but Trent noticed that Tim only ever referred to it as the guest room. Like: Will you be joining us for breakfast today, Trent, or lurking in the guest room? Tim didn't believe in privacy. He believed in open doors, good manners, family meals. He believed in keeping Trent's mother in beautiful dresses, in good shape, in close proximity.

"I see," Tim said, "that you've already helped yourself."

He stood at the bedroom door. Trent didn't look up from his article, but he could feel Tim's smile, peering over the screen.

"On days like this, Trent," Tim said, "it feels like we should all be together."

Tim liked nothing more than knowing something before anybody else. Trent glanced around his laptop.

"I'm sorry?" he said.

"Oh, Trent. You must have heard."

Trent opened a new browser window. There were already live feeds on the news websites. Politicians tweeted condolences. A police officer stood before a thicket of microphones, close to tears. There were photographs of people running, their arms held aloft. In one photograph he could see the lake, a glimpse of blue beyond the school fields.

"Your mother's been beside herself," Tim said. He had been comforting her all morning, of course. He comforted her in their palatial bedroom, looking over the old town. There were three spare rooms in the house, but Trent had been consigned to the only one that shared a wall with the master bedroom. At night, he played white noise from his phone.

"Stonesmere," Tim said. "Of all places."

He gave Trent a careful, tender frown.

"I should go now," he said. "I should be with your mother."

Stonesmere. It was the first place they had lived after his father died, when they were still reeling. When his mother still disappeared in the middle of sentences. When she spent most of her time on a message board for widowed military wives. When he still harbored quiet hopes of his father appearing at his classroom door, the way it happened on YouTube videos, to surprise him on his birthday.

He remembered little of the fabled beauty of Stonesmere. They had lived in a pebble dash house far from the lake. The house was usually cold. There was a vague impression of mountains, crowding the town like vultures. Of all the schools he attended, this was the hardest to crack. There were old orders in place, students whose parents had known one another since their own school days. People had hobbies he hadn't even heard of, canyoning and wakeboarding. Newcomers were as good as tourists. He spent many lunchtimes alone, perfecting a nonchalant expression. His mother worked at a café called the Teapotter, where the drinks were named after local writers. She had to wear a jaunty white hat with a teacup on the top of it. He found it one evening, the handle poking from her handbag, and turned it in his hands. She had never shown it to him herself. Had never once forgotten to take it off.

He spent the rest of the day reading the news on his laptop. The reporters seized the gristle they could find and chewed it. The bones of the story were close. They knew the shooter was a white male. They had devised graphics, demonstrating his route. They interviewed bewildered residents, who had not believed that such a thing could happen there.

At each quarter of the hour, they showed a girl, wandering from the scene with a foil blanket around her shoulders. She was angular and tanned and older than any of the children who were unaccounted for. She wore a short skirt, and her makeup was careful, crisp. She looked dead at the camera. If you watched enough times, you could see the reporter's delight, the glint of it when the girl stopped. "Now, tell me," the reporter said. She was solemn and sorry. She was pursuing the truth, but really: it pained her to do so. "Tell me. We saw you. You came from the hall."

He paused the video just as the girl opened her mouth. On the screen, he touched her face. Eyes wide, lips parted. He had the feeling he had seen her before, although he couldn't think of her name. Had only the strange sense of knowing her: could anticipate what her voice would sound like, just before she spoke. A school celebrity, perhaps. Every year had one. Those girls, who everybody wanted to know.

Over dinner, it was all Tim wanted to talk about. He sat at the head of the table, making pronouncements. Trent had passed whole evenings trying to catch his mother's eye, trying to cajole her into a new alliance. She remained disappointingly neutral.

"They're saying eleven people now," Tim said. "Eleven."

They had started to introduce the dead. Whenever Trent checked the news, the collage of victims was reshaped again, to fit in another face.

"Did you read," Tim said, "about the teacher?"

"No," Trent said.

"She was shielding the children," Tim said. "Under the stage, or somewhere. That's how they found her—" He shook his head. He ate his last mouthful of pie and lined up his knife and fork together. "What a thing," he said.

"There are always heroes," Trent's mother said. "That's what you see on days like this, isn't it? The good of the world."

"I don't know about that," Trent said.

"It could have been you," Trent's mother said. "It could have been us."

"If it had happened—what? Ten years earlier?"

"You know," Tim said, "what your mother means."

"We went to a performance there," Trent's mother said. "At the primary school. A kind of welcome show."

"I don't remember much," Trent said, "about that year."

He glanced at Tim.

"Other than Dad," he said. "Obviously."

His father sat in the final chair at the table, bleeding into the upholstery.

"Anyway," Tim said, "this teacher. This poor woman—the saddest thing is, there was an interview going around, earlier today, with this woman's daughter. Lead clip on every channel. She must have been there to watch this performance, whatever it was. In there, when the whole thing happened. They caught her just outside the hall, and she's talking about gunfire, and running, and saying she doesn't know where her mother is, she doesn't know if she got out. They've stopped showing it now, of course. Out of respect. Can you imagine?"

"I think I saw that," Trent said. "That video."

"Lovely looking girl," Tim said. "Poor thing."

He stood from the table, although Trent was still eating.

"I suppose that you'll write something, will you," Tim said. "On your little blog?"

The *Daily Stun* was still active. There had been no one at school enthusiastic enough to take it on, and so when Trent graduated, he took the newspaper with him. The *Daily Stun* was now online only, consisting of articles written by Trent that hadn't been picked up elsewhere. He expected that it would eventually host "The Dead Sea," although he hoped, still, that it might find a grander home. Every now and then, Tim opened the *Daily Stun* on his work laptop and read extracts from Trent's articles in a grandiose voice, a voice that would have made any article in the world sound embarrassing.

"It depends if I have anything interesting to say," Trent said, and Tim snorted. Trent could hear him in the living room, assembling himself in the armchair; then the noise of the television, of stern newscasters and speculating psychologists. The noise of shooting, captured on a mobile phone. Some viewers may find this footage disturbing. After a few minutes, his mother stood from the table and shut the kitchen door, and they sat together, the two of them, listening to each other eating.

DAY TWO

MARTY

The phone calls started just after midnight. By then, our number was on the forums. It was plucked from my dad's website, copied to Contacts and notepads. The ringing invaded the quiet of the house, down its corridors, into its crevices. It found us in our bedrooms, alone and awake.

I hadn't tried to sleep. Every time I lay down, panic crushed my chest. I sat with my back to the bed, surveying the room. The house made its usual noises. Plastic stars glowed from my ceiling, stars I'd been meaning to remove for some years. On my desk was the usual scatter of makeup, pens, a digital camera, a book lent by Leah and long forgotten. And yet none of it was familiar. It seemed, that first night, that it all belonged to somebody else.

I was glad of the ringing. It was a reason to leave the room. I hurried down the hallway, took the stairs two at a time. It had been a mistake, after all. She'd found a passage beneath the stage. No: she'd hidden within a treasure chest, left over from last year's performance of *Treasure Island*. She'd been waiting until she knew it was safe.

"Martha," somebody said. "Is that Martha Ward?"

"Yes. Hi."

"I'm calling," the man said, "to offer my condolences."

"Thank you," I said. How polite: Thank you.

"How are you doing, Martha?"

"I'm OK," I said. "Thanks." My dad was on the stairs. He came befuddled to the bottom and reached for the phone.

"I'm sorry," I said, "but who is this?"

"I'm helping to tell the story of Stonesmere, Martha. Martha, what was it like, being in that room? Did you see—did you see the shooter's face?"

I clutched for the hallway table and upended the bowl of keys. A pair missing now. Somewhere—in the hall, perhaps, or in a sealed plastic bag—there must be her purse. A small world of tissues, change, mints, lipsticks molded to the contours of her mouth. It felt good, recalling these trinkets. It felt good not to think about the shooter's face.

"Martha," the caller said. "Are you still there?"

My dad took the receiver and listened for a moment. "It's very late," he said. "Please—call us back tomorrow."

The next time it rang, I heard my dad's door. His footsteps were quick down the stairs. I found him there in the morning, dull-eyed, with the phone off the hook. "Nine calls," he said. "Nine calls, before I shut them down. Can you believe it?"

"Not really," I said. "No."

"One of them," my dad said, "was just some woman, rambling. A Stonesmere number, too. It's sent people doolally, Marty. I don't understand it."

"What number?" I said. "Dad?"

But he was already lumbering off into the kitchen. He stood, bewildered, at the island. A new frontier: cupboards, drawers, tools. He found the cafetière and scrutinized it like an artifact just unearthed.

"Dad?" I said. "This woman. What did she say?"

"We need coffee," he said. "Don't we?" And, as if it was nothing more than an unfortunate omission: "Nobody's made the coffee."

When my mother was killed, I was still a terrible optimist. My grandfather had died the year before, a Stonesmere native, a man who had propped up the bar at the Boaters for more than seventy years. I knew what grief was. It was lasagna and gift cards. It was an open house and friends in the garden. On the second day, I opened my wardrobe and dressed for the mourners. Black sweater, tartan skirt (and the way she waited on the other side of the curtain, ready to help with a strap or a zip; her face, when I emerged, more telling than any changing room mirror). I cobbled together dips from the fridge (here, see. You squeeze the lemon into your palm, and you catch the pips). I unlocked the front door (stepped over her shoes in the hallway: flat, bright, impractical. A stubborn quirkiness to them, which meant I sometimes kicked one beneath the hallway table as I passed).

I was ready to welcome them in.

But the only person who visited, that second day, was Leah Perry.

I watched her coming up from Crag Brow, her arms full of flowers. The steady, ponderous gait. With each step, she studied the drive ahead, as if she didn't quite trust that it would hold her. The seconds before the doorbell rang seemed endless, sitting on my bed in my uncomfortable outfit, wondering if she'd abandoned the flowers and let us be. Until then, I hadn't realized just how much I wanted to see her.

I spent a little time getting to the door, as if I might have been occupied with other guests.

Leah had been crying. I could see that right away. "God, Marty," she said. She held out the flowers with a kind of wince, as if somebody else had insisted she bring them along. "Thank you," I said. I hated her a little, for the tears. I was thinking of her mother behind the cordon, crowded by children. Leah: Leah had not been waiting outside that tent. It was unfair, of course. There were already news anchors crying for us, members of the public, people who knew the town only as a pretty place for a holiday. There was already a pyre of soft animals stacked at the town sign. And Leah had loved my mother. It was my mother, after all, who had first decided we should be friends.

She looked beyond me, as if to check that the hallway was clear. My dad was in the shower, because you have to keep a routine, Marty. You have to eat.

"I don't know what to say," Leah said.

"The flowers," I said. "They're nice."

"I drove into Penrith. The shops today—none of them are open. The whole town—it's just media. I got asked five times, just on the way here. If I wanted to talk."

She reached for the doorframe. "They've got the names," she said. "Your mum. Samuel, Samuel's in the hospital, they don't know if he'll make it. Kit—God. Kit Larkin."

The faces people have, when they're just about to cry—there's something of the child in them, if you know them well enough. I could see Leah at twelve years old, through the glass of a classroom door, when Amber Blackley decided to lock her out for the lunch hour. I kept wishing Leah would lope away to the library, make less of a big deal about it, but instead she waited in the corridor, her face looming and disappointed through the window. We had her bag—in the classroom, I mean—and for weeks after, I kept wondering what was in it that she needed so badly. Tampons, perhaps. Her glasses. I couldn't sleep, just thinking about it.

"The murderer," Leah said. "They have his name, too, Marty. Did you—"

I suppose there was something in my face that stopped her asking it, a kind of pleading. Whatever it was, it worked.

"Have you spoken with them, Marty?" she said instead.

"To who?"

"To the police."

"Only yesterday," I said. "When they told us—"

I shook my head.

"I'm sure they'll have questions," I said.

"Especially," Leah said, "after your interview."

She was looking at my feet, bare and vulnerable on the welcome mat. The nails were grubby from the lake bed, the garden. I'd need to find shoes, the next time the doorbell went.

"You saw that?" I said.

"Everybody saw that, Marty."

It was a little like waking up after a terrible night: one of the nights at the Boaters that descended to a fire at the lakefront and ended in the house of somebody you didn't know. That feeling that it might have been you this time: disclosing secrets, or captured on a phone, incoherent or half dressed. The feeling that you had been caught doing something terrible, humiliating; something that you couldn't really remember.

Although, as it happened, it had never before been me.

"Why did you do it?" Leah said. "Why did you say—"

"I think it was the shock," I said. "I saw it. What happened. In the hall."

"God, Marty."

"They asked me if I'd come from there. And then—"

"It's OK," Leah said. "You just need to tell them. You need to tell them the truth. You need to tell them everything you know."

I saw my hand reach from my side, extend toward her. A little betrayal of the body, weary with a night of no sleep. I managed to stop it on the doorframe. "Marty," she said again. If she stayed another minute, I knew I would say something awful, imploring. Tell me what to do. Tell me what to say. Her face was insufferable with sympathy.

"There are things I need to do," I said, "before everyone else arrives."

No lasagna; no gift cards. I took the stairs to my bedroom two at a time. The press were in Stonesmere; the interview was public. Leah's flowers trembled in my hands. I surveyed my gadgets, clothes, papers, bedding. I had squinted through enough magnifying glasses to know that each object could hold its own little version of the truth, and I knelt in the mess of them and started to sort.

I met Leah Perry twelve years before, when she joined my class at Stonesmere Primary School. Leah was a little like a new chair or a classroom cabinet: for a long time, people barely noticed she had arrived. She was the kid at the end of the lunch table, holding a book in front of her face, trying to prove she didn't mind sitting alone. She clung to the edges of conversation, trying to prize her way in. When letters went out to parents informing them there was a nit outbreak, it was decided that Leah Perry was probably patient zero. She was picked last in PE and last for British Bulldog at break time. My mother asked me to imagine what it would feel like, standing there, squirming. Imagine it, Marty. This was the same year I was immortalized by a formal amendment to the Cumbria Football Youth League Rules, which have, ever since, allowed any one boy *or girl*, having displayed exceptional and consistent ability, to be crowned Player of the Season.

It would feel pretty awful, I admitted. But there was little I could do about it.

"You could pick her first," my mother said. As if it was that simple.

It was my mother who invited Leah over. We must have been nine or ten then. She spoke to Mrs. Perry and arranged for Leah to visit one Sunday, when her mother worked a double shift at the Lakeview Hotel. Yes, Leah's other siblings were welcome. My mother would keep an eye on them, so the girls could have their fun.

"It's an hour, Marty," she said. It was an hour I'd been intending to spend with my dad, watching Sunday-afternoon sport in the rugby club bar. I was a mascot, of sorts. I had a regular stool at the bar. I drank orange juice on the house, listening to stories I'd heard a hundred times before.

"It's a lifetime," I said.

As it turned out, it was four hours. My mother had been a teacher for nearly a decade by then, and she had a good eye for unlikely friendships. Leah arrived with a large plastic bag and a herd of siblings. My mother shepherded the children to the garden. We sat at the breakfast bar, and I watched Leah looking about our kitchen. "You have a really, really nice house," she said, and I wanted to kick her. We took lemonade to my bedroom, and when we were alone, Leah upended the bag. It was her main birthday present, she said, and she hadn't shared it with anyone just yet. It was a young naturalist kit.

"Isn't that naked people?" I said, knowing it wasn't.

"You're always reading about nature, though," Leah said. "Right?"

She had an expression I had never seen, just before she smiled. Like her face was asking permission to do it. I read early in the morning when my mother dropped me off, or at the back of music lessons, while the rest of the class descended on the drum kit. I read, I guess, when I thought nobody was watching me.

"Sometimes," I said.

I took a magnifying glass from the box, a pond net after it.

In the evenings, at weekends, we came together. I still spent lunchtimes at school playing football. I still sat next to Amber Blackley in class and talked about fancying this boy or that. But I felt a kind of needling frustration, waiting for those hours to arrive. Leah and I took a Walks of Stonesmere map and circled patches for investigation. We dressed in boots and sun cream and set off into blue-sky Saturdays, and ice-fog dawns, and a Halloween evening when we didn't get past the edge of the woods for terror. My mother drove us to Martindale one September dusk, where we sat in the meadows and listened to the stags bellowing beneath us. We spent the summer between primary and high school out at St. Oswald's, watching a pair of otters bobbing in the shallows. Leah from the bank, because she couldn't swim; me, closer, in the water.

My dad said Leah was unathletic, a little dorky; she looked like somebody who spent a lot of time reading. But I could tell my mother was pleased.

We saw less of each other when it came to high school. I don't remember quite how it happened, only that Leah would try to talk to me, every now and then, about ospreys, or red squirrels, and always at the very worst times. I would be in the playground with Amber, or else on my way to football, and there she would be, lumbered with a rucksack full of books, appearing around corners with a nervous, crooked smile. It annoyed me a lot, the nervousness. As if I was somebody to be afraid of. My mother would ask why Leah wasn't invited to this birthday party or that occasion and would look disappointed with my answers. The fact was, Leah had started to spend evenings and weekends working at the Boaters, and I spent most of my time running around a litany of sport pitches across the north of England, surveyed by my dad. Those were our lives, that was how it was. And if there were times—passing the window of the Boaters—when I would slow down to check for the scrappy bun, the slice of hips across the bar—well. I didn't think too much of it. She was an old friend. I liked to see how she was doing.

———

We started talking again the autumn after we left school. Leah spent the whole of sixth form worrying about A levels, darting from this additional lesson to that. She was doing five subjects; of course she was. I saw her in the library every lunchtime, revising the same few paragraphs of her university application, looking like she should spend more time outside.

You only needed to do three A levels. That bought you free periods on the benches looking down to the lake, talking about parties, weekends. Amber and I spent most of our time designing our lives outside of Stonesmere. I talked about track facilities, about football initiations and pub crawls. There were times, sitting with Amber, when my mind was somewhere else entirely, when I listened to the two of us talking and marveled at the banality of it. I did not express to her what I had said to my mother: that Stonesmere was a small pond and university a bigger one.

All in all, I told Amber few of my secrets.

It was after exams were over, I guess, and the great debacle of results day. Leah had a place at Manchester, and I picked my way through the hysteria to congratulate her. My father taught me that: however miserable the defeat, you should shake the opponent's hand. Smile, with the hook through your cheek. Leah was posing for a photograph for the local paper, with our English teacher's arm around her shoulders. When Mrs. Lewis saw me, she gave me a sorry half-smile and sidled away.

"That's pretty amazing," I said, and Leah shrugged. She was trying to keep her happiness neat, contained, and I wanted to squeeze it from her skull.

"How'd it go?" she said.

"Me?" I said. "Oh." And what was the use in hiding it? Everybody would know soon enough.

"It was a disaster, actually," I said.

"A disaster? Marty. I'm sorry."

She really was sorry, too. There was a crinkle of sympathy between her eyes. Her arms twitched, as if she would have liked to take me within them.

"There's always resits," she said.

"It's fine," I said. "I'm sure it'll work itself out."

It didn't, really, although my dad made an awful lot of charming phone calls. As it turned out, it didn't work out for Leah, either. All I knew was that something happened with her mother in late August, some bout of illness or other, and Leah deferred her lectures and libraries and returned to the bar at the Boaters. She wore a special badge now, which read: ASSISTANT MANAGER.

It was a good summer, by Stonesmere's standards. Still warm enough to swim in September, if you were quick enough. But my failures spilled into the days, blotting their pleasure. It was all very well, lying in the sunshine with a few liters of cider and the golden members of my year, but in their bedrooms, these friends had open suitcases, reading lists. I attended Amber's farewell party, where she promised, drunkenly, that she would be back every other weekend. My mother scrabbled together a role at the school, where I would teach five-year-olds how to kick a ball and be paid next to nothing for the privilege. First the tourists were gone, and then the students.

By autumn, Leah and I were the last people left in Stonesmere. It was something of a relief: that now, we had to be friends.

DAY TWO

TRENT

The morning after the Stonesmere Massacre, he walked the two miles to work in summer drizzle. Beyond the valley, mist severed the ocean. Trent worked at the leisure center on the beach, selling goggles and apologizing to customers. The leisure center operated one of the worst apps Trent had ever encountered. He had spent hours of his life retrieving lost memberships, correcting bookings, canceling children's registrations for Geriatric Water Aerobics. He had once propositioned his phlegmatic manager with a new interface—something he would create, he offered, at his current wage—but the leisure center was owned by a chain, and improvement, his manager explained, was not an option.

He passed the nook to Smugglers World. No queue, this morning. Rain slid from the beard of the pirate mannequin. The mist skimmed the castle walls. He had spent whole walks speculating about the castle's strategic advantages, about where the moat must have been. Last Christmas, his mother had bought him a tome entitled *Castles of En-*

gland, and Tim had snorted into his Buck's Fizz. He wasn't a history man, Tim. No: he was a man of the future.

Warmth and chlorine burst from the sliding doors. A dank steam hung in reception. He worked the desk with a graduate, Ashley, who spent most of her time applying for better jobs on the leisure center computer. She raised her hand as he came in, but her smile was perfunctory. She watched the television hung over the turnstiles and shook her head.

"God," she said. "Can you believe it?"

Each morning, he had to update the Welcome whiteboard. He had become known for that, for illustrations themed around a particular celebration or promotion. Today, he drew a rough replica of the lake at Stonesmere. Had Ashley search for images, so he could capture the way the hills rose from the water. He wrote: "Our thoughts and prayers," in the same immaculate font the customers had grown to know. After half an hour, pained by the banality of it, he scrubbed the whole thing away. On the television, a presenter was guiding the camera through the streets of the town. He was, Trent suspected, searching for somebody to interview.

"Do you ever think about what you'd do," Ashley said, "if something like that happened? Like in Stonesmere? Like, say they came in, right now"—and she pointed to the sliding doors—"with a gun?"

"All the time," Trent said.

"Me too."

"So. What's your plan?"

"It depends, right?" she said. "It depends on the building. It depends on whether you're in the open or you get a chance to hide. It depends where the exits are."

"You wouldn't play dead?"

"Fuck no. These guys, they go around afterward, just to be sure. No way. I'd go for an exit, if I could. Not much good in Stonesmere, though. I read he locked the doors. There's already some pretty crazy stuff online."

"When I was younger," Trent said, "and I couldn't get to sleep—I would pretend that I'd been shot. Or beaten up or something. I'd pretend that I was sinking into it, you know. It always worked."

Specifically, he pretended he was his father. He lay on the latest cheap mattress and summoned the exact scene, a scene imagined with such loyalty that it felt like fact. His father was in a blocked alley that had once had an exit. He wore a thin coat of dust. Buildings craned over him, squeezing to see the scene. The sky was a bright, mocking blue. The sun burned out of sight. There was graffiti above him, in languages he didn't understand. He lay on his back with his head propped against a wall, as if he was reading in bed.

"That's the last thing you should do," Ashley said. "If you do get shot, I mean."

She studied him across the desk, disapproving.

"You should do everything you can," she said, "to try to stay awake."

Three hundred miles from Stonesmere, people were still swimming. He spent half the morning running a mother through the syllabus for baby classes and the other fixing a bench decimated by yesterday's school group in a fit of pre-holiday anarchy. By lunchtime, he had been away from the television for four hours. He ate a vending machine sandwich and rejoined Ashley at the desk, where she had just finished apologizing for a promotional image on the leisure center app that depicted a thirty-meter waterslide in Wisconsin.

"How'd it go?" Trent said.

"Her children," Ashley said, "were extremely disappointed."

"Well, don't believe everything you see on the internet."

She nodded toward the television. "You see this?"

"What now?"

"The shooter." She gave a slow sigh, blew her fringe from her eyes. She was looking between the television and some livestream on her phone. "He looks just like you'd expect," she said.

"They released the name?"

"They did."

And there he was. White male, mid-thirties. The image was a still from some YouTube upload, and his mouth was open. It must have taken them some time to capture the expression they wanted. Glee and spite. Trent rested his hands on the desk. The world shimmered, and he clung onto it. It was just the fug of the leisure center. It was just the heat.

"You see?" Ashley said.

He knew the eyes and their kindnesses. He knew the near-smile— the jowls baggier, sure, but still jocular, still ready with a quip or a compliment—and the widow's peak. He knew the house, revealed in the next shot, entombed by police tape and tents. The man was changed, but Trent knew him still.

DAY THREE

MARTY

Our second visitor was Sergeant Larkin. By the time he came, I was ready. I had mastered a look of stoic sorrow. I was wearing sensible shoes.

I couldn't understand how he was here, dressed and standing. I had expected him deformed, somehow. Mutilated by grief. Instead, he was pale and decrepit, just like the rest of us. At the time, I was impressed with his poise, although now it seems wretched: that he felt he should stand there, dry-eyed, being polite to my dad.

"Really, though," my dad said, "should you be here?"

They had announced Kit Larkin's death first. His face was on every website. He smiled from incomplete mosaics, with squares reserved for the rest of the dead. When I saw the photo, I knew right away that it had been taken after his mother died. Something about his caution. My mother always said that he was the oldest and youngest kid she had ever met, all at the same time, and when you looked at the photo, you knew just what she meant.

"It's a personal visit," Larkin said, though he wore a uniform and held his hat in his hands. "I just—I needed to walk."

I had only spoken to Larkin once before, on a trip back in primary school. My class had visited the Stonesmere Mountain Rescue Team, where Larkin volunteered. He reeled off a litany of stupid, dangerous behaviors, people hiking in the snow in Converse or setting out at two p.m. in November. There was a stutter to his voice, belying his gear, his weathered authority. I picked up on it, I guess. These were the days when I walked the school corridor with a loyal band of boys behind me, each hoping I'd favor them in the next football game. We had a spelling test that afternoon, and I hadn't revised.

"How do you rescue them?" I said.

"I'm sorry?"

"With rope?"

"Well, sometimes. It depends, really. Each situation is unique."

"So what if you had fallen down a cliff?" I said. "Say—you were lying there, at the bottom. Say you were squashed."

"Well, first—first of all, you would need to assess the terrain."

"What if it was muddy?"

And from some fawner near the back, catching on: "What if there was snow?"

We kept him at it for fifteen minutes, until the teacher swept in to save him.

Now I made the men tea, the way my mother would have done. They waited beside the table. Nobody seemed able to sit down. My dad was a head taller than Larkin, and even in grief, he had his posture. He had his early tan and the span of his shoulders, hunched over a kitchen chair. "However we can help," he said. "Truly."

"I appreciate that, Justin. I really do. As it is, I've got one question. For Martha."

We were out of milk. I paused stupidly in the glow of the fridge, surveying the remnants of my mother's last shop. Butter. Condiments. An unroasted chicken. A near-empty tub of hummus, which would rot there for a month, which neither of us could bear to throw away.

"Marty?" my dad said. "Well, Marty already spoke to the police. The day it happened."

"It's a quick follow-up. Nothing more."

I served the tea black, in little china cups. With it I served a smile prepared in the fridge, sad and compliant.

"I want to help," I said. "If I can."

"It's just a quick question," Larkin said. "About the last few minutes. Before you escaped the hall."

He didn't have a notebook. I sat in my usual chair at the head of the table. Larkin sat, finally, in my mother's seat; it was just the sort of thing he would do. For one strange moment, I thought I would scald him. I could imagine his skin: how fast it would change, under the heat.

"I understand," Larkin said, "that you were close to the front. When the performance started, I mean." He drew an invisible rectangle on the table. "If this is the stage," he said, "you were around here."

"This is a lot for her to think about," my dad said, "given it was only Friday—"

I closed my eyes. The Day One performance unfolded around me. The warm, dusty smell of the school hall. Old books, lost property, gym ropes. A glance from my mother as the first child stepped from the line. She was glad—she was glad that I'd come.

I pressed my fingertip a few centimeters from Larkin's hand. "Here," I said.

"Here. OK. And when the shooting started, you saw that the doors were rammed. And you proceeded to run down, to the side of the stage. Stage right—that would be here. Here. Near the stairs."

"Near the stairs," I said. "That's right."

"I only ask," Larkin said, "because it's where they think they found him, you see. Kit. It's where they found the body—"

"Larkin," my dad said.

"And so I just wanted to check, Martha," Larkin said, "if there were any additional details—"

My dad stepped for him then. He had his old rugby heft; a way of walking that meant people always parted for him on the pavement, and never the other way around. I had once shown Amber a photograph of my dad when he was our age, standing by the lake in short trunks, and when Amber whistled, I felt a kind of squirmish pride.

"She's nineteen years old," my dad said. "She's done enough."

"You're right, Justin. Of course, you're right. I'm just—I would just like—"

Larkin teetered on the brink of tears, and my dad looked to the floor. I had never seen my dad cry. His eyes were wet at the end of *Gladiator*, and on certain evenings in the rugby club, when they sang "Jerusalem" with their glasses held aloft. But it wasn't crying, so to speak.

The thought of Larkin, weeping in our kitchen: I couldn't think of anything worse.

"Anyway," Larkin said, "I should leave you be."

"I think that's for the best," my dad said. "I can drive you. Let's get you home."

He walked Larkin to the door. Then the noise of the Land Rover engine, and headlights swinging through the rooms of the house. I don't know what passed between them on that trip. Whether my dad spoke first, or Larkin; or whether they sat together in silence, watching the evening descend from the mountains and settle over the lake. That night, when I got into bed, I listened to the sound of my dad in the room next door, the weight of his body crossing the floorboards. The flush of the toilet and the twist of the tap. And I thought of Larkin, through the streets of Stonesmere, back in his cottage. I stuffed the sheet between my teeth and imagined him, stepping into the darkness of his house. To go inside—I don't know how he did it. How long did he pause at the doorway? How quiet were the rooms? I couldn't imagine a quiet like it.

DAY ONE

LARKIN

Their morning routine, refined over the months after Elsie died: a cuddle in bed, a cereal selection box for breakfast, teeth, into uniform. He'd reordered the last two steps, because Kit kept getting toothpaste on his school jumper. He had always wondered why Elsie dressed him at the last minute, and now—now he knew. The selection box had been introduced as a treat and begrudgingly remained. Kit took great care each morning to make the right choice, so that those mornings with a new eight-pack were considerably more hurried than those when only one or two boxes were left.

On the morning of Day One, Kit burrowed beneath Larkin's covers early. The room was already lit with white summer sky: Elsie had been the one to close the blinds each night, and there were days when he forgot. Or didn't forget, exactly: took an odd pleasure in the immediacy of her absence. When it was something that woke him, he did not need to remember it.

"It's very early, Kit," Larkin said. His son's body was warm, curled against his side. "It's very, very early."

"I couldn't get back to sleep."

"Yeah?"

"Yep."

"What were you thinking about?"

And Kit wriggled up the bed so that his face was pressed damp against Larkin's ear.

"The play," he said.

"Day One," Larkin said. "Of course. It's today." The morning was dawning on Larkin. The parts of the day that would pinch. He would drop Kit at school early, skedaddle to his own appointment, and be back in the hall for Day One. That would mean a long afternoon at work, making up the hours. Kit would be the last one at Afterschool Club, most likely, but that was OK, it was OK, he hardly ever had to go. Larkin would catch Mrs. Ward after the show, if he could, and would ask her to look out for Kit then. If she could stop him—if she could just prevent tears before Larkin arrived. That would be great. That would be something. He still needed to buy Special Dinner, oven pizzas, to celebrate the performance.

"You excited?" Larkin said.

"I guess."

"Not too nervous?"

"I don't know. Pretty nervous."

"Well, that's OK. It's a pretty nerve-racking thing."

He opened his eyes. Kit's face was a few centimeters from his own, pink-eyed and frowning.

"Give me a moment," Larkin said. He reached for his phone. Kit's face, again. There had once been the two of them, Kit perched on Elsie's lap in some tapas place in Majorca, each of them sunburned and jubilant. But Larkin had decided it mawkish.

It was five forty-five a.m.

"Any chance we're going back to sleep?" Larkin said.

Kit shook his head. "Can we practice?" he said.

"Your lines?"

"Yep."

"Let me get some coffee," Larkin said. "And then we'll practice. Deal?"

"Deal."

"You stay here. You get remembering them, OK?"

He could hear Kit all the way downstairs, lines practiced so often that Larkin knew them himself. He stood at the kitchen window, waiting for the kettle to boil, surveying the modest garden. Kit's little kingdom. There was a mediocre treehouse Larkin had spent the best part of a year constructing. A football post, a gentle slide. They spent many weekends out there, tending to the flowers. It was something Ava Ward had suggested, responsibility, and it seemed to be working. Kit conducted an evening slug patrol to ensure that the dahlias were safe. Last winter, he had inspected the Christmas rosebush on a daily basis, until it was deemed worthy to offer to Mrs. Ward. Larkin would watch him from this same spot, just out of sight, and there were days when he found his eyes filling with tears.

Kit: he found life so difficult, didn't he, with his phobias of everything from crossing the road to a twenty-second piece in the school play. He found life about as difficult as Larkin himself had found it as a child. He remembered school well. Looking at other boys in his year—Justin Ward, say—and marveling at how easy they seemed to find everything. Making catches, talking to strangers. They would fail a test and see it as a punchline, rather than a calamity. The kettle boiled. He fumbled for coffee, scattered grains over the countertop. In secret, he had hoped for a different son, one much less like him. There was potential for it, of course, because Elsie moved through life happily, taking people at their word, crossing roads with panache. But a few months after Kit was born, Larkin knew. He watched his son protest when he was passed to his grandparents. Watched him sitting contentedly on his mother's lap, playing with her hair. The boy would sleep only in his parents' arms. Those long nights, when Larkin was neither asleep nor awake, with Kit clung to his chest. He knew. His genes had trembled their way to the surface.

And here they were; and it was so much worse watching Kit, when Larkin knew precisely how frightening the world must seem.

Kit was waiting in Larkin's bedroom, hopping from foot to foot, with his hands behind his back. He wore Batman pajamas. He cleared his throat.

"An old teacher of mine," Larkin said, "suggested imagining the crowd in their underwear."

"No!"

"There you go."

"Even Mrs. Hutchinson?"

Larkin sat down on the bed, back against the headboard, mug between his hands. He had gathered Paddington Bear and Kit's favorite dinosaur, so the kid had an audience.

"OK, little one," he said. "From the top."

Kit nailed it, three times through, and Larkin ushered him down to breakfast. This was where things began to go wrong. Kit ate only a quarter of his Coco Pops (second choice). He held a hand to his belly. "I don't feel so great," he said. He took the stairs at a snail's pace, and by seven fifty-five a.m., when they had planned to leave the house, he was still sitting on the side of the bath, his toothbrush hanging from his mouth, complaining about a stomachache.

"I think," Larkin said, "it's just butterflies."

"But it hurts."

"It's a funny feeling, I agree."

"It hurts, Dad."

"Let's just get you into your clothes, and then we'll see how you feel."

Kit emerged from his bedroom with his eyes to the carpet. The label was sticking from his T-shirt, and Larkin tucked it away.

"All good?" he said.

"It wouldn't even matter," Kit said, "if I didn't show. Somebody else could do that part."

"Of course it would matter. Mrs. Ward"—and Larkin knew Mrs. Ward was a strong argument here, because Kit adored her; had spent the whole of Sunday working on a thank-you card he would present next week, on the final day of term—"she's counting on you."

His classmates, too. Larkin tried not to think too much about Kit's peers, rushing gleefully from their houses.

"Just then," Larkin said, "when we were practicing—you smashed it. Right out of the park."

"I did?"

"You absolutely did."

"OK, then."

"OK?"

"OK."

They tied their laces at the front door, Kit lost in thought, Larkin poised for another protest. But no: they were out of the cottage, through the front garden. Kit's hand was in his own. The cool at the cusp of a summer morning. Their shadows walked on stilts. Birds and insects rustled in the hedgerows along Old Oaks Road.

"And you'll be there for my bit," Kit said. "Just a few minutes late."

"That's right. Just a few minutes."

"Because you've got to catch a few bad guys first."

Larkin wondered how many people Kit had told: that this was how a policeman in Stonesmere spent his days.

"One or two, before breakfast."

"Dad?"

"Yes?"

Kit beckoned him down.

"What if they weren't in their underwear?" he whispered. "What if they were *naked*?"

Larkin laughed. He sent two wood pigeons heaving from the nearest tree. They turned onto Babbling Brook.

"That may be too much," Larkin said, "for anyone to handle."

"You'll be at the back of the room," Kit said. "Right?"

They had already been through this. Larkin was not permitted to sit too close to the stage; it would, Kit had decided, make him too nervous.

"That's right."

"Promise, though?"

"I promise."

Kit nodded, as if that was the best he was likely to get.

"How are you feeling?" Larkin said.

"OK."

"Your tummy's better?"

"It's a little better."

"It's no mean feat," Larkin said, "performing onstage."

"Is it brave?" Kit said. Bravery was one of his current occupations, along with pterodactyls and death.

"It's Herculean," Larkin said. And, when Kit frowned: "Brave as can be."

Larkin did not catch any bad guys that morning. Instead, he walked five minutes beyond the school, to the Stonesmere Community Hospital. He smoked a cigarette. He ducked under the austere stone entrance,

past a bronze plaque left by some minor royal or other, and upstairs, to
the office of his psychologist. Larkin had never considered himself somebody who may require a psychologist; had, in fact, only appreciated
the existence of this particular branch of medicine when he carried an
injured hiker past a poster in reception, eight months before. Are you
OK? the poster read, and Larkin, late to collect Kit and with the hiker
gasping wetly in his ear, couldn't help but smile.

On the way out, he stopped to read the small print.

And here he was, still, sitting before her. She had explained to him,
right off the bat, that she had little experience in grief: she was just out
of university and hoping to work with children. She would not be here
forever. She sat tilted forward, her expression expectant. Nothing he
said could surprise her.

"Well, then," she said. "How are you?"

Was he allowed to admit it: That this was the best part of his week?
Two chairs, gathered in the middle of a windowless room. A metal bed,
a curtain, a room designed for older medicines. Thirty minutes, when
all he talked about was himself. He closed his eyes. "The summer holiday starts next week," he said, and she smiled.

"That sounds like a challenge."

He had never talked like this. Not to his parents, obviously, and not
to his smattering of friends, and never to Elsie, although she had often
tried. All those times he had collected her from work, weary from a
late shift on the till, when she had asked about his day. She sat in the
passenger seat as they drove around the lake, passing snowy hills, or
new lambs, or blackberries hanging from the hedgerows, and however
tired she was, it was the first thing she asked. However tired—even
when the tiredness was right there on her face. When it had crept into
her bones and become a tiredness he should have recognized—

And what did he say? Fine. OK.

She would have listened, though. She would have listened.

Toward the end of the session, he thought he heard some commotion, down in the reception area. But he was talking about Elsie—about the way Elsie had been able to play with Kit, elaborate games of enemy invaders, boundaries and barrages, a suspension of disbelief that he, Larkin, had never managed—and soon, before he knew it, the hospital was quiet.

WEEK ONE

TRENT

The Stonesmere Massacre, if you were to believe everything you read:

At 8:30 a.m., Stonesmere Primary School opened its hall for the annual Day One performance. The seats were arranged in fifteen rows of twenty, split by an aisle. By 8:57 a.m., the hall was full. The audience spilled to the sides and back of the room.

At this time, the shooter was walking up from the lake. He had already destroyed his mobile phone and cast its remains into the water. He took a shortcut through woodland, overgrown and rarely used, and emerged on CCTV on Old School Road. He carried a bag of ammunition. He wore a military helmet with a visor, bought on Amazon for £39.99. He carried a Blaser R8 Black Edition. The shooter did not have a license. The origin of the gun remained unknown.

At 9:05 a.m., the first class took to the stage. The class teacher was Ava Ward, who watched her students from the front row. The children were ten years old. The audience was quiet, enthralled.

During this time, it was believed the shooter locked the fire escape of the hall using a steel hex security chain.

At 9:13 a.m., the shooter entered the hall. He killed two children onstage: Oliver Whitfield and Tessa Korrigan, ten. He killed three members of the audience: Marjorie Whittle, sixty-four; Alex Callahan, forty-two; and Leigh Vaughn, thirty-nine. He killed five students hiding in a greenroom below the stage: Kit Larkin, Charlie Malone, Julia Akner, Jade Gilbert, and Lucinda Oakwood, ten. Only one child in the dressing room survived: Alicia Morden, ten, who was shielded by the gunman's final victim, Ava Ward, forty-six.

The gunman shot a further twelve people, three of whom suffered life-changing injuries. Armed police arrived at the hall at 9:32 a.m. The gunman was already dead. He had stood in the center of the stage, facing what was left of the audience, and turned the gun on himself.

"Did you see the news?"

These days, it wasn't easy to talk to his mother. In the wake of Tim's salary, her hours at the hospital were reduced, and they ate a subdued dinner together most evenings. But Tim had procured her friends, the wives of his business partners, and Trent often found her engaged in appointed tasks: preparing a cake for some bake sale or other, or else replying to WhatsApp messages about fundraisers. They always seemed to be raising funds for a new extension to the golf club—raising money, as far as Trent could see it, for themselves—but when Trent suggested this, his mother accused him of being mean-spirited.

There was a time, Trent knew, when she would have found it funny.

His mother sat now on the damp patio, a glass in her hand, as the arcade lights emerged along the shore. Tim was late at work. There were moments like this when Trent pretended the house was theirs alone. In the night, when he padded the soft carpet to the bathroom. Three weeks before, when Tim had attended a great-aunt's funeral, and he and his mother spent a whole, glorious afternoon watching the extended edition of *The Fellowship of the Ring.*

"Stonesmere?" she said. "What now?"

"They identified the shooter. They've got his photo, his name. Everything."

He sat beside her. Tim's garden furniture was sodden, but she had found a dry patch, cocooned by a drooping willow tree. For a decade, it had been the stuff of their dreams: an actual garden. She had hung her wind chimes from the tired gazebo; wind chimes that were accustomed to windows, balconies, doorknobs.

"This is going to sound crazy," Trent said, "but I think that we knew him."

"Knew him?"

"There was a guy," Trent said, "when we lived in Stonesmere. Next door. Maybe not next door, but on the same street. He was living with his mother, too. He came around, when we first moved in."

"It was ten years ago," his mother said. She passed her glass from hand to hand.

"I know. But this guy—he actually welcomed us. And he helped around the house. The reason I remember it—he helped us with the Flood, right? On Christmas Day?"

The Flood was the stuff of their family folklore, up there with the overnight breakdown near Banbury—his dad stamping down the side of the M40 bearing a McDonald's bag like the enemy's colors; Trent, curled in the back seat with a Harry Potter audiobook, declaring this better than any hotel—or their first cat, Nelson, who detested them all day and yet came to their beds at night, purring.

Around Tim, his mother was reticent with such storytelling, so as not to leave anybody out.

"He was the one who brought us dinner," Trent said, "that Christmas.

But he kept coming round, in the new year. He must have been—I don't know. Twenty? Twenty-one?"

"Look," she said. "Yes. I remember there was a boy. He helped us around the house a little. You'd play football with him, every now and then."

"Yeah, exactly. Him."

"And you're saying," she said, "that he—?"

"It's not what I'm saying. It's what the news is saying. It's crazy."

She shifted across the patio steps, as if something in the remembering pained her. "And you're sure? It was years ago."

"I'm sure. I knew, as soon as I saw him."

"Trent," his mother said, "we barely knew him."

"You didn't, maybe. But I really did. It wasn't the most friendly of towns, right?"

"That," she said, "is quite the understatement."

"But this guy, he was decent. He always had time for us. I was this weird little kid, and he'd still play another round of *FIFA*, just so I could win a game."

"Well, people change. In all sorts of ways."

"Maybe. Or maybe—"

His mother gave a little shake of her head. It was a gesture she had acquired from Tim. Not quite imperceptible. As if the man had burrowed into her bones, too.

"You should see, though," Trent said, "what they're saying online."

"Trent."

"There are inconsistencies."

She reached a hand to his knee, cold from her glass. It had been some months since she had touched him. Her nails were neat and red and painted by somebody else.

"Not again, baby," she said. "Not again."

———

The Flood. The first Christmas without his father, a decade before. The effort his mother put in—the effort! She moved in a frenzy around the house, from the kitchen to the living room to the presents hidden in her bedroom, as if in her speed she could fill the rooms, leaving the impression of more parent than there actually was. She bought the same amount of turkey. She presented the same bottle of Buck's Fizz at breakfast, even if she had to pour half of it away. They watched *It's a Wonderful Life* in the same slot, before lunch, and she cried at the same parts. When George was sitting at the bar. At the ending. Everybody, she said, cried at the ending. The film had just finished when they heard it. A kind of gushing. They looked at each other across the sofa and rose in unison. The noise came from the kitchen, and when his mother opened the door, water drenched their socks. It was spilling from the washing machine, which whirred miserably in the corner of the room. From the buckling linoleum—from the rising waterline and the shoes submerged—it had been coming for quite some time.

He'd thought his mother would collapse. All the preparations, the purchases: and now pine needles were floating through the hallway. He could hear a noise coming from her, something he had never heard before—and he had heard so many strange, wounded noises in the months since his father died—but when she turned to him, her eyes were bright. She kicked a spray of water in his direction, and he squealed. Her face said that it was OK: he could splash her back. They spent half an hour chasing through the house, and they stopped, spent, on the stairs, their hair dripping, shivering a little. The boy next door saw the water coming down the doorstep and brought them round dinner in a Tupperware box, turkey with all the trimmings. Trent remembered the impression of him, arriving in their little living room, occupying the empty space on the sofa. He knew how to dry out the carpet. He knew who they could call. He looked around at the cardboard boxes, the own-label tins. The modest gathering of gifts, salvaged on a bookshelf. He knew what they were.

"Welcome to Stonesmere," he said.

WEEK TWO

MARTY

This is how it happened. First, the phone calls. The phone calls, we could live with. We were united in them, after all. My dad would check the machine each morning—the ringer long set to silent—and say some incredulous number, twenty-six or thirty-one, and we would shake our heads and return to our silent breakfast.

Next, the notifications. I had condolence messages from names I did not know. The interview from Day One, slipping into the homes of strangers. Newsfeeds, search results, Up next in three, two, one. There was not a second, I realized, when I was not being watched. On Facebook I was frozen behind a gray triangle, mouth open, just about to speak. *That's Martha Ward!* somebody had written, and beneath that comment were six hundred more: *My publication would love to speak to you to hear more,* and *RIP I'm so sorry for your loss,* and *You're a very beautiful girl.* When I looked at the still, I couldn't see much beauty. I was trapped in the frame, a dying animal. Contorted mouth, panicked limbs.

But it was OK. It was OK, because the audience wasn't real. Their icons were dogs, flags, middle-aged women drinking cocktails. I removed each social media app from my phone, according to a pamphlet issued by our family liaison officer. The pamphlet was entitled *Dealing with the Media*.

But then: then, they were at our door.

We had the kind of house people stop to admire. I would see them most summers, gathered on Crag Brow, tourists with baseball caps or paper umbrellas. They peered up the driveway—pointing out the long windows, perhaps, or else the flower beds leading to the front door—and discussed what their lives would be like, living up there. Maybe they discussed us, believing us eccentric or fabulously rich, rather than a small, lucky family.

"I can't even imagine what it would be like," Leah Perry had said, the first time she visited, "to grow up somewhere like this."

The house was part of my parents' mythology. They bought it in a probate sale. It was an old vicarage, white stone walls sagging with ivy. My dad gutted the place; called in a lifetime of favors around Stonesmere for the roof and the plumbing and the rewiring. For a new stained glass window, the length of the staircase. When he wasn't working, he was tinkering. He was examining the flower beds or else standing on the driveway, fixing a loose paving stone. From Crag Brow, you could see through the long windows to the lives inside: sport on the television; the glow of my laptop; my mother at her dressing table, touching her wrists to her neck. My dad liked the exposure, I think. He liked that people stopped on Crag Brow and called his name, hoping he would amble down to meet them.

They knocked, at first. From my bedroom, I watched them coming up the driveway, my feet crossed on the window ledge. They arranged their expressions on Crag Brow. Deep breaths, sympathetic eyes. Sometimes they sent a hopeful assistant, laden with cameras. I knew it was coming, but the doorbell still surprised me. I bet on how many times they would try it. I thought of my dad, straight-backed in the living room, the two of us melded to our chosen furniture.

It was Anoushka who answered the door. Anoushka was our Guardian Angel. Really: that was what they called them. She was, in fact, a family liaison officer, but enough of the families were left with small, siblingless children that they came up with a stupid name. Anoushka did not look like an angel. She sat still about the house like a loris; I could be in a room for whole minutes before realizing she was there. She brought us tissues and satsumas. It was Anoushka who rescued my mother's Le Creuset, left by my dad to cook a single portion of soup. It was Anoushka who found me by the washing machine at nine p.m., holding a sweater shrunk to a child's proportions, trying to coax it back to size.

"I can soak it," she said, though this didn't seem to fall within her job description. I held the sweater to my chest. The sweater said *Val Thorens*. I could remember stopping outside the window, pointing it out through afternoon snowfall. Ten months later, I unraveled it from a Christmas stocking while my mother smiled.

"Don't bother," I said.

Anoushka witnessed our little humiliations, and she answered the door. I would hear her voice rise up the stairs. No, the Ward family was not providing interviews. (OK, then: the Ward family was not providing *further* interviews.) They would appreciate it—they would appreciate it greatly—if their privacy could be respected.

It seemed to me Anoushka's fault, then, that they stopped ringing the doorbell.

The first time was ten days after my mother died. I sat alone in the garden, drinking a beer. At the end of the lawn was a fence built by my

dad, and beyond the fence was a scrub of woodland, sunbeams stirring within the trees. A teeming darkness between them, textured with
trunks and gnats; with helicopter seeds, dawdling to the ground.

We had been intending to host a barbecue, the same way we did
every year. The Wards' Last Day Party. My grandparents had started
the tradition when my dad was at school, and this provided the event
with a historical significance that meant people cared about being invited. My dad would preside over the meat, would reminisce with his
flatterers and teach the boys how to tell when something was ready. My
mother would make embarrassing conversation with my friends. She remembered you when you were *this big*. How were exams? Are you going
on holiday? Oh, Cornwall is lovely.

My mother detested Cornwall.

My dad dithered. He had made the order from the butcher a good
month before, and it wasn't fair to change it now. The butcher's niece
had been shot through the sternum and lay in a hospital bed in Newcastle, and I suppose my dad thought the cancellation of such a sub-
stantive order may be the final straw. But was it inappropriate—it was
inappropriate, wasn't it?—to host a barbecue, so soon after—

"I'm just not sure," I said, "that anybody's going to come."

"Your mother," he said, "she wouldn't have wanted us to cancel."

I felt pretty sure my mother would have happily canceled any one
of the prior twenty years of Last Day Parties, but I just nodded and
googled a recipe for potato salad.

My dad was bad at grieving. He fed off celebrations, company. He
couldn't make do with an empty house, with suit trousers and sandwiches and staying indoors. I woke that morning to the first inkling of
light, and from the bathroom I saw him, carrying charcoal across the
garden. Bloody parcels were laid on the grass. I wandered back down
the hallway in the thin dawn light. I would cry first, alone, and then I
would join him.

It was an excuse for him to do something, I think. Anoushka had advised us to stay put for a few more days. From my bedroom I could see the clutter of cameras on Crag Brow, people wearing sunglasses and lanyards, hoping we may appear. They would soon get bored, Anoushka said, watching, as she always was, from the living room window. But until then—

"The funerals have got to start soon," my dad said. "We can't hide away for much longer."

"We would never suggest," Anoushka said, "that you miss a funeral. I just want you to understand—it's something of a frenzy, out there. The media attention, when something like this takes place—it's a challenge."

"I've seen the Malone parents," my father said, "on the television."

"I appreciate that, Justin. But the situation with Martha, it's a little more delicate."

"She isn't delicate. She's the toughest kid you'll meet."

"Her interview," Anoushka said. "It attracted a lot of attention."

"As it should have done. As it should. Speaking that soon, after what she'd witnessed. Speaking to the world."

The afternoon crawled around. My dad loped hopefully around the house. "Maybe," he said, "it'll be a welcome distraction—" The worst thing wasn't even his hope. It was how tired he was of my company; that the two of us were so obviously insufficient. We assembled our plates and looked at the biblical pile of meat left on the grill, with little left to say. I told him the lamb was good, and he told me, gratefully, about the marinade.

Now, the vacant afternoon. Through the woods there was the road from Ambleside, subject to new checks, lined with flowers and soft animals, baking in the sunshine. I hadn't realized the comfort of the summer traffic, of motorbikes and caravans churning through our days. Leah was still working at the Boaters. She reported that every customer was a journalist or macabre. They offered you extra tips, if you would just tell them who you had known.

I ate a scrap of bun from my dad's plate, sodden with sauces.

That was when I sensed it. There was a movement behind the fence, heavier than a squirrel or a mouse. I stood, squinting between the trees, and I thought I saw the shift of a thing, craning away from me, into the woods.

My dad was coming from the kitchen with bowls of ice cream.

"Dad," I said, and pointed. There was something in the undergrowth, moving low and fast. I scrambled to the fence and clung to the top of it, but the sunlight shifted, and the spaces between the trees fell dark.

"Did you see it?" I said.

"What? A deer?"

"A person, I thought."

"Whatever it was, they're long gone."

"I guess so."

"A fairy?" my dad said. The word was strange in his mouth, and he seemed surprised that he'd said it.

"A fairy," I said. "Maybe." But he had already turned away, back toward the table, so that I couldn't see his face.

Those had been my mother's stories, told when I was young enough to set up a den and search for their inhabitants. The woodland was occupied, in turn, by dinosaurs, fairies, and Smurfs. The older I got, the more I doubted a mythical creature would make its home here, in a scrap of trees at the side of an A-road. But as a child? I'd repeat my mother's stories like my own little gospel. I told people about the lake gods of St. Oswald's for a whole term, until Amber declared, in a stern playground ruling, that lake gods didn't exist.

Only Leah had kept a straight face. We can go and look for them, she said. This weekend.

After dessert, my dad went to lie down. An amber flush spread from

the collar of his T-shirt. My ice cream melted in the sun. I pulled myself over the fence and picked through the bracken on the other side.
Wasps chewed at the tree trunks. There were nettles and cobwebs, and
brambles drying in the heat. The fairies had long since abandoned us.
I stepped toward the road, and a shrew shook the grass. In the undergrowth was something whiter than bark, whiter than anything I knew
in nature. I knelt and unfolded a sheet of paper, and written on the paper
was our address.

WEEK TWO

TRENT

Trent had grown up on the internet. The first computer lived in the lounge. His mother was addicted to a message board for military widows, and when she was online, he watched her face, pale and eager in the screen glow. There were whole compositions of empathy, amusement, relief, like she was sure the other Wives of Heroes could see her.

He would wait until she went to bed. He would move the old office chair higher. He stormed through chat rooms, giving his A/S/L as older and more interesting than it was. He watched snippets of pornography, the few free minutes before you had to subscribe. Flesh, tongues, devices. He curated immaculate playlists on Napster, until they started suing people; and on Audiogalaxy, until they shut it down; and on Lime-Wire after that. He perused photographs of corpses on Rotten.com, and in the time they took to load, he steadied himself, wondering if he would recognize his dad's face. He watched videos of fathers returning from time in the army, overseas, and the blind, stupid tears of their children. He found the LiveJournal of a man from his dad's regiment who had been honorably discharged, who now posted well-liked entries about the family dog. He left anonymous, snarling comments.

So: he knew where to look to find out what people were saying about Stonesmere. The internet had long convinced him that he was alone in nothing, no perversion or sadness or loathing; and he was sure that he was not alone when it came to Stonesmere, either.

The inconsistencies, as Trent gathered them, were as follows:

They would have you believe that a mourner would barbecue. He was photographed in some ostentatious garden, standing in the sunshine, his face turned skyward, his mouth broad with pleasure. The man was identified as the husband of Ava Ward.

A crisis actor, somebody said, *on his lunch break.*

Somebody said: *That is not what grief looks like.*

Somebody said: *Give him a fucking Oscar.*

They would have you believe that the boy had lived. That Samuel Malone—a mortal operating the stage lights—took a bullet to the head and survived it. That Samuel Malone would be squeezing hands from his hospital bed three days later. This, because everybody loves a survivor. They had the lack of imagination, said a poster, to ascribe this role to the brother of one of the "dead" children.

They would have you believe that a primary school teacher was found with her arms wrapped around her students. This, because everybody also loves a hero; and if that hero is a slight white woman with a nice profession, then all the better.

They would have you believe that the bodies were being examined as evidence. Not one body, Trent read, had been released for burial.

Somebody said: *Because they have to create the bodies, don't they.*

Somebody replied: *Gotta create before you cremate.*

They would have you believe that the local police sergeant, a man who had a child in that very school, did not receive the requests for backup; did not, in fact, emerge on the scene for a period of nineteen minutes.

They would have you believe that the shooter killed himself before the police even showed.

They would have you believe that the shooter was a man Trent had known. A man who had lived on the same road as he and his mother. A man who had—and Trent had to laugh, because you couldn't make it up—brought them his Christmas leftovers, when they were sodden and desperate. A man who would always give you the time of day, if you happened to be twelve years old and new to town, friendless and thin and preoccupied with video games and so lonely it was attached to you, at your heel when you entered each classroom.

It surprised Trent every time: the things people would believe.

All he did was gather them. This was what was said, later, in questioning. He was guilty of boredom, that July. Those long summer evenings, when his shift was over; when his mother and Tim were sitting beneath his bedroom window, their conversation just quiet enough to exclude him. Yes, he bought a domain name. Yes, the domain name was The-StonesmereExposer. His browser history confirmed the hours. He didn't deny his interest. He was, after all, an interested party. He knew the town, and he had known the shooter. Curiosity was not a crime, Trent's lawyer would say, as far as he was aware. At which the policewoman laughed. She was not suggesting that curiosity was a crime. No. The crimes: they came later.

WEEK TWO

MARTY

gave Anoushka the paper bearing our address. I handed it over with a kind of aha expression, expecting praise or intrigue, but she just peered from the paper to me and back again.

"It proves, doesn't it," I said, "that somebody—somebody's been searching. For us."

"Well, we know that already. We know that there's—speculation. The Larkin family has suffered the same. The Malones—"

"But it isn't just speculation, is it? If somebody was outside our house."

"It's one of the problems, Martha," she said, "of attracting publicity. Your father—"

She gave me a smile that looked like it came from a handbook.

"You focus on your family, Martha. Leave the eccentrics to us."

But there was little to do. For days, the bodies were missing. It was another of the things they talked about on the internet, when I ignored Anoushka's advice and searched for our names. Nearly two weeks, and not one funeral.

They were not missing, Anoushka said. They were unreleased. It was a nice way of putting it. In the daytime, I thought of my mother lying somewhere cool and clinical. She looked like her sleeping self from the days when I peered into my parents' bedroom, navigating the best route to get beneath the duvet. But in the nighttime, I knew what Anoushka meant. My mother was being examined, and after the examination, she would need to be repaired. A team hunched over her innards, stuffing and stitching.

Anoushka delivered details of the investigation in the same phrases I heard on the news. She asked us cautious questions and nodded at our answers. She surprised me only once, at the kitchen table, when she explained that she needed to show me a segment of CCTV footage. On her laptop, she played a video of a girl running along Old School Road, in the direction of the school. My dad watched closely, his hands on my shoulders.

"That could be anybody," he said.

"But my question, Martha, is whether it's you."

I watched the footage again. The girl's face was indistinct. She ran gracelessly, limbs flailing.

"I don't think so," I said. "What? Is it from Day One?"

"It is."

"It couldn't be me, I don't think. I ran out of the school, not toward it."

"That's what I thought, Martha. Thank you."

"I'm sorry," I said.

"Well, you have nothing to be sorry for."

If there couldn't be funerals, there could be lanterns. Katie Malone came to our door, holding a canvas bag that read: Bag Full of Goodies. By the time I got to the threshold, her arms were around my father. Her eyes widened over his shoulder, and she beckoned for me to join them; took us both in her embrace and squeezed. I had never seen Katie static. She was always in motion, coming down a school corridor or im-passioned at the sidelines of a football game. The skin at her neck was bunched, with nothing to crane for.

"I'm so sorry," my dad said. "I'm so sorry, Katie."

The youngest Malone, Charlie, had died in my mother's arms.

"No, no. I'm sorry for you. To grow up, Martha, without your mother—"

She pressed a hand to her heart.

"Samuel," my dad said. "How's he doing?"

Samuel had been helping with the lights on Day One. He was in an intensive care bed in Manchester, with bullets in his bones. His mother had released a photograph of him, comatose and wired, which appeared in newspapers around the world. I hadn't been able to look at it for very long. Could think of nothing more intrusive than to be splayed in print, with your mouth spread for the ventilator.

"Up and down, to tell you the truth. Up and down. The strength of that child—"

And she moved her palm from her own heart to mine.

"Of these children," she said. "Anyway. Anyway. That's not why I'm here. We must—we must persevere, mustn't we? All this weeping. What good does that do anybody? No good at all, that's what."

She held open her bag to display a stack of flyers. She took one and smoothed its edges and placed it carefully in my dad's hands. "Tomor-row," she said, pointing at the paper. "Prayers by the lake. We've or-dered eleven lanterns. Floating ones, you see. So we can send them off."

"We'll be there, Katie."

"Oh, good. Good. I expect the whole town will be." She looked from side to side, as if she would share a secret. "Well," she said. "Except for *her.*"

I studied Katie's flyer. She had added a clip art candle and a border of flowers.

"I should hope not," my dad said.

"I just had to do something," she said. "While they—while they're—"
Stuffing, stitching.

"Of course," my dad said.

It went without saying that we would go. If you were Justin Ward, it was what you did. You went to things. He bid on the largest items at the rugby club fundraiser, the weekend cottage or the case of champagne. He coached my junior football team, the year we won the Cumbria Youth League. He water-skied on the lake each year on the winter solstice, dressed in ski gear from the eighties, while I ran around on shore, serving hot chocolate to his sponsors. There was one year—I was nine, maybe, or ten—when Samuel Malone sought me out. He waited until I'd dutifully passed him the plastic cup, and then he pointed to my dad, halfway across the lake, a speck of fuchsia. "There's nothing he wouldn't do," he said, "if people would clap for him." I told Samuel Malone to shut his mouth. My dad, I said, had raised over one million pounds for charity.

I found his sponsorship form when I got home. The figure was eighty-five pounds and fifty pence. I added my name to the bottom of the list, a month of pocket money, to get him a little closer to a hundred.

What to wear for public mourning? My mother had understood clothes. There was a time when Leah and I spent days in her wardrobe, draped in scarves, rooting for Narnia. I parted the doors and my mother slipped out of them. The perfume she bought at airports. The smell of charity rails, combed for treasures. Flowers, polka dots, rainforests. There were the legs of the yellow dungarees, where I had hidden on the first day of something scary. There were black sequins, balding with age, which hobbled out for winter balls. There were the fine white shirts she resolved to wear each new term, and their stains, too, the grub of small, anxious hands. I took a hanger of black silk and held it to my body. It would be tight at the hips, of course, and short at the shins. But it would do.

My dad waited in the hallway in black jeans, black shirt. He looked like a cowboy.

"All set?" he said.

The end of our hibernation. The whole town, waiting for us to emerge.

We walked past the bed-and-breakfasts and into Market Square. I knew the dry-stone walls, each slate roof, the places where rain fell from overhangs. I knew which cobbles would shift. I knew the delay of the town hall clock and the chime of the hour. But there were little changes strewn throughout the town. Satellite vans parked across the pavements. The bunting down Main Street removed; scraps of it clinging to the streetlights, where it couldn't be disentangled. I saw the same picture taped to the windows of the cafés, the pubs, the shops; and it was only when we stopped at the crossing outside the butcher that I saw it was the class photograph.

My mother looked back at me like a mourned dictator.

The grass along the lakefront: everybody was here. It started with busier pavements, bowed heads, and by the time we stopped at the waterfront, the crowd was close and tight.

"She wouldn't actually come," I said. "Would she?"

"The mother? No. God, no. You don't need to worry."

But I looked for her, all the same. Someone had assembled a makeshift stage above the crowd, and on it was the priest, of course, Father Wicker, and a smattering of other mourners. There was Katie Malone, dressed in black ruffles, a poorly stuffed raven. Beneath the microphones there were a few twitchy children, the ones who had made it out, who stood there like this was another school play and they did not know their parts.

"We should be near the stage, I think," my dad said. People turned to us as we passed. Knowing that we were headline mourners; peering to see how grief had maimed us. There were so many people. People I didn't recognize, their faces replaced by cameras and phones. People with microphones for hands. I had the sense we were multiplying as we went, captured at new angles, condensed into captions. I wanted to cover my body with my hands. Here, I knew, must be the person who noted our address, who watched our sad barbecue from the forest. I was glad for the good dress; for makeup and the weight of my dad's palm on my shoulder. I was glad that Helen Sullivan had stayed at home, just as he had said she would.

When we were at the front, Father Wicker tapped the microphone, as if now, finally, he could begin.

"Stonesmere—" he said, but not like the name of my hometown. He said it like the name of an atrocity. He was opening his arms, his brow twisted with sympathies.

"Come to me," he said, "all you who are weary and burdened, and I will give you rest."

The touch of eyes to my right, and Leah, her arms around her siblings but her gaze nudging me. For a long, terrible moment, I was sure we would laugh. Father Wicker led the high school carol service and the assembly at Easter, and he always spoke for too long. He was one of those people I never could listen to, everything a long diatribe of Jesus and Bethlehem and repairs to the church roof.

I only knew he had stopped when the heads started to turn.

"Who," Father Wicker said, "would like to go first?"

Leah's face had changed. She shifted toward us. My dad's hand was no longer resting but clasping.

"The Wards, perhaps?" the priest said.

"You'll be OK, Marty," my father whispered. "Won't you?"

"I'm sorry?"

"A few words. About your mum."

"I don't know," I said. "I don't—"

But he believed that I could. He was here, waiting and proud. I took a step forward, out of the heat of the crowd. Silence settled over Stonesmere: the lake and the shops; the empty pubs and the islands out from shore.

My feet were still moving, taking the shaky stairs to the stage. And then my shoes were below the microphone stand, and I was opening my mouth.

Later, I told Leah—Leah, sitting incredulous in my bedroom, her voice kind while her expression asked what the hell I had been thinking—how I had thought it would go. I would say a few perfunctory words, my mother as the teacher of Year 5. I would speak about her as the abstract hero. I would pay testament to her bravery. I would reference her style. I would talk about the thank-you cards she kept in her bedside table, years of them, handcrafted by chubby fingers, shedding glitter and feathers each time she opened the drawer.

"My mother," I said, "was so brave."

But when I looked up, faces were starting to turn. There was some kind of commotion at the back of the crowd.

"My mother," I said, "was a hero." But more people were turning now. I shielded my eyes from the last, low sunlight, and I saw her. A late arrival. She was in her fifties. The bubblegum lipstick. The hair, resplendent, lifted from another decade. She was looking at me all the while, with small, swollen eyes, and when they met mine, she gave a fraction of a smile and lifted her hand.

I took a pace back. She was closer now, halfway through the crowd. She was not excusing herself, but bumping from person to person, as if she walked in her sleep. In seconds, she would be at the stage, and when she was at the stage—

I took the microphone from the stand.

"I know it," I said. "I know it's true. Because I was there."

I ensured I was just the right distance from the microphone. Faces snapped back to me, scenting a story. The woman came to a wobbling halt. And Leah: Leah was upon her, with platitudes and palms, steering her to the side of the crowd. I was not to look at them. I was to look only humble, stoic, pretty. I had bought myself time, and now I had to fill it.

"Let me tell you," I said, "exactly what I saw."

WEEK THREE

TRENT

The first thing he noticed about Stonesmere was a sense of nostalgia. He and his mother had lived there for less than a year, but he felt he knew the route into town, the way the trees craned over the road to inspect each new arrival. Bright front doors and baskets of flowers. There were shop windows full of things he couldn't believe anybody would actually buy, strange woolen cloaks and candles purporting to smell of seasons. There was a pile of teddy bears by the town sign, stacked in a way that made him shudder. There was no one on the pavements. The lake lay in its valley, unmoved, with hills of scree rising behind it.

To his mother and Tim, he was on a weeklong course arranged by the leisure center. Customer relationships, he said. Tim approved. Tim believed in hard work the way many lucky people believed in hard work. Hard work, for Tim, consisted of an air-conditioned office, free coffee, and a cake on your birthday. The fact they believed Trent's story indicated just how little they knew about his job.

He parked at the lakefront beside a skeletal little stage. They'd held some sort of ceremony a few nights before: a ceremony he had watched and rewatched. It was amazing what you saw, on the sixth viewing. On the seventh. He touched the steps they had trodden. Like stepping into a television set, just vacated by its cast.

Here he was.

If it hadn't been for the video, he wouldn't have come. The Stonesmere Exposer had been accepting submissions for only five days, and most of it was abuse or else deranged. Leave these poor people alone. He wondered how they had found the site in the first place. They asked for sympathy, didn't they—when they were the ones trawling for details.

On the fifth day: the video. It was sent by a woman called Susan Purcell, and the email was brief. I, too, am looking into the Stonesmere conspiracies. Perhaps this will be of interest.

In the video was an ordinary street. He could see pavement and tree trunks. A car jerked across the side of the screen. He watched a man in dark clothing emerge from between the trees. He was pale and tall. He wore a helmet with the visor up. His features were obscured by shadow. He carried a holdall slung over his shoulder. He was distant at first. Then the film jumped, and he appeared beneath the camera. The next second, he was gone from the shot.

Trent leaned back in his bed. It was footage he had seen before. The whole country had seen it. This was the shooter, three minutes from the hall. He had walked the cover of every national newspaper. Trent closed his eyes. It was two a.m., and another futile submission. He liked seeing the emails come in, the little crest of hope every time they did. But in the content there was always a dip of disappointment.

He opened his eyes. On the screen, coming closer to the camera, there was another person. She was in the video for only a moment.

He played it a second time. His eyes were raw with exhaustion. Two

minutes after the shooter left the screen: and there she was. She came
the same way the shooter had come, fast from the trees.

He played the video again. This time, he paused it. The quality was
poor, he could admit. She was blurred by speed. She was faceless. But
he knew her all the same. Knew the ponytail. Knew the outfit. In another tab, he searched for her interview. There she stood in her silver
blanket. "Now, tell me," the reporter said. "Tell me. We saw you. You
came from the hall? Are you able to tell us what happened?"

The girl nodded. "Yes," she said. "I was there—I was in the audience."

"And you saw the shooter," the reporter said. "You saw him, then,
coming into the room?"

"Coming into the hall," she said. "With the gun. Yes."

But she had not been in the hall. Had she? She had been minutes—
whole minutes—behind.

In the darkness he watched her run, and run again. There was something in her limbs, the purpose with which she moved. Something like
pursuit.

He touched her body, caught and mounted on the screen, small beneath his thumb.

Susan Purcell was fifty-two. She introduced herself as an administra-
tor and investigator. When Trent emailed her back, she replied with a
surplus of exclamation marks. Some of us are already in Stonesmere,
she said. We're looking into this!

She said: You should join us!!!

Susan was the first person he met in the town. He walked from the
lakeside to a pub overhanging the water. Wooden floors and green walls.
Oars mounted above the bar. A girl with glasses told him to sit anywhere he liked. She had the neat, bright smile of somebody who had
spent a while in the service industry. The bar was empty and the gar-

den dotted with journalists, speaking into phones, sitting before laptops. "Is it usually this quiet?" he said, and her smile changed, slowly,
into something sadder and true.

"What do you think?"

Susan was on the terrace. She had told him she would be wearing
pink, but otherwise, he didn't know what to look for. Her email avatar
depicted a bloodhound, which he guessed was symbolic. The pink was
a cardigan. She wore bootcut jeans and large sunglasses. When she saw
him, she opened her arms, already laughing.

"I've never met somebody," she said, "from the internet before."

He laughed. Some part of him had worried she would not exist.
"That video," he said. "It was—"

"Scandalous? Momentous? All of the above?"

The waitress gave them a bemused smile, sitting there: one white
wine and lemonade; one pint of Stonesmere Blonde. As he approached,
he had thought Susan younger than she really was. But the lines around
her eyes stretched beyond her sunglasses. The skin at her neck was a
ruff of freckles, sags.

"I recognized her straightaway," Trent said. "The police must've
done the same."

"The police will believe exactly what they want to believe," Susan
said. "If the young lady sticks to her sob story, there isn't much they
can do."

"Do you think," Trent said, "she was following him?"

"An accomplice? An actress? Who knows? That's what we're here to
find out."

She raised her glass.

"Trent Casey," she said, "of the Stonesmere Exposer. It's good to
meet you."

"And you."

"And what are you doing here?"

"Well—you know—"

"No," she said. She leaned over the table, and in her glasses he saw his face, timid and uncertain. "What are you *doing* here?"

How could he explain: the man who had lived next door to them. How he appeared on the doorstep on Christmas Day. Each time Trent considered the memory it was richer, as if in revisiting the day he extended its edges. The man hadn't just donated them dinner—had he?— but had sat with them in the living room, dignifying their predicament. The man said that he lived with his mother, too, and he gave Trent a knowing look, as if to say that he knew much about this business of living with mothers, and they would talk about it later.

"I lived here, a while ago," Trent said. "I knew the shooter. And I know—I just know—that it can't have been him. Not the way they said it happened, anyway. When I got your video"—and he was smiling, thinking of Martha Ward; thinking of the way she emerged from the trees in black and white—"it confirmed it. That somebody's lying."

"That's your theory, then, is it?" Susan said. There was something like disappointment drooping in her voice. "They got the wrong guy."

"So far, yes. Yes."

"If it happened," Susan said, "at all. That's another theory, doing the rounds. Ray Cleave—the politician, you know—you should hear the way he talks about this."

"Ray Cleave?" Trent said, grinning. Here, with his people. "You listen to his show?"

"Of course I do. And what Ray Cleave pointed out—some of these children—there's no trace of them. You take Kit Larkin, say. He isn't mentioned in a single school newsletter. I found them online, you see. Five years of attendance, and not a peek."

Trent considered his own school career. He had appeared in few newsletters himself. He knew what it was to be unremarkable. But he was enjoying sitting here, sharing theories: it felt like realizing a person he had long hoped to become.

"They're a special interest of mine," Susan said. "This Larkin family." And she settled herself in her chair, as if she had something to announce. "I've spoken to him, in fact," she said. "The father."

"The policeman?"

"That very one. His number's all over the internet. I picked up the phone and I said to him: If you're the local law enforcement, if your child's in this school—if you live a five-minute drive from the place— why did it take you nearly an hour to arrive? And did he have an answer?"

Trent, knowing his role: "I imagine not."

"No, no, no. He hung up—well. Faster than you would drive to your child's execution."

She gave a wild chuckle.

"And you," Trent said. "What are you doing here?"

"The children," Susan said. "It's for the children, you see. I lost my own daughter, quite some time ago. And to see these people—to see them make a mockery of something like this—"

"I'm sorry," Trent said.

Susan waved the words away with her glass. "Anyway. *Any*way. What's our plan of action?"

She had picked up a copy of the town *Gazette*, and she pushed it across the table, one pearl nail tapping at a box on the front page. There was a photograph, there, of the dead teacher. She and Martha Ward shared no features he could point to, but you could see this was her mother. It was a mutual haughtiness, Trent decided. He knew their type. They would share a glance over your shoulder and turn back to you with a smile.

The box was a funeral notice. Open to all who knew and loved her. There was even the family address, where the wake would take place. It took a certain kind of arrogance, to open your grief to an audience.

"Tomorrow," Susan said. "We'll go, shall we?"

He said nothing. This was different from sitting in a bar and basking in suspicion. He tried to imagine them there, an unlikely duo, bearing flowers at the Wards' front door.

She gave him a cheerful little jostle and leaned closer. "Don't worry," she said. "Between us, I know the Ward house rather well."

"The photograph," Trent said, "of the father?"

And Susan bowed. "We're here to find the truth, Trent. Aren't we?" And she nudged his glass with her own. "The Stonesmere exposers," she said. "Right?"

"OK," Trent said. "OK."

Susan clapped her hands together, the newspaper flattened between them.

"The gall of it," she said. "To invite us in."

The town was not as quiet as he had thought. In the evening, the pub began to fill with a strange carnival. First came the media, reporters with anodyne faces. They all knew one another, Trent guessed, after many nights like this one. Their exchanges were quiet, but every now and then they burst into raucous laughter. Laughing at the rest of us, whispered Susan. The media were the worst of the lot. Whatever happened here, Susan said, the mainstream media were in on it.

"They'll sit around for a year," Susan said, "waiting for the inquest. Waiting! While we're out in the field, doing their job for them."

"That woman, there," Trent said. "She isn't a journalist."

At a corner table, a woman in an olive green suit, earrings to her shoulders. Trent knew her face.

"No, no. That's Rose Meaden. She's been communicating with the children, you see. Reporting back."

She was the most famous of the psychics, Susan said, but the town was full of them. There had been a séance in the pub one night that culminated in a man falling to the wooden floor and shouting for his mother in a high, tinny voice. She heard that the Malone mother was going through them, one by one, to find out if her son would walk again.

"That's pretty depressing," Trent said.

"Oh, it's grotesque."

Next to Rose Meaden there were passive smiles and water on the table. Here, Susan said, were the Christians. A niche branch of them; she didn't know the name. They set up camp outside the church each day and handed out leaflets. The children were in a better place now, read the leaflets. Now, they were angels.

Once the pub had closed, he walked back to his car and stood a moment in the silent lot. The keys rustled in his pocket. He could start the engine. Could be home by morning, eating one of Tim's lauded breakfasts. Sadness seemed to dust the town. He had passed a woman sitting on a bench overlooking the water, staring at nothing. She wore slippers, and her hair hung in tangles across her face. He had seen two men carrying a great arrangement of flowers along the main road, roses dyed blue and white, their faces drained against the childish colors. He sat in the driver's seat and closed his eyes. Across his lids came the girl, running. The girl, who could not have been in the hall.

He reclined the seat. What was one more day, in a life as small as his?

DAY TWENTY-TWO

MARTY

They left my mother's funeral to last. Saturday afternoon. My dad talked a lot about it being my mother's favorite day of the week, as if that didn't apply to most of the population. I never did find out if the parents of the dead children had got there first, or if Father Wicker recognized that Ava Ward was a hero, the subject of headlines and editorials; that this would be one of the big ones, and it would be good to end the whole sorry business on a high.

I woke that morning with a dream stirring away from me. I had a sense that it had been happy, and for the first long seconds of the day I was still, trying not to disturb it, like it was a pet slumbering beside me. For months after my mother died, I would come to fever-wet and smelling of the worst of myself, sweat and mouth. It was my mother who had changed the sheets. I looked around the room. A fan playing at the curtains, touching old medals and the photographs pinned above my desk. Leah had offered to stay, but I had told her to come in the morning. After my speech at the lakeside, she looked at me with an expression I couldn't stand. It wasn't quite pity, and nor was it disapproval. I reached for my phone. Dismay, perhaps. It was five thirty a.m.

I dressed in the half-light and winced down the stairs. My dad slept in the living room, his face white in television glow. On the screen I saw Stonesmere from above, the sun rising over Old Man's Edge, and alongside it a still photograph, a photograph of my mother. The reel read: STONESMERE FUNERALS. I hadn't seen the photograph before. They had something of her that I didn't know existed. She sat on the school field in a white dress. Sports day, maybe. Though she may as well have been in Antibes.

I turned off the television. Took the keys from the pot and edged them into the lock. I had the sense that the drone may find me, zoom in on me stepping from the house.

Instead: on the threshold was a man.

I flailed at him. This was it: The creature from the woods. The bearer of our address. The reason for Anoushka's warning: Do not leave the house.

But I could make out a uniform, raised arms, the new, terrible thinness.

"I'm sorry," Larkin said. "I was just about to knock."

"Sorry," I said. "I'm just—"

"I know. I know. The town's full of strangers."

"You're early," I said. "There are still hours to go."

"I don't have much else to do."

"Just waiting for funerals?"

"That sounds about right."

"I'm just off on a walk," I said. The invitation was in my voice before I could consider it. A walk with Larkin, with plenty of time for questions.

We avoided the center of town; cut down past the campsite, squeezing past nettles and foxgloves. From the stiles I could make out satellites, perched on vans along the lakefront. When we reached the shore, we turned east and walked for ten minutes, unspeaking. The sky was light but sunless. The lapping of the lake and birds beginning to stir.

"How are you doing?" Larkin said.

He looked to me with a grim smile. I could feel my face getting hot. It was too early in the day for tears, I decided.

"Oh, pretty great," I said. "Yeah."

"That funereal feeling?"

"How did you find Kit's?"

"The funeral? I don't know. I don't remember all that much about it. I had thought—it was me, who asked people to wear bright colors. It seemed more joyful, somehow."

"That's nice," I said, although it had been terrible, like the guests for a wedding had wandered into the wrong church. In his hand, Larkin had held a dinosaur figurine, the tail peeking from his fist.

"And then there I am," Larkin said, "in the mirror that morning. Putting on a red tie. Thinking—what am I doing? Everyone—everyone should have been in black."

"There were lots of people," I said. "He made a big impression."

"Not people I knew. Just—stragglers. They all gather—don't they? The best and the worst of them. I've had the strangest phone calls. I had a clairvoyant, the other day. Messages from Kit. She couldn't disclose them unless I put down a deposit."

"What? Did you do it?"

"No. I felt pretty confident that he wouldn't have chosen the psychic from *The Star*, if he was trying to get in touch."

Once Larkin started laughing, I knew that I could, too.

"Anyway," he said, at the same time as I said: "Mr. Larkin?"

"Go ahead."

Here the path tapered into woodland, and I stopped in the sunlight.

Insects were circling our shins. The sun fell over Old Man's Edge and shadows rose from the ground.

"Mr. Larkin," I said, "I'm really, really sorry."

"That's OK," he said. "I'm sorry for you, too."

"Katie Malone's setting up a support group for the relatives."

"So I hear."

"Are you going to go?"

"I don't think that would help me very much, no."

"Anyway," I said, "what were you going to say?"

"It was what I mentioned the other day, actually. With your father. About the hall. It's the reason I came by so early, Marty. I was hoping we could talk."

I could feel the change in my skin, as if it fit, all of a sudden, one size tighter.

"I appreciate, Marty," he said, "that it's unprofessional. Don't—don't think I don't know that. But it's what you think about, isn't it? When you're awake in the night. Those—those last few moments. How long they might have been."

This close, I could smell the grime of him, leaking from his creases and joints.

On my worst days, this is the conversation I come back to. You may think it would be the first interview, or else the interview that came later. And for a little while, that was true. I would think about how many people had seen them—it was no exaggeration to contemplate the millions—and I would think about how these conversations would outlive me: that once I was buried myself—and in these thoughts, my funeral was always impoverished and unattended—people would still be able to go on YouTube and find me out. I worked hard not to think about the interviews. I haven't watched them for many years. But Larkin: Larkin, I come back to. His face was pleading. My mother had helped him, and I could help him, too. There was little I could do or undo. But for Larkin, I could make it better.

My grandmother used to talk a lot about a good funeral. She would sit in her favored chair in the living room at Crag Brow—which was, inevitably, my mother's chair—and opine on her latest trip to Stonesmere Parish Church. The music (lovely, at best; unsuitable, at worst); the eulogy (the best you could hope for was elegant), and the food (which was, invariably, disappointing). She would not have approved of Larkin's request for bright colors. My dad must have listened to enough reviews to take note, because by the time Larkin and I returned, the house was filling. Caterers were removing our food to make room in the fridge. A gazebo had arrived in the garden. There was a coven of my dad's friends in the kitchen, solemnly bearing beers. I recognized the taper of Nick Moran's hair and turned on the threshold. The last time I had seen him, spread across our sofa in the early summer, he had slowly appraised my legs, torso, chest, and said: "Well, look at you."

Outside my room, sitting with her legs stretched across the hallway: Leah.

"Is there anyone left in Stonesmere," I said, "who isn't in this house?"

To which the answer, obviously, was plenty. All of my old friends were home from university and many of them would be attending my mother's funeral, but it was only Leah who was here, now, clambering up from the carpet.

"Come on, then," I said. "Help me pick an outfit."

"I'm renowned," Leah said, "for my sense of style."

I sat on the bed. Leah rummaged in the wardrobe. "You have a lot of trainers," she said. From the floor, she gathered a black dress, nipped at the waist, short to the thighs. I'd been forced to buy it for work experience at Lakeside Law, the only solicitors in Stonesmere. My dad knew the partners. The dress smelled, now, of year-old sweat. I held it for a moment, remembering the last time it was worn, touched, removed.

"Not that," I said.

"It's really nice, though."

I took it from her hands and bundled it into a drawer.

"No," I said. "It isn't."

And then, after the long morning, it was time. The hearse was in the driveway. The undertakers waited, holding their hats. My mother was dead. She would be buried at St. Oswald's, rather than in the center of town. She would make us cross cowpats and thistles just to see her off. There was already sweat on the back of my dad's jacket. Leah held my hand to the car: "I could come—" she said, when she saw the space in it, how small we looked. No, no. We'll see you there. And still she held my hand through the window, until the engine started and we pulled away from the house. My mother was dead. The drive was no more than ten minutes, but I wished it could last forever. The cold quiet of the car, where my dad rested his hand on my knee and clutched me as if he needed to. We drove through Stonesmere with the windows open and warm sunlight filling the car, and as we drove people stilled on the pavements and watched us pass. My mother was dead. Outside the church was a crush of cameras, jostling as respectfully as they could, and my dad took off his sunglasses and held them out to me, and when we stepped into the heat, into the clicking and the requests for comments and the flowers pressed into our arms, I understood it: they were mirrored and ridiculous, sure, but they were something to hide behind.

DAY TWENTY-TWO

TRENT

Of course: of course the house stood alone, cradled by hedgerows, distant from its neighbors. Of course the flowers spilled from their beds. Of course there were good smells, charcoal and meat, greeting them on the driveway. A half-moon of gravel and impossibly green grass. The windows were long and occupied by mourners, moving between the rooms. He and Susan slunk up the drive behind two sweating cameramen, lenses slapping their thighs. "You don't think she'll already be here?" one said to the other.

"No, no. You see her at the vigil? She'll make an entrance."

There were families and friends staggering across the grass, dispatched from taxis or pulled up along the driveway. He saw Kit Larkin's father, alone, in the daft pomp of his police uniform. He saw the mother of the comatose kid, the Boy Who Lived, holding her husband like a frame. There, at one of the long windows, was the waitress who had served him the night before.

The journalist was right. Martha Ward arrived just as they did, fresh from the graveyard. Susan took his arm, let out a giddy kind of squeal as the car pulled up. Beneath sunglasses, the girl's face was impassive. She was smaller than she had been on the television, diminished by the occasion. It was affecting her, perhaps: tending to the lies. Arranging them, just so, to grow in the right direction. Susan took his hand, and he found himself walking alongside the girl, just for a moment, as they made their way to the front door. She wore an ill-fitting suit, her body glimpsed at its hems, and he reached forward and brushed the skirt of it, held it in his fingers for a slight, strange moment as she passed. Real enough, for now.

They crunched to the door where the Wards had stopped to greet their guests. Three steps to the threshold. There was a flutter of panic in his throat. Susan turned back to him. She had prepared a smile that could be taken for sympathy, which he already knew to be glee.

Observation they could get away with. But within the house, he knew, and into these foreign rooms: they were beyond the pale. On the second step, he paused. Behind the girl there was a staircase laddered with sunshine. Susan's hand was between the man's fingers, and then Trent was before them both, extending his own.

"I'm sorry," he said. "I'm so sorry—"

The girl's hand was cold. "Thank you," she said. She didn't look at him. Not really. She was already glancing over his shoulder at the next person in the queue. But he—he looked at her. He could see all the little imperfections lost on the screen. Freckles: spring on the lake, too arrogant for sun cream. Scars: chicken pox, an old vaccination, an accident, carving a fine line through one eyebrow. The gap between her front teeth, which made her look like a child.

"I'm sorry," Justin Ward said. "How did you—"

"My son," Susan said, and gestured to Trent. "He used to attend Stonesmere Primary School."

"Ah," Justin said. "You remember her as Mrs. Ward, then?"

"She was a great teacher," Trent said. Everything he had read confirmed this to be true. He had read testaments from every type of kid, the lucky to the cursed. If he had been taught by Ava Ward, perhaps Stonesmere would have seemed different.

"She was," Justin said. "Thank you, anyway. For making the effort."

What they were looking for, he and Susan had concluded, was evidence. That was what investigators did. At breakfast in Stonesmere's cheapest café, Susan had produced a gel pen from her bag and refined their objectives on a flowered pad. If Martha Ward was not in the hall, she wrote, where was she?

Why lie?

The house unraveled in tall, white rooms. On the walls were photographs of Stonesmere, the lake and the mountains, printed in black and white to look more impressive than they were. In the kitchen there was a great wooden table, laden with food, too long for a trio. Susan lifted a blini to her mouth and licked a finger.

"Did you see their eyes, there, at the door?" she said. "Completely dry."

Had he cried, in the weeks after his father died? He couldn't remember. Susan took another blini and crushed it, steadily, into the table slats.

"They looked," Susan said, "positively jubilant."

They turned together across the garden. And although Trent struggled to buy Susan's theory—that nothing had happened at all; that the Ward family were actors appointed to reside in a beautiful house, mourning prettily—he understood it. It seemed that everybody was coordinated. Everybody knew somebody; each body fitted civilly into its own little circle.

His father's funeral—that! That was a funeral. The pub, smelling of dogs and hops. His mother had instructed him to shake hands the way his father had taught him: eye to eye, with a steady wrist. He remembered a particular man in uniform, the way the room bristled as he moved around it. He knew this was somebody impressive. The man's chest was broad with medals. This: this was somebody who required a handshake. He'd built himself up before he approached. "Hello, son," the man said, and Trent prepared his hand: "Hello." "I liked your father," the man said, "a great, great deal." And Trent—bolder, now— said: "Thank you."

Trent said: "He was a hero."

He had expected acquiescence. A war story, perhaps. Had stood there in his little suit, waiting for it. Instead, the man had smiled a strange, sad smile. "Aren't we all," he said, and turned away.

In Stonesmere, there were no medals; only brooches.

"Where do you think they keep the skeletons?" Trent said. And Susan's eyes moved to the ceiling, to the bronze spotlights, and past them, to the rooms above.

DAY TWENTY-TWO

MARTY

can tell you, with some confidence, that my dad's eulogy was not the best. It was no great surprise people balked at it when the recording came out, several weeks later. During an evening expedition to the fridge, I had discovered a notebook abandoned on the kitchen table. The drafts were tedious and generic, like he'd googled a eulogy template.

My wife, Ava Ward, was full of life.

As so many of you know, Ava made a wonderful impact on so many people's lives.

Ava was a wonderful wife, mother, and teacher.

On one page, he had just written Ava, and admitted defeat.

I didn't volunteer. For all my years of halftime speeches, I didn't know what I would say. I had survived twenty-two days without my mother, and survived them, for the most part, by thinking about anything else. What words were there—for my childhood? For how well she hid her tiredness in the evenings, standing eager in the kitchen, listening to my latest essay? An essay on castles in Wales or the corries of Stones-mere. What words for the bathroom cabinet, quietly stocked with tampons, or for the right dress, ironed for that weekend's party and awaiting me in my wardrobe? The good, clean smell, pulling it over my head.

What words for last year—the year after those disastrous exam results—when we barely talked at all? For every small, wasted moment— passing in the kitchen, listening to her slippers ascend to bed—when I could have told her everything?

My dad ran the final draft past me, a few nights before. "I'll do it standing," he said, "like the real thing." And there he was, with the television on mute and a tatter of notes in his hand. Behind him, I could see the two of us in the great living room window, dwarfed beneath the high ceiling. My face looked cynical and old. It seemed impossible: impossible that this was our family now. I assembled the expression he would need when he next looked up, and it turned out it wasn't particularly hard to cry at the right parts, when it came down to it.

After the service, the house was full of people and Tupperware. Every person I had ever met seemed to be waiting at the door. They were sorry, they were sorry, they were sorry. I took hand after hand. Whenever people got near the front, they rearranged their faces to remove any vestige of humor. I noticed food smears on skirts and the smell of clothes worn on repeat. Some of these people had been to a funeral a day for a week.

My mother had asked for champagne to be served. She had left an envelope with her solicitor, specifying champagne, canapes, and a dress code of Fabulous, which my dad refused to enforce. The circumstances, he said, were not what she had had in mind. She had written the note after my birth, when she was twenty-eight and death had been funnier.

"Marty! Oh, Marty."

Amber, flanked by her parents. During her first year at university, Amber had started to create videos about makeup for YouTube, which

I watched loyally, while I was doing something else. Today, she was wearing false eyelashes, and her eyebrows were immaculate. I wondered if she had created a video that morning, and if yes, what she had called it.

"Hi," I said. "Hello."

"Here she is," Mr. Blackley said. "How are you doing, Martha?"

I was prepared for this question. "OK," I said. "Yep."

"The woman of the hour," Mr. Blackley said.

Amber wasn't looking at me. She stared at her father with rigid intensity, as if he was saying something difficult to follow. This, from a person who had lain in this garden, summer after summer, reading problem pages and *Forever* and—to please some educated future love interest—Nietzsche.

"We've been thinking about you," Mr. Blackley said. "You know that."

"OK. Thank you."

"Amber wanted to come right around. Didn't you? But we said: Give them time. We didn't want you overwhelmed."

"There weren't so many people, after the police cleared out."

"All those questions," Mrs. Blackley said. "You poor girl."

"We saw the interview, of course," Mr. Blackley said. "You did a fine job. We can't imagine what you must have been going through."

The Blackley family surveyed me.

"What you must have gone through," Mr. Blackley said, "being in that hall."

The invitation hung between us. I felt the weight of eyes across the kitchen. Anoushka stood close to the doors to the garden, watching me. Our resident angel.

"Excuse me," I said.

"Do you know," Anoushka said, "when we'll be finished?"

"With the party?"

"That's right."

"A few hours, I imagine. Why?"

"We'll need to be finished by then. OK, Marty? It isn't anything to worry about. It's just a minor development. But I'd like to be able to fill you in."

I could see Leah at the kitchen counter, laying out desserts. There was a medicinal deftness in the way she cut the brownies, blondies; divided them in the baking tin and served them like a chessboard. It was just like Leah, to inadvertently join the catering team. She'd always handed out the worksheets in class, or organized lunchtime clubs nobody attended. She lifted four plates and wove her hips through the crowd, heading for the garden.

"I'm sorry," I said to Anoushka, "I need to go."

I followed Leah, past the kitchen table, keeping her bun in sight. At the patio doors, I stumbled, and Katie Malone caught my elbow.

"Miss Ward," she said.

Leah stepped down to the garden, out of sight.

"It's a good turnout, isn't it? It's a good turnout, indeed."

She turned to a small husband, tucked at her side.

"Nearly as many as for Charlie," she said.

The youngest Malone had been buried a few days before.

"He loved being in Mrs. Ward's class," Katie said. "He was always talking about it."

Her voice carried across the polite conversation. Necks stirred; eyes shifted. I wanted her to stop speaking.

"It was standing room only," Katie said. "Isn't that something? There was a queue at the doors. We ran out of wine at the reception. Would you believe it? We had to send Howard down to Booths, to keep us stocked."

The husband was nodding. "It was really something," he said. I thought of him waiting at the checkout, still in his suit.

"They think that Sammy'll be ready for visitors in the next few weeks," she said. "He would love to see you, Martha. We're going to arrange a little trip, as soon as we can. The school said we could take the minibus. They just need to put us on the insurance."

Loud sobs started to retch from her throat. I knew that I should say something, that I should reach for her, but to do so would make me part of the tableau, the thing that people would talk about on the walk home.

"We'll save you a seat, should we?" Katie said. And what answer was there to that? Samuel Malone had lost some of his popularity in the years since he started high school. He had a paunch and a sneer, and he wasn't quite as clever as he thought he was.

"Sure," I said. I was looking for somebody else to talk to. I knew, even then, that they wouldn't fill the bus. My dad was trapped by Anoushka, laughing at something she had said. Anoushka was frowning, but Anoushka was usually frowning. He passed by with a fogged beer, and I caught his eye. Into the conversation he came—my old savior— with one finger raised.

"A moment, Katie, with my daughter."

In the garden, he gave me a thumbs-up.

"It's going well," he said. "Do you think?"

He looked so hopeful I couldn't imagine doing anything other than agreeing with him.

"Once today's over," he said, "we can start getting back to normal."

I smiled at that. He got the same smile I'd always taken to school. It had only ever been my mother who got the snarl. My mother: she got teeth.

"I'd like that," I said.

He was looking to the side of my eyes. I saw Nick Moran, hovering at the edge of our conversation. Katie Malone held court at the kitchen counter, surrounded by a small band of mothers, serving stories about surgeries, extractions, physiotherapy. Hands patted her shoulders, or else covered their own gasping mouths. The ladies of Stonesmere, ready with their cocktail sticks.

"What did Anoushka have to say?" I asked.

"Oh, nothing. Nothing. Something about ensuring we finish on time. But she doesn't know the Ward family. Does she? No. We'll finish exactly when we want to."

He raised his glass and scooted for Nick. For a moment, I stood there unmoored. My nearest shelter was Amber. She tried to squeeze past me, a polite smile beneath her hair, but I blocked her way. I was a head taller, and always heavier. There was something satisfying in the way she shrank. Amber, with her fragile limbs: limbs I'd envied, now and then, folded beneath a school skirt or bared before a party.

"I haven't heard from you," I said.

"Oh, Marty. I know. I'm sorry. It's all just been—overwhelming. Hasn't it? I only came back this last weekend."

She touched my shoulder. Her hand was limp. She had a look of curiosity, but curiosity close to disgust, a look for a spider or worm.

"A phone call," I said. "A phone call would have been nice."

"I'm sorry. I really am. But—"

And she entwined her fingers, with a look of managerial tact.

"When I heard what happened at Day One," she said, "I didn't quite know what to say."

"I'd have taken sorry," I said. "I'd have taken—God. I'd have taken a euphemism."

"Of course I'm sorry, Marty. Obviously. That isn't quite what I mean."

"Then I suppose you should tell me. Shouldn't you? Exactly what you mean."

"There have been rumors, Marty," she said. "This last year. That's all."

"Go on, then," I said. "Rumors?"

"Oh, this isn't the day for it, is it?" Amber said. "Oh, Marty. Your mum. I'm so sorry."

She gave me a sweet, swift kiss on the cheek. "And I'm sure," she said, just as she turned, "that none of it's true."

I followed her into the house. I had tried confrontation, and now—

now, I supposed, I would beg. But there, instead, was Leah. Leah, holding an empty platter. She saw me coming and smiled.

"Can I have your attention," Larkin said.

He was standing on a chair at the kitchen table. I saw my dad's face, comically aghast, and somebody close by—a middle-aged woman I didn't know—said, "Oh, my." There were too many people between me and the table, and besides: Larkin was already speaking, had already raised his glass.

"A toast," he said, "to our hostess."

Tears sprouted from his eyes. Leah was at my side. Her whole face was creased in pain, and I remembered one of the things I liked about her the most: Leah never reveled in other people's embarrassment, but was cursed to endure it with them.

"Martha," Larkin said. "Oh, Marty."

His glass found me, and I smiled in spite of myself. It seemed like something you might be expected to do.

"What she hasn't told you all—" Larkin said. "What she won't tell you—and what I want—what I want you all to know—is that she was there. Right at the end. With Kit, you see. He was the youngest—and she was there, with him. In the hall. Right at the end. She was able to tell me—to tell me what he said. She's a credit to this town, Martha. A credit to her mother."

A murmur warmed the room. "To Martha," Mrs. Hutchinson said; and then my father's hand was heavy on my shoulder, and in his other fist was his beer, raised to the ceiling.

"So thank you," Larkin said. "Thank you, Marty. Thank you."

My smile congealed. There were other hands now, pawing my elbows and back. To Marty! It seemed impossible that they could touch me without knowing the secrets of my body; without seeing the handprints, accumulated as on an unwashed window; and the lies, beating beneath them.

DAY ONE

KIT

What happened was that Mrs. Ward came into the classroom looking very serious, almost as serious as the day after the whole guinea pig incident—which he was still trying not to think too much about—and took a big red hat out of her bag. She said she had a plan for Day One, that it was going to be the best Day One performance anybody had ever witnessed. Bar none.

And *bar* was an old way of saying *except*, Mrs. Ward explained. And so from that day on, at his request, that was how he and his dad said *except* when they were at home. Like: Yes, all the sides, bar broccoli.

Anyway. He was one of the last to approach the hat, which was OK, he didn't mind. And from the hat he pulled out a piece of paper and on the piece of paper it said "Spain." That was kind of great because he knew Spain. Had actually been to Spain. He told Mrs. Ward about it after the bell. The best part of Spain was the water park, followed by the airplane, followed by being allowed to stay up until nine thirty p.m.

The only part he didn't tell Mrs. Ward about was how on the way home, just before the plane took off, he looked over and Mum was crying.

Don't worry, she said. It's happy tears. Which was something he hadn't really understood, back then. He was only seven, just a little kid. But now, at ten—now, he got it.

His dad said it was OK to cry, but Charlie Malone didn't agree with him. The day after the guinea pig incident, Charlie called him not just a murderer, but a pussy, too.

For Day One, it wasn't enough to talk about his holiday. He had to learn how to speak Spanish and how people in Spain liked to do things. Mrs. Ward explained that they'd be talking about their countries in front of the whole of Stonesmere, not just the other kids but also the parents and governors and people who hadn't even joined the school yet. That meant he had to say things slowly, clearly. Like he was speaking to someone old, Mrs. Ward said, although he wasn't supposed to repeat that to his grandparents.

He'd been practicing for what felt like forever. He'd practiced in the bath, where his voice sounded as if it was in a cave, and he'd practiced on the walk to school with his dad, and he'd practiced at break time, when he tended to take a stroll around the edge of the playground or maybe read a book. British Bulldog wasn't really his thing, and the way everybody played football had got so much more serious this year. Nobody passed to you unless you could score.

He didn't mind.

And now—it was here. Day One. His onstage debut. He'd been awake since it was dark, and in summertime dark was really, really early. He only went into his dad's room when it was nearly six a.m., the way he'd been told, by which point he had tidied his room, made two emergency trips to the bathroom, finished *Five Have a Mystery to Solve* (the part in the well was OK, but who was stupid enough to get stuck on an island? It was a two-star read), and ran through his lines five times over.

What he knew was that his dad would make him feel better, and that was exactly what happened. When they were together, he'd look

at the clock and see that whole chunks of time had flown past. A few
hours would go by—a few hours of selecting cereal and chewing the
fat and toothbrushing and running through his lines for the billionth
time—and he wouldn't have thought about anything bad at all.

But the problem with that was that Day One went from being three
whole hours away to being just fifty-five minutes away before Kit knew
it. He made a last emergency trip to the bathroom and went as slowly
with his laces as he could. And then—

Then—it was time to skedaddle.

There was some boring adult reason, Kit knew, as to why his dad
was dropping him at school and returning for the performance. That
was what happened when somebody died: the grown-ups spoke a lot in
hushed voices and made secret appointments and told you that you could
talk to them about anything, when they were actually lying to your
face. It was one of the reasons Mrs. Ward was pretty great. She didn't
try to brush Mother's Day under the carpet, or pretend like it wasn't
kind of awful, having to watch the mothers' race on sports day. She'd
always be there, asking how he was doing or saying: Why don't you
come and help me set up the egg and spoon?

And that morning, she saw Kit as soon as he came into the classroom. It was like she saw exactly what was happening with his insides,
that they were twisting and turning, not so much butterflies as caterpillars, crawling around his tummy; and when he told this to Mrs. Ward,
she laughed and said that was a much better way to put it.

He'd expected that last hour would be the worst, but there was so
much to do. There were props to find, there were outfits to pin, there
were hats and tears and glitter. There was Oliver Whitfield, who had
brought along a plastic sword and had to be coaxed into surrender.
There was Alicia Morden, who vomited into the Lost Property bin but
insisted the show must go on. There was Mrs. Ward, announcing that
it was time to leave for the hall, instructing them to get in line. From

the moment they walked in, she said, they were good as onstage, and so it was important to be silent and smiling. It was important, she said, to be professional.

And the best thing was, everyone did go quiet. They got into their pairs, and Kit was next to Charlie Malone, and even Charlie was serious. Charlie took Kit's hand and nodded and said good luck, and Kit tried not to smile; had to try pretty hard, because it was the first time Charlie had spoken to him in a year. Maybe this was the start of it, Kit invited to swim in the Malones' pool in the summer, Charlie offering to teach Kit how to score from a free kick, and Kit saying, Sure, like he didn't mind either way, until the day he got so good he was picked for Stonesmere Primary First XI and Charlie got left on the bench.

Anyway. Mrs. Ward swept to the front of the line, and on the way she crouched down to Kit and smiled.

"How are the caterpillars?" she said.

"They're OK."

And they were OK, for a little while. They were OK all the way out of the classroom, down the school corridor, out across the playground. But when he caught sight of the hall, they started to twitch. And by the time they walked in—when he had seen the hundreds of people, all turning to gawp at them, and the height of the stage, the stage he would be on, any minute now—they were back to inching around his belly.

He put a hand on his T-shirt. Quiet, little guys.

He took the one, two, three steps up onto the stage.

Well. Whoa. Here they were. What was it his dad had said? To picture them in their underpants. Not Mrs. Ward, because Kit liked her far too much for that. But Mrs. Hutchinson, who was wearing pink bloomers and an elaborate brassiere. And Mr. Heron, who would be wearing something tight. Something where you could see—

OK, then. OK. He couldn't laugh on the stage.

The headmaster said a few boring words about the joy of traditions, about the community of Stonesmere, blah blah blah. Kit peered around him, hoping he might see his dad. If his dad wasn't there just yet, that was OK. He'd timed the period from the start of the performance to his part, and it was a whole three minutes, forty-three seconds. That gave his dad three minutes, forty-three seconds to show, plus what was left of the headmaster's speech.

And it could be the case that he couldn't see him. There were at least two thousand people there, Kit would guess. So it was possible, wasn't it? That his dad was just tucked away at the end of the row or right at the back of the room? And Kit hadn't spotted him?

People were doing their lines quicker than normal. Mrs. Ward had warned them that this could happen, that nerves made you rush through, and so Kit and his dad had practiced saying his lines like he was stuck in a vortex.

Charlie was already up. He was perfect, obviously. He even managed to remember a little bow at the end, while Kit's caterpillars were throwing themselves off the wall of his stomach.

Charlie—Charlie was done.

And Mrs. Ward was in the front row, giving Kit the biggest smile he'd ever seen.

And here he was, stepping forward.

What happened next—it was like something out of the movies he was only allowed to watch with his dad. Like *Die Hard* meets *The Avengers*. That was how loud it was. He knew from the first shot that it was a gun. And what did you do, if someone had a gun? You ran.

Everybody knew that.

Mrs. Ward was already there. She was at the side of the stage with her arms open, and he ran right for her. There was another shot as he was running across the stage, but nope, not today. Not today, you ass clown. The shooter had missed, he had dodged the bullet, and what would his dad say, when he told him that?

His dad. Right then, Kit would've bet, his dad was behind the man with the gun, preparing to take him down.

He collided with Mrs. Ward, and that feeling—the feeling of her arms, scooping him from the stage—it was the best feeling in the world. Grown-ups were the worst, sure, but they also knew the best hiding places, the best ways to beat the bad guys. They gave the very best hugs.

Mrs. Ward had him in her arms, and they were running. Down the stairs at the side of the stage. Through the door to the greenroom, which was actually painted white. They burst in, and Mrs. Ward gathered them in a corner and held them there. Kit had peed himself, which he hadn't done for months by then; hadn't done for years, he'd like to point out, until his mum died. Must have done it onstage, when the bad guy started shooting. It was OK, it happened. It happened, when you were under enemy fire. Mrs. Ward was speaking in his ear. Her voice was muffled and warm.

But her tactics—Kit wasn't sure about her tactics. They were cornered, for one. And they were bunched up together, which would make it harder to fight. And fight—that was what they were going to have to do. Mrs. Ward was good at lots of things, spelling and numbers and art and knowing just the right moment to put her hand on your shoulder. But when it came to tactics—

The door was rattling.

Kit darted from the corner, giddy with courage. He'd tackle him. He'd wrestle the gun from his arms. He'd seen enough movies; he knew how it was done. You used the element of surprise. You—

What was he doing? Oh, God, what was he—

In the small room, the gun was a hundred times louder. The noise popped right through his eardrums, and for a moment, he could hear nothing. The bad guy—OK. He could admit it. The bad guy was bigger than he'd expected. He had no face, only a helmet. He was taller than Kit's dad, and when Kit ran at him, he didn't give way.

Plan B. Plan B was to get out of there.

He ran for the stairs. He'd never been great at football, but he was a decent runner. That sports day, he'd come in joint second in the Boys' one-hundred-meter. The certificate was still pride of place on his desk. His dad had ordered a frame. It was pretty annoying, the way they never put cross-country in the school newsletter, whereas football—

There was something wrong with his tummy. He gulped. He would lie here awhile, and get his strength back, and in no time at all—

It didn't hurt too much.

It didn't hurt as much as the day Charlie Malone tripped him on the way out of school—

When all the class parents saw, his dad included—

And he'd thought his dad would be so embarrassed, that day. He'd thought his dad would tsk and go red and make some joke about being the father of the clumsy kid. But it didn't happen that way at all. Instead, they walked home together the way they always did, Kit limping a little, his dad not noticing, or at least pretending not to notice. That night, his dad made Kit's favorite meal, spaghetti bolognese, a meal he had managed—with some help, and quite a lot of feedback—to make about as good as Kit's mum used to make it. When they were sitting at the table, his dad rolled back his trouser leg and showed him a scar below his knee and said that some kid called Justin had once tripped him over, when he was just a little older than Kit himself. And his dad said something then that Kit had never in a million years imagined his dad would say.

"Fuck them," he said.

And Kit, laughing, said it too.

Fuck them.

The scar—it was pretty great.

The shooting has stopped. His dad—his dad probably had something to do with that. There'd probably be medals. Wouldn't there?

There'd probably be a whole ceremony. Every time they went outside he and his dad would have to stop, graciously, to tell people about it.

He looked up the stairs. He could see shoes hanging from the top step. The fire doors were open, and between them was a glimpse of blue sky. He thought he could see somebody there, peering into the hall, and he tried to raise a hand, to let them know he was there. To let them know that there were others, down in the greenroom, who needed help. His arm wasn't working. Dust motes turned in the breeze, but all else in the hall was still.

DAY TWENTY-TWO

TRENT

This was their moment. The mourners still weeping over old Larkin's speech. Martha Ward surrounded, soon to be sanctified. Susan went first, and he followed her. Up the quiet staircase to the hallway, dark with closed doors.

The intimacy, here, in the private rooms of a home. They had a particular smell: what their occupants would smell like, if you were close enough. He opened the first door and stepped inside.

It was the master bedroom, the curtains heavy and unopened. There was a sketch of a woman's form above the fireplace, and clothes on the floor. A photograph of the girl on the dressing table. Toothless smile and dungarees, a football at her feet.

Susan opened the wardrobe. He watched her fingers skim the dresses. She opened a drawer and held up a bra, tufts of lace at the cups. There was something in her face he had not seen before, a pant of excitement. He thought of her avatar, the droops of the bloodhound's jowls, and shuddered. What were they doing? All he cared about was the girl: the girl, and why she was lying.

"We don't have long," he said.

The next room was a bathroom. He watched himself in the mirror. The investigator. Surprised to see his own face, peering into view.

The next: a kind of office, wood-paneled, with two leather armchairs. They entered beneath a stag's head mounted upon the wall. He fumbled with the desk drawers, but each of them was locked.

"See?" Susan said. "They keep their secrets."

The girl's room was last. Polite conversation still chattered up the stairs. The smell of the house was strongest here. Deep: deep in the enemy's den.

It was an ordinary teenage girl's bedroom. Or what he expected, anyway; it wasn't like many had invited him in. There were open pots on a dressing table, applied that morning. There were plastic medals hanging from the wardrobe, shaped like footballs or athletes. There was black underwear on the floor. Glasses lined her windowsill, fogged with fingerprints. Her laptop was decorated with white silhouettes, stickers long-removed.

In the wardrobe he found clothes with labels he had never contemplated. Susan was at the laptop, trying passwords. The wallpaper was a photograph of the girl and her father. Some square white hotel behind them.

He was in her bedside table now. His fingers clumsy among earrings and ticket stubs. He tried to read them, looking for some inconsistency, but his hands were shaking and the paper fluttered away from his fists. Then—there. Something lodged in the darkness at the back of the drawer. He fumbled for the glint of metal, encased between the drawer and the frame. He wrapped the strap around his fist and pulled. Susan was above him, dancing with anticipation.

"No password," she said, "for that."

It was a pink digital camera, the kind all the worst people at school had used. Capturing each tedious night in town. He was just about to turn the thing on, his finger on the button. He looked to Susan, expecting elation. Instead, her hands were at her mouth. She was flailing. He heard it then, too. The party had fallen silent, and there were footsteps, quick, coming up the stairs.

DAY TWENTY-TWO

MARTY

People were dispersing back to their own sad houses, but my dad had coaxed an audience around him, and he would not let them leave. He kept them rapt: beer, whisky, old Stonesmere stories. I saw Anoushka approach him again, and the mockery in his rebuttal. What Anoushka didn't understand was just how lost my dad would look once everybody had gone home. I took champagne in one hand and quiche in the other, and walked to the bottom of the garden. No fairies, this evening. The wood was still and close to darkness.

I suppose I had hoped Leah would join me, and it didn't take long. She never could resist admonishment. I smiled, hearing the lollop of her coming along the grass. Cheap shoes, hands in her pockets. She wore her waitressing trousers and a shirt I didn't recognize. Gaping at the shoulders. Her mother's, perhaps, or the castoff of some other ancient relative.

"I'm sorry," Leah said. "I really am . . ."

"But?" I said.

"But what are you doing, Marty? Kit Larkin? What were you thinking?"

"You don't understand. Larkin, he asked me—"

"He asked you? He asked you for the truth. He didn't—he didn't ask for this."

"He needed something. And that—that's what I gave him. I made it right. You saw him today. You heard what he said."

"No, Marty. You can't—you can't just say whatever you want, hoping you'll make someone feel better."

"And why not? Why not, if it means that—that Kit Larkin didn't die alone?"

"There will be an inquest," Leah said. "You know that. There will be an inquest, and they'll ask you there, and then—"

She reached for my wrist. It had been a long while since somebody touched me with that kind of care. My mother always was the family's resident hugger. I could feel an embarrassing ache, spreading from her grip across my skin. The hope that she might embrace me.

"If this is atonement," she said, "then you can drop it, Marty. Day One—it wasn't your fault."

I shook her off. She stepped away from me and looked back to the house. She had the same face then as the rest of them. Pity. I'd learned by then that you had to catch it before they knew you were looking; otherwise, the face changed, settled into something more palatable.

"I could come with you," she said. "To the police. We could go together. We can tell them everything. They'll get it. They'll understand."

"Do I look like I need help?" I said.

I didn't want to do it, really. But it was so easy, when you had known somebody since they were a child. You'd found the chinks before they could even fit the armor. I looked back to the house, and Leah looked there, too. The windows glowed through the evening, as if they had taken some of the day's sunlight and cradled it still.

"Do I look like I need help," I said, "from you?"

Leah never wanted me inside her house. It was in the part of town my dad called the Sprawl. The houses were thin and gray. Whenever Leah emerged, she kept the door tight behind her, shielding the inside from view. Behind her, I'd spot plastic flung across the floor, some sibling chasing another, cereal bowls and television. It was always noisy, the Perry house, and never still, and some days I wanted to beg her to invite me in.

"Oh, the shame of it," Leah said, "to need a little help."

Her voice seemed louder than it had been a second before. There was a hush spreading from the doors of the house. Leah's eyes widened. When I turned, they were already in the kitchen. Police, four or five of them, their faces polite but their bodies commandeering the room. Leah looked at me, and I looked back at her, and I knew she was thinking the same. My lies were at an end. It would be bad for a while, and then it would be better. I had always come out of things well enough: a sporting defeat or failed exams. Everybody—everybody—loved a comeback.

But they had not come for me.

Instead, they walked from the kitchen to the top of the garden, where my dad stood, a soft, sloppy smile on his face. He hadn't seen them. I was too far away to call to him—to get to him in time. The distance of a nightmare. He didn't see them until they were on top of him, reaching for his shoulders.

Leah eased my fingers from her shirt. I hadn't realized I was holding her.

He turned to find me, my dad. His face was bewildered. His smile was stuck. Every mourner watched us. Every mourner saw. At the kitchen table, Mrs. Hutchinson's lips were twitching. An arrest at the Ward funeral. The Wards, with their beautiful house and their saintly mother. I could see the tale of it, pacing through the town, across the cobbles, along the front of the lake. It took its seat in bored living rooms and quiet bars. "Dad," I said, and ran for him. Anoushka had me by the shoulder. He looked to find me. His great hand shook in the air. The police turned back through the kitchen, and my dad followed, obedient, among them.

MONTH TWO

TRENT

How was he to return to Tim's house, after everything they had found? How to stand behind the desk at the leisure center, pacifying a woman who had just lost a pound to the vending machine? How to watch his mother's careful simpering over this glass of wine or that package deal? When he had been in the Ward house, just outside the girl's bedroom, as police stormed the place. Out, please. Everybody out. When he had watched the father escorted from his own home—seen that feeble, sorry smile in the flesh.

When Martha Ward's camera was on his desk, among the notes and the diagrams, the printouts and theories.

When it seemed, to all intents and purposes, that he and Susan had discovered something, the stuff of headlines and glory.

When Trent's mother asked him about the customer service course, he said it had been instructive.

Susan called each day. Strange—to miss somebody he had known for only a few days. What it was, Trent decided, was the fact that Susan occupied the same world he did: a world where things were not as the mainstream media narrated it. Were not as they were in Tim's living room, reclined on a John Lewis sofa, nodding along to the news at ten. Without Susan, that world also dimmed, seeming distant, improbable.

"Have you come to a decision," Susan said, "about the pictures?"

He looked to the camera. The strap was curled beneath his papers, like the tail of a pet. "Not yet," he said.

"You've not decided," she said. "Or—"

"Oh, I've decided," he said. "I've decided."

He heard the clap of her hands, joyful down the line.

"But not yet," he said. "Not just yet."

It was just like Tim, to raise the news over dinner. There was the usual explanation of the food, because it was not enough for Tim merely to cook. Tim needed to espouse his techniques, his sources. He needed to ridicule the other ways of doing it, so you knew just how lucky you were. Then: to politics. Tim believed in debate so long as that debate consisted of Tim, sharing his views; Trent, silent; Trent's mother, nodding.

Trent was usually able to remove himself from the conversation. Tim would be talking about ragù, or else the right to protest, and Trent would find himself in a different reality, where his father sat at the head of the table. They would have long, elaborate conversations. His father was always doing something interesting, in these imaginings, had retrained as a vet or a doctor, and regaled them with stories of contrary farmyard animals or brain surgery. More recently, Trent found himself back in Stonesmere. He was standing in the Ward hallway. The tall, white walls. Darkness curling down from the upper floor. The thrill of that—

When Tim mentioned the name of the town, he landed, hard, back at the table.

"Nobody could believe such a thing," his mother said.

"You say that," Tim said. "You say that—but you don't know these people. The sheer capacity for delusion. They're bonkers. You look at somebody like Ray Cleave—"

Tim shook his head and lined up his cutlery. "They're ghastly," he said.

"I'm sorry?" Trent said. Tim blinked, as if surprised to find that Trent continued to exist.

"It was just on the news," Tim said. "These people in Stonesmere—people who've already lost their children, may I add—they're being hounded. Hounded on the internet."

Tim talked about the internet as if it was a place he knew well, when Trent was fully aware he still had a Hotmail email address.

"Trolling," Tim said. "Comments, beneath the memorial posts."

"Maybe they have a point, though," Trent said.

It was worth it, just to see the hang of Tim's mouth. Tim, for whom surprise was a sin of the unprepared.

Tim looked to Trent's mother.

"Excuse me?" he said.

"There've been lots of reports," Trent said, "of inconsistencies."

"And you think that's a good enough reason to hunt these people down? To say to a mourning parent, 'Your child didn't exist'?"

"No," Trent said. "But I think it's a good enough reason to ask questions."

"Tell me," Tim said, "from your combat experience—vast, I'm sure—if you'd expect every account to align. People who ran for their lives. People who were trying to save their children. If you'd really expect everything to line right up."

Trent thought of the girl. The photographs on the camera. He must have been smiling, and that was all Tim saw.

"Isn't this something," Tim said, "you ought to have grown out of?"

Trent looked to his mother. His mother looked to the remains of her dinner.

"Grown out of?" Trent said.

"Well, yes. You were quite involved in one of these little conspiracies in the past. Weren't you?"

"He was a child," his mother said. "He was twelve, Tim."

"You said," Tim said, "that it was an obsession."

An obsession: there was some truth to that, Trent could admit. It had started when they lived in Stonesmere, but it had continued for some time after. He had never been able to find the details of his father's death online. He had spent many hours—hours that would form not just days, but weeks, months—searching for the story of it. The alley, the ambush. Searching for multiple combinations of words; for his father's image; for the location of the place, one dusty Street View at a time. Whenever his mother had found him searching, she had always said the same thing: His father's work had been secret. His death—that needed to be secret, too. There would be nothing for him to find.

"Didn't find anything that time, either," Tim said. "Did you?"

He hadn't. What he might have done was determine his own version of events in an essay he published online, which speculated that his father had uncovered significant state secrets and been murdered by members of his own battalion. He might have submitted that essay for an assignment at Stonesmere High School, which required a journalistic study of a topic close to your heart.

Trent's mother had been called into school to discuss the piece, and Trent remembered only that she had emerged from the head teacher's office looking slight and sad; that he had expected to be in trouble but was instead taken for ice cream.

"The boy should know," Tim said. "Shouldn't he? It's why you're meant to tell the truth in the first place, you see. Otherwise, children— they fill in the blanks themselves."

He looked to Trent with a slow, sorry shake of his head.

"They get things wrong," he said.

Trent was no longer thinking of Stonesmere. He was here, stuck at Tim's table, before a wooden salad bowl and a place mat depicting a carrot.

"Tim," his mother said. "Tim. Please."

"What are you talking about?" Trent said.

"It's a miracle, really," Tim said, "that you haven't uncovered it yourself."

"Uncovered what?"

Trent looked to his mother, and Tim looked to her, too. Tim looked to her as if they were at one of the eternal middle management meetings that Tim liked to narrate, verbatim, for dinnertime fodder, and she was about to make Trent redundant.

"I'd only spoken to Tim," she said, "because I'd decided that now was the time. The time to tell you."

A smile stirred on Tim's face. Trent had a desperate urge to leave the table, to retreat to his room and the mailbox of the Stonesmere Exposer. He held to the underside of his chair, and waited.

"I said to your mother, in fact," Tim said, "that she should have told you earlier."

"Your father's death," she said. Tim was dissolving, now, into the beige of the kitchen, and it was just the two of them. "It wasn't enemy fire, Trent. The reason there were no details, no articles—"

Her eyes were filling with tears.

"He did it to himself," she said. "Now that we're here—now that you're old enough—it was always the plan—"

"A terrible business," Tim said, pleasantly.

Trent tried to laugh, although the noise was shrill, pained.

"Of course he did," he said.

He forced himself to lift his fork. The spaghetti clogged at the back of his throat, like hair at a drain.

"What?"

"It was pretty obvious," Trent said. "Wasn't it?"

"You're saying," his mother said, "that you knew? You—you always knew?"

"Not always," he said. "But eventually. Yes."

"But you didn't—you didn't want to talk about it? With me?"

Trent looked to Tim. If he could just keep his face still—for a few seconds more. "It would always upset you, wouldn't it?" Trent said. "Talking about him."

Through the evening he heard the undulations of their argument. His mother in the bedroom and Tim appeasing her. His mother's footsteps, weary down the stairs. Tim's slippers following, apologetically. The touch of glasses; and other touches, Trent was sure. He could not breathe. He could not stay in this house. Tim? Tim was a bit part. Tim barely mattered. What he could not think about was his mother. His mother—Christ. How many years had she kept her faces straight? How many times had he reenacted battles, combed the internet, boasted in class—

When all the while, she was a conspirator. A liar. One of them.

To calm himself, he reached for the camera and looked again at the face of the girl. The girl, undressed. The girl, embraced. You could not trust a person in the world, but you could trust pixels, timestamps, the memories of machines.

DAY TWENTY-TWO

MARTY

I sat dumb in the garden while police spread through the house. Anoushka sat with me, breathing deep and slow, telling me to breathe along with her. There had been a moment, just after my dad left, when it felt like I'd forgotten how to do it, when Anoushka had taken me by the shoulders and said, Easy, Marty, easy. You've got this. You're OK.

The police were gathering a few bits and pieces, Anoushka said. Familiar objects, made foreign in transparent bags.

It was a formality, Anoushka said. I was not to worry.

Beside me, Leah gave a look of cartoonish alarm. I looked away.

"Where's my dad?"

"It's just a few questions, Marty. He'll be able to explain everything as soon as he's back."

"You humiliated him," I said, although I knew that Anoushka wouldn't get it. For my dad, humiliation was as good as death.

"I tried," Anoushka said. "I tried to get everybody out."

Leah was the only person who stayed. She lingered into the evening, dog-faithful, long after the police had gone. Her face asked questions I didn't want to think about.

It was only when she left that I jogged up to my room. The door was parted. The place was changed, somehow, though there was nothing I could point to. My laptop remained. My medals chimed in the breeze. Yesterday's underwear was still on the floor, twisted and streaked, and I scrunched it into my fist. I reached into my bedside table. If they had left the laptop, they would have left this, too. I clutched the sides, the corners. It would be here, somewhere. The wardrobe maybe; though I knew exactly where I'd hidden it. They could have unsettled things. Switched things around. I unfolded clothes, opened exercise books, unpacked sports kits, tore birthday cards. Unearthed nail varnish, a lava lamp, my previous phone. "Please," I said, fumbling beneath the bed. "Please." But there was only a handful of tissues and a bear wearing a football strip. *Christopher Ronaldo*, christened the day my mother got the name wrong.

By the time my dad opened the door, the house was quiet and dark. My bedroom was neat. I sat on the stairs, and I saw his face before he knew I was there. The terror of it. I had let the night surround me, too weary to turn on a light. This was the house we didn't usually see. The hallway had turned to shadows, the furniture looming and strange.

"Dad," I said. I came down the stairs and into his arms, and his body remembered me. His arms met around my back, his chin rested on my head.

"The gun," he said.

I thought he must be able to feel my face, changing against his chest. I'd leave some imprint on his best shirt: wide eyes, mouth contorted. A memory burst into the hallway. Another man, standing on our doorstep, and how frightened I had been, approaching the door.

"The gun," my dad said. "The gun—used in the attack. It was mine."

"How?" I said.

"I don't know."

He was holding me tighter than he knew. We staggered together into the living room. When I eased him onto the sofa, I had a sense that we were both much older than we were. A preview of a time I didn't want to imagine. He eased his weight from my shoulders and took his face in his hands.

"So, what?" I said. "It was stolen?"

"I don't know. They have my alibi. The shooter's dead. But—how—" He trawled a hand over his face. "It isn't that I'm a suspect," he said. "But they don't understand how he could have got it. How. Why."

I remembered what Anoushka had said. Easy, easy. I had this. There could be other explanations—other ways—that were not my fault.

"People know you hunt, Dad. People around town."

"Him, though? We barely knew him."

I sat beside him, where it was harder for him to see my face. I had always thought it was my dad who knew me best—our happy silences, driving to county trials; our evening games of keepy-uppy, until we could no longer see the ball in the dark—but if he could sit there, unknowing, with his hand on my head—

It seemed impossible that he knew me at all.

"I hadn't even noticed," he said, "that it was gone."

The gun: a family joke, of sorts. On reflection: not so funny. Locked in a wooden cabinet in the dining room, wielded for the Stonesmere old guard. It was my mother's cue to leave a dinner party. My mother, the pacifist. The next morning she would always be distant, disgusted, and it would be a year before the gun emerged again. I shot it one Christmas morning, when my dad and I drove to Old Man's Edge under the cover of darkness and the guise of a stroll, and I pulled the trigger with purple fingers. It had killed grouse, hare, a pine marten. Once, in the Highlands, a doe. My dad returned from that weekend heralded a professional huntsman. "Just ask him," Nick Moran called, from the car window, "about that shot." My dad was laughing, then; was laughing when he came into the house and dropped his bag and kissed my forehead. But when I passed the kitchen late that night, my parents were sitting at the table still, long after dinner. My dad looked troubled. "You can't take it back," my mother said, and my dad said he knew that. What was done was done. All the same, it had not felt how he hoped it would. "No," my mother said. "I imagine not."

YEAR EIGHT

MARTY

fter the gun, things changed for my dad in Stonesmere. He didn't leave town for several more years, but he no longer held court at the Boaters. There was no more waterskiing on the winter solstice, and he quietly resigned as chairman of the rugby club, with no farewell occasion. A few weeks after my mother's funeral, somebody broke into the office he kept on Main Street. They painted the window black and took hammers to the place. The floor, the desk, the shelves. There was a rumor it was Oliver Whitfield's uncle and a few of his friends, although if somebody in the town knew, they never came forward. Most people assumed it was one of the first violent acts of the truthers, although I didn't buy that. It wasn't their style. Either way, my father didn't go to the police, and he never mentioned the incident to me, although he must have known I would find out. He left the house early for a week, to work on the repairs, and we added it to the list of things we didn't talk about.

By the time he left, he had spent fifty-four years in Stonesmere. His little kingdom, with fond subjects and a befitting castle. He had done nothing wrong. What people didn't seem to understand was that wrong-doing was irrelevant, when it came to my dad and me. You heard the Ward name in Stonesmere, and what did you see? My dad, escorted by police from his wife's funeral. The next day's headlines, recasting him as the villain. Me, besuited and diminished, taking my seat at the inquest. Our faces, hoisted behind Ray Cleave, while he questioned our demeanor, the eulogy, our posture in the hearse.

Wrongdoing, guilt: those were just the details.

My dad moved to Ravensglass. The house was gray and weather-battered. The windows were misted with salt. He adopted a decrepit greyhound, Stenmark, who often gave up halfway through a walk and demanded to be carried home. I suppose that was what people thought of my dad, now: the bearded hermit who carried his dog along the beach.

When I saw the news, he was the first person I called. I waited until ten a.m., when I knew he would be awake; and not just awake, but ready to talk. Something about the move unsettled him, so that when I visited I found him ever slower, a little befuddled. The mornings were worse. He would open three cupboards before finding mugs for tea. He would wander to the toilet and return surprised—just for a second—to find me at the table. And he would let me do things for him, too, in a way he would once have resisted. I cleaned the windows. I made Stenmark appointments at the vet. I cooked bland meals and stored portions in the freezer.

My dad picked up right away, the way he always did. It had been one of his business philosophies: you don't leave a customer waiting.

"This is a nice surprise," he said.

"Yeah?" I closed my eyes. I liked to picture him, still. When I did, I made the house a little grander than it was. Stenmark fitter, and my dad younger. "What were you doing?"

"We're out front, watching the boats come in. It's a beautiful day up here. How's it with you?"

"It's pretty overcast," I said.

"You'll have to bring the sunshine."

To my dad, I was still somebody with the charisma to change the weather.

"You didn't see the news," I said, "did you?"

"You know I can't watch that stuff. They never tell you anything good, do they?"

"They don't tend to."

"What did the old fool miss?"

"There was something today," I said, "about Trent Casey. He's out."

There was a long silence. There he was, standing at one of the fogged little windows, while the fishing boats returned creaking, as if from another time.

"Well, Marty. It was always going to happen. His sentence—"

"It wasn't so long when it came down to it. Was it?"

"No, I suppose it wasn't. Good behavior, I imagine."

"Impeccable."

"It is what it is. There's very little we can do about it."

"What he did, Dad—to us. To you—"

"Oh, we're doing all right, aren't we? We're doing OK."

I looked out of the kitchen window, to the courtyard below. There was a playground there. *Playground*: a generous term. A plastic slide and a pair of swings. A wobbling blue horse. There were always notices in the stairwell, pleading for people to keep it clean.

"Your mother, Marty," he said. "She'd have had no interest in grudges."

It was really something—to evoke her now. After the funeral— after that Hallmark eulogy—months had passed without his mentioning her name. The internet told me that he was grieving privately, that he'd grieve in his own time, but I don't believe he knew how. For a long time, I'd thought him stoic, but when I'd offered this explanation to

Leah—my father, keeping the family screwed together—she'd given me a long, crumpled look and said: Marty, your dad's the saddest man I know.

"Have you been back?" I said. "Recently?"

"To Crag Brow? No. No. Why's that?"

"I may call by sometime. I don't know."

"Well, you're welcome any time. It's still your home."

"I'll keep you updated," I said, "if I come up."

Though I knew that I wouldn't, this time, for fear that some of his softness would stay with me and stop me from what I had started to plan.

"I'd like that." And I heard the pat of his huge hand on Stenmark's back. "We'd like that, wouldn't we?"

"Goodbye, then, Dad."

"Martha—this thing. About Casey. Him, Cleave—you're best to forget them." And he said it this time to Stenmark, the way people speak to animals in empty houses, when they're really talking to themselves: "We're all right."

MONTH THREE

TRENT

He moved out two weeks after he learned of his father's suicide. Little had changed in the house, although Trent felt Tim's smile more often, glimpsed across the hallway or from a window to the garden. Whenever he looked up, Tim raised a cheerful hand. Trent could survive this only by clutching to the secret of his departure. He unfolded it each night, to finalize the plans.

He would move to London, and he would write. When he shared his intentions with Susan, he could hear the precise face she was pulling against the phone. "London's a miserable place," she said, "full of terrible people."

"On the plus side, though," Trent said, "no Tim."

"Oh, there's Tims aplenty."

But she sent him five hundred pounds on PayPal, a mortifying amount of money to come from somebody he had met only once. When he said he couldn't accept it, Susan typed for over a minute, but all she said was: You can't take it with you.

He remembered her lost child and thanked her again.

He had money saved from the leisure center. He had a note, written over two days and left on the dining room table, which explained that he had secured a role in journalism and would be back for Christmas.

He had all of this. And he had Ray Cleave.

The Stonesmere Exposer had never been busier. It had baffled him for a few days, until Susan sent him the link: "Ray Cleave Tells the Truth About Stonesmere."

Trent knew that Ray Cleave had run for parliament and lost to some dull incumbent. He knew that Ray Cleave had come from little, that he had once delivered speeches to three sleepy attendees from the back of a hired van, that his first two businesses had folded. That whatever they had said to him—however hard they laughed—he never, ever gave up. He knew that Ray Cleave had finally made his own fortune, enough money to fund his political campaigns: that his fingers, ringed, were spread between many pies. He knew that Ray Cleave was ridiculed by the press. Ray, with his classic cars and his endorsements for balding treatments. Ray, with his little radio show.

And Trent knew that Ray Cleave was the first person to challenge what had happened in Stonesmere—or, at the very least, the first person who mattered.

In September, Trent watched Ray on *Question Time*. The question for discussion was how to stop an event like Stonesmere from happening again. Cleave faced the crowd of a university town with good humor and grace, sandwiched between a cardigan feminist and a stunned academic. They booed him, hissed like he was some kind of pantomime villain, while he sat there with a good suit and an affable smile. Cleave was ready. Cleave was prepared. When the presenter asked if he was honestly proposing that the Stonesmere Massacre had not taken place, Ray Cleave clasped his hands, smiling still.

"There are questions," Ray said. "There are questions. That's all I'm saying."

When Trent thought of Ray Cleave, he was always smiling.

"I've got questions for Martha Ward," Cleave said. "Martha Ward. Justin Ward. Justin Ward—the owner of the gun, no less. Sergeant Larkin. Samuel Malone. The inquest—the inquest's coming. And the people will know the truth."

"And don't you think that these people," the presenter said, "these people—people who are grieving, people who are trying to work out how to live without their loved ones—don't you think they may have better things to be doing? Better things—than answering your questions?"

"That's what we do, though, isn't it," Ray said. "Us journalists."

He found just the right camera. He smiled humbly.

"We ask questions."

MONTH THREE

MARTY

After my dad's questioning, Leah visited most nights. She brought strange offerings from the Boaters, leftover bread rolls or thirds of good wine, and set them on my bedroom carpet like a picnic. When I told her about the gun, her face wrinkled with concern. She pretended to study a thread in her skirt, then the skin flaking from her hands. Anything, if it meant she didn't have to look at me. When there was nothing else to observe, she raised her eyes miserably to my face.

"But how did he get hold of it?" she said.

"It was in my dad's study. But he hardly ever took it out. It could have been taken any time, the police said—any time in the last few months."

"Months?"

Anoushka had come to us with her theories. Come spring, my dad was in the habit of leaving the door open for friends passing by. It would have taken only a few minutes for somebody to slip up the staircase. The shooter had worked with my mother. Might he have called by, unannounced, when only she was home? He had just been let go by the school, and my mother was kind; perhaps he had come asking for her support.

"Marty?" Leah said.

"They don't know. My dad hadn't used it since New Year's Day."

"You, though, Marty," Leah said, "do you know?"

"No," I said. "I don't."

Autumn came late. The ospreys lingered into September. Wasps lagged at our windows. Stonesmere Primary School quietly reopened for the new term. I went along loyally each afternoon and set up the football drills. I placed fluorescent cones on the grass and waited for the children to traipse from the changing rooms. If the headmaster wasn't so pleased to see me—if the Ward name was burdened with the ownership of the gun: not quite suspects, but no longer innocents, either—he didn't have the heart to say so. At home, I kept the house. I searched for the best bathroom cleaning products. I searched for how to do laundry properly. I searched for *when will grief get better.*

By September, Samuel Malone was talking. I knew that because he delivered his first interview in the middle of the month, a four-page feature in *The Sun.* Samuel was thinned by hospital food, by the beginnings of physiotherapy. He had cheeks sharp enough for television lights. I heard from my dad that Samuel had received multiple interview requests; that the whole family had agreed to sit on the *BBC Breakfast* couch and were planning their next move.

"Did you read it?" Leah said, when she next visited.

"Not yet."

"I wouldn't bother."

"Well, then. I'll have to read it now."

"Seriously, Marty. Don't—"

I pulled out my laptop. Leah pretended to look at a photograph of Amber and me, wearing signed white shirts on the last day of school.

"He talks," I said, "about my mum."

"He does," Leah said. "A little."

"'A lot of people,'" I read, as close to Samuel's conceit as I could muster, "'have said that Ava Ward was the hero of Day One. I don't think it's OK for anyone to be held up as a hero. I know this isn't what people want to hear. But there weren't any heroics that day. You take Ava Ward, and she actually ran right past me. This was when I'd fallen from the stage rafters, when I had been hit—and Ava Ward, she essentially left me there, to save herself.'"

I could feel tears in my eyes, and a terrible giddiness. It was the giddiness of hatred, an excitement I was coming to know. Over the laptop, Leah was still and imploring.

"Will you be visiting him?" I said. "On the Malone Megabus?"

"Marty—"

Give me Samuel. Give me his hospital room, late at night, strung with implements and wires.

"Maybe I'll pay him a visit, too."

"Come on," Leah said. "Calm down. The only reason Samuel said anything was Ray Cleave."

"Ray—what?"

"Ray Cleave. He's a politician. Or wants to be a politician, anyway. He's got a radio show, I think. He's mentioned Stonesmere, once or twice. Conspiracy theories, questions. That's his style. And Samuel wanted to respond. He wanted to make sure we got to tell our side of the story."

I typed the name into the search bar and opened Ray Cleave's site. Leah stood at my shoulder, reading faster.

"It would seem," she said, "that Ray Cleave doesn't believe you actually exist."

"Sadly," I said, "I continue to do so."

———

Ray Cleave? Truth be told, I had barely heard of him. He seemed like the kind of person my dad's cousin talked about. My dad's cousin was fifty-nine, divorced, and spent Christmases alone, preparing for the annual apocalypse that would come on the new year. Ray Cleave started focusing on Stonesmere in the autumn, once the graves were settled and the grief was dulled. Once the inquest was announced. We'd fallen from the headlines, below the fold. We'd fallen low enough to touch.

MONTH THREE

TRENT

He found a flat over a Chinese restaurant on Jamaica Road. The landlord showed him around. She was called Anita, and she talked about her portfolio of property. Trent said that he had a portfolio of articles, in a plastic wallet in his room, and Anita gave him a bemused little blink and moved on. She wore billowing trousers and a blouse. She had gray hair and a plain, inscrutable face, the kind of face you could hide things behind.

He thought of her flattening people, paper-thin, and tucking them into her books.

The staircase to the flat led right up from the restaurant, behind a curtain emblazoned with a dragon. "You'll never be far from dinner, will you?" Anita said.

She glanced at the plastic menus. At the paper lanterns, blazing low over the counter. She smiled, kindly.

"Bless them," she said. "I rent to them, too."

The flat was just refurbished, which meant there was a new mattress and the walls were white enough. He looked down from the window to the huddle of bins below. Across from the flat was a concrete block with rows of identical booths. The same office chair tucked beneath every desk. He could see a cleaner, walking a vacuum across the carpet, and he felt the tic of his arm, rising, as if he would wave to her.

"It's a wonderful location," Anita said. "Very up-and-coming."

Anita was a lawyer. She had a place in Hampstead. "You have to buy," she advised, "at just the right time."

The day after he moved in, washing-up water regurgitated into the bathtub. He sat on the toilet, watching his lunch scraps filling the porcelain.

The only good thing that happened, that first week, was the cat. One evening, from behind the courtyard bins, he heard a person strangled. He arranged himself for combat. He saw a flash of a headline, "Man Fights Off Rapist," and raised his fists. "New Londoner Comes to the Rescue," perhaps. He stumbled his way through the restaurant, scattering chopsticks to the floor. Behind the skip there was darkness and piss. The cries continued.

He shifted a sodden filing cabinet and a few crippled chairs. Beneath them was a suitcase, and in the suitcase was a black, writhing thing. As soon as he opened the zip, it swiped for him and staggered back into a recess. It was a kitten, half dead. The kitten peered at him, miserably, and he stared back.

"Come on, then," he said. He lifted the suitcase whole and carried it back to the flat, and in the corner of the living room he arranged a den from his spare sheet and the pillow from his bed. In the light, it was in a sorrier state than he had thought. Its fur was matted to its frame, so you could see the scrawn of it, the little bones. There were sores on its belly, and its eyes were sealed with gunk. He warmed a cup of milk, and for the first time, he turned on the heating.

———

The kitten would live. "She's older than she looks," the vet said, which was really something, because the kitten had the wizened face of somebody a hundred years old. "And tougher, too." The vet put the kitten on a heated IV while Trent sat in the waiting room, watching an array of creatures come through the doors. Everybody in the place seemed to be called something stupid and pretentious. It took an hour for him to realize that when they announced the next appointment, they were using the name of the pet.

Three hours in, the veterinary nurse called him through. She had a counter of tablets and a plaster around her thumb.

"It's an occupational hazard," she said. "She's pretty ferocious."

She was typing, looking from the screen to the keyboard.

"We have really good plasters," she said. She smiled. "Have you named her?"

"You know," Trent said, "she isn't actually mine."

"I know. But can you keep her?"

He thought of Anita's paltry five hundred square feet and the clause that would be in his lease—he didn't even need to check it—prohibiting pets.

"It's better than a shelter," the nurse said, "if you're willing."

"I don't know. Maybe. I guess, yes."

"If you find that you can't," she said, "you can bring her back. But either way, she needs a name."

"I don't know. I mean—what do people call them?"

She laughed. She had a serious face, and her laugh felt like a triumph.

"People call them all sorts of things. Some of them, they have, like, seven names."

She peered through the bars. The kitten was tucked into herself, the kind of enviable sleep he had forgotten.

"She's come back from the dead," she said. "You could work with that."

"Zombie?" he said.

She hit return.

"People are pretty awful," she said. "For what it's worth—even if you do end up bringing her back—it was really cool, what you did."

He was exhausted. He was buoyed with her laughter and with the kitten alive. "You could come round, if you want," he said. "Some time. I don't know. To see how she's doing."

Right away: mortification. The humor drained from her face, left it pale and sour.

"Actually," she said, "I'm not that single right now."

"Oh," he said. "That's OK. That wasn't really what I meant."

What *had* he meant? He didn't know. She was talking to the kitten now, filling Trent's hands with pills and instructions. There were other animals waiting. She should really go. She slid a finger through the bars and stroked the kitten's head.

"Bye, Zombie," she said.

The second week, he got an interview. An online magazine. The office was in north London, with windows over the canal. Rain stirred the water. He thought of a taller, luckier version of himself, striding through reception in six months' time, nonchalant to the view.

A man called Max collected him. He wore a suit with Converse, and he kept a pen tucked behind his ear. They sat on an electric pink sofa, and Max asked about his work. Trent had brought along his portfolio, printed on Tim's ancient LaserJet, and he handed it over.

"'The Dead Sea,'" Max said. He touched the paper, traced the headline. "I like that. You grow up around there?"

"We moved there," Trent said, "when I was a teenager."

"My parents live that way."

"Yeah? You ever go back?"

Max smiled. "I try not to."

He turned the page. Here, a summary of the work Trent had done for the Stonesmere Exposer.

"Stonesmere?" Max said. "Jesus. Did you get up there?"

"I did. I wanted to report from the scene."

"That's admirable stuff. That's how we like to do it."

It seemed to go well. At the lift, Max took the pen from behind his ear and touched it to his fist. "Do you have the URL?" he said. "For that website? The Stonesmere—what was it?"

Trent spent the week unlocking his phone, as if he might have missed the notification. For a few days, he could justify the silence. Working at a place like that, you would be somebody with plans. You would have client drinks on a Friday night, starting in the early afternoon. You would have a good table in a loud bar. You would be hungover Saturday. You would lie in bed with a tablet and the noise of your family lilting around the house. In his imaginings, Max's house looked like the Ward house. Same white duvets, same bifold doors. The smell of a family, long settled into linens and wardrobes.

By Wednesday, he had run out of excuses. If he wasn't going to be a journalist, what did it matter? It could be demeaning. It could be dull. He spent four days on the phone. Could he make cocktails? Was he competent with Excel? If he was a superhero, which superhero would he be, and why?

He got the call two hundred pounds into his overdraft. A magazine publisher. The reception job he'd applied for was gone—there had been a nice girl, a graduate, who had just that little bit more experience—but there was security work available in the evenings.

He worked four nights a week. His job title was Evening Supervisor. He was expected to patrol the floor of each different publication. The cover models smiled beside the lifts. Computers hummed. Every now and then, an anxious intern rushed down a corridor. He read Post-it notes, passwords, to-do lists. He lifted desktop figurines and photographs, things he supposed people displayed to mark them out as interesting. He took pleasure in placing them back at different angles.

What the job gave him was time. He could clear all six floors by midnight. He set himself up at the reception desk, glancing every now and then at the CCTV, unpopulated corridors and vacant doorways, empty desk after empty desk. He opened his laptop. Each day, he emailed Ray Cleave's people. We strongly believe that the public account of the Stonesmere Massacre is false. We have visited the town ourselves to gather evidence. It was two a.m., sure, and Ray's team probably didn't work through the night. All the same, he liked to keep his inbox open. It was a pleasant buzz: the knowledge that at any moment, his life could change.

MONTH THREE

MARTY

cycled to Lake View before sunrise. The water was gray and unmoving, the kind of day when I wasn't sure it would give way. Samuel's family lived in a white house, with wooden beams my dad had attached to the sides. It was a house my mother used to ridicule. Sticking black wood to your house, she said, doesn't make it Tudor. I knew that the Malone family had a summerhouse and a pool, and that Samuel used to secure company on that basis. Like: It's a *pool* party.

The minibus was pulled into the driveway, and Katie Malone stood outside, holding a sheet of paper, glancing from side to side down the road. The bus wasn't full. Not even close. There were one or two silhouettes at the windows, and Samuel's father up front, next to the driver. All I wanted in the world was to cycle on past.

"Martha Ward," Katie said. A warm welcome, when she had surely sat beside him, listening to the interview. When I could see just how she would have nodded, smiled, clasped his fingers in her hand.

"It was a terrible business," she said, "what happened at your mother's funeral."

She patted me on the back.

"You can tell, can't you," she said, "what the police are doing. Trying to prove that they're investigating. When in fact—it's much too late."

From the bus, Leah watched us with a worried little frown.

The hospital looked like any other. There was a tired receptionist and a thousand vending machines. We stood a sad troupe at the desk while Katie signed us in. "All for Samuel!" she said. The receptionist gave us a pained smile. Samuel's last form teacher was there, Mr. Denton, wearing ill-fitting jeans and carrying a present. He had taught me in my final year at school, when he had told me, carefully, that I could do with spending a little less time on sports pitches and a little more time in the library.

"You'll be off to university soon, will you, Martha?" he said. "At last?"

"That's right," I said. It wasn't a conversation I could bear.

"Should we have brought a gift?" Leah whispered. I gave her a baffled look. If either of us knew hospital etiquette, it would be Leah.

Samuel's parents went in first, and Leah queued for chocolate. I sat tucked on a plastic chair, reading the hospital posters. My mother hadn't been taken to a hospital. If you were shot three times in the back—if you bled out in a windowless room, with corpses in your arms—they didn't tend to check for a pulse. She was laid out, I guessed, in one of the polite white tents in the school car park. Some nights, I would wonder if they had undressed her, and the thought impaled my skull. My mother's body—the private curls of it, the moles and the scars—exposed for clinical review.

"Did you know him well?" I said, when Leah was back. "Samuel? At school?"

"We did some clubs together. Creative Writing. Further Maths. He's a pretty smart guy. He was meant to be heading off to Oxford next month."

"I never heard he was that nice a person," I said.

Leah hung her head back over the chair. "Well, then, Marty," she said, "I don't know what you're doing here." This close, under the bright bulbs, she looked neater than usual. She wore her hair straight, a T-shirt I hadn't seen before. She had concealed the urchin skin beneath her eyes.

When Katie Malone came out, she was crying. A small crowd congregated around her, nurses and receptionists, arms outheld. Waiting for the collapse. "Go ahead, girls," she said, and Leah and I took the corridor together, watching the colors of ourselves moving ahead over the vinyl floor.

Samuel was propped up in a complicated bed, surrounded by machines. Like this, with him at the center of a small, bleeping universe, it seemed as if his body powered the technology, rather than the other way around. A frame supported his skull. Plastic tubes curled from his nostrils. Somebody had gelled his hair, badly, and I imagined Katie crouched like a sculptor, agonizing over every tuft.

"Hi," Samuel said. He looked at me with a strange, flat smile. "I wasn't expecting you."

"You look well," Leah said. She fanned the chocolate bars on Samuel's bedside table and presented them with an awkward palm.

Samuel laughed: "All things considered?" he said.

"It was really nice of your parents," Leah said, "to arrange the trip."

"Nice?" Samuel said. "I suppose."

"I'm sorry about your brother."

Samuel looked to his hands, bruised with needles, resting on the bedsheets. "Thank you," he said. And despite everything, I had an urge to lie beside him then, among the machinery. I would tell him how tired I was of the euphemisms, and we would whisper them to each other, cruelly: she passed away; he went home; we lost them, fuck knows where.

"I'm sorry about your mother, Martha," Samuel said. "She was the best teacher I ever had."

"She was the best mother I ever had," I said, and Leah flinched.

"What's it been like," she said, "stuck in here?"

"It could be worse. You get special treatment, being one of the Stonesmere children. I mean, they really need us to live. It's a matter of national morale, at this point."

"Have you graduated yet?" Leah said. "From critical to stable?"

"Oh, I'm stable. I'm stable, but I'm life-changing injuries. I'm stable, but I'm fucked."

He saw Leah's face, and cleared his throat.

"Anyway," he said. "How are you getting on?"

"We're OK. Marty's back at the primary school, doing her coaching. I'm about to head for uni. The campus—it's not far from here, actually."

"English?"

And Leah smiled: some old joke, crafted in clubs for students who dreaded break time: "Of course."

"You'll have to visit. When you have a chance."

"Will you defer?" I said. Samuel turned to me, the brace turning with him.

"What do you think?" he said. His fingers spread at his sides, and he presented his body, the sheets concealing the worst of it.

"I've seen a lot of you, Martha," he said, "doing the rounds."

"I'm sorry?"

"Your speech. At the memorial. Very rousing. You were with Kit Larkin, I hear. At the very end."

Leah was completely still.

"Tell me," Samuel said, "what do you remember?"

"I'm sorry?"

"I'm just curious," he said, "about your account."

"I'm sure you've watched the interview, just like everybody else."

"You were so calm," Samuel said. "Weren't you? Walking from that hall."

"Everything I've had to do," I said, "was unprompted. Whereas you—"

Accompanying the interview there had been two photographs. The first: Samuel in a coma, a spider of wires. The second: Samuel smiling from his hospital bed, with his parents perched on either side of him. His older brother cradling the headboard. The whole room full of family.

"My mother," I said. "Really? What was she—an easy target?"

"Your mother stood on my hand," Samuel said, "on her way out the door."

"My mother stood on your hand on her way to save her class."

"I'll tell my truth, then. And you can keep telling yours."

"It isn't the truth," I said. "It's just a different way of remembering things."

"We'll see," he said. "Won't we? I hear there's an inquest on the way. I'm sure we'll all get another opportunity—another chance—to set things straight."

He gestured for a glass of water, stagnating on the bedside table, and Leah fumbled it to his lips.

"Until then," Samuel said, "I'd be careful, Martha. If I were you. The publicity—there's been an interesting response. There's something I could show you—"

There was an awkward dance to find it, buried at the bottom of a pile of cards stacked on the windowsill. No, not that one: this one. The bedsheet shifted, and at his waist I saw a hang of pale, emptied skin.

"There were so many cards," he said, "when I got out of the coma. It was nice, actually. Cards from all over the country. But this one—"

The card read: With deepest sympathy, above a weeping cartoon dove. Inside, it read: You sick crippled cunt do you really expect us to believe you would have lived.

"Jesus," Leah said.

"Some people," Samuel said, "don't think the Stonesmere Massacre happened at all."

"A few lunatics on the internet," I said.

"That would be nice," Samuel said. "Wouldn't it?"

I looked to a clock over the bed. On the bus, Katie Malone had warned us that our visits should be brief. Samuel could become exhausted. He was still recovering. He was easily confused. I touched Leah's shoulder and tilted my head to the door.

"It would be nice," Samuel said, "but it isn't true."

"I think we should probably get going," Leah said.

"You'd do well to listen to Ray Cleave," Samuel said. "To understand what we're up against."

I stood as fast as I could. My coat was caught on some complex feature of the bed, and I couldn't dislodge it.

"If anybody's lying, Martha," Samuel said, "they're going to bring the town down with them."

On the bus home, Katie Malone talked for ninety minutes about the hospital food, the wait at reception. It was a travesty. There were people she could write to, as soon as she was back in Stonesmere. There were people she knew. Her husband nodded. Leah stared out at her new city. There was rubbish on the street, ragged market stalls. "Looks pretty glamorous," I said, and hated myself the whole motorway home.

My dad was sitting in our vast, motherless lounge, reading BBC Sports on his phone. A Harry Potter film was playing, but I didn't know which one. Leah: Leah would have known. Leah and my mother. The sadness submerged me for a moment, and I looked at the television, waiting to be able to speak.

"Dad," I said, "I'm thinking about talking to the press."

For three months, there had been journalists on the phone. My dad would mention them, every now and then, with his usual faith. I would charm them. I had my old gap-toothed smile. I had my pluck.

"What Samuel Malone's saying," I said, "about Mum. He shouldn't be able to say those things."

He looked at me as if I had only just come into the room. At last: the girl he knew.

"You'd be able to explain the gun, too," he said. "Wouldn't you? The theft."

He smiled at me, from one sofa to the next.

"I saw what you did to the crowd," he said, "that day by the lake. They loved you. They loved you, Marty."

You loved me, anyway. It was the moment I always thought of, when I heard him ascend the stairs to bed. His face, beaming from the crowd. He came to bed late now, a lot later than he used to. Sometimes it seemed like his footsteps passed his bedroom and stopped just outside my door. Come in. Just for a moment. I would pretend to be asleep, of course. I would save us both the awkwardness of conversation. It was just the thought of it. The weight of his body at the bottom of the mattress. What it would mean—that I was the last thing he wanted to see in his day.

A month later, I was sitting in a greenroom of my own.

DAY ONE

SAMUEL

Samuel Malone sat waiting above the stage. The hall was full, and the first class was ready. They were dressed in—well. He didn't really know. A bunch of terrible outfits. It was a little distasteful, Samuel thought, but whatever. This was Stonesmere, and taste wasn't the town's forte. His brother's costume was up there with the worst of them. His mother had spent two months making Charlie a black hanfu. There'd been a whole saga of color changes, fabric orders, adjustments. Which was what happened if you fell in love with an accountant, gave up your teaching career, and dedicated literal decades of your life to stitching Malone labels into sweatshirts. A school play became the highlight of the year.

He could see his mother, too. Right near the front, obviously, having barged a few new families out of the way. She was jostling her knees in anticipation. There was literal knee jostling, right before his eyes. He checked the switches, just to look away, and once he had checked the switches, he scanned the hall for something less mortifying to look at.

Always, always: Ava Ward.

The worst thing about the Wards wasn't that they thought they were better than everybody else. It was that—in the world of Stonesmere, at least—they were right. Samuel could remember, quite clearly, his first impression of Ava Ward, walking down the corridor at Stonesmere Primary School. There was a train of excitable children hurtling behind her, and she wore clothes that looked like rainbows; clothes that he had since traced to Pucci or Moschino, fashion houses so distant from Stonesmere that they may as well have been on the moon. He'd spent five years waiting for Mrs. Ward to be his teacher, and as soon as he'd stepped through her classroom door, he'd known it would be the best of years. Mrs. Ward didn't mention Benjamin Malone, for one. She recommended books befitting his reading level. She didn't fawn over the football players. She spoke to some teacher at the high school and secured him a weekly visit to their Maths club, a Maths club of which he later became, in turn, vice president, secretary, and president. Those early days, though. He'd pretended to know exactly what everybody was talking about, while making a string of baffled notes to research at the weekend.

Would return on Monday, like, I'm pretty sure technological advances mean we'll see the Collatz conjecture solved in our lifetime, though.

When he contemplated the acknowledgments note to his debut piece in *The Lancet*, Ava Ward was the person he thanked first.

When she looked up to him, he jumped. But she was just motioning for him to switch on the lights. He flicked on the PARs and lit the first kid beneath the spotlight. Bonne journée! Jesus. They'd hear it in Carlisle. His mother clasped her hands in glee. The hall made the kind of noise usually reserved for baby animals.

Alone in the rafters, Samuel rolled his eyes.

Mrs. Ward's face was still serious. That was just like her, to give the kids a little dignity. He'd once tumbled in the mud on some stupid field

trip to Old Man's Edge. An observation of the corries. It had been raining, naturally, and he ended up with a great patch of mud across the
ass. Mr. Heron had joined in with the jokes, but Mrs. Ward had taken
off her anorak and tied it around his waist, and pretty soon the class
had forgotten all about it.

Not his mother, though. Oh, no. He remembered standing in the
vast hallway, down to his pants, while she examined the stain. Those
were new jeans, Samuel. How did you get to be so cumbersome?

Mrs. Ward would never have said something like that. And—in spite
of that—Martha Ward wasn't even here. Hadn't even bothered to show.
He'd expected to see her darting in late, elegantly disheveled. Marty
Ward, still in Stonesmere. That was how the mighty fell: not with any
great ceremony, but with a handful of Cs. Had he been happy, hearing the news? Happy—that was a little unfair. Satisfied? Maybe. He'd
once asked Leah Perry why she hung around after somebody so full of
herself—Leah, of all people, who was one of the greatest minds Stonesmere had ever seen—and all Leah had been able to say was that there
was more to Marty than met the eye.

"Even more," he had said, "than a ponytail and football?"

He had always wondered what happened to girls like that—these
small-town celebrities—once their own mediocrity caught up with them.
And now he knew. Every time he saw Marty Ward, her big, gappy smile
looked increasingly desperate, the last overpriced doll left on an ever-
dustier shelf.

He shifted the spotlight along the row. The kid representing Germany was holding a plastic pretzel. Jesus. This town. How he'd come
to hate it. He hated the smug little shops, flogging items that looked like
they'd been made by a Sylvanian Family. He hated the bravado, men
who thought themselves Edmund Hillary because they'd once walked
up Scafell Pike in winter. He hated the eyes watching at the pub bar
and the chemist counter. He hated the weather, the tourists, the rugby

club. Give him gowns and spires and people who could see past Lancaster.

He'd kept a countdown clock in the corner of his laptop for the last
few months. Stared at that clock through exam revision, through the
tedium of the last few weeks at school. Unlike Marty Ward, he had no
concerns about getting the grades. In October, he would pack a few choice
belongings and leave Lake View for good. He would make a dignified
annual appearance at Christmas. He would spend dinner texting a series of intellectual women he had met in tutorials, all of whom were
skilled at puns and vaguely resembled Leah Perry.

On the morning of Day One, the clock had read: 92 days, 8 hours, 32
minutes.

There was a scuffle at the back of the room. Samuel glanced up from
the stage, and the spotlight jerked in his hands. There was a man in body
armor standing at the door to the hall, holding some kind of replica—

A gun.

Samuel craned over the lights. Something Mrs. Ward had planned,
perhaps. This was probably some poor bastard in costume, a character
the kids would know. Although it hadn't been part of the rehearsals. A
kind of—what? A surprise? An end-of-term surprise? If there was a
surprise, Mrs. Ward should have briefed him. He could have come up
with something special. Brought out the Fresnels.

Beneath him, one of the spotlights exploded.

He stood. No costume. No replica. The man had a gun. He had an
actual gun. The stairs down to the stage were a few footsteps away, and
there was nothing in his head but to run, run, run. He took one step,
and a shot hit the rigging. He stumbled and lost his balance. Cumbersome. Never sure-footed; never a footballer. He landed on the stage with
a terrible, bony thwack and fell from the stage to the floor of the hall.

He'd need to move. The man was right there, coming down the
aisle. Taking his time. Time enough. Time enough for his mother to

find him. It was embarrassing, wasn't it? Eighteen, and waiting for your mother. He tried to sit, but there was something wrong with his legs. His hair was warm with blood. He scrabbled for a weapon. Found a chair leg but couldn't grasp it. Where was she? With Charlie, maybe. She was getting Charlie to safety, and then—

One of his eyes rested against the floor, but from the other, he saw a woman appear above him.

Not his mother, but Mrs. Ward.

Of course. Of course it was her. The flash of her skirt, yellow and blue and red. Who else? He raised a hand, the easier for her to lift him, but instead of her fingers he felt the slam of a single pink brogue. Heard the snap of another few bones. Couldn't feel them, though. That was something. Stress-induced analgesia. He'd done his reading. He watched the soles of her shoes, slapping away across the hall. He could feel only his heart. A terrible quaver beat. 92 days, 6 hours, 55 minutes. Other footsteps now. Before his face came great black boots. He could not have begged if he had wanted to. No mother to save him. He turned his eye upward. The man wore a helmet, and the gun was on his shoulder.

MONTH FOUR

TRENT

A Ray Cleave clinic, only a quick train ride from London. Ray announced the dates on Facebook. In the accompanying photograph, he sat at his desk behind an oversized microphone, frowning. Above him, bold type: WE TELL THE STORIES THEY FEAR.

Ray called them clinics, but they were held in pubs, barns, hotel ballrooms. Trent had seen photographs on Ray's website. There were young men with their arms around one another's shoulders, lifting pints, posters, Ray himself. There were photographs of beautiful women wearing T-shirts of Ray's face, his features stretched across their bodies. In some of the photographs, people were dancing, fists raised and mouths wide, and Trent thought of those golden army dances, glinting from his childhood.

"The energy," Susan said. "It's beautiful."

She had attended twelve clinics across the country. At the tenth, she was welcomed to the stage and awarded a little shining badge.

The clinic was on a Sunday. He had no other plans, after all.

He took a silent train out to Bexley, squinting from his shift. Early sun pummeled the windows, but the heaters were down, and he could see his breath in the air. Susan waited for him on the station platform. In the bright winter light she looked swollen, and older than he remembered.

"I know," she said. "I know. I should get to bed more early."

She rummaged in a tight pocket and emerged with a packet of catnip.

"For your new roommate," she said.

"I have to admit," Trent said, "I'm a little nervous."

"Oh, don't be nervous. Don't be nervous. You'll never meet a friendlier bunch."

Ray was speaking at a hotel. Two redbrick stories, surrounded by car parks. At the reception there was a sign for the Clinic, and they followed printed carpet, walls striped in different shades of beige, to Ballroom 2. Beneath her coat, Susan's T-shirt read: We are all being played.

From within Ballroom 2 came a roar of chatter, and he opened the doors, cautious, as if he might let something out.

But inside there were only warm handshakes. There was a gathering at the threshold, asking for his name, where he had come from, how he had found them. They were so very glad he had made it. One man shook his hand with particular vigor. He was a head taller than Trent, and he smiled with more teeth than his mouth could hold. His hair was combed, painstakingly, to cover his scalp.

"This," Susan said, "is Trent Casey. Trent Casey, of the Stonesmere Exposer."

"The Stonesmere Exposer," the man said. "We know your work. The things you've written about the shooter. Your experience—"

And he held up his arms. Trent, a prophet.

"I work with Ray," the man said, "on his radio show. Aidan McGee."

Trent knew Aidan. Aidan usually spent the show spluttering, in laughter or incredulity, at whatever Ray had just said.

"Do you have a particular theory?" Trent said shyly. He was still braced for ridicule. It was a habit, he supposed, that he would need to break. He could not wrangle the smile from his face. It was like the land he had inhabited for four months—occupied, for the most part, by avatars, by emails—had residents, customs, a rare, shared language.

"It didn't happen," the man said. "That much is clear."

"None of it?" Trent said.

"Look at the parents. You saw the husband, right? He's hosting a barbecue a few days later."

"But how—" Trent said, and stopped himself. Who cared? They had greeted him as one of their own. There would be time for nuance, analysis: this was the time for celebration.

"You don't need to know exactly what happened," the man said. "Do you? But you need to question what you've been told."

The lights were dimming. Silence spread across the windowless room. Trent had always shied from a front row, but Susan was on her way, bustling toward the stage. It was hard not to smile, watching her go. She complimented the people in the aisle seats: your hair, your shoes, your cap. She flopped down and patted the seat beside her. On each chair was an envelope for donations.

Help us, the envelope read, to tell the stories they fear.

"It's money well spent," Susan said. Her purse was in her hands.

Ray Cleave came out to "Suspicious Minds," and although the crowd was modest—although there were empty rows behind him—Trent felt the change in the room. Some people, they charged the particles. It was a power he would have liked. Who wouldn't? Ray wore a fine suit, double-breasted, with a Union Jack pinned to the lapel. He stood before a projector screen, emblazoned with a younger version of his face. He wore a red tie and a winter tan, and he carried a beer, full, and drank it at the microphone, drank it deep, so you could hear the lip smack just before he started to speak.

"Listen," Ray said. "Listen. The fact that you're here—you're here,

in spite of everything that's said about me. About us. I know that I'm
talking to a discerning crowd. I'm talking to the curious. I'm talking to
the bold. I'm talking to people who read the stories everybody else reads,
and see them differently. I'm talking to the brave. I'm talking to the
freethinkers. Let's talk today, then—about the stories they fear."

He looked to Susan. Her hands were clasped, close to prayer. Trent
smiled and leaned forward in his seat.

Ray didn't talk about Stonesmere right away. He started with the
house prices in London; with whole families displaced by foreign wealth.
"You will not hear the word *deportation*," Ray said, "in this context." He
visited those lawless estates where they ended up, the places other politicians didn't dare to tread. He spoke to good families, traditional families; families banished from that metal kingdom. He met a man who'd
lost an arm for his country, who lived now beneath a shop awning. A man
who had been ridiculed, burgled, abandoned. And did you see this man—

"Did you see this man, in the mainstream media?"

"But I saw him," Ray said. "I saw him."

And Trent found he was standing, with his hands together.

"Now," Ray said. "Listen. Let's talk about the great massacre—the
terrible atrocity!—of Stonesmere."

Ray said that people called him a conspiracy theorist. As if—as if
that was a bad thing! Behind him, on the screen, a flurry of headlines.
Project Sunshine. Bin Laden, located by a vaccination rollout. Manning: the pale, tired face, indignant over Ray's shoulder.

"If this is what it means," Ray said, "to be a conspiracy theorist—I'll
take it. I'll take it, and happily. I'll take it, and proudly. Let them say it.
Let them come."

He took the microphone and stepped from the stage. Now the whole
room was on their feet; and Ray was walking along the front row, embrac-
ing his followers as he went. He took one of Trent's hands in both of his
own, and Trent saw something like recognition warming Ray's face.

"You look at Boston," Ray said. "You look at Paris. You look at the good people of this country, the modest people, who saved all year for that one holiday—that single week of sunshine, the one that gets you through the winter, that week where you go to the bar and order a pint and don't consider the cost of it—in Tunisia."

They needed a new narrative, Ray said, and that was how they ended up with Stonesmere. They ended up with a different face above the headlines, and it was a face that suited them. Look at the facts. All of those wandering children, each with a muddled account. The parents suspended behind police tape, each with the same catalog bewilderment. Ray's staff—his brilliant, relentless people—had traced six of the actors to other atrocities. Their images appeared behind him, enlarged until they no longer showed people but pixels.

"There are folks in this room," Ray said, "who are gathering evidence. Who are challenging the Establishment. Who are conducting their own investigations."

Trent's smile tightened. What would he say, if Ray summoned him to the stage? He saw Ray catch his eye and nod, and he knew that he wouldn't be summoned, not just yet; that this small, private acknowledgment was a more precious thing.

"You may have heard," Ray said, "that the teacher's daughter is giving an interview. That the interview will take place a week on Monday, at nine a.m. That the whole country will be watching.

"That's an opportunity," Ray said. "That's an opportunity."

What Trent liked most of all was the very end of the event, when Ray walked between the rows, kicking chairs aside, getting to the people he had missed. At the back of the hall there was a man in a wheelchair with medals pinned proud to his jacket, and Ray clambered over the final few rows to reach him. Beneath the medals, the man's jacket was tatty, stained with old meals. Ray spent five minutes knelt at his side, while Aidan took photographs with an analog camera.

"How does he know that," Trent said, "about Martha Ward?"

"Oh, he has his friends in the mainstream media," Susan said. "They pretend to shun him, of course. Of course they do. But they can't quite resist—"

"It's pretty bold," Trent said. "Isn't it? An interview."

Susan looked to him. She was flushed with the warmth of the room. Ray must have recognized her: he had held her in his arms for a good few seconds as he did the rounds.

"You could call it," Trent said—and he was starting to laugh, the plan emerging as if it had been waiting here all along—"an opportunity."

Susan danced from one foot to the other, clutched her cheeks in her hands.

"It's perfect," she said.

MONTH FOUR

MARTY

A waitress at a state dinner accuses a royal of sexual assault, and he wishes to clear his name.

Or else an ailing pop star invites the press to his ranch, where he keeps cheetahs, leopards, lions.

Or else a departing prime minister, accused of lying to the House, gives his final interview in office.

Always, always: Rebecca Gleeson.

Leah left for university two weeks before the interview. She didn't throw a farewell party. She spent her last night in Stonesmere standing over my bed, trying to dissuade me from talking.

"Where you are right now, Marty—" Leah said. "It isn't a bad place to be. There are some fringe skeptics, sure. There's Samuel Malone, telling his version of events. Fine. Who cares? You haven't even been summoned to the inquest. You're—you're good as free."

This was what I told her: I was doing it for my family. If there were people who doubted our version of Day One, this would fix it. Fifteen minutes: no more, no less. I would repeat the facts everybody already knew. My mother would be a hero. My father would be unlucky. I would be dull and likable. When I returned to Stonesmere, people would touch my elbow in the supermarket and whisper: Well done.

I lay down on the bed. Outside, it was long dark, and the stars on the ceiling were starting to glow.

"Tell me," I said. "What does Freshers' Week have in store?"

"Marty—"

"Come on. Let me live vicariously at least."

Leah gave a long sigh, and acquiesced. "There's a foam party," she said.

"I can just see you, in the center of the dance floor."

"The party doesn't start," Leah said, "until I walk in."

I wanted, then, to ask her not to leave. I could have used any number of lines: Who else will suffer me, other than you? I like to think I could have persuaded her to stay. I could see the nerves, twitching beneath her eyes. The prospect of drinks receptions, lectures, a hundred introductions. It wouldn't have taken much.

I got my own way, I suppose, several months later, but it didn't feel as good as I had imagined.

"What are you going to say," Leah said, "if they ask you about him?"

"They won't," I said.

"How do you know?"

"No one talks about him," I said. "Do they? They don't even use his name." I hauled myself from the bed and looked to her, tired and worried at the window. "It's like he didn't even exist."

The night before the interview, I lay awake, reading old reports of Day One on the internet. I enlarged bird's-eye graphics of the hall and scrolled between the rooms. Leah messaged after midnight. I was hoping for a dire warning, for an outlook wise and bleak enough to call the whole thing off. But she must have been busy or else doused in foam. All the message said was Good luck.

Rebecca came to meet me in the underbelly of the studio, where I was gowned in a chair and incapacitated by hair rollers. She had a scalpel bob and quick, nimble hands. She looked like somebody who would never get sick.

"Martha!" she said, and opened her arms. "Martha. We were so delighted when we heard your dad was in touch. Our producers, they tell me they've been wanting you for months. The elusive Martha Ward. There are very, very few people, Martha, who've been through what you have. And that makes your voice precious, and it makes it important, and it makes me so happy to have you with us today."

"I think," I said, "I just needed time."

"Of course," Rebecca said. "Of course. That makes complete sense. How could anybody not need time?"

Beneath her arm was a clipboard, and she turned to it, touching her glasses as she went. I craned to see the contents, but she held it just out of view.

"What we'll do, then, Martha," Rebecca said, "is run through everything the producers discussed. And we'll have one or two callers on the line, too, as we always do, with questions we've screened."

She tapped the clipboard with a neat, unpainted nail.

"Now, what I'm here to check," she said, "is whether there's anything out of bounds. Anything you don't want to talk about. You tell me, we strike it. You just say."

"Did you see her at the memorial event?" my dad said. I had thought that we hated London, but he'd been jubilant since we arrived. On the train he bought a small bottle of champagne and poured it between plastic cups. He took photographs at the studio door. He asked the makeup artist about celebrities she had encountered. Who was a diva? Who was just as nice as they seemed?

"This girl," my dad said, "can handle anything."

"Open your mouth, please," the makeup artist said. "Just there."

My lips were parted and plumped. In those mute, gormless seconds, I tried to think how to phrase it. I didn't want to talk about my mother, obviously. I didn't want to talk about the things I was afraid of forgetting, as the days started to pass (her hands, ever ink-stained, or gummy with children's paws; or the certain look we exchanged when Dad talked about wood types; or the nights we would meet in the kitchen for tea, when neither of us could sleep). I didn't want to talk about how sad my dad was, a sadness hidden behind baseball caps and beers, so you could only catch it in certain lights (first thing in the morning, say, when he sat gazing at my mother's chair with a spoon limp in his fist). I didn't want to talk about what happened in the hall. I didn't want to talk about the wonder of Samuel Malone's survival. I didn't want to talk about—

The makeup artist nodded. My face was ready. "All of it," I said. "I'm happy to talk about it all."

Rebecca Gleeson sat in her infamous pink chair. I sat on a couch that looked far comfier on television than it actually was. I'd pictured the moment in my bedroom, in long showers, in the train toilet. Here we were.

"What would you like people to remember about your mother?" Rebecca Gleeson asked.

I could see myself in a multitude of cameras, and I looked OK. I looked composed.

"A lot of people are going to remember how she was found," I said. "I know that. And—you know what? They should remember. She could have got out, right? She was quick enough. She wasn't hurt. But she didn't. She went to her class. She saved Alicia Morden's life. She did everything she could—everything—to save the rest of them."

I rearranged my shirt (black, silk, two buttons undone), and swallowed.

"But she was also a really great teacher," I said. "The kids in her class, they loved her. She would spend whole weekends, thinking up the next cool thing for them to do. We'd run into her old students, every now and then, around town, and they'd always remember some chaotic field trip or a mad science experiment or an elaborate World Book Day costume."

Rebecca Gleeson looked calculatedly confused. "That's her as a teacher. But what about—as a mother?"

(No: not the smell of her, dressing at her bedroom mirror, surely the most beautiful person in the world. Not how seriously she took my questions; questions about periods, body hair; how she dignified them with her full attention. Not her forgiveness: I don't know what happened, Marty. But it's certainly nice to have you back.)

Behind the cameras, my father's eyes shone in the darkness.

"She was wonderful," I said. "She was the best."

"But there have been comments," Rebecca Gleeson said. "Haven't there? That your mother's bravery may have been exaggerated."

"Look," I said. "People in Stonesmere—people have been through hell. It's to be expected, that some of them may be—"

I smiled, graciously.

"Confused," I said.

"Would you say," Rebecca Gleeson said, "that you were close?"

So close I couldn't stand it. She was one of the few people in the world who knew that I was neither happy nor lucky; who knew my recent failures were not a blip but a kind of terrible culmination. She knew that I had a weakening knee, that after a game I had to sleep with it raised. She knew that I wasn't revising, that I was listless, that I was tired of being good. She knew that I was bored in a way that was dangerous, a boredom that was also a vacuum, the kind that doesn't care what fills it. She knew all my secrets, and kept them.

I had paused for too long.

"Yes," I said. "I would."

Rebecca Gleeson gave me a bemused smile, as if she had been hoping for more. I smiled back.

"OK," Rebecca Gleeson said. "OK then, Martha. What I want to talk about now is how things unfolded for you. I'm sure, Martha, that you don't want to think about Day One too much, in your everyday life—but I'm sure that it's with you, all the time."

That much, at least, was true.

"All the time," I said. "Yes. It's there, you know, when you first wake up in the morning. Almost as if it's been waiting for you. Like, overnight."

But I wasn't there to be another sob story, like Samuel Malone.

"But I'm more in control now," I said. "I feel like I can face it a little better, every day."

Rebecca Gleeson checked her notes.

"You were in the audience," Rebecca Gleeson said, "when the shooting began."

"That's right."

"And how did you come to realize what was taking place?"

I'd imagined it enough that it had become like a memory. It had its own colors, blind spots, sounds. I had been just where I should be. I had been at my mother's side. I had thought, at first, that the shots may have been part of the performance. A sound effect released too early. I only knew the truth of it when one of the children on the stage collapsed. The shooter was behind me, at the back of the audience, and I had seconds to decide whether to hide or to run, whether to play dead or to fight. I panicked. I could admit that now. I ran from the next few rounds, aimed at the crowd trying to open the fire escape. I took cover at the side of the stage—

"And it was there," Rebecca Gleeson said, "that you encountered Kit Larkin."

"Yes," I said. "At the side of the stage."

The studio was still. I could hear the hum of the cameras. The blink of their small, cold lights.

"Kit was the youngest victim that day," Rebecca Gleeson said. "And it must have been your natural response—something very similar to the traits people talk about in your mother, in fact—that made you stop there, by his side."

"I'm sorry," I said. "I haven't really—I haven't talked—"

"And we don't need to talk about this today, if it's too painful."

But she said nothing else. She left me there, in the long silence.

"He was still alive," I said. "He was just very—very tired. It can't have been much more than a few seconds, I don't think, but it felt—it felt a lot longer. I held his hand. I said, you know, that I was here. And he asked me if—"

Larkin's face, on the day of my mother's funeral: the way relief had eased the new, graver lines.

"—if we were going to be OK," I said. "I said, Of course. We'll be just fine. It's going to be OK."

"Thank you," Rebecca Gleeson said. "Thank you for sharing that."

They would be able to see my heart, beating beneath the nice new clothes.

"I'm sure you're aware," Rebecca Gleeson said, "that there are some malicious parties, on the internet, who would challenge your version of events. You've got your famous skeptics, your conspiracy theorists. And you've got a lot of individuals, too. They're on the message boards, they're posting about inconsistencies, about suspicions. They call you an actress. They say the bodies should be exhumed. They say the shooter was an innocent man. And you—you're one of the focal points of these discussions. Are you aware of that?"

I heard my voice, strange and otherly, as if it came from the studio walls.

"I've heard rumors of that," I said. "Yes."

"And what would you say, Martha, to people who believe the Stonesmere Massacre was a hoax?"

I took one hand in the other to cover the curl of my fingers.

"You can speak," Rebecca Gleeson said, "to the camera."

"We've been through enough," I said. "Haven't we? I don't know what kind of person—what kind of person you are. I don't know what happened, to make you see the world that way. But you've got things wrong. I would ask you—I would tell you—to leave my town alone."

My dad raised a single, triumphant fist.

"Now, we've received many comments," Rebecca Gleeson said, "from our viewers. And I want to read some of them to you, because I'd like you to know the impression you've made today. Cassandra from Tonbridge says that you're an emblem of bravery yourself, somebody of whom the whole country should be proud—"

I was nodding gracefully. At the side of the studio, a producer held up a single finger. It occurred to me that I still needed to talk about the gun, to clear my dad's name, and instead of listening, I waited to speak.

"Now, this isn't a question we were expecting," Rebecca Gleeson said. "But it's an important question, I think. And that's from Trent, calling from London. Trent. Welcome to the show."

I was so close, now, to my dad's arms. There would be congratulations backstage, and in Stonesmere, there would be praise. How eloquent I had been. How honest.

When the caller spoke, he sounded younger than I had expected.

"Hello, Martha," he said.

There was silence in the studio.

"My question," he said, "is whether you knew Rowan Sullivan."

I saw the tilt of the cameras. Behind them were strangers in shadow, expectant. Rebecca waited with a long, still gaze. I thought of Leah, watching from her dorm with a pillow between her teeth.

"And to be clear, for our viewers," Rebecca Gleeson said, "you're re-ferring to the shooter, there. Rowan Sullivan."

"I'm referring to the man named as the Stonesmere shooter. Yes."

"I knew of him," I said. "Yes. I think—I think everybody knows that. He used to work at the school. I worked there, too, over the last year or so."

"And that was the extent," Rebecca Gleeson said, "of your relation-ship?"

"That's right."

"Because we've received a photograph, Martha," Rebecca Gleeson said, "sent to us anonymously. It's a photograph we believe you took. And we wanted to share this photograph with you, to understand how it came about."

And there it was: on the screen behind us, enlarged for the audi-ence. Held, too, between Rebecca's dainty nails. I had been so careful to avoid his face, and the press had helped. He would have no fame; he would not be named. In the photograph he smiled gloriously, with his arm around my shoulders. The lake glittered behind us. Memories burst across my body. The minutes before the photograph was taken. The hours after it.

"I don't know—" I said. "I don't understand—"

I remembered my own smile, then. In the remembering, I knew that it must have faltered, but I couldn't bear to think, just yet, about what might have replaced it.

"Yes," I said. "Yes. I suppose you could say—there was a time when we were friends."

YEAR EIGHT

MARTY

Let me tell you something embarrassing. I know, I know: What could be left of me? But this fantasy is still private. Every few weeks, I would think about killing him. When I first got back to Stonesmere, after speaking to Rebecca Gleeson, I would consider doing it myself. I was young enough, I reasoned. I was fit. I didn't have a great deal left to lose. I would hire somebody to seek him out—Trent, calling from London—and for a long time, I would watch him. I'd imagined him, in those days, as a hulk; and so the killing, when it came, would be noble. Do you know, I would say, what you've done to us? Do you know that the school has dismissed me—until things die down—and that there are mornings when I can't climb from my bed? Do you know that my dad no longer sleeps? That he patrols the house, waiting for one of your kind? That neither of us can acknowledge it; because if we acknowledged it, it would have to be true?

I spent quite some time refining this speech.

After he was sentenced, the fantasy became more elaborate. I had to involve prison guards, insiders. I would find myself entangled in a whole mob saga, just to reach him. It was always worth it. The look of surprise, when they finally did my bidding—

Before I left my flat in the city, I took a cruel little paring knife from the kitchen drawer and set it on top of underwear, chargers, a jacket warm enough for Stonesmere. It was how I passed the drive, once I'd spoken to my dad. Five hours straight. Contemplating: the knife, or piano wire?

I reached Stonesmere in the late afternoon, but I wasn't ready for Crag Brow. I fought for a parking space at the supermarket, cracked every joint in my body, and took a hobble around town.

A lot of people thought Day One would be the end of tourism for Stonesmere. Nothing says summer holiday like a school shooting, after all. But at the close of the inquest, Katie Malone—who was, unsurprisingly, a member of the Stonesmere Tourism Board—delivered an impassioned address to the public, imploring them to keep visiting. On the second anniversary of Day One, they launched a new campaign, We're Still Beautiful. They used Alicia Morden in the publicity materials. The only person who survived the greenroom, standing by the lake and eating an ice cream, with an old bullet hole showing below the hem of her skirt. I don't know if it was charming or ghoulish, but either way, it worked.

It was the middle of September, and although the families were long gone, there were couples walking hand in hand past the shops on Main Street, pointing at fleeces, bobble hats, the stuff of autumn walks. The day's hikers had just descended from the hills, and they huddled hungrily over the tables in the square. Low autumn light slipped down the alleys. The rush of the river down Babbling Brook, the postcard turnstiles creaking in the breeze. I sat awhile, watching people changing shoes, dogs hopping into car boots, picnics unpacked across the grass.

My town.

Two men were collecting for the Mountain Rescue, accompanied by an extremely persuasive trail hound, and I stood for a moment, thinking of Larkin.

I left ten pounds in their bucket and headed for the car.

My mother once told Leah and me that the Romans used exile as an alternative to capital punishment, and Leah gave her great, Leahnine laugh, as if those things couldn't possibly be equivalent. Leah got most things right, especially when it came to the human condition. But I know, now, that she was wrong about this.

Once it was dark, I drove to Crag Brow. I preferred to come to the house at night. Swinging from the road, like this, around the driveway—the place was unchanged. The two rows of windows were still stately. You couldn't see that the curtains had long been closed. My headlights caught in the windowpanes, and at a squint, they might have been lights glowing from within. My mother in the kitchen, or one of my father's famous parties. You could see only that the flower beds were abundant, and not that they were neglected. The gravel sounded the same, stirring beneath my shoes. I glanced back before I turned the key. An old habit. Nobody would bother to watch me now. Above me, the stone arch was still stained, where some years before—when the house was already empty—a truther had daubed LIARS above our front door.

MONTH FIVE

TRENT

Rowan Sullivan. At last, they were using his name.

The triumph of the interview lasted a month. As soon as Martha Ward was off-air, Susan was on the phone, laughing so hard he couldn't understand a word she was saying. A day later, Ray Cleave dedicated his entire weekly show—two and a half hours—to scrutinizing the interview. "Here—see here. This is when she knows her time's up." Trent lay on his bed, and Zombie lay on Trent, and they listened to it twice over. Ray speculated, in turn, that Martha Ward was an accomplice, an actress (a poor one, at that), and a mastermind.

"Let's talk through," Ray said, "what she's wearing. We've got immaculate makeup." ("Immaculate!" said Aidan.) "Eye shadow, lipstick, the works. We've got a black shirt that our people have managed to trace. A one-hundred-and-fifty-pound shirt." (Aidan whistled.) "And what I would say to you good people is: Is this a girl who is grieving?"

"She and her mother," Ray said. "Maybe they had a disagreement. Maybe she thinks, this Rowan guy, he'll do my bidding." ("We've all heard," Aidan said, "of Lady Macbeth.")

Ray said: "Let's not forget. This is the girl whose father supplied the gun."

When the owner of the Chinese restaurant asked Trent what he was so happy about all of a sudden, he said, "Nothing."

He had more material for the Stonesmere Exposer than he had ever expected, and he and Susan spent their days sifting through the content. Kit Larkin was unlikely to have been a sex trafficking victim, kidnapped at birth and murdered as part of an elaborate cover-up, but they would take the piece about his father, who had confessed to attending a psychologist appointment while his son was murdered but had refused, point-blank, to provide the medical notes.

In which case: How was that an alibi?

Winter flurried into London. The offices where Trent worked were not heated at night, and his breath stirred in the still rooms. He was more daring, these days, when it came to the empty desks. He kept a note of the passwords he found, scrawled on Post-it notes, stuck inside desk drawers. He stepped into the shoes—expensive, probably tasseled—of his rightful role. He typed log-in details and browsed inboxes. Party invitations, billboard arrangements, interviews with people he hadn't heard of. He ordered Zombie a crate of premium cat food from some editor's Amazon account. When he returned to the flat, he was always wet. Zombie played with rivulets on the small windows.

It was in winter that Trent tended to think about his time in Stonesmere. He and his mother had lived there November to April, then fled back south for the spring. He had never been so cold. His clothes were designed for beaches, fens. They hadn't had the money for new ones. By December, the hills were mottled with snow. For days, low clouds slept in the valley, curled around the ridges and peaks.

He remembered now the evenings he had spent with Rowan. Their Christmas savior. His mother would go to bed early. He would dress in her jacket—Rowan never commented on it, though it was purple and absurd—and cut across the gardens, to the red door a few houses down. He had no memory of knocking, ringing: the door was always open, and Rowan's mother was rarely there.

"Where does she go?" Trent asked. They sat in Rowan's lounge, playing *Vice City*.

"Well," Rowan said, "she's a whore. So. Who knows?"

Rowan's mother had always seemed pretty decent to Trent. She spoke to his own mother, at least; no one else in Stonesmere seemed to. When he passed Rowan's house, he would know she was in by a great bouffant of blond hair, peeping from behind the sofa.

"Your dad was in the forces," Rowan said. "Yes?"

"That's right."

"That's a proper father. That's an actual fucking man. You miss him?"

"He wasn't around very much."

"Oh, come on"—and Rowan paused the game and held his bottle like a microphone—"you miss him?"

Trent laughed. His face was hot with pride. He had the sense he could tell Rowan everything. His mother's sadness, the army's silence, the long nights online in pursuit of clues. That Rowan would sit there, on the flowered sofa, getting it all.

"OK," Trent said. "Then yeah. I miss him."

"Good lad."

When Rowan finished a bottle, he threw it like a ninja star in the approximate direction of the kitchen bin. Half the bottles shattered en route.

"You know your dad?" Trent said.

"The Deserter?" Rowan said. He scoffed. He smacked the controller against his thigh. "My dad's girlfriend," he said, "is a year younger than me. So, you know. The less said about him, the better."

He unpaused. They were in Little Haiti, near the bay. Outside, it was raining.

"People act like you're defined by him, right," Rowan said. "Your father. Don't buy it. I'll tell you that for free. Well, look. Buy it if you want. Maybe you can afford to. But me . . ."

He laughed, although his eyes were wet. Trent looked away.

"The only thing I remember," Rowan said, "was this shitty school play, right. My mother, she can't come. My dad, he's got his one task of the year. And I'm dyslexic, right. I can't remember a fucking thing. I've got one line, and it gets to my turn, and I freeze. Just—fucking freeze. Right there onstage. Some cunt says it for me, in the end. And after the performance, all the parents are waiting in the classroom. It's a little party, right. To celebrate. And at first, I thought my dad wouldn't be there. I thought he'd be fucking furious. A waste of his time, right? But he's there, he's in there, he's waiting for me. You know what he does?"

Trent slowed his car. He turned to Rowan.

"He congratulates every other kid. There must be, like, twenty of us, and he's remembered everyone's part. He speaks to them all. Every single one. 'Oh, you were wonderful.' 'Oh, you're a star!' Everyone. Except for me."

Remembering it, Trent still felt a miserable sadness. Rowan had been a grown-up then, the same age Trent was now, and this was the story he chose to tell. He was such an easy target for a conspiracy. Wasn't he? Rowan, who had never belonged.

"I like you," Rowan said. "You're better than the rest of them."

Trent looked back to the cars. He was smiling stupidly, and he didn't want Rowan to see it. He would carry the words warm in his belly, past the fog of the Teapotter window, down the school corridors, to his desk. When he chanced a glance, Rowan was watching him, grinning, knowing it all.

"I mean it," he said. "Don't let this shithole grind you down."

MONTH FOUR

MARTY

My dad spoke little on the train home. We were in Lancaster before he could ask it. "How did you know him?" he said, and I explained that we had met when I started working at the primary school. "It was professional," I said.

It was nothing.

"Someone must have leaked it," I said. "Someone from the police. To press us, maybe. I don't know. To give people somebody to blame."

"The police?"

"My camera," I said. "It was a photograph from my camera."

"Why would the police have your camera?"

"They took it, the night you were questioned."

My dad shook his head. Slow at first, and then faster. "They provided a list of those things. They had to. Your camera—they didn't—"

"Are you sure?" I said.

"What would the police want with your camera?"

"I don't know."

"They only took a handful of things. My laptop. A book of appointments. No camera."

"I'm sorry," I said. "There must have been—some kind of misunderstanding."

A misunderstanding, or else a theft. I thought of Trent, calling from London. I thought of standing at the door, greeting my mother's mourners. The people I knew, and the people I didn't. Everybody had received the same grateful smile. Our house, open to all.

My dad turned to the window. The first purple hills came from behind the clouds. I didn't feel any of the usual relief, the sense of coming home. "Let's just get back," he said, as if it was still a place we could hide.

The morning after the interview, we received two items of post.

I lay in bed, listening to my dad downstairs. The television was on, and the radio, too, and so the house was full of strangers' voices, muffling its silence. Dread was multiplying in my stomach. I could feel it pressing against my heart, spreading to the bones. I had turned off my phone in the taxi from the studio, and I wasn't sure when I would turn it on again. I opened a book Leah had insisted I borrow, a collection of Wordsworth poems I'd planned to read over the summer. On each page, I could see the photograph, projected on the television behind Rebecca Gleeson. Other photographs, taken soon after.

My dad came for me at ten a.m. He didn't believe in moping. A breakup, an illness, national humiliation: you got up, and you pulled yourself together. He opened the curtains and looked to me.

"I'm sorry," I said. It was all I seemed able to say.

"This came," my dad said, "for you."

He handed me a white envelope, already torn.

"I opened it," he said, "just in case—"

In case of spite, powders, blades.

"Just in case," he said.

In the envelope was a printed letter, summoning me to speak at the inquest into the shooting at Stonesmere Primary School, of the fifth of July. The inquest, the letter said, would take place over two weeks in July, approximately a year after the atrocity. I would be notified of my required day of attendance closer to the time.

I set the letter down on the duvet and swung my legs from the bed. My dad was supposed to be working over at the Malone house, laying a ramp for Samuel's return. Instead, he was in the kitchen, cleaning the fridge. I could imagine Katie Malone on the phone, first thing this morning. Perfectly polite. We've decided to go with somebody else. Nothing personal.

Nothing to do with you.

I heard something fall on the doormat, and the quick crunch of gravel. Not the postman. The post had long come.

We reached the hallway at exactly the same time. On the doormat was a newspaper, face down.

"Marty," he said.

For a long moment we looked at each other.

"Don't, Marty," he said. "Don't look."

He knelt down, keeping his eyes on my face, as if I might be about to pounce. He snatched up the paper from the floor.

I held out my hand.

"They don't know what they're talking about," he said.

"Dad? I'd rather know."

He shook his head. He handed over the paper, folded. He gave me a few last seconds in a world where I hadn't seen it.

And it was really something—to see my own face, looking back at me. I had the sense, for a second, that I was no longer real; that the printed girl, smiling from Rebecca Gleeson's sofa, was the one living, breathing. Dread crippled my fingers. The paper shook.

The headline read HERO OR LIAR?

"Martha Ward purports to have been a hero of Stonesmere," the byline read. "But an uncovered photograph suggests she may have something to hide."

"Don't read it, Marty," my dad said. "Don't bother. It's a rag. Come on, Marty. Please."

I knew the exact moment they had captured. *We wanted to share this photograph with you.* I was ugly with the shock of it, caught somewhere between panic and indignance.

My dad took the paper from my hands. The printed girl in one arm, and me in the other, our faces pressed tight against his chest.

MONTH SIX

TRENT

In early December, he returned from the corner shop to find Tim smiling placidly from the window of the Chinese restaurant. Trent was so baffled that he stood a moment in the street, buses flecking him with puddle. Tim, who had known about his father. Tim, his mother's confidant, who had always observed Trent with such disdainful sympathy. Poor, oblivious Trent, thinking his father the hero—

He could retreat. Could trudge the afternoon in Southwark Park and turn up early for work.

But Tim was already waving.

At the threshold, Trent mustered his nonchalance. Tim's laptop was plugged into the wall. He drank from a glass of ice water. The owner of the Chinese restaurant gave Trent a long, tired look, and he waved an apology.

"Hello, there," Tim said.

"This is a surprise."

"I was in town for a conference," Tim said, "and I just thought—"

He gave a cheerful shrug. It was unclear to Trent what Tim could possibly have been thinking.

"Come on up, then," Trent said.

Zombie trotted to meet them at the door. "Oh," Tim said, and stepped from the cat's greeting. "Quite a place you've got," he said. Trent unpacked the shopping. He had bought cat food, chewing gum, biscuits, sliced bread, and two cheese sandwiches with impossibly long expiry dates. Even to him, the items seemed indicative of existential loneliness.

"How are you doing?" Tim said. "How *are* you doing?"

"Fine," he said. "Pretty good. How are you?"

He would have liked to ask about his mother. She'd been disappointed by the way he left. Had said as much, in a series of formal text messages sent the week after he arrived. From the tone of the messages, Trent gathered they were subject to extensive peer review. Now, she texted only on Sunday afternoons, wishing him a good week. Accompanying the good wishes were reports of her weekend, which were always pleasantly mundane, Got new pots at M&S sale, or Badger in the garden on Friday. Trent looked forward to the messages more than he cared to admit.

"Oh, we're very well," Tim said. "Very well indeed. 'Tis the season, and all that. Your lovely mother, she's been dressing the house. The tree! The tree that woman's ordered. I've never seen anything like it."

"Well," Trent said, "she loves Christmas."

A lump of sadness tightened in his chest. He couldn't remember a year when they hadn't traipsed to some garden center or other. Garden centers in December: they were the coldest places on earth. She'd find the tree with a crooked top or a few bare branches, and begin negotiations.

"How are your Christmas plans panning out?" Tim said. It was a question that assumed there were extensive preparations to be made.

That he was spending his free time writing cards and wrapping gifts, instead of analyzing photographs on the internet.

"I'll probably leave the Friday before," he said.

Tim gave him a sweet, befuddled smile.

"Right—right. And where are you heading?"

This, the moment where Trent would spend the night. He was so unsuspecting—so fucking foolish—that he lay down in the trap and snapped it closed himself.

"Home," he said. "I mean—if that's OK."

The smile stayed, but Tim's other features were changing. Reddening, sharpening.

"We've been discussing this, Trent," he said. "Me and your mother. It's actually—it's actually the prime reason I'm here. To see you, too—of course! But also. Christmas. The thing is—you're making quite a name for yourself up here. Aren't you?"

"I work security," Trent said.

"Oh, I know that. I know. I'm referring to your side project, you see. To your little appearance—with Rebecca Gleeson."

"Ah," Trent said. He and Susan had spent some time discussing whether he should use his real name. To not do so, Trent had concluded, was the type of cowardice he condemned. The photograph would need to be submitted anonymously, but the question—of the question, they could be proud.

"These kinds of politics, Trent," Tim said, "they're not welcome in my home."

Trent's laugh was intended to be carefree, but it came out wet and sad. Zombie turned to him from the windowsill, startled.

"The politics of—what? Honesty? Integrity?"

"Come on, now," Tim said. "It's delusional, Trent. It's the stuff of wackos. It's—I'm going to say it. It's mentally unstable. Those folks in Stonesmere, they've watched their kids gunned down. They're griev-

ing. And now—this? You know how she found out? Your mother? Somebody at the golf club. 'Don't you have a Trent, too?' She had to watch it
on her phone in the ladies' room. Can you imagine?"

"You don't get to do this," Trent said.

"To do what?"

"To use her—"

An old curse, to cry when he was angry. That time in the playground, in his third school, when George Strout—God, that he could
still remember his name—had announced that Trent's mother couldn't
afford a car. Had seen him changing into his trainers, one day after
school, for the two-mile walk home. And the hot, horrible tears, impossible to hide—

At that point the memory faded, but he was pretty sure he had
claimed one of Strout's teeth. His mother once told him his father did
the same, cried with rage, and for a while that dulled the humiliation.
He was always scavenging for the ways they were the same.

He turned from Tim and dragged at his eyes.

"Does she even know," he said, "that you're here?"

Tim was already at the threshold.

"When you're done with these conspiracies, Trent," he said, "then
we can talk. When you're done, we'll welcome you with open arms. But
until then—"

He shook his head. A painful task, sure, but something that had to
be done. At the station, Tim would buy a celebratory gin and tonic for
the train home. Trent could see it—Tim, stepping into the warmth of
the house. His mother, waiting at the tree. Her exhausted cardboard
boxes, dragged from house to house: the best baubles, the average baubles, the baubles that needed to be hidden at the back.

"Anyway, Trent," Tim said, "Happy Christmas."

MONTH SIX

MARTY

The best Christmas card I received was from Leah. The stock message wished me a merry Christmas and a happy new year. Maybe even better, Leah had written, than the last?

Other cards—and how I wished I could show them to Leah; that we could ridicule them together, until they became funny—hoped that I would be dead by Christmas.

After the interview, I only left the house in the dark. It was less restrictive than it sounds. The Lake District in December: it was dark for most of the day. I had always liked the way Stonesmere looked, this time of year. The lights of the town huddled together beneath Old Man's Edge. The sky blackening each hour, until the mountains disappeared. There had been some kind of ceremony—there was a ceremony for everything, these days—at which Samuel Malone, on leave from the hospital, had turned on the Christmas lights. I hadn't attended, but my dad reported that Samuel was very dignified. He did a stellar job.

"They all came on, then?" I said. "The lights?"

But my dad was already gone, up to his study. He was humorless, these days. He was about the house more, but I saw him less. I hadn't told him that the primary school had let me go. It could wait, I decided, for the new year. When we were together, we still tried to talk about our favorite things, the football scores and Stonesmere gossip. But when we were quiet, I felt him looking at me, as if there was something more he would like to say.

I ran into Samuel Malone myself a few days before Christmas. He came down Main Street with a gift bag wrapped stubbornly around his wrist, picking between cobbles with his crutches. He stopped to rest outside the butcher, chest heaving. He had the clean, sallow skin of somebody who hadn't been outside in a while. I'm not sure whether I went to him out of kindness or spite.

"Can I help?" I said.

"No, thank you."

"Gift buying?"

"For Leah, actually," he said. "She'll be back on Saturday."

"I know," I said, although I didn't. "What did you get?"

He made to shield the bag, but I'd already seen the logo. "A book?" I said.

"Fine. Romantic poetry. She's studying it next term."

He looked at my face and sighed: "It was a literary movement."

"I'm sure it was. Either way. I can take the bag."

"Oh, fuck off."

He was smiling. He straightened from the wall and matched my pace.

"That was quite a ride," he said. "Rebecca Gleeson."

"That's one way of putting it."

"And quite a photograph, too."

I saw the two of us in the window of the Teapotter. My expression was well-pitched: sympathetic but firm. "I don't think it's a crime to have known him, is it? A lot of people did. We used to work together. We took the odd trip to the lake."

"From what I heard," Samuel said, "Rowan Sullivan hated everybody. I heard he mostly kept to himself."

"Most of the time, maybe."

"He made an exception, then, did he," Samuel said, "for Martha Ward?"

I gave him the same smile I saved for small children, or my dad's cousin, kicking off a new monologue on Princess Diana. "Whatever you say."

"My mother receives letters," Samuel said, "telling her that she's never had a son. That she isn't a mother, she's a trickster. That she's mad. They ask for my brother's death certificate. His birth certificate, too, some days. Do you know—do you know what that can do to a person?"

In his fury, he was slower. We were off Main Street and heading for the roads that rose above the lake. Only a few meters, and I could turn for Crag Brow.

"I'm sorry," I said. "But that's nothing to do with me."

"Isn't it? Every time you pop up, you make everything that little bit worse."

He stopped at the junction. The shops had petered out, and with them the streetlights. Crag Brow curled up the hillside.

"Did you get your invitation?" he said.

"Invitation?"

"To the inquest."

"Yeah. I did."

"I'm looking forward to it, myself. It's a chance, isn't it? A chance to set the record straight. To prove these lunatics wrong. Your testimony. I'm looking forward to that."

It was easy to like Samuel, the way he looked today. The way he looked on breakfast television. The careful hair, stoic jaw, vulnerable bones. But this close, I could see the lines of older, crueler expressions.

"Another opportunity," I said, "to slander my mother?"

"Another opportunity," he said, "to tell the truth. Bird's-eye view, Martha. I don't know where you were that day. But I know where you weren't."

MONTH SIX

TRENT

On Christmas Eve he caught a train to Oxenholme, and from there a smaller train to Stonesmere. The first train was full of Londoners returning home, presents on their laps and cases crushing their knees. The second train was quiet, and he was the only person to get off at Stonesmere. The train lights caught in the frost of the platform for a few noisy seconds, and then the station fell dark and quiet.

On Christmas Day he ate lunch at the Lakeview. It was the oldest hotel in town. There was a bell at the reception desk. There were thick carpets in the restaurant, and the napkins were folded into elaborate, unidentifiable shapes. They kept his wineglass full. He finished before any of the other guests, and in the falling evening he walked around the lake, toward the lights of the town.

Even in grief, the place was quaint. The whole town was dressed for Christmas, as if by a single, enthusiastic artist. The same golden lights hung from the pharmacy, the butcher, the pubs along the lakefront. The shop windows displayed nice, miniature lives. There were ballerinas at the newsagent, dressed for *The Nutcracker*, and at the Teapotter it was Christmas morning. Featureless dolls crouched around the tree. At the doctor's surgery there was a row of eleven angels: ten of them small, and one a little bigger.

He knew he would end up there. This time he stuck to the shadows of the walls, his hands damp with moss and sleet. The Wards drew their curtains late. It was like another of the shop miniatures, only engorged, in motion. The resplendent tree and the gifts beneath it. The family, too. If that was what they were. The father wore a jolly jumper, and his hands were always full. He held pints, kitchen knives, party food too small for his fingers. Trent saw flashes of crisp pastries, of grease on lips. They ate in the same way, the father and daughter, as if they might never eat again. Trent stood there long into the night, with damp boring into his coat and skin, and something hotter rising within him, a kind of fury worse than fury, because it was also longing. To be back in those rooms—in the light, brilliant hallway. There would be holly on the staircase—wouldn't there?—and the smells of pine, meat, butter, dusting the house.

All the same: he might not have done it if it wasn't for Sergeant Larkin.

A man came up the driveway with a parcel in his hands, and Trent shrank to the wall. Kit Larkin's father, at the Ward house, on Christmas Day. He fumbled his phone from his pocket. It was too dark to capture a photograph, but he sent a message to Susan, who replied right away.

Of course he is.

The father welcomed Larkin with open arms. Trent watched them congregate in the living room. They sat a trio around the fire, heads bent conspiratorially close, mouths parted in laughter. They raised triumphant glasses. What else? Champagne.

MONTH SIX

MARTY

On the big day itself, we kept to the living room of the house on Crag Brow. There, the fire was lit, and we just about filled the space. The decorations all seemed wrong—the hang of particular baubles, the arrangement of the lights on the mantelpiece, the modest pile of presents—and although I adjusted them each time I passed, I seemed only to make them wonkier, and further from what I remembered.

We took turns opening presents. My dad couldn't wrap. You could see parts of the boxes, the books, where he hadn't provided for enough paper. I opened a travel guide entitled *The World*, where the paper was taped to the book itself.

"You know that Amazon would have wrapped it for you?" I said. I grinned, and he grinned back.

"That one," he said, "is from your mother."

"It is?"

"She always started buying in January. You know that."

"Are there others—" I said. I touched the cover. "Others that she—"

The rug, he said. She'd thought it would brighten a university room. The running socks. I'd asked for them in March, but they were too expensive for an everyday purchase. She had picked up the earrings on some class trip or other, but he couldn't remember where from.

"Why didn't you tell me," I said, "before I opened them?"

"I don't know. I didn't—I didn't want to bring the day down."

I was gathering them from among the paper, a little shrine of items she'd chosen herself.

"I'd have liked it," I said. "I'd have liked to know."

The other surprise of the day was Larkin. As soon as the doorbell rang, I stood. A journalist. Maybe a truther. Not today. Not today—of all days. It was important to get to the door before my dad; it was important he didn't see me eviscerated. I could just about bear it, if I was alone.

But there was only Larkin, huddled close to the light of the door. My dad rested a slow hand on my shoulder, and we exchanged a strange, grateful glance. These days, in Stonesmere, there was always somebody a little sadder than you.

"Room at the inn?" Larkin said. "I won't be long."

He held a bottle of champagne, clutched between thick gloves.

"Of course," my dad said, and stepped aside. "Happy Christmas," he said. "I can't imagine it's been an easy one."

"Not the best," Larkin said. "No."

I hadn't seen him since the Rebecca Gleeson interview, but all the same: he didn't seem to be here to scalp me.

There was the clown dance of him removing his shoes while we hovered, waiting to catch him. He shuffled ahead of us, touching the walls as he went. His waterproofs squeaked together. At the kitchen table, he set down the bottle and opened his arms. Ta-da.

"I remembered it," he said, "from the funeral—"

Closer now, he smelled of other, cheaper bottles.

"Well," he said. "Cheers."

My dad's smile was gentle and pained. "We'll open it, then," he said. "Shall we?" He set an arm around Larkin's shoulders and steered him toward the living room. "Marty. Do you want to get the glasses?"

I collected three flutes from the cupboard. There was dust on the rims. The cork burst from the lounge, and I clutched for the kitchen counter. I hadn't cried that day, but standing there, in the dark room, I took the marble in my hands and clung to it, waiting for the hell to subside. Waiting, waiting.

In the lounge, Larkin sat on the sofa, dripping onto the fabric. "What can we toast?" my dad said, and I laughed. He would always find something to celebrate. He gave me a hurt little glance and remustered his smile.

"We survived the year, I suppose," Larkin said.

"We can do better than that."

"To Ava, then," Larkin said. "And to Kit."

I saw a line of sadness furrow my dad's face, and then it was gone, replaced by banal cheer. He raised a glass.

"Yes," he said. "Of course."

Larkin kept to his word. He drank fast. No, he didn't have other holiday plans. He was putting something together, he said, for the new year. These rumors, he said—and he looked at his socks, threadbare on the rug—something had to be done. These—truthers. There was a war to be won. We understood that, didn't we? A war.

He stood, dull-eyed. He would be in touch.

"You'll be all right," my dad said, "getting home?"

"Oh, I could do with the walk. I could do with the walk."

My dad lit the drive for him, and we stood together, watching him leave.

"That guy," my dad said. "Jesus. That poor man."

He closed the front door.

"He really knows," my dad said, "how to bring down a party."

Long after he was asleep, I jogged slow through the streets of the town. I wore my new socks. The pubs were closing. The Stonesmere Christmas tree, sanctified by Samuel Malone, was bright and dripping wet. I found myself out at the Sprawl. I passed the Sullivan house and ran faster. A boy passing wished me a happy Christmas, and I called back the same. At Leah's place, I stopped to rest on the curb. There was a hideous blow-up Santa Claus, swaying in the Perrys' front garden. Behind the curtains I could see a warm, golden light and people moving within it. I hauled myself from the pavement and headed for home.

MONTH SIX

TRENT

He couldn't speak, think. In his head, they raised their glasses, and raised them again. To deception, to prosperity. To getting away with it.

He could not bear the dinge of the hotel. He could not return to London. He could not see his mother. He walked blind through the sleet. It was some way to their old neighborhood, but he could recall the route. No views of the lake, here. No bay windows, no gravel drives. The houses were smaller and hidden embarrassedly in the depths of the valley. There were pebble dash fronts, and television on the curtains. Here, here: this was the place.

He had thought there might be security or police tape, but the house was quiet. There were no lights on inside. Rowan Sullivan's home. The garden boggy, the hanging baskets empty. There was a gap in the fence, and the curtains were drawn. It had been a good house when he'd last seen it. One of the smartest houses on the street. Rowan had designed the number on the door. He had assembled fencing along the boundaries and a proud little gate from the street, which he shut behind him as he came and went. As soon as it was spring, he was in the garden, heaving bags of compost or scraping weeds from the dirt.

"Your garden," Rowan had once said, "is a fucking shitshow." And Trent, returning from another bleak day at Stonesmere High, had been surprised by just how much this hurt.

"It is?" Trent said.

"It's the problem," Rowan said, "with renting. Most tenants, they don't give a shit."

Trent had looked back to his own house. The grass was patchy, but his mother had set a pot of daffodils by the front door, and yellow flowers grew along the borders.

"Those flowers there, though," Trent said. "They're pretty nice."

Rowan sat back in his own resplendent grass and howled with laughter.

"They're dandelions, you muppet. It's a weed."

And Trent must have bristled then, because Rowan became softer. He held out the trowel, laid across his palm like some ancient inheritance. "I can show you," he said. "If you want."

They planted sunflowers and dahlias and love-in-a-mist (which neither of them could say with a straight face). Rowan brought round his mower, and they tidied the grass. He had to water the beds, Rowan said, every evening, and Rowan lent him a great red watering can. They stopped slugs at the borders. They sprinkled them with salt—a little, Rowan advised, and then a little more—until they turned to puddles. At the end of these days—and there couldn't have been more than a handful of them, though Trent remembered them as whole seasons— Rowan emerged from his house with two beers, dripping cold, and removed the caps with his teeth. Trent and his mother left town well before the flowers bloomed, but he liked to think of them, even once they moved away. The house, transformed.

He knew, now, where he would go. With the knowledge came fear, of course, but also a thrill. This, the evidence they needed. He could see himself in Ray Cleave's studio, adjusting a microphone. In the imagining, he wore a suit. "We have a very special guest with us today," Ray said. And Trent cleared his throat—his voice was deeper, in this fantasy—and began.

He found himself shouting happy Christmas to a girl stopped on the curb, and to his surprise, she shouted it back.

MONTH SEVEN

―――――

MARTY

All through the holidays, I had been waiting for it. When I searched for my name—and I searched for it more than I cared to admit, that Christmas, with nobody to see and little to do—links about the conspiracy had advanced to the first page. *Whore liar hoax was never really there.* I lost whole days reading the comments underneath Ray Cleave's blog posts. *Actress boohoo the truth deluded stuck-up bitch.* In my bedroom, I spoke to myself the way Anoushka had spoken to me the day of my mother's funeral: a calm, stroking tone that felt like it reached from a memory. You're OK. You're OK. You're OK. When Leah called around on Boxing Day, holding a battered copy of *Love Actually,* I saw the state of myself in her expression. *When we get hold of her—*

"Marty," she said.

"Don't say it," I said. "Let's just have"—and I laughed—"a nice time."

"All I was going to say," Leah said, "is that it's good to see you."

Somebody needs to do something.

When it came down to it, there was no vigilance required. It was the second day of January. I had finally entertained my dad's pleas to get out of the house. I wore an anorak of my mother's, with the hood pulled up. I walked up to Old Man's Edge, relishing the pain of the climb: an easy, familiar pain, which meant I couldn't think about anything else. I found a decent lump of scree and ate turkey sandwiches sitting by the tarn, hands purple-cold and trembling. Here, close to the edge, there were islands of ice, shaking in the currents. I'd done the walk the past spring, a few months before my mother died. We had swum that day, the tarn turned a deep, brilliant blue beneath the sky. But there was some sourness to the memory, the nausea of old humiliation.

I swallowed my last half of sandwich and hoisted up my pack. It was a stupid place to have come.

As soon as I turned from Crag Brow, I saw the disturbance. The front door was open, and my dad's car was stopped in the middle of the drive.

I held to the fabric of my pockets and came to the house.

I touched the door and watched it swing into the hallway. I had the sense of stepping into something long-imagined. There was some relief to that. It wasn't that the worst thing had been avoided, but that it had happened, that at last the waiting was over and we'd come to the thing itself.

"Hello?" I said.

I looked up to the landing. Gray light shifted along the walls, sent shadows scuttling from stair to stair. I set one foot into the house and tried to summon the other to join it.

"Hello?" I said, and from the kitchen I heard a stagger, and then a hush.

"Marty," my dad said. "Marty. Don't come in here. Do not come in here. Stay where you are."

He appeared from the kitchen. I froze there, seeing him. His face was wet with tears. He touched his eyes, as if he hadn't yet realized, or had realized only when he saw my expression. I'd have taken a home invasion. I mean it. I'd have taken mutilation, broken bones. Anoushka was behind him, and she was telling me that I needed to sit down, just here, and she would let me know what had happened.

Out at St. Oswald's, somebody had attempted to exhume Ava Ward's corpse. They had not got far, no more than a foot or so, but the grave would need to be repaired. And the stone—the stone would need to be replaced.

"We believe," Anoushka said, "that this act was probably committed by somebody who denies the Stonesmere Massacre ever took place."

I sat there, retching for breath, while my dad followed Anoushka from room to room, asking how she could have let this happen. When I couldn't listen to them anymore, I climbed the stairs to my room and called Leah.

I don't remember much about the hours after. When I called, Leah said, I sounded as if I was struggling to breathe. There were no words, just the panic of it. You sounded—I don't know, Marty. Like you'd reached the end of something. I knew that you needed somebody. I mean. I knew that I had to come.

She arrived within an hour, and for the next few months, she didn't really leave. It said a lot about my frame of mind, that I only remembered where she should be when it was the middle of January and too late to do anything about it. "When are you going back to university?" I asked, from the bedsit I'd made of the sofa, and Leah, carrying hot mugs of tea from the kitchen, said, "I'm not."

MONTH SEVEN

TRENT

He thought, at times, that evidence of what he had done must be visible, there on his face. The morning receptionists would see it as soon as they swung in. Zombie would recoil at the threshold. On the third of January, it was the lead item on *BBC News*, and he waited, stunned, for the newsreader to point at him from the television.

"It's a slow season," Susan said. He was not to worry.

It was only Susan he told. When he said he had news, he heard her adjust her body in the chair. She settled in for the story. The graves had grown crooked from the earth, unsettled by tree roots and split by frost. As he went, he read the inscriptions. Grandfather, Mother, Son, Friend. The dead defined by their company. He saw a grave for a child of eleven and a half months, a Daughter and Granddaughter and Sister, and he felt tears in his throat, damp and croaking. Too much wine at the Lakeview. Something about that half month—as if it counted.

"The teacher's grave, though," Susan said. "Tell me about that."

He found the spade in a shed attached to the church. The Ward stone was flowerless and already weathered. Green grime in the curls of the letters. Whoever had come up with the wording, they'd been concise. Wife, Mother, and Teacher, the grave read.

It saved them crafting a personality, Susan guessed.

He stuck the blade into the earth.

He wasn't sure what he had expected. Some kind of divine intervention, perhaps. Instead—nothing. The spade stopped a few inches past the surface, and the impact hurt his hands. He tightened his grip. Dug harder. But the ground was stubborn. By the light of his phone, he could see a glaze of frost, set beneath the grass.

He lifted the spade higher. Plummeted the thing into the earth. Sleet spluttered against his face. Like the weather had conspired to keep their secrets.

He kicked at the stone, and when it didn't budge, he took the spade and swung at it. The top of the grave cracked. He dealt another blow, and the thing started to crumble.

"I only wish," Susan said, "that you'd have told me. To be there—"

How to explain? That it was uncalculated and desperate. That he told it with a flourish but could no longer sleep at night.

"There'll be other chances," Trent said. "The inquest, for one. You saw, right—that they've set the date?"

"Oh, I saw. I saw."

"I've been thinking," Trent said, "about what we should do."

Better this: the warmth of the flat, Zombie deadening his leg, Susan rapt on the line. Better than the graveyard on Christmas night, where he had felt like the last man on earth. He had left the stone a stump. If he could not reach the body, he had planned to destroy the thing, but he decided instead to leave it, depleted and pathetic. Something hard to look at, amid their cobbles and hills.

YEAR EIGHT

MARTY

In the old house, I always slept badly. I tended to take a sofa in the living room, which didn't help. A leak had set in above my bedroom, and there was a bucket in the corner, catching the droplets. I had decided my dad would fix it when he next visited, and perhaps he'd decided I would do the same. The bucket had overspilled to the carpet. Mold sprinkled the wool. I poured the water down the sink and set the bucket back in place.

The house hadn't been heated in some months, and cold had set into the walls. I took the duvet from my parents' bedroom and closed the living room door. Behind it, I could feel the looming of the empty rooms. The silence of the place. I missed the soundtrack of the flat, traffic and planes, televisions and other people's phone calls. I tried to sleep an hour longer, and then I gave in, turned on the light, and called Leah.

"Marty?" she said. Leah always answered my calls that way, like she expected somebody was phoning to say I was dead.

"Are you asleep?" I said.

"The evidence," Leah said, "would suggest otherwise."

"Where are you?"

"I'm home."

I closed my eyes. I would be able to sleep, now. Knowing that she was just there, up in the Sprawl. She could be here in twenty minutes, if I wished.

"It's Francesca's sixteenth," she said, which stunned me more than anything. Those small barbarians, tumbling from the Perry house. Teenagers.

"Is this," Leah said, "about last week's news?"

Unlike my dad, Leah was a loyal follower of current affairs.

"Maybe. I wanted to come up. To see the town. Get some— country air."

"Country air," she said. "I'm sure."

"Are you free?"

"Now?"

"I'm not that desperate. Tomorrow?"

"A little desperate, then," she said. There was a long pause, as if she was checking for other appointments. "I could do eleven," she said. "Before the party."

"The Boaters?"

"Really?"

"We don't have to," I said. But we'd so often met there, at the end of her shifts. I liked the idea of it, the two of us back at the bar. Leah would make immaculate coffees, and we would eat kitchen scraps, exploded croquettes or deformed brownies.

"Lattes," I said, "on the house."

"I don't work there anymore, Marty. You know that."

Again, she was quiet.

"But OK," she said, at last. "The Boaters."

When she hung up, the silence was worse than ever. I summoned an ancient playlist on my phone and fell asleep to Fall Out Boy, The 1975: the music I had grown up to. I would play it in the bar, when the customers had long gone home. One morning, the manager had come in with the early delivery and stopped at the threshold, laughing.

"What are you?" he said. "A sixteen-year-old girl?"

My phone died in the night, and I woke to the disquiet of silence. There were still many hours before I would see Leah. I left the house and wandered Main Street. The heavyweight gear was already in stock. Mannequins wore bobble hats and gloves. I bought a bad coffee and took one of the alleys to the lake. Clay gray and nicked with rain.

They set the memorial a few meters out from the shore. Eleven metal flowers, craning for sun. It was opened a little while after I left town, and everybody had an opinion. A truther once tried to take the flowers out with a boot full of bricks, and CCTV of his failure went viral. Each anniversary, Katie Malone walked into the water and threaded flowers around the steel. I wondered what Samuel thought about that.

During construction, the thing looked ugly, strange. But now—I wasn't so sure. Ten of the flowers were shorter, carved so the petals weren't quite open. Stuck half formed, waiting for light. The eleventh flower rose above them, in bloom. I looked at that stupid flower for a long time.

Two girls, eighteen or nineteen, sidled along to the next bench. I had the old, queasy sense of scrutiny, but when I looked over they were absorbed in each other and hadn't noticed me at all. I was bedraggled and badly dressed. I was practically middle-aged. I wouldn't have given myself a second glance.

"Do you think they'll be boring?" one girl said to the other. She wore tight black jeans and pristine mascara, and I found that I was smiling. You had to admire it, for a morning by the lake.

"Oh, probably," the second girl said. She was taller. Her sweatshirt read Stonesmere High Leavers. She spoke the way you do, once you've survived being a teenager. Like you've seen it all and been right about every bit.

"But not as boring as here," she added.

"Well, obviously."

The shorter girl nodded to the memorial. "Did you decide what you're going to do?" she said.

"I talked to Denise. We talk about it all the time, obviously. But, like, about this—" The girl hung her head back over the bench and stretched. "So. What we decided is, I'm not going to volunteer it. I'm going to see how it goes. If there are people I really, really like, and I trust them, then maybe. Maybe. But Day One—it's not going to, like, define me. If that makes sense."

"That makes a lot of sense."

"And Denise does these video calls," the taller girl said, "so it's not like—"

"Of course it isn't."

"It'll just be different."

"Different," the shorter girl said. "But good different."

"Do you know what Denise said?" the taller girl said. "She said it's like a really, really expensive present. The sharing of it. You don't want to go handing them out to any old person, but just now and then, it could actually feel pretty good."

"I like that."

"She said, 'Alicia, don't you give that gift out willy-nilly.'"

The shorter girl snorted. Alicia threw back her head and gave a great bark of a laugh. It was a laugh older than she was. If they had seen my face—if they could have seen it. I'm pretty sure my cover would have been blown. I took a look as long as I dared. There was a great toad of a sob caught in my throat, and I swallowed it back down and adjusted my hood. Alicia Morden at eighteen, with her school leaver sweatshirt and her nails painted black. She wore Doc Martens, and each ear was pierced twice. I wanted every detail. To sit there with her. To implore her: Tell me everything. Every year. Every mundane achievement. I would have made all sorts of unreasonable demands. Tell me—tell me you'll have a good life. Tell me you'll be happy.

You were the only thing she managed to save.

Instead, the shorter girl suggested the Teapotter—how many more opportunities would they have to sample Cumbria's worst Kendal Mint Cake, after all—and hauled Alicia from the bench, and they sauntered away, talking about driving lessons.

MONTH SEVEN

TRENT

L ike most of his triumphs, the investigation of the grave was short-lived and soon spoiled. He returned from the night shift in early January, and Zombie didn't meet him at the door.

He searched the corners of the flat. The shower stall, the mean wardrobe. He poured food and tapped the bowl. He lifted ridiculous pieces of furniture. On all fours, with his head beneath the bed and his T-shirt chilling with sweat, he heard a ping from his laptop and scrabbled for the kitchen.

Dear Trent, the email read.

He sat at the table and scraped his eyes into focus.

> As made clear from our lease (attached for reference),
> pets are prohibited in the Property (as defined herein).
> During a routine inspection, I discovered a cat residing in
> the Property. I removed the cat and left it outside, where it
> seemed quite content. I would ask that you please refrain
> from allowing any further pets in the Property in the future.

The email ended: Best regards, Anita.

There was something rising in his throat. He seized the bowl and took the stairs two at a time, out onto Jamaica Road. Workers and traffic, heaving into the morning. He tried not to look at the tires.

It was OK. She was discerning, untrusting. She wouldn't have gone far.

He straightened his back. He would search the blocks. She would be curled in a porch or on a stranger's sofa.

He was out there for six hours. By the end of it, his voice was cracked, and his teeth chattered. He could sense his reflection in the faces of the people he approached. They were sorry, yes, but they did not have time to assist a lunatic.

Returning to the apartment, he had the delusion that she could be waiting for him. Maybe she'd taken a seat at the Chinese restaurant and charmed herself a free lunch.

But the apartment was empty.

It was just a cat. Just a stupid cat.

He thought it enough that he found he was saying it, a continual whisper to the still apartment, the way a child might comfort themselves before stepping into darkness, and as soon as he heard it, he latched a palm across his mouth, and stopped.

MONTH NINE

MARTY

I f it had ended with the exhumation, I suspect some people in Stonesmere would have said the Ward family got what they deserved. Flaunting our grief, posing with the enemy. The mystery of the gun. It was enough to hate us, just a little. If you had long been bored of my dad and me, jogging golden down Main Street, or basking on the Boaters terrace as if the rest of the punters were there by our invitation. If there were truthers in town, filming a new video. If there were letters on the doorsteps of the dead, requesting autopsy reports, birth certificates, proof. If Ray Cleave was touring the country, the Truth Tour, calling on us from fields, fairgrounds, market squares—

They needed somebody to hate.

But in the springtime, the truthers' campaign spread across the town, and it was decided that something must be done. It started with Larkin's fight, but it had been coming for a while. The sentimentality of Christmas was over. There was only the damp new year and all the years that would follow it, childless and imperfect.

For much of January, I didn't leave Crag Brow, and when I did, it was always to visit the Boaters. Leah was trusted now to count the cash and lock up. The best part of my week—the one part of the week I really looked forward to—was walking up the steps to the restaurant, late on a Saturday evening, when there were just a few tables left. I sat at the bar. The customers lingered over dessert, too full to notice me. Leah gave me a look of relief, as if she was glad, every time, that I was still standing. When the last diners were gone, she would produce some half-finished bottle of wine—who spends thirty quid, Leah said, and doesn't even finish it?—and we'd talk into the night. It was Leah who told me the story of Larkin's fight, the day after it happened.

Larkin had been drinking, Leah said, just here. She wasn't averse to being part of the legend, and I grinned, watching her tell it. I didn't blame her.

Get a cab, Leah had said, and Larkin had promised he would.

On Main Street, he had the misfortune of coming across Chadwick McKinsey, who had flown over from Oregon the week before. Seventeen hours in the air, just to get to Stonesmere.

When the police searched McKinsey's hotel room, they found two hundred pages of research, printed at Crook County Library, into the hoax of Stonesmere.

"We're going global, then," I said, and Leah said: It would seem so.

McKinsey had been following Larkin all evening. He waited outside the Boaters doors for two and a half hours, armed with binoculars and a picket sign. The picket sign said: YOU DO NOT EXIST.

At first, Larkin ignored him. McKinsey pursued him with the sign held aloft, shouting so loud that Leah opened the Boaters balcony to check on the commotion. "Where are the bodies, then?" McKinsey yelled. "Why were you late?" All the while, Larkin walked with his chin tucked into his fleece. One foot in front of the other.

McKinsey was breathless. "Your silence," McKinsey shouted, "speaks volumes."

He touched Larkin's shoulder with the corner of his sign.

"Kit Larkin," McKinsey said, "did not exist."

Then—then, Larkin turned. He hit McKinsey so hard that blood flecked from his mouth over the alley wall. It stayed there for two weeks, attracting children and dogs, until a rainstorm washed it clean. Larkin left McKinsey gathering his teeth from the pavement. Like a beggar, Leah said cheerfully, collecting change. Larkin submitted a successful plea of self-defense, based around the intimidation of McKinsey's sign, and was released a hero. My dad condemned it as needless violence, but he was one of the only people in town who did. From the way the story was told—and told again—Stonesmere had started to see Larkin in a different light.

After Larkin, there was the Malone party. Samuel Malone was fully discharged from hospital, and everybody was invited. Katie Malone was calling it the Homecoming, which I refused, for a long while, to entertain. It was all anyone was talking about, Leah said. There would be cocktail dresses and caterers. It would be the opposite—the very opposite!—of a funeral.

"I think we should go," my dad said. "Certainly."

He had opened the kitchen doors that weekend, to let spring into the house. He looked at the garden, rather than at me, and his voice was pompous with hope. I had been ready to nod, agreeably, and select my most amenable dress. I had been ready to leave the sofa. But I couldn't. I couldn't do it.

"Why?" I said.

"I think it would do you the world of good, Marty," he said, "to get out and about."

"Half the country," I said, "think that I was friends with Rowan Sullivan. They think that I knew, Dad. That I knew something—"

He frowned. It was harder to be optimistic, with the name settling across the room.

"Well, you'll show them. Show them just how wrong they are."

I didn't know it at the time, but I think I went for him. My dad, waiting at the bottom of the stairs, with a pink bow tie and flowers for the Malones. I knew it would be a disaster, and I went to prove him wrong. Mr. Stonesmere, my mother had called him, when she wished to be cruel, and that was what I thought, coming down to join him. Hello, Mr. Stonesmere. I wore a dress unmistakably my mother's, a kind of venomous green, decorated with tiny deer.

"That's a strange choice of outfit," he said.

I went because I had started to hate him.

I hadn't been to Lake View since the hospital visit. At the Malones', the windows had been cleaned, the grass mowed in stripes. The flowers along the drive were just planted. But there were little sadnesses, roosting in the frame of the house. There were rails, flanking the steps to the door. There were cameras at the gates.

Caterers beckoned the guests to the garden, beneath a canopy of roses and early bees. The pool was sealed with its winter cover, although it was spring. No pool parties that day. There were fewer guests than I had expected. My dad waved to Nick Moran and patted my shoulder. He was so glad—so glad I had decided to come.

"I'm sure I'll find you later," he said, "tearing up the dance floor."

There was a checked square of linoleum in the middle of the garden. A cellist was plodding through pop songs. It had been so long since I'd been to a party that I couldn't remember if I enjoyed or endured them. Leah detached herself from a sibling and joined my side.

"You look nice," she said. "I wasn't sure if you'd come."

"Neither was I."

"Well, I'm glad you did. There are classic cocktails with a Stonesmere twist. Imagine if you'd missed it."

Samuel stepped from the house, worrying his sleeves, one hand close to his hair.

"I'm going to go say hi," Leah said.

"OK."

She took a few steps and looked back at me, and I stared right back at her.

"OK, then, Marty. Have it your way."

I stood by the bar, drinking Stonesmere Slings. "It's a Singapore Sling," the barwoman said. "Only worse." She took to preparing my next drink before I ordered it, so I always had something to do with my hands. I walked around the garden, pretending to be on my way to greet somebody. I went to the toilet twice. I watched Katie Malone request that the bar staff slow down the pace of service (it was a garden party, not a *party* party). The barwoman nodded, merrily, and poured larger measures. She was my favorite person at the Homecoming so far.

"Do you always do private houses?" I asked.

"Weddings, usually," she said.

"This is a little different, then."

"A little." She looked around and shrugged. "I don't really know what's going on," she said.

"I mean," I said, "have you ever been to a house as sad as this one?"

Samuel Malone gave a speech. He must have been used to public speaking by then. I was just out of the hog roast queue, and I kept eating. The first act was about his family. The second was about Day One. The days in the hospital, he said, were when he realized who his real friends were.

"No one was there for me more," he said, "than Leah Perry." His sentiment dulled to white noise, and I found I was watching Leah instead. I could tell what Samuel said by the beats of her face, the little pulses of humor and sadness. I swallowed the last of the bap and licked my fingers, and when I returned to the speech, Leah was in Samuel's arms. They kissed to cheers. They looked good together, I thought. Both intellectual, and perpetually disappointed. My dad was clapping sincerely. I returned to my friend at the bar.

"Martha Ward," Katie Malone said. She wore a great candyfloss concoction and eclipsed the last of the sun.

"Oh," I said. "Hi."

"I'll be quite honest, Martha. I'm surprised you came."

I tried to stand a little taller.

"Aren't we all?" I said.

"Have you heard the news?" Katie said. Her eyes stuck with her son, talking to Leah at the busier end of the garden.

"The news?"

"He's been nominated for an award," Katie said. "The Pride of Britain."

"You must be very proud."

She gave me a ferocious look. It was new to us both. I took a step away from her, and my back touched the bar. Around us, conversations softened.

"These truthers, Martha," she said. "These people, who call us in the night. Who wait—they wait, Martha—for us to leave our house, every morning. They hold signs. They—they send us letters. Horrible things, Martha. Unspeakable—unspeakable things—"

My dad was coming through the crowd, brushing aside flutes and handbags. Good. See: you were wrong.

"Can we talk," I said, "somewhere more—"

"No. No, Martha. You like an audience, don't you? This is where you like to be."

Her whole body was trembling. "Now, this is something you've created," she said. "You've lied, Martha. I don't know what happened, at Day One. I don't know where you were or what you knew. And let me tell you the honest truth: I don't really care. But you're going to have an opportunity, Martha. Aren't you? Very soon, in fact. You're going to sit at the inquest, and the coroner is going to ask you some questions. And you need—you need to tell the truth. For Samuel. For all of us. Whatever you did or didn't do. You need to make it go away."

"You were in the hall, too," I said quietly, and Katie, buoyed with daring, bobbing from sandal to sandal, said: "Please, do speak up."

"You were in the hall, too," I said. "I suppose there must have been things—things that you didn't manage to do."

I enjoyed a few seconds of satisfaction, watching her expression change. Watching my dad, face anguished above the crooked bow tie. I had known for a while how good it felt, to say or do the worst kinds of things; but I knew, too, how it felt to recall them the morning after.

"I think it might be time for you to leave," Katie Malone said.

My dad gave a small, treacherous nod over Katie's shoulder.

Walking around the house, I heard a rustling from the trees. I had the dull bravado that came with five Stonesmere Slings, and I raised my fists. I would end the night like Larkin, with blood on my knuckles. Instead, a woman stepped delicately into the streetlights. She wore a little pink skirt and a top adorned with sequins. She moved with a cheerful jangle, earrings on necklace, bangle on bangle, but her smile was sloppily drawn and hard to look at.

"Oh dear, Martha," she said. "You weren't welcome, either."

"Hello, Helen," I said. Girlish perfume covered long, curtained days. My skin shuddered, as if it would like to crawl away from her.

"I'm just on my way home," I said. She gave a long, mocking mmm.

"I haven't seen you, Martha. Have I? You haven't been to pay your respects."

"I'm very sorry," I said, "for your loss."

"That's nice. That's very nice."

"I'm going to get on my way."

"Oh, I bet you are. That's you, through and through. Always some-where better to be."

I willed my hand to comfort her. I rested it on her arm, the skin of it freckled, vulnerable, a little bulge where it met her top. I suppose I thought a lot of myself: that I would be so tender.

"You should go home, too," I said.

"Don't you pretend you're any different," she said. "I know you. Oh, I know you. I've seen you, just the way you are."

"Helen," I said. "Go home."

"How does it feel, Martha? To be out here in the cold? Out here—with the likes of me?"

She bared her teeth. She had me—how she had me. And when she smiled that way, she reminded me of him. I took a pathetic little step away from her, and she pretended to lunge after me, as if we were playing tag and she could make me It. I don't know what would have happened—if I'd have pleaded or socked her—but instead there was a snap behind us. We turned together, back to the Malone house, customized and curated for nine months by then, and ready to welcome the Pride of Britain.

There were flames behind the windows, engulfing the great, fake beams.

And for a moment I thought it must have been her, some terrible act of grief or vengeance. But her face was incredulous. Helen wasn't an arsonist; was only exiled and sad. Something brushed my arm, and I saw it was her. For a moment, there, she had reached for me, as if we could still, somehow, help each other out.

MONTH NINE

TRENT

Trent did not know the waiter who started the Malone house fire, and this, he said to Susan, was the best thing about it. The two of them scuttling around Stonesmere: that was an initiative. But this? This was a movement.

Ray Cleave started his latest radio show by denying responsibility for the crime. Still, he appreciated the spirit of the boy who had done it. He was an entrepreneur, Ray said. He was a freethinker. He was a good kid, driven to violence by his desire to expose the truth. Ray announced a crowdfunder for his legal fees, and Trent made a modest donation. He would have liked to give more. In the mug shot published online, the boy looked younger than eighteen. He was still wearing his name badge, which read: I'M HAPPY TO SERVE!

When Trent told Susan what had happened to Zombie, silence hung on the line. For a moment, he thought Susan was crying. Then he heard a fast rasp of breath. She was not sad. No. She was excited.

"Do you know her address?" Susan said. "This landlord?"

Susan traveled to London for the occasion. Trent took pleasure in the fact that they did it from the flat on Jamaica Road. Inside Anita's own portfolio. They sat at separate laptops and worked through the night. They registered Anita for every mail catalog delivery they could find. Package holidays, cheap clothes, plastic surgery. At the bottom of her email was her office address, and so they requested brochures be sent there, too. Charities saving donkeys, diabetics, dolphins. Free subscriptions to magazines about sheep farming, politics, girls next door, heavy metal, tattooing. The later it was, the more creative they got. She would receive invitations to fetish events of London, interpretive dance, hot tub speed dating.

At three a.m., they raised glasses across the kitchen table. "To the underdogs," Trent said.

"To comeuppance!"

For the next month, Susan sent triumphant missives whenever she found another suitable mailing list. When Anita conducted the next of her surprise inspections, she looked harried. She asked Trent if he had received any strange mail to the flat, and he gave her a puzzled smile. No. He didn't believe so. But he would keep a lookout.

He tried his best not to look at the empty space in the kitchen, where Zombie had slept upon a nest of his clothes. All the same, he couldn't quite bring himself to tidy them away. He checked the courtyard each time he left the flat, and sometimes, when he had a night off, he would sit an hour by the dustbins, hoping she might turn up. These night shifts: he didn't know if he would ever sleep again. He would lie in bed, listening to the traffic, the taxis and the night buses, the shrieks of an ambulance. He usually ended up turning on Ray Cleave's show. There was something comforting about Ray's conviction, bursting from the radio to fill the dark little room. When Trent was too tired to follow the stories, he still enjoyed the sound of certainty.

But whenever Ray spoke of Stonesmere, Trent started, as if somebody had called his name.

"Tonight," Ray said. "Tonight, we've got news."

Trent reached from his bed and turned the radio up.

"Legal action," Ray said. "Legal action. We're used to that. Aren't
we? It's the curse of our service! And where does this claim come from?
I hear you cry. Stonesmere, ladies and gentlemen. A lawsuit, blown down
from the north. Stonesmere, of all places. We seem to have upset them.
And by 'them,' I mean our complainants. Who do we have, who do we
have? We have Larkin, of course. That's Larkin, a police officer, a sergeant, no less, who—let's not forget it—turned up half an hour late to
the school. We have the families of the eleven. They've suffered violence, suspicion, and slander. Which is another way, ladies and gentlemen, of saying they've suffered scrutiny."

Ray's microphone snuffled with laughter.

"Listen," Ray said. "All I'll say is this: We'll be fighting. We'll fight
for you, and we'll fight hard. But we'll need your help. These lawyers—
they're an expensive business. Fill our coffers, and we'll fight them off.
Fill our coffers, and we'll keep bringing you the stories they fear. Fill
our coffers! You know the number."

Trent's phone hummed with a message. Susan: Are you hearing this?

"As ever," Ray said. "We send our condolences."

Trent picked up his phone. Susan sounded entirely awake. He could
see her, hands folded atop a flowery duvet, bespectacled and small in
her bed.

"Do you think they'll come," Trent said, "for the Stonesmere Exposer?"

"Oh, let them try. They can't trace us to the camera, Trent. They
can't trace you to the grave. We're curious innocents, aren't we? We're
curious innocents, and we also happen to be right."

"You're not worried?" Trent said. Lawyers: lawyers were expensive.

Even Ray acknowledged that. In his bank account, Trent had two hundred and thirty-seven pounds. Would that buy him an hour? Two?

"No," Susan said. "No! I'm not worried. If anything, I'm incredulous. I'm baffled. This thing's going to drum up all the publicity in the world. Just before their precious inquest. Worried? No. If anything—I have to admit—I feel a little sorry for them."

She gave a pitying chortle. Trent lay back on the bed, his heart steadying, soothed.

"Because we know, don't we," Susan said, "what's coming next."

DAY ONE

KATIE

What Katie Malone had built was what everybody, in fact, wanted. Oh, people would tell themselves they wanted other things, trips around the world, passion and art, but when it came down to it, when those people were older and wiser, they looked at lives like Katie's and wondered where they had gone wrong.

Take, for example, the fridge. The fridge was double-fronted, purchased during a pleasurable outing to the Trafford Centre's John Lewis. The fridge had a camera that enabled any member of the Malone family to check on its content from their phones. You could be in Andalusia, say—in Andalusia!—and confirm whether or not there was milk at home. In the fridge door, Katie kept a chilled bottle of prosecco. There was always some success or other to be celebrated, that was the kind of family they were, and a mother—a mother had to be prepared.

On the outside of the fridge was a compendium of those successes. There was Howard, besuited at the British Accountancy Awards, holding a trophy for Small Practice Innovation of the Year. There were Charlie's Star of the Week certificates, three from Mrs. Hutchinson, one from Mrs. Ward. (What could she say? Mrs. Ward was an odd one.) There was her eldest son, Benjamin, in his graduation gown, his arm around his girlfriend, who was obscured by an invitation for Oliver Whitfield's tenth birthday party.

From the fridge, Katie removed two packed lunches, prepared the evening before. Charlie carried his lunch in a red Marvel box. Samuel carried his lunch in transparent Tupperware. She liked the boxes to be ready when they came down for breakfast, so they had plenty of time to pack them. Not once had Katie been summoned to school to deliver a forgotten lunch, and this was a record she intended to maintain.

On the stairs—a tour of the Malone boys through the ages, freckles and bowl cuts ascending to uniform, braces, a certain kind of charm— she heard the fall of reluctant feet. She drew back her shoulders and busied herself with the washing of Howard's morning coffee mug, which had been left, again, to ring the marble.

"Good morning," she said, brightly, to which there was no response.

"It's nice out there," she said.

"Breakfast?" she said, and Samuel parroted: Breakfast.

"It's the most important meal of the day," she said, and Samuel laughed. He was standing at the bifold doors, an eyebrow raised to the morning. Benjamin: Benjamin had always eaten breakfast at the island, Katie his audience, with some anecdote about the previous night's party or a difficult teacher.

Whereas Samuel—

She could not remember the last time Samuel had deigned her with a conversation.

He took bread from the freezer, and they stood in their usual, unpleasant silence, waiting for it to emerge from the toaster. Katie supposed she should ask about his role in Day One, what he intended to do with the stage lights, but she couldn't quite bring herself to do it. This was typical Samuel, after all: to find an odd niche, to take up something that meant he had even more of a reason to spend time in the dark. She watched his back, buttering toast, shorter than Benjamin and thinner, too. He looked like Katie's brother, who had broken her collarbone as a child; who occupied their parents' old flat and filled it with cigarettes and grime.

"Perhaps," Katie said, "we could go out this evening. Celebrate Charlie's big moment."

"Celebrate—what? His three seconds of fame?"

"It could be nice."

"Could it?"

The toast popped. She tried to keep the relief from her shoulders. He buttered it without a word and all but ran from the room. She heard his voice on the stairs, some sly remark or other. Some impression of her hopefulness. As if it was such a bad thing—to be an optimist. To wake up every morning, hoping that today would be the day he had grown up. She lingered there, alone at the breakfast bar, and with a trembling hand she took an extra Tunnock's Teacake from the pantry and added it to Charlie's lunch box.

And of course it was worth celebrating, because Charlie was the star of the show. She sat toward the middle of the hall, watching the children onstage, a bristle of nerves in her belly as it came closer to his turn. But it was Charlie, wasn't it—Charlie Malone, the youngest member of Stonesmere Primary School's First XI, purveyor of a total of three dimples, crafter of Valentine's and Mother's Day cards which always came imprinted with the logo of his own publishing house, CM Productions— and so of course: he knocked it out of the park. He was articulate, expressive. He was very clear. He gave a little bow just before he stepped back into the line—all those other, shyer children, waiting their turn— and Katie heard an audible *aw* from the audience.

She wondered if they wished, secretly, that their child had that kind of charisma.

Subconsciously, perhaps.

She heard something just beside her—a latecomer—and turned to scowl. Katie had been one of the first in her seat. You couldn't be late, could you? Not for something like this. It disrupted the moment, and besides: little Kit Larkin was up soon, and that child needed all the help he could get.

The next thing she knew, there was a tremendous popping. Like fireworks, she would say, in the police interview, and in every interview afterward. Oh: somebody had let off fireworks early, fireworks that must have been intended to celebrate the last day of term. And it was a shame, a real shame, because the kids would have loved them.

And then—what? She was running. Oliver Whitfield's mother had Katie's wrist in her hand. She could not recall who had seized the other. The room was a fumble of chairs and limbs. She could see a green exit sign overhead. She had not yet understood what they were running from. She should—she should get to Charlie. Samuel would be safe, wouldn't he? He was above the stage; he was hidden. But Charlie—

She tried to turn, but behind her was a crush of people, still running, as if they would move through her. Her arms were at her sides, sealed by other bodies. My son— she said, but the space left by her inhale was filled with elbows, shoulders, and no words came out. She was tall enough to see that the stage was empty, empty but for two shapes she could not accept. She was tall enough to see other faces, deranged in the stampede, furious and terrified and panicked, the whole comical array.

The shapes, faces: these, she would not talk about.

Something gave. The bodies in front of her began to move. She freed a hand to steady herself, and before her there was light, light, the brilliant greens of the grass and the hills. They burst onto the school playing fields and she stumbled. Her dress was around her thighs. Mr.

Heron lifted her beneath her arms—kindness could resume, now that they had ceased crushing one another to death—and dragged her to her feet, and although she was screaming her children's names, he had her by the elbows. She could not have gone back. Could not, although God, she tried—

It was only afterward—a long time afterward—when she considered how she must have looked, dragged across the field with dirt on her knees. She told it to Samuel, hoping it might make him feel better about his own predicament—his mother, degraded, too!—but he said nothing. Only turned his body as best he could, to face the hospital wall.

Howard arrived an hour after the end of it. Seeing him, finally, huffing his way up Old School Road, tie wagging behind him, she felt a loathing so strong she could have clawed him. The thought of him, driving safely home, encased in air conditioning. Driving at the speed limit. When she—she'd been prostrate. Indignities he couldn't—couldn't even imagine. She had pleaded for information; she had linked her fingers and begged. She had seen children emerging from behind the police tape, bundled in twos and threes, guided by people in uniform. Some of the children were too stunned to walk. They were passed from the arms of strangers to their parents, where they were received like food for the starving.

And every time, every time it was not Charlie—

Every time, she hated them. She hated every mother who rushed to the front of the queue with her arms open. Couldn't they be a little more dignified? Couldn't they understand what it felt like—when your child was not the one to come out?

"Where are they?" Howard said, and she said it, the awful truth: "I don't know."

They did not know for five hours. All the while a scene of tragedy was assembled around them. The white tents unsprung. The tape un-raveled. The screens unfolded. Blue suits unveiled, and occupied by people with jobs she couldn't bear to think about.

There were fewer and fewer people waiting, as the hours passed by. Oliver Whitfield's mother was still there, although Katie didn't feel she could talk to her; did not know what to say, when a few hours before each had been willing to use the other as a shield. She nodded hello to Justin Ward, who sat on the pavement with his daughter's head in his lap. Martha Ward didn't even look up. You had to laugh: that the girl still had the gall to be arrogant, on a day like today.

And then, at last, they called the Malone name. At last, at last: the boys were safe. She sprang to her feet and followed the policeman—nice enough, now that it came down to it—and entered his little tent, turning in circles to find her children.

"Your son," the policeman said, "was killed in today's attack. I'm so very sorry."

The words came to her then, as if they had been living within her bones. Not Charlie. She didn't think them so much as feel them, welded in some hot place within her body. Not Charlie. Please. And once the words were there, they couldn't be unthought.

She hoped it so fiercely she could not breathe.

"We had two sons," Howard said, "at Day One. Samuel and Charles. Samuel and Charles Malone."

She could not look at him. He would see—wouldn't he?—what she was thinking.

The policeman's eyes were red. "Ah," he said. He wore sunglasses on his head, with brash blue lenses. She could only assume he had put them there earlier in the day and forgotten all about them.

"Right," the policeman said. "Right. If you'd just wait here. You'll need to give me a few minutes."

He ducked from the tent. As soon as he was gone, Howard gave a gasp of a sob, a noise that made her think of opening a bottle of soda. It occurred to Katie that she was not crying. It seemed something must be terribly wrong with her, to have heard the policeman's words and still be sitting there, dry-eyed and calm. That was an old fear, wasn't it? That motherhood was not for her; how could you be a mother, when your own mother—

The policeman returned. He confirmed that a teenage victim had been airlifted to Manchester Royal Infirmary, where he was undergoing surgery. The body on site, he said, was believed to be that of Charlie Malone.

"We'll arrange a police car to the hospital," the policeman said. "Let me arrange that, right away."

They sat in the back seat. Her thighs stuck to the leather. Howard held her hand, and in his other hand he held his face. She did not know how he could bear to be so close to her—his knee, careless against her own—after the things she had thought. She crossed her legs and shifted herself away from him. The car was leaving Stonesmere. The sun was starting to sink. Samuel, bleeding in a helicopter. Samuel, writhing. That boy—her son, too. A boy who had been afraid of the most ludicrous things. A boy who had been afraid of the utility room. Afraid of the dark. He still slept with his bedroom door open, didn't he? And it had been going on so long she had started to think of it with irritation, a reason for him to rail against the family for waking him up. When that wasn't—that wasn't it at all.

What would she do when she saw him? She would not leave his bedside. She would spend a lifetime apologizing for that thought. If it was a lifetime of quiet atonement—well. So be it. She would dress wounds, turn him in his bed, handle his limbs with gentle, motherly hands. She would do anything.

MONTH TEN

TRENT

He had always trusted that one day the reply would come, but how sweet it felt when it finally did. A tepid Monday, midday, and the Office of Ray Cleave in his inbox. Thank you for getting in touch. We're so grateful for all your hard work. Ray would love to speak with you to hear more.

The meeting would take place at an event in Essex, over Easter. A kind of rally, said the Office of Ray Cleave. There would be speeches. Festivities. Bring a guest, the email said. Ray is extremely excited to meet you.

He and Susan drove east out of London, talking little. Spaces opened between the buildings, slight and then gaping. He wore a suit found on Commercial Street, shinier than he would have liked. The tailor had popped from the till like a dime-store genie and told him he looked dapper. Dapper: who used a word like that, and meant it? Now, the label scratched scab-like at his neck. He felt the prickle of coming sweat.

"Are you nervous?" Susan said.

"Yes. A little."

He opened the window, and the motorway drowned their silence.

The event was at a pub in Brent-on-Sea. The Never Surrender. As they passed, music filled the car. The houses were gray and spattered with old storms. The streets were crammed with cars, Union Jacks blaring from the bumpers. "Busy," Trent said, and Susan said: "Of course."

They passed a strip of bin bags, innards split toward the flood barriers. There were nappies and peelings, bottles and toys. There was a sofa, frothing yellow foam.

"The beach," Trent said, "it's beautiful."

"Yes. It is."

They parked beyond the last of the precarious houses. Net curtains dangled at the pub windows, and behind them Trent could see a crush of bodies, slot machines, lights. There was a queue at the door, and the old excitement was in his belly. At the threshold, Aidan embraced him. He could feel beer spilling onto his new suit, but it didn't matter: what mattered was Aidan, greeting him like an old friend.

"You'll be here," Aidan said, "to meet Ray."

Inside: Ray Cleave, shaking hands. The pub carpet was yellow, and there was a band playing, set up on a small, spotlit stage. Susan excused her way to the bar. This was his moment, and his alone. Aidan guided him into the hot heart of the place. Ray was talking to a blond woman, nearly beautiful. Today, he wore a houndstooth suit and a white shirt, translucent with sweat. Aidan seemed to move the woman aside, and then Trent was there, before Ray Cleave, having taken her place.

"This," Aidan said, "is Trent Casey." And his voice became shrill: "Trent, calling from London."

"Trent," Ray Cleave said. And it was true what Susan had always said: that when Ray looked to you, the rest of the room fell away. He pummeled Trent's hand, smiling. "Welcome!"

"It's Trent," Aidan said, "who runs the Stonesmere Exposer."

Ray nodded. Of course—of course he knew him. He had been biding his time. Waiting for just the right event to ask Trent along. "We should go somewhere," Ray said, "a little more quiet."

En route, Ray set down his empty glass and replaced it with Trent's elbow. He held open a velvet curtain beside the sound system, and Trent ducked beneath it, backstage. Backstage was a wooden table, a bottle of Grey Goose, a popped packet of tablets, a suitcase fallen open on the ground. Inside the suitcase, Trent could see the private shine of underwear, and Ray, clocking him looking, kicked it closed.

"I need to thank you, Trent," Ray said, "for everything you've done for us. The website. The evidence. Rebecca Gleeson. It's remarkable. And I don't use that word lightly." Into two smeared glasses he splashed the vodka, quarter pints, and clunked them together. "To us!" he said. "To you. To the stories they fear. And by God, they should fear us. By God, they should."

"Thank you," Trent said. Ray's eyes were crinkled with gratitude. He smelled the same as Trent's glass.

"The photograph," Ray said, "sent to Rebecca Gleeson. Martha Ward, yes? Laughing—with poor Rowan. Her face, Trent. Her face, at the end of that interview."

He gave a comical gape, which narrowed to pride.

"Don't tell me that was you, too?"

"That was us," Trent said. Ray waved his bashfulness away. Come, celebrate: another glass.

"How the hell did you wrangle that one?"

Trent paused. He and Susan had always agreed that the funeral was their morbid little secret.

"Trent," Ray said, and he said it like he was talking to an endearingly mischievous child, a child he knew and loved.

"OK," Trent said. "OK."

There he was, in the midst of Ava Ward's funeral. He exaggerated the canapes: added caviar, oysters. He rose from his chair, the better to demonstrate the ascent up the stairs. As he talked, Ray reclined, a deity receiving his prayers. At the denouement—the camera, safe in Trent's pocket—Ray gave a slow, firm clap of his hands.

"I like you, Trent," he said. "I like your style."

Ray fell silent. The pub hummed from behind the curtain. "I wish you could have seen us," Ray said, quietly, "in the early days. You'd have loved it, Trent. There weren't that many of us then. Me. Aidan. A few fine stragglers. We had a different approach. We were scrappy. We could afford to be. Hungry—we were starving. We'd get our megaphones, get our pamphlets, and we'd corner them in the most magnificent places. The lobby of the opera. A commuter train. Just one or two of us. Their faces when they heard us. You'd see it in real time. When we finished up, I'd have spit on my back. A torn jacket. But you don't get that angry, Trent, unless you know you've been fooled all this time."

"Your show," Trent said. "I'm a big fan."

"You are? You tell me. What do you like about it?"

"I like—" And Trent paused. "The conviction," he said.

Ray gave a roar of laughter. "The conviction," he said. "That's wonderful. That's what we like to hear."

He stood from his chair and peeled the shirt from his back. The bulk of his body filled the room. Overstuffed with blood, pleasures, heart. Beneath the fat were tired muscles, jostling to be seen. Trent looked away.

"I'm glad," Ray said, "that you hear it."

From the suitcase, he took a fresh red shirt and shrugged it over his shoulders. "I'll let you in on a secret, Trent," he said. "Advice, if you will. It's a burden. They're always looking to wound us. They're out there with their pitchforks, their pyres. You know that." And he whispered then, as if they really were there, on the other side of the curtain. "Being the one to tell the truth, Trent—it isn't easy. It takes sacrifice. And you have to be ready for that. Sacrifice. Are you ready? You tell me."

"Whatever it takes," Trent said, "to get to the truth."

Ray's buttons were fastened. His glass was empty. He took Trent's cheeks in his hand and kissed him upon the forehead.

"Now, then," he said. "Let's go see our people."

Ray Cleave stepped onstage amid billows of colored smoke. Red, white, blue. He raised his arms, and silence descended. His whole body was shaking. Beer spilled over his glass, and he licked at his fingers, his wrist. "Brent-on-Sea," he said. "Thank you. Thank you."

It was all photographs, Ray's presentation. The landlord had wheeled an overhead projector out among the crowd. Martha Ward, stretched behind the stage, the day of the Massacre, her mouth wider than Ray's arm span. You could see pores, eyelashes. You could see the inside of one cheek, the color of her tongue. You could see the early lines—the premonition of an older face—at the corners of her mouth. You could see the wear of that morning: mascara scum in the caruncle, and hair caught on a lip.

"This girl," Ray said, "is a liar. This girl wants the world to hate— to hate men like us. Shame on her. Shame on the people propping her up, the people letting her go unchallenged. Shame on the mainstream media, telling her story."

You may have heard, Ray said, that Stonesmere was mounting a legal case against him. They'd been petitioning for a criminal investigation, too. Let them try, Ray said. Just let them try. These people: they believe in human rights until they don't. They believe in human rights, just not freedom of speech. They believe in human rights unless those rights belong to us.

The most exciting announcement, Ray saved until last. "I want you to guess," Ray said, "where our next gathering will be. This—this is going to be big. A rally. The Truth Rally! There's a birthday coming up. Isn't there? There's the first birthday of the biggest fraud this country's ever seen."

Trent looked to Susan, and Susan looked to Trent. They had written the script; and this, their stage.

"I'll see you there," Ray said. "Won't I? I'll see you there."

He drank with Susan for two hours. They added flourishes to their plan. Set the final arrangements in place. Aidan joined them outside, on a rickety pub table, and entertained them with his impressions. He could do Martha Ward, open-mouthed on Rebecca Gleeson's couch. He could do Larkin's tears. He could do the Malone mother, her great swoon outside the school. He rolled beneath the table, bawling.

Susan retreated to sleep in the car, but Trent wasn't ready for the day to end. There was the woman Ray had been speaking to before. Entirely beautiful, now. How effortless it was to talk to her. How easy: here, in this warm, welcoming world. He was so drunk he could not focus on her face without it multiplying, veering away across the room. Trent was talking about Rowan. Aidan was there, too, of course. Aidan was asking for more. Trent was telling them about the photographs; all the photographic proof that Martha Ward was a liar. The grave? That was him. And the inquest? Just you wait. Seriously. Wait and see.

The woman lived in a caravan along the seafront. They didn't turn on the lights. "You know him, do you?" she said. "Ray Cleave?" There were headlights moving across her body, cars and people passing outside, the last stragglers stumbling home.

"Yes," he said.

"So, you," she said. "Are you famous?"

"Not yet," he said.

He left the next morning, while she was still asleep. White light

pounded the grubby windows. He could see the ocean, dirty and churning, and the caravan shifted in the wind. He was thinking of "The
Dead Sea"—all those months spent conducting interviews, traipsing
the beach—and in thinking of "The Dead Sea," his mother slipped
through the flimsy door. She surveyed him, sadly, as he looked for his
clothes. That was the problem with hangovers. The melancholy. It was
time to go. Fumbling with the lock, he saw that there was a child asleep
on the sofa, wrapped beneath blankets, no more than three or four. "I'm
sorry," he said, although he hadn't woken them; although they would
never know he had been there at all.

MONTH TEN

MARTY

T hey're coming," Larkin said. "And there's nothing we can do about it."

He stood at the front of the town hall. The first slide was already up. I found myself smiling, seeing Kit's face. It was hard not to. In this photo, Kit's mother was alive. You just knew it. He had the unselfconscious grin of a kid of seven or eight. He still had missing teeth. The town made a small, fond noise and settled into their chairs.

Until then, we'd all been a little hesitant—to gather in a hall.

The story went that Larkin wasn't allowed to investigate the Malone arson. The fire had started in the hallway, beside the lift installed for Samuel's return. It had burned through the work to relay the crooked floors and left the living room blackened and smudged. The smoke alarm had been unscrewed, the battery removed. The arsonist had requested the Homecoming job after attending a Ray Cleave rally in Newcastle the month before. When they arrested him, he refused to believe he'd done any damage. His victims were actors. He had done nothing but dismantle a set.

Leah had served the news over the bar at the Boaters, and waited for me to speak. The restaurant was quiet, that night. She was mostly polishing cutlery. I looked at the photographs of Stonesmere's old sailing squad; at the chalkboard of specials hanging above the bar; looked anywhere, in fact, to avoid having to look Leah in the eyes.

"What?" I said.

"Don't you think," she said, "that it may be time to say something?"

Leah was more distant than I could remember. She didn't talk the way she used to: not about books, and not about gossip. She had stopped removing the manager's errant apostrophes from the chalkboard. The only time I had seen her happy in months—really, gloriously happy—was when her sister was accepted into a private school in Penrith, on a complete scholarship. She spent her free evenings at the Malone house, where there were long family dinners. Where board games were played to completion. She'd been welcomed with open arms, which closed tight. She was invited to participate in each of Mrs. Malone's hobbies: to embroider, to cook, to walk around the lake with pumping arms, talking about Samuel's day, diet, state of mind.

"The inquest," I said. "It's only a few weeks away."

Leah shook her head. "For fuck's sake, Marty," she said, and returned to her forks.

Days later, flyers had landed on each doormat in Stonesmere. Larkin invited us to a meeting about the campaign of hatred against the town. The paper was cheap, but the flyers used the same photograph we were looking at now. The room was filling.

"It isn't just one person," Larkin said. "But there are people—there are people who are far more culpable than others."

The next slide: Ray Cleave, and a selection of headlines from his blog.

I stayed at the back of the hall. All I wanted, really, was for Larkin to have a full house. I would have done anything. People bumped me, packing down the aisle. I could feel the evening chill of their coats as they passed. There was a constant bustle at the doors, and those already sitting had to shuffle from seat to seat to make room for the rest. Larkin walked from one side of the room to the other, and something about him—on the balls of his feet, moving easy through the silence—reminded me of my mother.

"This man," he said, "does not believe that we exist."

Larkin started with the legal action. If they won, he said, Ray Cleave could be bankrupted. Could be left—and Larkin rubbed two fingers together, as if Cleave was ground between them—with nothing. In the meantime, he was doing everything he could to encourage a police investigation. Investment. Manpower. The phone calls, the fire, the grave. These things were not unconnected.

But there was a more pressing question, Larkin said. This Truth Rally. A mob, descending for the inquest.

"We have to decide," Larkin said, "what kind of town we want to be."

Katie Malone was the first person out of her seat. Her clothes hung deflated from her frame. Leah reported that she rarely ate dinner, only worried about Samuel's food. There were evenings, Leah said, when he looked at his mother's oblation, served on his favorite plate, and ascended, silent, up the stairs.

"A counterprotest," Katie said. "That's my proposal. I want to look them in the eye. I want to look them right in the eye and tell them exactly what I think of them."

"And what then?" Larkin said, gently. "When they're shouting right back at you? When they're insisting that Charlie was a fiction?"

"Nobody," she said—and her voice was quieter than I had ever heard it—"nobody could say that."

"I know, Katie," Larkin said. "I know. But these people . . . You—you, more than anyone—you know what they are."

She opened her mouth, but there were no words left in her arsenal. A strange, sorry silence spread across the room. Her husband touched the small of her back, and she sat back in her seat.

Suggestions erupted across the room. Oliver Whitfield's father wanted to flatten them. Alicia Morden's mother wondered if the inquest could be postponed altogether. Leah, looking surprised to find she was standing, proposed some kind of legal measure, an injunction or a prohibition, to stop them from coming in the first place.

I watched Larkin, gracious and rehearsed. I knew then that he had long decided—alone, in some quiet room of his cottage—exactly what Stonesmere should do.

"I have one further idea," he said, "for your consideration."

He waited for every head to turn. This: the man who had stuttered his way through mountain safety.

"Suppose we do nothing," he said.

"Nothing?" Katie Malone said, the word half a sob, and a ripple of disappointment spread from her seat across the hall.

"They come here with their banners," Larkin said. "With their masks. They come with their miserable posters. They spit at people in the street. They throw their stones and shout their slogans. They have a beer in the car park, and if we're lucky, they drive straight off Westpoint Bridge on the way home."

The room gave a collective little snort. I'd given enough team talks to know that he had them.

"On the internet," Larkin said, "they have a little mystery. But here? Here, in person? Let them come. Let them come and show themselves, just the way they are."

At the end of the presentation, Larkin was cocooned in attention. I took a handful of biscuits and slipped down the steps into the square.

The mountains were the faint lilac of clouds. I tried to summon some of the joy this time of year once held, with winter behind us and tourists returning to the town. My bike carted out of the garage; my mother reading in the garden.

"Marty? Marty!"

I braced myself, these days, hearing my name. But it was only Larkin, escaped from the crowd. I swallowed the last glob of biscuit and dragged small tears from my eyes.

"Hello, Marty," he said. I was braced for fury, but Larkin came gentle across the street. He raised his hands from his side, as if he was afraid I might flee. Larkin, living in a world where I was still an acceptable human being. The photograph was a one-off; the CCTV was a case of mistaken identity. It was a kind of marvel. Your family was obliterated, and you could still believe that people were honest and good.

"Hello," I said. "Up there, on the stage—you were great."

"That's very kind of you. Thank you. How are you doing, Marty? I know that things can't exactly have been easy."

"I don't know," I said. "I'm OK."

Exhibit A. I wore my dad's sweatshirt, with my hair tucked down the collar. I wore tracksuit bottoms with a lost string. The closer you got to my skin, the worse it became. I wore a sweat-crusted sports bra and gray knickers, holes at the seams.

"About Rowan—" I said, and Larkin raised a hand.

"You don't need to explain yourself," he said. He cleared his throat. His voice was scratchy from the presentation. "These people. They seize on anything, don't they? It's desperate."

I looked from the pavement to his face. "Thank you," I said.

"Anyway, Marty," Larkin said. "I won't keep you. But I wanted to tell you. I did it. I went to a group."

"The Malone thing?"

"No. No. Nothing to do with Stonesmere at all, in fact. No, I went to Manchester. I needed the distance. You had to have lost a child. That was the only requirement."

"A mother," I said. "What? That's not quite tragic enough?"

He flustered his face into an apology, but I was already smiling. I waved him on.

"For the first three times," he said, "I didn't talk at all. Can you imagine? They asked me to introduce myself, and I didn't say a thing. I'd have liked to tell them to fuck off, to be entirely honest with you."

"I think I'd have liked that, too."

"It was about purpose," Larkin said. "That's what I picked up. The other people in the group, they had something already. They had their other children, or this job that meant the world to them. Something like that. And when I thought about it—I've got nothing. They're asking me about my friends or hoping I need to renovate the cottage. We're getting desperate, right? Janet's got three other kids and a shop on Etsy, and I've got nothing. Week after week, they're looking a little more worried."

"But now?" I said, and nodded back the way we had come. There were silhouettes gathered beneath the clockface, waiting for Larkin to return.

"I don't need to tell you, do I?" he said. "A few letters at first. An email or two. That's easy to ignore. But the radio? The websites? People waiting in the street, shouting his name?" He gave a dogged nod and wiped a hand across his face. "That," he said. "That's a purpose."

I could see Leah's expression, stern over the Boaters bar. Who deserved the truth more than Larkin? Larkin, fighting for us all. I glanced up the road. There was nobody close enough to hear us. Say it. Come on.

He was turning back to the town hall. "We'll get them," he said, although standing there, the people of town buoyed and smiling as they passed, I thought of Larkin's purpose, and wondered what would happen if we did.

MONTH ELEVEN

TRENT

The last hour of the night shift. Five a.m. He had become complacent. He sat at a desk in the office that was not his, finalizing the last few details of his and Susan's plan. He entered the usual flourishes, cheerful emojis and a spate of kisses after the signature. He was about to send the email—was contemplating the precise message he would leave for Susan, as soon as it was done—when a stranger crashed from the lift. She carried a thermos and an umbrella. The office lights sprang on ahead of her, lighting his horror.

When she saw him, she let out a cartoonish gasp. "Oh," she said, in a way that made it clear it was for him to explain himself. He clung to the fact he was not sitting at her desk; knew, in fact, that she was the intern who occupied a dim bay a few rows over.

"IT issues," he said.

"IT issues," she said. "At five a.m.?"

He entered a Run command and hoped the code looked convincing enough.

"I try to resolve things overnight," he said, "to minimize disruption."

"OK," she said. And, frowning: "Is this a new thing?"

"We're always working," Trent said, "to improve our services."

The intern flopped down at her desk. "They work you guys hard, too, then," she said. Trent hit Send. The intern scrubbed her mouse across the desk and blinked in the laptop light.

"They do."

"We should start a revolution," she said. Trent smiled. He deleted the email from the Sent folder and deleted it, in turn, from the Bin.

The intern sniffed and began to type.

She could have saved him. Could have done any number of things. She could have mentioned him, for example, to Sally Meynard-Hirst, News Editor, at whose desk he sat. A kitchen exchange, a meeting at the water cooler. The IT team have really stepped up their game, right? The whole thing would have been scuppered. He thought about this encounter a lot, after the inquest, and when he did, he contemplated the intern with something like fury.

Who were these people, who took everybody at their word?

The intern: she probably never thought about that morning again.

MONTH ELEVEN

MARTY

By June, there were news cameras back on the streets of Stonesmere. Somber-faced presenters stood before the lake. I was back in the news. Stills from the first interview outside the school accompanied articles and opinion pieces. Nearly one year on, what have we learned? In the newsagent, I saw myself staring from the cover of a tabloid, shrunken beneath the headlines. I looked very, very young.

Anoushka talked us through the inquest. She brought extra satsumas that day. You will arrive at the town hall by police escort. I will be with you, in the car. We expect a crowd. We expect cameras. We expect— comments.

You will walk past them, up the steps. Yes, yes: we will guide your way. You will take seats reserved for you, close to the front of the room. Usually, yes; usually, members of the public would be welcome. In light of the circumstances in Stonesmere, there will be restrictions. Only the families and select members of the press.

You will be called on the first day. You will sit in a chair at the very front of the room. The room will be full. Behind the chair there will be a screen, and on the screen there may be documents, images, things relevant to the coroner's questions. The coroner will ask you about Day One. We expect the questions to be simple, factual. They will ask what you saw and what you did.

It's OK, Marty. Breathe. Do you want to stop?

Kit Larkin? Yes. I expect they will.

You must remember: there will be no apportionment of blame. This is not about blame, but clarity, prevention. This is not about blame, but truth.

I'd always thought Anoushka a robot, but in the hallway she paused, halfway into her jacket. My dad was still in the kitchen. On her face was an expression I hadn't seen before, an expression you would not find in a training deck. "Are you going to be all right?" she said, and I was so taken aback that I answered her honestly. I didn't know.

YEAR TWO,
DAY ONE

TRENT

He would catch a train to Susan's house, and the next morning they would drive early to Stonesmere. He had only one appointment before he left London, and he wasn't sure if he would attend it. In his dithering, he was fifteen minutes late, and he knew, as soon as he arrived, that she had been early.

His mother sat at a table outside, her hands cupping a mug. They were two blocks from Tower Bridge. There were whole alleys of delicatessens, the kinds of places that sold coffee for children and dogs. But he had chosen the cheapest café he could find. He had hoped she would find herself out of place, but instead she reclined, her hair hanging over the hard silver chair, her face to the sun. He had forgotten how adaptable she could be, that she had learned to change herself with the flick of a lipstick, a tweak to her shoulders.

He made to sit beside her, but she stood and met him in her arms.

"Hello," she said.

"What are you drinking?"

"Tea. Decent tea, as a matter of fact."

At the counter, he ordered the same. He could smell bacon, chips, batter. Black, black coffee. Smells of his adolescence, dingy flats and stubborn camaraderie. Something within him was giving way. He should have gone for a deli.

He sat beside her. They looked together across the street, where a crane presided over the promise of luxury housing. Along the boundary were pictures of young, beautiful families, cycling and eating dinner.

"How are you?" he said.

"How am I? I'm livid, to tell you the truth. I've hardly heard from you, have I? And when I do, it's—what? A television appearance?"

"Oh, I'm sure Tim keeps you updated."

"That's unfair. That has nothing to do with me and you."

"I don't know. I feel like you moving in with a dickhead had quite a lot to do with me and you."

"He's given us a decent life, these last few years," she said. "He's given us a life we always said we wanted."

"I don't know how you can expect me to believe a single thing you say," Trent said. His mother flinched. He was good at this, now. He was good at speaking directly, and saying the thing that would hurt the most.

"I did what I did," she said, "to protect you."

"You did what you did because you're just like the rest of them."

"Who, Trent? The mainstream media? Stonesmere? The police? No. Don't tell me. The government?"

Her voice cracked. Trent looked hard at the construction site. He read the safety notices twice through. He couldn't stand it when his mother cried. In his belly was a cramp of shame, shame so painful it made him crueler.

"You've chosen your side," he said, "and I'll choose mine."

"There's something happening there, isn't there?" she said. "Tomorrow. In Stonesmere, I mean."

"Of sorts. They're finally looking into what happened."

"But that isn't all that's happening," she said. "Is it? I know—I know. You think I'm ignorant. But I know who Ray Cleave is, Trent. I know where to look, to see what's being planned."

He squirmed at this. The idea of his mother trawling Ray Cleave's blog. Scrolling slowly through Facebook, Reddit, with her glasses perched in her hair.

"All I can do," she said, "is ask you. Please. Don't go."

"I know what I'm doing."

"No, Trent. I don't think you do."

Her hand crept across the table toward him, a tired, gentle creature.

"I know who he was now," she said. "Rowan Sullivan. There were so many photographs on the internet. Photographs—all the way back to when we knew him. I remember him well enough."

"He was my friend."

"No. He was so much older. It was odd, Trent. The way you would follow him around. The way he let you. It made me—I don't know. It made me a little sad."

He crossed his arms and left her hand to curl up on the table.

"I'm not pretending," she said, "to remember this well. It was a decade ago, wasn't it? I've slept since then. But there was a night—there was a night, I'm sure of it—when this man's mother came to our house. I don't pretend to know the specifics. But I remember. Something had happened next door. Some argument. And what I do remember—what I don't think I could forget—"

He wasn't sure just how, but he knew what she would say next. He could sense the discomfort of a memory, seeping into those long, easy afternoons at Rowan's house.

"She was in her underwear," his mother said. "The woman next door. His mother, I suppose. She was locked out of the house, in her underwear. There was snow—Christ—there was snow on the hills. And the two of us—I think we laughed about it at the time. This strange woman, turning up on our doorstep, hopping from foot to foot. We got her a dressing gown and a hot drink, and we must have laughed about it, once she was gone. But now—Trent. Now—knowing what we know— it doesn't seem very funny at all."

And he did remember. There was an image in his head of Rowan Sullivan's mother, standing at their door, her arms clutched uselessly around her body. Her flesh was purple-white and shaking.

"She said it herself," Trent said. "She was locked out."

"You don't believe anything, baby. Surely—surely you don't believe that?"

She sat there for a while, staring at the side of his face. Waiting, he guessed, for a response. Let her sit. After a few minutes, she settled her mug on the table and stood, and before he could stop her, she pressed her face to his hair.

"You can do what you like," she said, "and I'm sure you will. But I'd like to make sure you're doing it for the right reasons."

"I appreciate your concern," Trent said.

Before he left London, he stacked a bowl with cat food and set it, ceremoniously, behind the bins. He sent a message to Susan; he would be with her in a few hours. He hesitated at the door and looked a final time around the little flat, unsure who he would be when he returned to it.

YEAR TWO, DAY ONE

―――――――

MARTY

"All ready, Marty?"

I had tried to cross unnoticed from the stairs to the living room. I was doing my old kitchen shuffle, refined with Leah when we were in need of another snack. Stick to the walls, think like a doe. Even then, we'd almost always been caught. I rested my head against the banister and adjusted my face.

My dad stood at the kitchen counter, salting steaks. His hands were damp and pink. He was still flecked with paint. He'd been awarded a new contract, a family from out of town. He left the house, diligently, before eight a.m., and came home only when he was hungry.

"As ready as I'll ever be."

"Not long to go now," he said, "and we can start getting back to normal."

I just stood there, in the middle of the kitchen.

"You said that before," I said.

"Did I?"

"The day of the funeral," I said. "The exact same thing."

"Well, there you go. I'm getting old."

Night had closed across the windows. I could see the two of us in the glass, faceless, and there in my pajamas, in socks and a ponytail, I could have been no more than twelve or thirteen.

"It won't do, though, Dad," I said. "Will it? It won't go back to normal."

The worst thing was just how crestfallen he looked. It was as if I had said something he really didn't know. Had ruined what would otherwise be a perfectly pleasant evening, with good meat and the cricket highlights.

"No," he said. "No. Maybe not. I just hoped, I think—that things could still be good."

I waited for him to breeze on through to the living room. To fumble for the griddle pan, perhaps, and clatter the moment away. Instead, he rested his hands on the counter, his head hung, looking at nothing.

"We used to do so much stuff together," he said. "Didn't we?"

We did. There had been nights my mother turned on every light in the kitchen so we could still see the ball. He'd supported me the way people supported their very favorite team, forever enthusing about my victories and blaming my failures on just about anything else.

I went to him then. I laid a hand across the crags of his back. "I loved it, you know," I said. "I loved growing up with you."

Same long fingers, bulbous veins, shabby nails.

"It was like everybody in town knew you," I said. "And when I was little—I don't know. That was like everybody in the world."

He took me by the skull, my head small between his palms. "Come here," he said.

I didn't have the heart to argue with him. And it felt so good, shrinking between his arms. I thought I might step out of them a decade younger, and still his favorite person.

"But after the inquest, Dad," I said, "I don't think I'll stay here much longer. Not just Crag Brow, I mean. Stonesmere. I don't know if I can live here anymore."

"Of course you can, Marty. We'll figure it out. The two of us. We'll pull ourselves together. We're still us, aren't we? We'll find a way to live."

Why not give him a few more days? The last scraps of our life together, there in our tired palace.

YEAR TWO,
DAY ONE

TRENT

Susan lived on an estate of two hundred houses built the decade before. She had told Trent the story. When she reserved the house, Susan had been presented with an extensive list of customizations that would distinguish her property from the rest. She could choose only two. But Susan—with fierce negotiation and several strongly worded emails—had wrangled four.

It took Trent fifteen minutes to find Susan's house, which had a bay window, a utility room, outdoor lighting, and a tree.

She ushered him from the doorstep and patted his shoulders. "Nearly there," she said. "Nearly there." Her doormat read: Welcome to the madhouse; but the house was quiet and dark. He knew she kept the lights off to prevent surveillance; that she used dim lamps bought on the internet, which resisted any attempt at photography. "I'm still recovering," she said, "from Brent-on-Sea." She puffed out her cheeks. "What a day," she said. "What. A. Day. To have Ray Cleave—Ray Cleave!—welcome you. Oh, Trent. What a day."

"Your place," Trent said. "It's really nice."

"Oh, it's not much. Let me show you around. The grand tour, if you will."

If you didn't look closely, the house was ordinary. The carpets were beige, the walls were cream. But in the corners, at the windows, you found her: Susan. The back windows were taped with black gauze. There was no television and no microwave. In her living room, there was a framed newspaper: "Hero or Liar?" the headline begged, above Martha Ward's crestfallen face. She led Trent up a carpeted staircase, narrowed by cardboard boxes.

"Are you having a clear-out?" Trent said.

"Oh, no. No. Let me show you."

She opened the first door upstairs. "This is you," she said.

Trent had the impression of a library. The basement where the rogue cop would be assigned in a bad police drama. Each wall was shelved from floor to ceiling, and on the shelves were boxes. Susan pulled the lid from one with a silver service flourish, and inside he saw files, dated with care. "This was an inquiry," she said, "into government corruption. My daughter got friendly with the daughter of the local MP, you see. Big dog. Huge. The things I could show you. The things"—she rapped on the folder—"in here."

"And Stonesmere?" Trent said.

She kept Stonesmere in the next bedroom along. There was a small bed and a pretty white bureau, imprisoned by boxes. He wanted to ask her if this was where she lived, the only few feet not dedicated to her investigations, but when he tried the question in his head, he couldn't bring himself to say it aloud.

"Anyway," Susan said, "a drink?"

They drank a lot that night. He was drinking, he supposed, to forget his mother's face. Susan cradled her laptop on her belly and refreshed the Facebook page for the Truth Rally. Another attendee! A whole agenda, uploaded by Aidan. When would Ray arrive, did he think? What was Martha Ward doing, this very second? She couldn't sleep, surely. She wasn't asleep, knowing they were on their way.

"Is that your daughter?" Trent said. He pointed to a child captured in a homemade frame, the clay indented with flowers and stars. The girl had a fringe from another decade. She wore a checked school dress. She looked the same age in the photograph, Trent thought, as the Stonesmere kids.

"That's her."

"I'm so sorry," Trent said.

"I am, too. But she made her choices."

He started, drink halfway to his mouth. "Oh," he said. "I thought—"

"That she was dead?" Susan gave a quiet, humorless laugh. "Oh, well. I suppose it's not so different."

She tilted her glass this way and that.

"No," she said. "She lives in California, of all places. I'm afraid I was an embarrassment." She pointed through the ceiling. The weight of the boxes. Folder after folder, page after page.

"You raise somebody," Susan said. "You do everything you can for them. Everything. And they decide, one day, that they can't stand you. Your ideas, your dedication. Your life's work. How about that? How about it?"

She opened her arms, as if he might comfort her. This odd half-mother, folded in her chair. He wanted to pity her, still, but he had the uneasy sensation of having been fooled, and he did not leave his seat.

"I'll tell you," Susan said. "It feels a little like a death, Trent. That's how it feels."

She looked back to the laptop. She was typing, once more, and her face started to soften.

That night, he did not sleep. He kicked off the embroidered duvet and sat up in the strange room. The boxes towered around him. He would have liked to go for a walk, but he wasn't sure he would find his way back. All these houses, sold as different. They all looked exactly the same.

YEAR TWO, DAY TWO

MARTY

heard them coming before I saw them. And they came so softly at first. I woke before dawn and watched the window emerge from the darkness, sure they were close. The curtains turned from gray to white. I could not move from the bed. What would happen—if I just stayed here? Pitchforks, perhaps. I would be dragged from the mattress. I would be led by a mob through the streets of Stonesmere and burned before the town hall.

"Are you up?" my dad said, on the other side of the door. His refusal to enter my bedroom had been respectful once, but it had become its own kind of neglect. I lived in my bed as a kind of island, shipwrecked amid clothes, plates, books, letters. There was a small spray of mold, new to the ceiling.

"Yes," I said.

"Anoushka'll be here, pretty soon."

And others—others had already arrived. A murmur through the bathroom window. A chatter beneath my bedroom. I wore a drab black dress. I wore my hair in a plait. I did not open the curtains. Coming down the stairs, I saw the glint of lenses lined on Crag Brow.

"Breakfast?" my dad said. I sat before a plate of eggs but could not lift the fork. From across the garden, there was a kind of roar. I imagined car after car, bonnet to bonnet, filling the street into town.

At the doorbell, we clutched for each other. My dad laughed, clownishly, as soon as the moment had passed.

"I'll get it," he said.

I did not move until he returned. It was not Anoushka, but Leah. She stepped into the kitchen carrying a cardboard tray of coffees. She looked faintly surprised to find herself there, in our house. "I thought we could do with refreshments," she said, and for the first time in many days I started to laugh.

"How long do we have?" I said. Ten minutes, my dad said. Give or take. He touched the buttons of his shirt. It was open low at the neck. I could see hair, freckles, the wear of fifty-two summers. It pained me, that Leah would see this, too.

"I'll get my tie," he said. We listened together to his socks on the stairs, waiting for the creak of his bedroom door.

"So," I said. And Leah, with a juddering sigh, said: "So."

"They're already here," I said.

"I know."

"I thought you would be with Malone."

"I don't think he needs me," Leah said. "Honestly? I think he's looking forward to it."

"Whereas me—"

Leah gave a weak grin. "Whereas you—"

"Did you ever tell him?" I said. "He must have asked."

"He asked," she said. "But no. No. Not for the reasons I'd like, though. Whenever I'd tell it, in my head—I'd realize. I come out of it a monster."

"Come on, Leah," I said. If we worked to Leah's standards, I thought, every person in town became a monster.

"There was so much more," Leah said, "that I could have done. I had months. Months, when I could have just said to you—"

I liked that she thought I'd have listened. That she thought me so much less of a fool than I was.

"Do you know," she said, "what you're going to do?"

I tried to give her a reassuring smile. I really did. But somewhere between the idea of it and my face, the thing changed. The old panic was coming, emptying the room of air. I heard myself saying her name. She steered me to the kitchen table and sat me in my mother's chair, and she sat down in my usual place and held my hands. Better here, I thought, than in the town hall. Better here, with Leah.

Leah: she knew how to keep a secret.

DAY ONE

LEAH

Leah had started at the Boaters at fifteen, washing pots. On her first day, she put on her uniform—black T-shirt, hair cap, trainers—with the view that she would get some good life experience. Orwell in Paris, Guevara on the motorcycle. It soon transpired that this attitude was romantic. The hours were long and the chefs were cruel. She smelled, always, of batter; would frown each time it drifted through the next day's lessons. Alongside the pots, she had to check, on an hourly basis, that the toilets were acceptable for use. She signed her initials on a sheet attached to the wall, beneath hour upon hour—month after month—of former signatories.

Whatever. Pots, toilets: she would not be defeated. The owner of the Royal Oak was a pervert, and the pay at the Teapotter wasn't even legal. She stayed. She clambered her way past gap year waitresses and grand reopenings and eight head chefs, and here she was: nineteen years old, seven a.m., Friday morning, opening for breakfast.

Breakfast was the best shift. The chef was placidly hungover. The customers were workers or tourists, and grateful for coffee either way.

It was quiet enough to keep a good latte in the kitchen, which she returned to every chance she got. This morning, she had four American
campers, a birdwatcher in khaki, and the Whitfield family, the kid dressed
in something resembling a suit of armor.

"That's quite an outfit," she said.

"It's Day One today."

"Ah, yes. So it is."

"Did you do it? Day One?"

"I did."

"What were you?"

"This is very embarrassing," Leah said, "but I don't actually remember."

"You don't re*member*?"

"It was at least a hundred years ago, to be fair," she said, and the kid
snorted and picked up his straw.

This cursed town. Of course she remembered. On Day One, she had
been cast, prophetically, as a restaurateur. When the intrepid explorer—
played, with winning enthusiasm, by Marty Ward—needed a bite to
eat, Leah held out a laminated menu and said: Perhaps you'd like to try
one of our locally sourced delicacies? The worst thing was, she had actually rehearsed this line. Had rehearsed it—well. OK. More times than
she cared to admit. Enough times that her whole family repeated it,
verbatim, for the rest of the summer.

Just past eight a.m., she darted to the kitchen. Finished the latte and
picked up her phone. And there it was. The contact she always hoped for.

The intrepid explorer herself.

There were many types of love, Leah knew, and the love she held
for Marty Ward was nothing remarkable. It was not the stuff of novels,
poetry (and God, there had been days—there had been whole years—
when she'd tried). There was nothing to declare. During one of many
lunchtimes spent in the English block, when they were supposed to be

discussing that week's Further Reading assignment, Samuel Malone had asked Leah why she liked Marty in the first place, and she hadn't known what to say. How to phrase it: that all the best memories of her childhood went back to Marty. That she would pretend, as they walked up to Crag Brow, that they lived there together, in splendor, and never went to bed. That Leah had once peed herself laughing, listening to Marty recount a kiss with Roland Trapp, who had walked straight into a lamppost after they said farewell. That Marty could sit in the undergrowth for three hours, waiting for a red squirrel to pass, but could also run rings around eleven sniffling boys on a football pitch.

That she was the only person at school who had ever invited Leah over to her house.

Leah had mumbled something about hidden depths, and changed the subject.

Her mother thought Leah was a fool. She'd made it clear enough after Marty first wheedled her way inside. Even Leah had been able to tell it. The way Marty looked at the clutter of plastic in the living room. The movement of a single eyebrow when she understood there was only one bathroom, all the way upstairs.

"That girl," her mother said, "thinks a great deal of herself."

"You can do that," Leah said, "when you're good at everything."

"You're good at lots of things, too."

"Not the things that count."

"You just make sure, Leah, that she's nice to you."

Her mother always defended them. She wasn't necessarily joyful, which was what Leah had once wished. She didn't have Ava Ward's energy. But she was first to the headmaster's office the day Amber Blackley scattered Leah's gym kit from the art block window. For a term before Francesca's scholarship test, she sat by her daughter's side as she completed the weekly practice paper. She knew the best shops for sturdy shoes, thick coats, books on offer.

The day Leah's mother broke the news of her diagnosis, Leah first promised not to tell her sisters. Then she phoned the admissions office of the University of Manchester, and asked to defer her place.

"Marty's a lot nicer to me," Leah said, "than everyone else is."

And sure: there had been slights, over the years. But they weren't intentional. They weren't malicious. They were things Leah didn't believe Marty even noticed. The very idea of it—that Marty Ward would be struck by the cruelty of locking somebody, briefly, from a classroom, when Marty wasn't to know that Leah's eczema cream was inside, that beneath her school shirt her skin was weeping and raw; that Marty Ward would remember forgetting to invite Leah to her eighteenth birthday party, which Leah only knew about because she served Marty's parents at the Boaters that evening, banished from their own home—

It was entirely improbable.

Marty's message said: He's asked me to see him. What should I do? And, ten minutes later: I'm on my way. Am I being an idiot? Be honest.

Leah sank back against the silver station. "Watch the eggs," the chef said, and Leah said: "Truly, a masterpiece."

This whole business with Rowan Sullivan. Leah was tired of it. Secrets were often more boring than their subjects realized, and Leah found this particular secret the most boring of the bunch. Had Rowan Sullivan distracted Marty from her exams, from any academic work whatsoever, leaving her floundering in Stonesmere, teaching children how to kick balls? He had. Was Rowan somebody who spent the majority of his time watching shitty videos on the internet, dumb ideologies and misogynist comedians, videos Marty was expected to find funny? He was.

Was the prospect of Marty resurrecting this particular dalliance a terrible mistake? Of course.

She carried the eggs to the Americans, considering how much of this to say.

She had tiptoed around the issue for the last year. She had been gentle and careful and said all the things Marty wanted to hear. Yes, he was mature (he was thirty-three, after all). He was tall and somewhat handsome. He had a sense of humor, lackluster though it was (as if this was an achievement, rather than a general human condition).

And why? Why all the tact?

What Marty couldn't see—what Leah would never say—was that it was all so disappointingly typical. There was some part of Marty, Leah knew, that was tired of being golden, a part that was done with charity runs and the Stonesmere Rugby Club ball and holding court with who-ever happened to walk up Crag Brow. This, Leah understood. Who wouldn't be done with Justin Ward? A man who literally, honestly be-lieved Stonesmere was the greatest place on earth? But there were so many other ways—so many more interesting ways—to show it.

She typed out the letters and examined the message.

Don't go.

There were other things she could say.

Don't go, because you're smaller, these days. Because he's not just a loser, but cruel with it. Don't go, because I spend whole nights think-ing of the stories you've told me, whispered from behind your hair: of the walk to Old Man's Edge, and how he speaks to his mother, and what he said about your thighs. Don't go, because you're Martha Ward. Because—

There would be a day, soon, when she and Marty would laugh about it. Of this, Leah was sure. She would return home from university, and Marty would be studying to retake her exams. They would lie on Mar-ty's bed, while Leah talked about all the people she had met in halls, the bores and the lovers, and Marty would say: God. Remember when I went out with Rowan Sullivan?

And Leah would say: How could I forget it?

Not my finest hour, Marty would say. And Leah would say: More red flags than a matador convention.

The chef hit the serving bell, obnoxiously, and Leah cleared the empty plates from the Whitfield table.

"Godspeed, soldier," she said, and the Whitfield kid said: "I'm a samurai." She set the plates back in the kitchen and returned to the message.

The chef stood at the fire escape, trying to light a cigarette.

Don't go.

Marty would be angry, obviously. She would be frustrated. She was already on her way. She would message back, asking why not, and they'd spend the morning in an angry exchange. It would be whole days before they were back to memes and slighting the people of Stonesmere.

This last year, the two of them had been closer than ever. And some of that—

Some of that, Leah had to admit, was down to Rowan. It was Leah who heard the secrets, the things he would do to her, things she felt sort of bad for liking, but that felt so good, honestly, she had never known how good it could be.

It was Leah who climbed into her bed the day he hit her. More like a knock, really, and only once, but hard enough that they needed to craft a cover story, an errant football, an apologetic kiddo, a whole comedic revision. It was Leah who curled around her, nose to neck, knee to knee, like a shield.

Character by character, Leah deleted the message, and typed out a new one.

You may as well hear what he has to say.

She stood there a moment, in the quiet of the kitchen. Then she sighed, and sent it.

YEAR EIGHT

―――――――

MARTY

The Boaters was a lot blander than it used to be. There was a menu for tonic. The waiters wore these stupid little earpieces, as if they were in the secret service rather than a gastropub. I ordered two goblets of gin and stood hovering at the bar. I had this fear that I might not recognize her. We had emailed each other often, in the years after I left Stonesmere, but I had seen Leah only once or twice. She had moved to Cartmel. The house was on the river, and purchased by the Malone family. There were corridors of cream rooms, gaping for children. Leah would write to me about the tips you got at L'Enclume, about a new night course and a variety of madcap diners. I would write to her about my dad and the sex life of the couple next door. She wrote little about Samuel, other than to say he was getting by. There was usually an impending surgery, a new pain. On Sunday evenings, Katie Malone joined them for dinner, and Leah reported her weekly slights.

She came in wearing a white shirt and cigarette trousers, and she held me for longer than she needed to. "It's good to see you," she said, with a smile. "It really is."

She settled into a barstool, although every table in the place was free. I hauled myself up next to her. The windows were utterly gray, as if the world outside had dissipated altogether.

"I've spent more hours here," Leah said, "than I've spent in my own bed."

"Is this what you have to wear now?" I said. "Even on days off?"

"There's a clothes budget," Leah said, "and I make the most of it."

She glanced down at herself, to check that everything remained in place. Leah would never have my mother's easy style. There would always be a button hanging or a little tell of toothpaste.

"I'm atoning," she said, "for a lifetime of sartorial mishaps."

"You were never that bad."

"I hit rock bottom at the funerals, I think. Immortalized in the world's press."

"You had your charm."

"Come on, Marty."

Work was OK, she said. She told an elaborate story about a lost delivery of mussels, Leah sprinting through the puddles of Morecambe's fish market with her shoes in one hand and a cool bag in the other. I only knew we'd reached the punch line from the rise of her eyebrows. It wasn't that I didn't listen to what she was saying, just that I enjoyed watching her talk.

"Katie wants me to give it all up," she said.

"Because her life turned out so well."

"Marty."

"I don't know," I said. "I always thought you were going to be—like, a great English professor. The world's premier expert on the Romantics."

She gave a small shrug. "These things happen. The money's good, right. I get to buy Francesca a handbag for her birthday. A good handbag. I get to go on holiday. I get the best free food known to man. There are worse lives, aren't there? Than mine."

"You're still doing the online thing, though. Right? The diploma?"

"You sound like my mother. Yes. Yes, I'm still doing the course."

She picked the grapefruit from her glass and peered at it, bemused. "I think I'm probably the dumbest person," she said, "in the whole class."

I hated hearing her talk like that. I couldn't stand it. Even at school, she'd had this conviction, whenever she raised her hand. Whatever people thought of Leah, she'd usually been right, or close enough; and she'd always known it, too.

"Come on," I said. "Tell me about the party."

If she wasn't there, she couldn't trust there would be a party at all. Leah's mother was in and out of hospital, and her father was ineffectual. Half the time, Leah said, he moves like he's underwater. She had spent the morning mixing the weakest cocktails she could devise. She had procured a cake from work, candles from Katie.

Beneath her sleeve was an elegant rose gold watch. Half our time was gone.

"You," she said. "How are you doing?"

"I'm still in the flat. I'm still at the bar."

She gave me a slow, skeptical look, as if that wasn't what she was asking at all.

"The panic attacks?" she said.

"They're under control. You don't need to worry."

"Don't I?"

"Do you know who I saw?" I said. "Today? Alicia Morden."

"Alicia Morden? She was one of the Day One kids?"

"Yeah. She was in my mum's class. She was the only one who made it out of the greenroom. My mum used to go on about how clever she was. She'd point her out, like: 'Oh, that's Alicia. The genius.' Anyway. I saw her by the memorial today. She was a literal adult."

"She'd be going to university now, right? Eighteen?"

"Eighteen."

Neither of us knew what to say to that. Leah peered around the bar and waved for another drink and said: "You wouldn't have got away with this in my day," as if she was a Stonesmere institution. Once the drinks were served, I took a glug and set down my glass.

"I'm going to visit him," I said. "Trent Casey."

"What?" Leah said.

"I'm going to pay him a visit."

"OK."

"Really?"

"What do you want me to say, Marty? What am I meant to do? Beg you not to go? Console you? Tell you it's a stupid idea? Which it obviously is, by the way. No. No. You do what you want. You always have done."

She looked around, surprised by her own indiscretion. The room was still empty.

"That's why you're here, is it?" she said. "To say goodbye."

"Yes. I guess it is. I don't expect he'll be particularly happy to see me."

"Before you say it," Leah said, "I appreciate the irony of this. I get it. But there are days when I feel like you've spent the whole of your life—every moment, since it happened—stuck in that hall."

She looked into her drink.

"Did you ever read his statement?" she said. "Casey's?"

"At the time, I think. I don't really remember."

"He was a kid, too, Marty. He was a stupid, stupid kid. And he happened to run into Rowan Sullivan, and he happened to listen to Ray Cleave. He fucked up—God, he fucked up—but—"

"But?"

"He didn't kill your mother."

"Oh. Thanks. Thanks for clarifying that."

"It was Rowan, Marty. It was Rowan Sullivan."

His name still felt like a wounding.

"I try not to think too much," I said, "about Rowan Sullivan."

"Of course not. I mean—God. What he did to you. I'd imagine it was easier to think about almost anything else."

She reached out and fumbled me against her.

"But that wasn't Trent Casey's fault," she said. "And it wasn't yours."

I clung on to her. I would have climbed inside her, if I could. Even now, a whisper in my skull told me that I was terrible, embarrassing, clinging like this to Leah Perry. Our cheeks crushed together. I could feel the drag of her lips against my jaw. It wasn't your fault, she said. It wasn't your fault.

She had time for a walk, she said, although it was long past midday. We sidled away from the lake. We were heading for Old School Road, although neither of us acknowledged it. At the gates, we stopped and looked together at the school. Through the drizzle, the classroom lights enclosed children, teachers, desks, chairs. There was paint on the windows, flowers and ladybirds. There were puddles gathering across the playground.

"I miss it, actually," Leah said.

"Really?"

"Yeah. It was just—I don't know. I'm probably being stupid. But we had a good time."

"People weren't particularly nice to you," I said.

"People? Like you?"

I couldn't really argue with that. And there was relief, too, in hearing Leah say it. I'd once consoled myself that I hadn't been cruel. A little self-interested, maybe, but the most gracious of the class. A tight, sympathetic smile, when the rest of them were cawing.

How had she borne to look at me, meeting her on Crag Brow for a Saturday hike?

"Yes," I said. "People like me."

"I'm sorry. I didn't mean it like that, really."

"That's OK. I deserved it."

I looked again across the playground. "Anyway," I said, "you've got a party to get to."

"They'll all be unbearably young," she said. "And insufferable." She reached for me a final time and kissed me on the cheek. There were little eggs of rain, laid among her hair.

"Leah," I said. "You're not the most stupid person on your course."

"How would you know?"

"I just do," I said. "If it hadn't been for Malone, you'd have graduated years ago."

"Samuel?"

"When you dropped out," I said. "That Christmas. When you came home."

"Samuel?" she said. "Come on, Marty."

"What?"

"I didn't do it for Samuel," Leah said. "God, no. I left university for you."

There was a time when I would have laughed it off. I suppose I could have denied that Leah had it right. Perhaps she had misremembered, exaggerated. I tried to open my mouth, to say something funny, but nothing came out. Leah was looking at me as if she could see right inside, through the dreary clothes and cold skin, flesh and ribs. It was all I could do to hide that my heart was just about breaking.

"How could I leave you?" she said. "Right after the grave? You were so lonely, Marty." She was silent for a moment. She gave a small, self-deprecating shake of her head. "I couldn't have left you," she said, "if I'd tried."

I managed a sorry sort of shrug and patted her, fondly, on the shoulder.

"It was a strange time," I said. "Wasn't it?"

"That, it was. Anyway, Marty. The party—"

"No. Of course. Goodbye, Leah."

"Goodbye, Marty."

"And the course—"

"I know. I know."

YEAR TWO,
DAY TWO

TRENT

When Susan emerged that morning, he did not know her. Her clothes were angular, immaculate. She no longer wore glasses, but jewelry. Her nails were painted scarlet, and she tapped them on the dashboard as she drove.

They stopped at a service station outside of Stoke and sat on a grass embankment eating breakfast. Susan was watching the car park. There was a hunch of men, dressed in black, drinking beer from the bonnet of a Ford.

"Them," Susan said. "Do you think they're with us?"

"Maybe," he said. For the past week, he had been contemplating how the Truth Rally would look. In some of these imaginings, there were five or six people, humiliated before the town. In other versions, there was a teeming mass of masks, loud enough to wake him.

"We best be on our way," Susan said.

He knew the landscape of Stonesmere so well by then. Signs for free-range eggs, inns, trails. Trees gathered in the valleys. Rock and scree bared on the hillsides. There was none of the banal weather of London, but spotlights of sunshine roving across the lake. Thin clouds moved around the ridges, adjusting the horizon.

There was a point, after the first signs for Stonesmere, when he began to notice the cars. At the bends in the road, they slowed behind other vehicles. Vehicles unsure of the route. They passed a cluster of cars pulled into a lay-by. Men walked toward one another, their arms outstretched. They overtook a woman driving alone, a Ray Cleave sticker on her window, and Susan shrieked. There were press vans, too, laden with satellites. In the traffic, he felt in the midst of a great, crushing tide. It no longer mattered what he thought or hoped. He could only wait to see where it left him.

The meeting point for the Truth Rally was the car park by the lake. They would march along Main Street and gather at the town hall, where Ray Cleave would make his speech. Trent opened the car door, and the lake wind nearly took it from its hinges. In those first few minutes, it was as terrible as the worst of his dreams. There were a few cars, their occupants waiting shyly in their seats. It was impossible to believe that anybody else would join them, and looking at Susan, a frown cracking her powder, Trent saw that she thought it, too.

And then, impossibly, they came.

The first was a carload of men, distinguishable only for being early. The next was a woman and her daughter, come from Eastbourne over-night, with a stop at a Travelodge en route. The woman greeted Trent and Susan as if they were family, gathered them into the talcum folds of her arms and whispered: Ray, he changed my life. And then there were two cars bouncing onto the grass of the beach, and another parked nonchalantly in the middle of the lot, and then three more.

"Where is he, then?" the woman said. "Ray?" Trent said that he didn't know. He was sure—quite sure—that he was on his way. Ray on the outskirts of town, driving one of his better cars, rehearsing his speech as he went.

Trent could see him.

Others arrived hooded, and more in balaclavas. There were number plates obscured by paint. There were plastic bottles passed from hand to hand. There were banners unfurled. There was Ray's name, repeated and whispered, a kind of prayer. There were the bold crayon colors of the Union Jack. It was almost time. If they were to arrive before the witnesses, if they were to greet them at the doors—

There were thousands of them: Trent knew that. A noise built within the crowd, something that started in a rumble of feet and fists and ended in a howl. Trent was standing in the very heart of them, and he felt it in his boots and his skull, felt it beating in his chest. He saw it in Susan's laughter, the wildness of teeth, spit, gums. He couldn't help it. He howled along with them.

YEAR TWO,
DAY TWO

MARTY

I t was easy enough to pass the press on Crag Brow. As we pulled from the drive there was a flurry of handprints spattering the windows. I watched Leah, left empty-handed outside the house, until she disappeared behind the trees. I sat between Anoushka and my dad, where I was harder to photograph. We came cautious between the dry-stone walls and down the hillside. Anoushka held a phone to her ear, talking in code. The men in the front seats said nothing.

"They've blocked Main Street," Anoushka said. There wasn't code, I guessed, for that. "We'll need a different way round."

The driver nodded. He swung for the narrow roads above the town. Bed-and-breakfasts, footpaths to the mountains. "Better hope," my dad said, "that we don't meet anything." He said it all jocular, but his hand fumbled across the seat and found my knee. We passed the mill, the stunted industrial estate. Old Man's Edge was blurred with clouds.

"We need to turn back toward the hall," the driver said. Anoushka was studying something on her phone.

"We may just beat them," she said. "Come on."

"What will happen," my dad said, "if we don't?"

The car turned down a narrow track and bumped back toward Main Street. I took my dad's trembling hand. Anoushka held her radio to her chest, clutched like a charm. The track was cluttered with cars, abandoned by journalists or truthers. "It's hard to pass," the driver said, and the man beside him said: "Do it anyway." We chipped a mirror, sent metal clanging across the road.

The driver peered onto Main and turned. Anoushka craned through the rear window and her face changed.

"They're coming this way," she said.

I sat dead still and listened. I could hear them now, somewhere behind us. What was coming? Bellows, weapons. There was a shrieking of alarms. The town hall came into view. The old clock tower, the steps to the door. There were cameras assembled around the cobbled square.

"Park up, please," Anoushka said. "Just here." My dad doubled his grip, harder.

We bumped up to the hall. Anoushka's door was already open. When I stepped from the car, I could see them, coming fast behind us.

"Inside," Anoushka said. "Inside, please." She hurried me in front of her with a hand to my shoulder. My dad panted behind us. At the doors to the town hall, I turned to look at them, just as they reached the square.

From the noise, I had expected an army, but there were fewer than one hundred. Some of them were ordinary, and many of them were old. They had little of Ray Cleave's vitality. They wore military fatigues. They wore white polo shirts and sunglasses. They wore helmets: helmets. They had spread out, as if to cover more ground, but instead they looked patchy and disarrayed. One or two broke from the others, to tap at a window or bellow for support; but they always retreated, I saw, when they found themselves alone. I saw a man lose his flat cap and bend to collect it from the road. I saw Ray Cleave's slogans, illegible and incoherent. I saw homemade masks and flames already extinguished by the wind from the lake. They wielded sticks rather than torches. I thought of them in dull houses the night before, stenciling slogans onto sheets. Careful not to get paint on the carpet. I thought of their parents or children downstairs, watching the television, preparing for bed.

I squeezed past the people gathered solemn at the threshold. The only person I knew was Larkin. He was turned away from the town hall, not waiting to enter but making the most of the vantage point. He surveyed the gathering with a slight smile. I knew exactly what he was thinking. They had come just as he hoped, rabid and frothing, and snared in a thousand lenses. There was no happiness in Larkin's face, and no sadness, either. There was only satisfaction.

YEAR TWO,
DAY TWO

TRENT

He walked at the back of them, down the road into Stonesmere. Traffic was at a standstill, vehicles abandoned, occupants fled or eager. There was a mass of flags and color, squeezing between the bollards and onto Main Street. Somebody wailed Ray's name, and it turned to a chant: Ray Cleave. Trent couldn't hear his own voice. Hands gathered him into the tide, pinches and fists.

The cenotaph was daubed with paint. They passed the chalkboard for the Teapotter. Breakfast, Morning Coffee, Lunch, Afternoon Tea. He remembered his mother's hat and fought an urge to kick the thing in two. The street glinted with broken glass. There was a car siren wailing, and there were snippets of graffiti on the shopfronts. Not a single one decipherable. Susan was laughing. Sweat dripping, lips stretching, flags waving, bottles flying, fists rising. He could no longer move now, kept tight in the shoal. He wasn't sure whether it was glee or dread moving in his blood. They passed a blond woman with a straight back who held a sign that read: GET OUT OF OUR TOWN. Shame on you, she said. Shame on you. A man passing spat in her mouth, and Trent saw her flinch. Susan chortled. The woman behind them now, her sign snatched and torn.

They were coming to the town hall. The gathering place: the place where Ray would be waiting. Beyond the crowd were the people of Stonesmere, filing up the steps to the great wooden doors. They stood patiently, with their backs to the Rally. Why weren't they fighting? The nutcase behind the lawsuit, and the Boy Who Lived, and Martha Ward. All of these phonies who had spent the last year proclaiming their grief and rage. Here they were, sad and still.

There were more cameras than he expected. Not just the press, but scatterings of tourists, residents. They wielded phones like shields. He looked about to see what they would see. There was a billow of flags for causes he did not know. There were teenagers thrusting chairs toward the media. There were masked faces, and no resistance to them, and in that void, he knew. He knew exactly how it would look.

Susan took him by the shoulder. Her eyes were gleeful and clear. If she noticed his dismay, she had no time for it. Not now.

"We need to go," she said. "We can't get too close." He nodded. She held tight to his wrist and led him from the crowd. They stumbled on glass, over rubbish and cans. He could hear the din of the Rally, trying to breach the town hall.

"It's beautiful," Susan said.

"It's a mess," Trent said. "Ray—"

Trent knew only that it was the end of things. That there would be no great exposé, nor investigation. In the evening headlines, there would be condemnation. There would be photographs of the brutes who had harassed a grieving community. On Twitter, people would ridicule their banners. There would be odes to Stonesmere's grace.

"He's not coming," Trent said. "Ray. Is he?"

"What does it matter?" Susan said. She touched her hair back in place. "We're here," she said. "Aren't we?"

She gestured to the back of the building. There, the catering door.
A police officer stood outside, checking names from a list. Two days
earlier, Trent had retrieved the email from Sally Meynard-Hirst's account. A map. An arrow, directing journalists from the site of potential
protests. There it was: the press entrance for the Stonesmere inquest.

The coroner would begin proceedings, she said, with a minute of silence. The room paused for the dead. He and Susan sat in the gallery
above the witnesses. Trent used the silence to survey the cast. He could
see hair partings, notes, hands clasped in laps. Martha Ward sat just
below him. He could not see her face.

"Let's begin, then," the coroner said. He had expected her robed,
but she wore a trouser suit and delicate glasses. She looked as if she had
occupied her chair for many months: that when the court adjourned,
she would remain in her seat, owlishly awaiting the next of her duties.

Who was up first? Larkin. Larkin, the claimant. Larkin, who had
knocked three teeth from the mouth of one of Ray Cleave's most loyal
supporters, and had the gall to sue him, still.

Trent had heard most of it before. He'd read the interviews. He'd
listened to Larkin tour the podcasts, straddling a whole bunch of genres
with oblivious charm. Grief, Family, Current Affairs. He awaited the
stock lines: *Just because I lost my child, I should not lose my right to confidential
medical treatment*, and *In one way, they're right, I should have been there.* The
boredom only lifted when the coroner asked Larkin how Kit had found
life at Stonesmere Primary School. Larkin hesitated. Kit hadn't been
particularly happy, he said. He had never found it easy to fit in.

Unhappiness: it was not part of the Stonesmere narrative.

"Kit lost his mum," Larkin said, "the year before. And after that—
well. There was the business with Percy."

"Percy?"

Larkin was smiling now. "He was a guinea pig," Larkin said. "The class guinea pig. They took it in turns, you see, to keep him over the weekend. This is months before Day One, you understand. Months and months."

Larkin shuffled in his seat, and made himself comfortable.

"It was Kit's turn, this one time. Kit, he decides Percy should have some fresh air. He was an early riser, Kit, and it's Saturday morning, long before I'm even awake. And Kit takes Percy for a walk around the garden. Well. I'm sure you can imagine what happened next."

The room gave a collective little groan. A security guard seated at the end of Trent's row was rapt. Trent had to give it to him: Larkin could tell a story.

"It was a total disaster," Larkin said, "at the time. We spent the whole day searching. Most of the night, too. Head torches, spinach. Everything we could think of. We didn't have much luck. As you may imagine. And there was a very tearful phone call on Monday morning, to Mrs. Ward. I thought that would be the end of it. But Kit—Kit, he was always keeping an eye out. Things like that—he could never quite forget them. I like to think that one day—someday—he would have found life a little easier."

"Thank you," the coroner said. "And I'm very sorry, Mr. Larkin, for your unquantifiable loss."

"Can I say one more thing?" Larkin said. "Just the one. I know this'll be reported, you see, and I want—I wanted to say something, for the record. To those people, out there, who think that my son didn't exist."

Trent waited, the breath caught in his throat. It was easy to believe that Larkin looked to him, up there in the gallery; but wasn't that how all good actors made you feel, just before they spoke?

"I wish that they were right," Larkin said. "That's all. I wish he were a fiction. I mean, Christ. How easy would that be? If I'd never known him at all."

And though he could sense the roll of Susan's neck, though he knew that the speech must have been rehearsed, time and again, with this exact reaction in mind—Trent felt the ambush of tears in his eyes.

"Let's take a break there, then," the coroner said, "before we move on to Martha Ward."

YEAR TWO,
DAY TWO

MARTY

t was a long walk, to that chair. Past my dad, who made as if he would like to stop me, but folded his legs to his chest and let me go. Past the Malone family, the four of them remaining. Past Larkin—God, Larkin—who sat with a still face, looking at nothing I could see. Past so many faces, known since I was a child. I took my seat. The chair was wooden and plain. It was still warm from Larkin's body.

I gave my full name for the record. The coroner thanked me for being here today, and I said, by default, "No problem."

"Now there may be various documents, photographs, things shown to you. And they'll appear on the big screen at the front of the room."

"Thank you," I said. How I wanted her to like me, this calm, orderly woman. If she could just like me, for a few more minutes—

"Were you, on the day we're concerned with," the coroner said, "an employee of Stonesmere Primary School?"

"That's right," I said. "Yes. I coached sport there, in the afternoons."

"And how long had you been in their employment?"

"Nearly a year," I said.

"And, in addition, your mother—that's Ava Ward—was a teacher at Stonesmere Primary School."

"Yes."

"Thank you. What I'm going to ask you, Miss Ward, is a series of questions about the Day One performance, which was where the deaths of the eleven subjects took place. Is that all right?"

"Yes."

"What time," the coroner said, "did you arrive to watch the Day One performance that morning?"

"I didn't," I said. I said it so softly that the coroner gave me a great, comforting smile, as if I might have stage fright or else a very quiet voice, neither of which had ever been a problem.

I was scared, though. I suppose that was it.

"Please could you repeat that answer, Miss Ward?"

"I didn't," I said. "I didn't make it."

The texture of the room changed, just like that. It was still silent, but the silence was different, terrible, full of words.

"Ah," the coroner said. She turned, frowning, to the file on her desk.

"That seems to be inconsistent," she said, "with your previous statements."

"It is," I said. "Yes."

The coroner removed her glasses and laid them on her papers. "We'll need to take a little time, I think," she said, "to get to the bottom of this. But first, Miss Ward, I'm going to ask the obvious question."

I nodded. It wasn't scary anymore. It was done.

"If you weren't at the Day One performance, Miss Ward, I'll need to ask you where you were."

From across the quiet room there came a beating. I guessed it was something internal, the blood in my ears or heart. It was only when the coroner frowned that I realized everybody else could hear it, too. I had thought myself the finale, but I was wrong.

YEAR TWO, DAY TWO

TRENT

didn't make it," she said. How long—how long had he waited? There
had been so many months, when this was all he wanted to hear. Martha Ward, a liar. The headlines were printing in his skull. "Ward
Confesses; Sullivan Is Innocent." He could see Ray Cleave, welcoming
him to the stage. He could see Tim, pontificating his way around the
facts. He could see his mother, standing before a Christmas tree, of all
things.

Welcome home, baby.

You were right.

He had waited, but all the same. Martha Ward was so small, sitting
at the front of the room. She was small and hunched and deflated. And
he was relieved, too, that she had saved herself; that she would never
know just how close—

He looked to Susan, expecting glee. Relief, too. But instead, she was
occupied. The projector was in her hands. He had bought it with the
last of his security money, and tenderly checked the settings.

"Stop," Trent said. There was no space to whisper, in a room like this. The journalist beside him glanced from her notes. "Stop. We need to hear—"

Susan gave a little shake of her head, and settled the projector on her lap.

"Stop," Trent said. "She's telling the truth."

"We've come this far," Susan said. And the projector was on now, and pointing at the great white screen. He made an ill-fated snatch for the thing. The whole row of reporters was turning. "Please," Trent said. Because what was it now but cruelty? And they were not cruel, had never been cruel. The security guard lumbered toward them. Too late, Trent thought. Too late. The photograph burst onto the screen. Martha Ward, and Rowan, too. The embarrassment of human bodies, stretched larger than they were. Rowan looked at the camera, but Martha looked only at Rowan. The security guard was nearly upon them. Trent clambered over the back of his chair, crashing past laptops, papers, knees.

The girl sat below her own naked self. He had thought she may run, bellow, but instead she turned back to the coroner. It was the last thing he glimpsed. Her face, tired and resigned and just that little bit defiant.

"Please," she said, "could you repeat the question?"

DAY ONE

MARTY

Sixteen months before Day One, she met Rowan Sullivan. It was late February. Snow on the mountains. Darkness pincering the school day. She was waiting for her mother in the playground of Stonesmere Primary School. Waiting there, admittedly, so her mother could see precisely how cold it was possible to be—how inconvenienced—if she kept her daughter waiting for twenty minutes to get a lift home. It was a crisis, her mother had said, but it was always a crisis: as if she were the prime minister, rather than a primary school teacher. Her crises, Marty knew, consisted of vomit, knee scrapes, lost property.

Marty watched the breath hang from her mouth into the darkness. Her hands were lilac. She tucked them into her sleeves.

She was in her final year at Stonesmere High School. Three months left of a shirt, a blazer, the skirt rolled twice at the waist. Some weeks later, when she was in Rowan Sullivan's bed, a bed in a pebble dash two-up two-down close to Leah Perry's house, he said he had thought about that uniform all night. The way the skirt fell, he said, demonstrating what she liked to think of as his attention to detail.

Honestly, he said, on top of her. I'm still fucking thinking about it.

But that day in February, he was polite. He came from the primary school hall carrying coils of climbing ropes. She knew who he was right away, because he was a recent topic of discussion at the Ward dinner table. His main offense was shunning the middle-aged women in the staff room. He did not accept their offers of hot drinks, nor conversation. He sat alone, drinking water.

Just think, Marty said, of what he could be missing.

"Are you lost?" he said. He looked as she had expected. He was tall. His hair fell under his collar, like he had just got dressed. Amid the ropes, his arms were bare and hard.

"No," she said. "Just waiting."

"Ah. Mrs. Ward's kid. I know you." He shook his head. "Your mother, she talks about you all the time."

"What does she say?"

He held up his arms mockingly, as if she was some self-declared deity. "I hear," he said, "that I'm in the presence of a head girl."

"That was just democracy," she said. As if he was interested in the nuances of Stonesmere High's prefect election process. He was closer now. In the light of the classroom windows, his eyes were narrow and curled like smiles.

"Your mother'll have to watch out," he said, and although she didn't know what he meant, not really, she said: "I don't think it's up to her. Do you?"

He laughed. Certain laughs, you would debase yourself for them. You would be the joker, the clown. Paint your face, eat the pie. The things you would do—

"No," he said. "As a matter of fact, I don't think it is."

He was a nice thing to think about. She would be sitting on the benches, listening to Amber talk, or else lacing her boots for the latest football trial. And there he would be. He smiled from the darkness, the climbing ropes snaking from his arms. When her mother mentioned his name, she flinched, secretly, and listened.

She next saw him outside the Royal Oak. One of the first weekends of spring. She should have been revising. She had been revising. Had been inside, reading about—what? The shape of birds' wings, the honeycomb structure beneath the feathers. For what? So she could sit in some other room, confined, reading something different? She wore old football shorts and a graying vest. Her dad came to the door and told her to take a break. Get outside. Kick a ball. It was not just a suggestion. That winter, she had put in a series of dismal performances for Sunderland Ladies, her first season playing in the women's league. A chasm had cracked between those players who were truly gifted and those who were merely very good, and she found herself on the wrong side of it, and toppling.

All this working, her dad whispered, quiet enough that her mother wouldn't hear. You'll become a bore.

She had lain down on her bedroom floor, face to the carpet, warm in the afternoon sunshine, and come twice, thinking about faceless men, a multitude of them, wielding her limbs like tools. She had made some toast. She had discovered a trio of tennis balls left by her dad on the kitchen table, and tried to juggle.

She was so bored.

She took a walk. He came from the Royal Oak with his face swollen and amused. In the daylight he was older. The skin around his eyes had started to pucker. There were shallow lines in his forehead, which deepened when she said something he didn't like.

"Miss Ward," he said. "Hello."

He smelled of cigarettes. That good, dirty smell. More exotic in her life than she cared to admit. You could not, under any circumstances, smoke cigarettes and come first lady in Stonesmere's parkrun.

"Hello," she said. She said it in a voice she had been working on, the voice she intended to use at university. None of the old shrillness left. "What happened to you?"

"This? I had an encounter. Didn't I? People don't like it, do they? When someone's a little different."

"I'm sorry."

"Ah, well. You should see the other guy, and all that. Where are you off to?"

"I'm just out for a walk."

"A walk? Do people still do that?"

"I do."

"OK, then," he said. "Show me how you do it."

He walked behind her for a moment, watching, and she felt every part of her skin new beneath his eyes. She worried that the calves were too defined, that the muscles of her thighs were touching.

"You're very good," he said—and he started laughing then—"at that."

"Thank you," she said, laughing, too.

"Let's sit by the lake," he said. "Enough of this—this walking business."

"And do what?"

"And talk. The lost art of conversation."

And they talked. She had imagined their first conversation for some time by then, but it was closer and longer than she had hoped. What did they talk about? Oh, she couldn't have said. Leah asked the exact same question once, but she could recall only the sensation of it, that she was finally becoming a person she had always longed to be.

She took a photograph of him that afternoon, and in the photograph he reclined in one of the free deck chairs set up each spring on the grass along the lake. "Don't you know," he said, "that cameras are prone to stealing your soul?" He held a cigarette in one hand and marked his words with the other. He wore a black fleece and the same jeans he always wore, and his mouth was curling toward ridicule—a photograph, of all things—and even if you knew all that would happen, you wouldn't be able to deny it, that in this photograph he was one of the most beautiful people you had ever seen.

She heard later that he had been in a fight at the Royal Oak; that he had threatened to bottle a member of the bowling club.

You had to laugh. Didn't you?

She slept with him a week later, in April. She had planned to keep him waiting, but fuck it, who cared? She walked the school corridors with her open, ordinary face, greeting this teacher or that. She delivered a speech in assembly encouraging more girls to give sports a try. Each evening, she undressed in his bedroom according to specific instructions. Turn around, slow, yes. No, no, leave the skirt. "You're so good," he said, when she came to him, and he said *good* as if it was something he both detested and faintly admired.

"What do we do now, then," he said.

"What do you mean?"

"Are you going to make me your boyfriend?"

"I don't know. Is that what—I mean. Is that what you want?"

What she did not tell him: she knew little of boyfriends. Oh, she knew fumbles, sucking, wet earth, cold hands. The things she'd done at parties, ever since she was thirteen years old. But nothing of love. When Amber had got a boyfriend, aged sixteen and a half, Marty had spent several mortifying evenings trailing Stonesmere behind them, wondering whether she was allowed to speak.

"Your mother won't like it," he said. "I'll tell you that for free."

"No," she said, "I imagine not."

His head was pressed into the mattress, so she saw only the corner of his mouth, rising into view. "But you're not going to tell her," he said. "Are you?"

She gave him a slow, conspiratorial stare, and he rolled onto his back, laughing: "Your secret boyfriend, then," he said, and this was how he referred to himself, ever after.

In May, the last weekend before exams, her parents decided to drive to Northumbria for the weekend. She told him as soon as the hotel was booked. She worked hard to remove the exclamation marks from her message. He replied right away.

Dirty weekend at yours, then.

Her mother checked and double-checked that she wouldn't need any emotional support. The weekend was some belated birthday surprise from her dad, of course, who had brazenly failed every exam he took, and look how much harm it did to him. "I'll cook everything before-hand," her mother said, "so you won't need to think about a thing." Marty already knew the menu. Overnight oats, quiche, lasagna. A litany of fa-vorites.

She messaged Rowan back: Filthy.

In the week leading up to it, she thought of nothing else. There were times when she imagined the house through his eyes and detested it. The embarrassment of candles. The throws, rolled in a basket in the living room, as if her mother was expecting—any day now—to wel-come a family of cold refugees. The twee, obvious art. His house was clean and bare. He lived without such affectations. He needed only good, simple things.

"Fuck," he said, when she opened the door. "What are you? A mil-lionaire?"

She had imagined Friday night spent in her bedroom. The luxury of hours, rather than minutes. She had bought underwear online, delivered in discreet packaging, and tried it on late at night when she wouldn't be disturbed. The knickers were black lace. She removed them slowly before the mirror, down over her thighs, knees, ankles, feet, replicating the care with which she hoped he would do it. All she needed, in those days—all she needed was the thought of him.

"Come on," she said. She nodded to the staircase and took his hand. But he shook his head.

"No," he said. And he led her through to the kitchen, the great expanse of the garden beyond it. "Here," he said.

"Here? Where?"

"Here."

Her thighs touched the table. He pressed her shoulders to the ground and lowered her jaw with a finger. She made to unbuckle his jeans, but she was too slow. He brushed away her hands. Her head was pinned between the table leg and his body. Each time she choked, he looked a little more pleased.

"Come on, then," he said. "Get up."

"They could come back, though."

"And? Get on the table."

He came on her stomach, but most of it went over the wood, a tiled coaster her mother had picked up in Portugal. He wanted to lie on the couch, but she could think only of getting the stuff off the table. He walked around her, naked, while she crouched and cleaned. "It's the stuff of romances," he said. "The postcoital cleanup." And when she returned to him, he shrugged from her hands and took a knife from her dad's block.

"What are you doing?" she said.

He laid his hand on the chopping board and pierced the spaces between his fingers, fast as he could.

"I bet these knives," he said, "cost more than I make in a month."

"I don't know."

"*I don't know.* Well, of course you don't. Of course you don't know."

The day was falling through her hands. "My dad does have some cool stuff, though," she said. Grasping for it, spooling it from the ground.

"Like what?"

The table was clean. She polished a good smile, the smile everybody liked, and clambered from her knees. "He has a gun," she said.

"He does?"

"Yes."

"Have you ever shot it?"

"I have."

He gave her a long, quizzical look. How sweet it felt, to have confused him. "I don't believe you," he said, carefully.

So she showed him. She retrieved her dad's key from his desk, while Rowan slugged from a bottle of good whisky; a bottle that did, in fact, cost more than he made in a month. She opened the wooden cabinet in her dad's study and checked the safety, and she held the rifle to the light.

He took it tenderly, like it was a living thing, and weighed it in his hands. She had thought he would want to shoot it, was braced for him to joke around. Bang, bang! Instead, he turned it this way and that, curled a finger along the trigger and stroked the barrel.

"Show me, then," he said. He passed it back to her. "If you're such an expert."

She rested the heel against her shoulder. "Like this, you mean?" she said. She stepped quick to the window and crouched as if she were on a sniper mission in one of the games she watched him play. She disengaged the safety and loaded. "Like this?"

He was laughing. "Come here," he said.

She knew the day was salvaged, then. He took her in his arms and

kissed her on the forehead. She returned the gun to the cabinet, the
key to the pencil pot.

She only remembered the underwear that night, when she saw it
fallen small and unfamiliar to her bedroom floor.

There were always things, she told Leah, that made her feel uncomfortable; that made the smile hesitate on her face. His mother was often
there, in the house, and sometimes it seemed like he was trying to be
loud, would position Marty's body so that the bed would rock or his
desk would drum the wall. When she didn't get the grades for university, he gave a great spit of a laugh and said: How does it feel, your first
taste of failure? She knew none of his friends. Knew only the inside of
his bedroom, where the shelves were bursting but ordered, and he kept
the curtains drawn. When they passed in the school playground, he
gave her a slow, appraising stare, but said nothing at all.

He liked to photograph her. It was revenge, he said, for the very first
photograph. A soul for a soul. But Rowan's photographs were different.
He arranged her limbs like the components of a still life. He muddled
them with his own and shot them together, tangled upon his bed. When
she took the camera from her bedside table and looked at them, she
recognized little of the girl in the pictures. She saw flesh, hair, fat. She
appraised her body as if it belonged to somebody she did not know.

Her dad procured her a dreary few days of work experience. Lakeside Law. The printer churned tiredly through the afternoon. That whole
week, Rowan called her Your Honor. He ordered her to the desk in his
room. To bend. Bent, there—waiting—in the smart black dress she had
chosen with her mother. He prepared the camera. While he was doing
so, she imagined the disclosure of the photographs, a wide distribution
to her family and friends. Ah, yes, they would say. Of course. This: this
is the kind of person she is.

———

And then: the walk to Old Man's Edge.

She had known him for a year. Had known him for long enough to understand that it was her fault. An indelicacy. As they came to the tarn, she was talking about exams. She was about to book in for resits. She was confident, this time, that she would do it. She could hear her own excitement, rebounding from the crags.

"Are you doing it for yourself, though," he said, "or because your parents told you to?"

She should have known, really, that he might get upset. She was talking of a time beyond him, and talking of it carelessly.

"It's an interesting point," she said.

"I just know," he said, "how desperate you are to please."

She was glad that he was in front, so he couldn't see her turning red.

"Then what?" he said. "University?"

She tried to imagine how it could work. He'd come to visit her, perhaps. She'd meet him from a bus and they would sleep together in her single bed, and she would take him to parties where he was a decade older than everybody else.

She knew, when it came down to it, that this would never happen.

He decided that they should swim. It was already midafternoon, and March. She looked to the sky. A few thin clouds stirring in the valley. More, heavier, on the horizon. The light would soon be poor, then dim, then absent.

"OK," she said. The cheer trembled in her voice.

The water was black and still. Within it, her body looked cadaverous. There was late snow in the shadow of the ridge. She swam far out, hoping to impress him, but instead he beat her back to the bank and snatched a handful of her clothes. "Rowan," she said, and he said, "*Marty,*" which he only called her in ridicule. She had told him the old story thinking he would find her vulnerability sweet, endearing; that when she had not managed the *th*, her mother had come up with a workaround. That's the Wards, isn't it? Rowan had said. When you can't speak, you just get your own language.

He scattered her clothes, and she retrieved them hunched, naked, shaking them for dirt.

That would be the end of it, at least. She thought longingly of the house on Crag Brow, where she would be admonished for her absence. The warmth of the radiator in the hall. Her mother would have saved her a whole plate of Sunday dinner. Her mother, standing at the living room window, looking for the swing of her ponytail over the wall. Her dad, appeasing her, saying nice, meaningless things. *Any minute now*, and *A watched pot never boils.*

"Come on, then," Rowan said. "We're going up."

"What? But you just said—"

"It was our plan, wasn't it? Think of the sunset. The sunset, it's going to be perfect."

From nowhere came the memory of Sergeant Larkin, standing before her class, delivering his compendium of walkers' stupidity.

"No," she said. "The weather. It's coming in."

"What are you? A weatherman?"

And so she had gone. He walked too fast for conversation. Cloud closed around them, erasing the view. Old Man's Edge was a tightrope of rock. Nowhere for your hands but air. In the dimming light she could see only the land beneath her boots, but not the step ahead of it. There was mist lapping at their shins. She was cold and frightened. "We should go back," she said, a few meters across. He turned to her, his face floating in the gloom. "Pussy," he said. A few outcrops farther, his foot slid, and she scrambled to catch him.

"If I fell," he said, "what do you think would happen?"

She could see a tremble to his hands. The aftershock of the fall. That little vulnerability. It was enough to keep her dogged at his heel.

"You wouldn't miss me," he said. "Would you? You wouldn't miss me at all."

"Of course I would," she said. "Come on—"

"You'll have such wonderful friends, won't you," he said. "Intellects. Imagine. Imagine the men you'll be fucking."

He turned before she could respond. She muddled after him, testing each rock with outstretched fingers. He didn't look back until right at the end, where the scree turned to grass and the land spread, softened. He waited for her, whooping in triumph. She clawed the tears from her eyes and staggered the last few steps, and he took her ponytail in his fist and dragged her to standing, and kissed her there, laughter tumbling from his mouth and into her own.

There were ways, Leah advised, of doing it kindly, though it was not what he deserved. Marty washed the clothes she had borrowed. She had slept with some of them, mortifyingly, in her bed. She gathered the books he had lent to her, nonfiction, strange ideologies, none of which she had read. She turned up to his house with a neat bag of his belongings, wearing leggings and a sweatshirt, ugly enough to soften the blow.

She and Leah had laughed, practicing the speech. "We're very different," Marty had said, and Leah had said: "Because you're a dickwad, and I'm not." But here, before his house, it was no longer funny. His mother came diffidently to the door. There was a quiz show on the television, the contestant opening boxes for money.

"He's upstairs," his mother said.

It went well, the speech. She needed to focus, she said, on these exams. (Studious, dull.) She had messed them up once already. (Self-deprecating.) It was not fair to keep him waiting, when she intended to leave Stonesmere anyway. (And gracious, too.) He sat on his bed, head bowed, listening. She had never seen him so still. He, who was always narrowing an eye, cracking a knuckle. When she was finished, she sat beside him and looked at the carpet.

"OK, then," she said. "I should probably head home."

"I'll bet it was your mum," he said. "Wasn't it?"

"What? No. I never even told her."

He turned to her and kissed her, gently, on the mouth.

"OK," he said. "Whatever you say." But he kissed her again, and she felt his hand close around her thigh.

"What are you doing?" she said.

"Come on," he said. "Please. The last time."

"No," she said. She stood from the bed, but he stood faster.

"I should know," he said, "when it's the last time."

He pushed her, gently, back to sitting, and when she stood, he pushed her again.

"I'm going to leave now," she said. She stood, a third time.

She watched him draw back his arm, close his fist, and hit her in the face. Martha Ward, head girl, football protégée, daughter of Justin, Ava. She just watched. All the while, thinking stupidly: he is not going to do this. He did. And she could have laughed, in incredulity. He really did! She saw a flurry of lights and grasped wildly at the pain. She had landed heavy, her torso on his bed, her legs tangled on the floor. While she was checking that her eye was still there, intact, he was coming toward her. In the tilt of his head she saw a terrible softness, close to love. When his hand touched her cheek, it was tender, as if he was examining a wound inflicted by somebody else.

She was making terrible deals. Get me out of this room, and I will be good, modest, repentant. Please, God. Get me out of this room.

There was a brisk knock at the door, and his mother said: "All OK, Rowan?"

What would have happened, if it hadn't been for his mother? She did not know. She spent hours, afterward, basking in the not-knowing. In her luck. She was on her feet. The door opened; his mother was at the threshold. Marty saw the landing and staggered toward it. She said something, she knew, shamefully polite. Thank you for having me! She walked down the stairs and into the small living room. The television was still on, and loud. She took her coat from the hooks at the door. On the television, an audience applauded. She pulled on her trainers and stepped into the day, unchanged, just as she had left it. There was a dainty little gate, marking the front of the garden, and she slammed it behind her with such force that it snapped from its hinges. Then she was running, running; and this, she knew how to do.

She told her parents a good story. Funny enough. A flyaway football. A groveling child, begging for forgiveness. At the school, she pulled hideous faces and sent the children squealing across the field, arms askew.

For a long time, she could think of nothing else. And then, in less time than she had expected, she could. When Leah said, There will be a day soon, Marty, when he won't even cross your mind, when you're the captain of the university football team and he's still living in his mother's house, she knew, determinedly, that this was true.

He lost his job at the primary school at the beginning of summer. She heard about it from her mother. They were sitting together on the sofa, watching a program about people looking at houses in the countryside. Every time they watched it, they enjoyed how much the house hunters hated the countryside.

Marty was still wearing her coaching clothes. Rounders, today. The six-year-olds. They always made her laugh. The way they dawdled out across the school field, falling over their feet. It took half the lesson, just to get them to the pitch.

There had been erratic behavior, her mother said. Rumors about a girl, younger than she should be, who hung around the shed where they kept the PE equipment.

"I feel sorry for him," Marty said, not looking up from the television, and to her surprise, her mother said, Yes. She did, too. They sat a few minutes in silence, and when it was time for the adverts, her mother set the TV to mute.

"I saw you, once," she said, "going into his house. I was dropping off some ancient books from the classroom. Something I thought Leah could read to her sisters. And I knew, just from the glimpse—"

She could feel her mother's eyes on her cheek. That awful, beautiful knowingness. It was the knowingness of absolute vulnerability, of tears and shit and birthdays, Christmases and stupidity, celebrations and vacations, vomit and tantrums and humiliation, and loving somebody, wearily, through it all.

"I don't pretend to know what happened, Marty," her mother said. "But it's certainly nice to have you back."

She did not hear from him until two weeks before Day One. He came to her house on a Friday morning. Her parents were at work. She wore a T-shirt and pajama shorts. No underwear. She could feel the bare, vulnerable places beneath her clothes. She was afraid, and the fact of the fear was terrible. She had spent so many months, mistaking it for other things.

"Hello, there," he said. He looked good. He wore the clothes he ran in, black shorts and a tight gray top. He carried a bag on his shoulder.

"I brought you these," he said. From the holdall he pulled a clean pair of socks and a jumper she had long forgotten. She pictured his mother at the dryer, pairing and folding.

"Thanks," she said. "You didn't need to."

"That's OK. Would it be OK to get some water, do you think? I'm training."

He did not say what he was training for. She nodded, and he followed her through the hallway. The floorboards shifted beneath his trainers. She reached for a glass from the cupboard, conscious of his body behind her. She turned back to him. He leaned against the kitchen island, his arms folded.

"I'm sure this place gets bigger," he said, "every time I visit."

"I don't know about that."

At the fridge, she filled the glass with ice, then water.

"You look beautiful, by the way," he said.

"I'm not sure about that, either."

"Well, you never were. But you should be."

Standing here in the sunshine, with the warm morning drifting through the house, she examined her fear. He had hit her, yes, but only once: once, when he was defeated and frightened himself. Leah's horror: that wouldn't have helped. "Were you reading?" he said, nodding to her chair on the patio, and they talked a little about the book, something Leah loved—ah, the ingenious Leah—that she couldn't get into. He asked about her mother, how preparations for Day One were going, and she thought it a little sad, that he still kept up, so closely, with the school calendar.

"You know what it's like," she said. "The kids can't wait. Why?" And she gave him a kind, bemused smile. "Are you going?"

"I don't know," he said. "I may make an appearance."

There was so much she could have said. Is that really a good idea?

or What the hell are you thinking? But she couldn't muster the effort. She looked back to her chair, tilted for the sunshine, and he looked there, too.

"I bet your mum hasn't shut up about it," he said, and where Marty would once have smiled, admitted it, she said: "Well, she really loves this class."

"I should leave you be," he said. She made to follow him into the hallway, but he waved her back to her book. No, no. Not to worry.

Remember?

He knew the way.

In the week before Day One, she spent evenings helping her mother with the backdrop. There had been an ordering mishap. What had looked like a banner of flags online turned up in twenty pieces, accompanied by a spool of thread. Her mother stood in the hallway, the tricolore fluttering from her fingers. "How hard can it be?" Marty said, and that was that: she was recruited.

Marty was skilled enough: she could cascade-shuffle a deck of cards; perform an Elastico; do a decent impersonation of Mrs. Hutchinson at the edge of her temper. What she couldn't do was sew one piece of material to another.

Her mother snatched her time after dinner. They arranged the flags across the table and worked beneath the pendant lights. They didn't look at each other. She stabbed the needle through the nylon and dragged it through. She pricked her fingers and presented bulges of blood, evidence of cruel and inhumane treatment. Child labor, at the very least.

"You're overage now, I think."

It was the night before Day One, and late. No time, now, for unpicking. Her mother stood from the table and filled their glasses with a good, cold wine. The smell of dinner was subsiding, and Marty started to relent. "When did you know," she said, "that you wanted to be a teacher?"

"I don't know," her mother said. "For a long time, to be honest. I'd teach the children down the road. Make them take their seats in the garden. Teach them back what I'd done that day at school."

"It must have been nice. To know."

"A little dull, maybe. But yes. Nice enough."

"I did a quiz today," Marty admitted. "A career quiz. I was a falcon."

"Is that a profession?"

"They start by allocating you an animal. Then they make up a personality for the animal, and they assign it a career." She laughed, hoping her mother would join her. "It was really stupid."

They were quiet. She knew her mother was hoping she would continue to talk, and contrarily, she let the minutes pass.

"It said that I could be an offshore roughneck," she said, finally. "Or a lighting technician."

"Just like you always dreamed."

She held her work up to the lights. Behind it, she waited to stop grinning.

"But you, Mary," her mother said. "What do you want to be?"

"Exams didn't exactly go well. And it doesn't look like I'm going to be a professional sportswoman, either."

Her mother's face was pained. If you attacked yourself viciously enough, Marty knew, you could also hurt the people who liked you. She fumbled with the needle and sucked at her thumb.

"What if I wanted to be a hand model?" she said.

Her hands were like her dad's, indelicate but quick. She liked them for that. The long, crooked fingers. White webbing between them, closed from her tan. She had broken her middle finger when she was eight years old, in the hinges of a balcony door. They had sat in a Cypriot hospital for three hours, under slow fans, until she insisted on returning to the swimming pool, and her dad set it himself.

"Most people," Marty continued, "know already. You look at someone like Leah. She's going to be—what? A literature professor? And she's already read every book in the library. She's basically there. You—you're great at your job. People in my class—they still talk about you. Whereas me . . ."

"Whereas you? People love you, Marty. They always have done. The girls come in from PE, and they say they want to be you when they grow up."

Marty tried to keep her face glum enough for sympathy, but she knew she would remember those words for a while. Would take them out on listless afternoons, polish them, set them proudly back in place.

"You could still resit your exams," her mother said. "Next year, or the year after that. Or you could do something—something entirely different. Something where you can always be outdoors. Something to do with nature. Maybe you'll end up working right here. You see the park rangers, don't you?"

"Maybe I'll look into it."

"Maybe you should."

"Sometimes I miss being little," Marty said. "Like the kids in your class." And she missed, too, how things had been between them. Other people got her mother for a year, but she had her for life. How many hours had they spent here, sitting at the kitchen table, while she told her mother about her and Leah's latest discoveries? Four red squirrels. An otter pup bobbing in the shallows. A fairy in the garden. There was a hard lump in her throat. She watched her fingers pinching the needle.

"Sometimes I miss that, too," her mother said.

They worked awhile more, threading and cursing.

"Will you come tomorrow?" her mother said. And Marty said: "Sure."

———

On the morning of Day One, she lay in bed and listened to her mother leaving the house. The engine puttered beneath her window. She smelled petrol and cold, the smells of so many school day mornings. The front door opened, closed, opened. The banner was finished and folded. She knew her mother had put a lot into it, this performance. A difficult class come good. She supposed she would go. It would be sweet to see the kids bellowing out their lines. From the color of her curtains, she could tell the window would be full of blue.

She lifted her phone and saw the shape of his name, waiting on the screen.

I'm leaving town this morning, he said. It would be nice to say goodbye. St. Oswald's, half eight.

She lay there, still, looking at it. The day was changed. Here, right here: a banquet of the worst things about him. Assumption, secrecy, understatement. Was he really leaving town? That didn't seem likely. He was a Stonesmere native, just like she was, and the town tolerated its own. Here, he was an eccentric. Somewhere else, he would most likely be a threat.

She climbed from the bed and started to dress. And how she hated it—that she chose a short, short skirt. That she spent five minutes of her life applying just the right amount of makeup. Before she left her room, she sent Leah some desperate missive. Leah: Leah would know what to do.

The beach in town was laden with armbands and paddleboats, but St. Oswald's was for locals. The only way down there was through the wood on Old School Road. You could see the spire, rising beyond the trees. Just past the church was a grassy bay. The lake bed tilted slow, silty. You could walk to your neck. She stopped a moment where the trail trod off between the trees, and glanced to her phone.

You may as well hear what he has to say.

She was only a little scared. And she had always been scared, coming down through this wood. She used to have to hide it from Leah, every time they wandered this way. Marty would march ahead, clutching the straps of her backpack, complaining about how slow Leah was going, when all she really wanted was to get back into the sunshine. Even now, she hurried. She skittered at the birds. Her trainers sent up puffs of earth, kept dry beneath the trees. She crushed bluebells, ants, beetles.

When she saw him, she felt a residual little flutter. The last of the butterflies, flapping around on the floor of her stomach. Maybe that was just how it went. Once you had loved somebody, you were stuck loving them, just a little, for the rest of time. He looked strange, though. Looked like somebody from a budget movie. He wore an outfit she had never seen before, urban camouflage meets RoboCop. True to his word, there was a bag at his feet.

"This is unexpected," she said. She walked—slow, now, set on steadying her breath—to meet him.

"I know," he said, generously. "I'm sorry."

"So," she said. "What's going on?"

"It's like I said. I'm leaving town. Today. And I wanted to see you."

"Where are you going?"

"I'm not sure. I'm not sure just yet. But I wanted to say goodbye."

"OK," she said. And, before she could stop herself, "Thanks."

"I liked you, Marty," he said. "That's all. I didn't want you there."

She frowned. She was careful, still, to be gentle. "I'm sorry?"

"You should stay here," he said, "for a little while."

He lifted the bag to his shoulder.

"I don't have any idea what you're talking about," she said.

He only smiled. He was backing away from her then, stepping carefully through the bracken. He touched the trees as he went.

"You'll have to live with it forever, now," he said. "Won't you? That I was the one to save you."

He turned from her, then, and she watched him moving away into the wood, slighter and smaller, until he was replaced by trunks and shadow.

She stood there dumbly for a few minutes. The mist was lifting from the lake, and she wandered down to the bank and touched her hands to the water. None of it made sense. None of it. And now she was late for Day One, and her mother—

He'd been talking about Day One, hadn't he? And it was a strange coincidence that he would decide to leave today. She had a suspicion so terrible that it didn't really worry her. That kind of thing didn't happen in the world where she lived.

All the same.

All the same, she should really get going.

What was it he had said? That he would save her?

She walked fast, at first, and then she started to run.

She arrived at the school as if moving through a dream, slow and sick with fear. Coming this way, she could see only the back of the hall. She could hear sirens close by, and coming closer. She walked around the corner of the building, and the playing fields fell into view. On the field there were two sacks, one red and one blue, fifty meters from the hall. Left from sports day, perhaps. Although sports day—that had been a good few weeks ago. She could see a group of people beyond them, moving fast, heading for the car park. The fire doors at the side of the hall hung open, banging the bricks with each burst of wind. She walked slow to the threshold.

She saw a black chain at her feet, attached to a door handle snapped clean from its frame.

The hall came into view.

She could hear a noise like crickets, and it was only when she was at the doors that she understood it was the ringing of mobile phones.

She saw the chairs upended, legs splayed like fractures. She saw the twitches of fingers and shoes. Somebody said: Please, help me. Down the stairs at the side of the stage she saw a small boy with a white T-shirt turned black.

She saw shoes and cameras, glinting on the wooden floor. She saw Rowan's holdall, set calmly in the aisle. She did not see her mother.

She was on the field and running.

She passed the sacks and saw they had clothes, limbs, faces.

She was in the car park.

"She came from the hall," the policeman said. It was true. She had come from the hall. She looked at the crowd gathering behind the police cordon. Everybody—everybody had seen it. Martha Ward. There wasn't a person in Stonesmere who didn't know her name. There wasn't a person who didn't like to see her, running on Main Street in her old Stonesmere High School T-shirt, ponytail shooting behind her like some comical sketch of speed.

That was her. Martha Ward, come valiant from the hall.

That was who she would be.

YEAR TWO

TRENT

He was back in London for only three days before they found him. He spent most of the time reading Martha Ward's testimony, and reading it again. He and Susan were noted only by parentheses.

(Pause; minor disruption in the gallery.)

They came knocking through the fug of sleep. Blue lights turned behind his curtains. For half a second he entertained resistance. A shattered window, an abseil by sheet. Puffing down Jamaica Road in his pajama bottoms. The slowest car chase in the world.

"I'm coming," he said, or something like it. His mouth wasn't yet working. He clutched his way around the bed, the doorframe, the kitchen table. He opened the door.

There were two police officers standing in the hallway. They were showered and composed. Envoys from a land of civilization. Behind them, on the stairs, the owner of the Chinese restaurant gave him a quizzical stare.

The woman held up a badge and said names he would not remember.

"It was a protest," Trent said. "It was a peaceful protest."

"Peaceful," the man said, and laughed.

"There's nothing illegal about that, is there?" Trent said.

"We're not here about the protest," the woman said. "But we appreciate your transparency."

"No," the man said. "We're here about a series of crimes, in fact. Crimes committed over the course of the last year. Theft. Criminal damage."

"I don't know anything about that," Trent said.

"We'll need to ask you some further questions," the woman said.

"Here?" he said. He was thinking of the small shames scattered around the flat. His papers, documenting the events of Stonesmere. Zombie's bed and bowls, and no cat in sight. He would need to ask for a moment, he decided, before he allowed them in.

"Not here," the woman said. "No. We'll need you to come with us."

"We'll need to collect your laptop, too," the man said. "Laptop and phone."

"What?" Trent said. "Why?"

He contemplated the guts of the things. A whole year of investigations. He realized that he did not know what they could glean from them. Could they find each comment? Each search? Or just the things he had saved? These were things he should have known. Weren't they? These were things he should have looked into.

"No," he said. "I'm afraid—I'm afraid that isn't possible."

"I'm afraid it is," the woman said. "I'm afraid it's very possible."

"Inevitable, in fact. We have a warrant for these searches, Mr. Casey. And a warrant for your arrest."

For a terrible moment he believed he would cry. He had never felt lonelier than at this threshold. He closed his eyes. The man was still talking. This section, that Act.

"Can I call somebody?" he said.

The man and woman looked at each other. They seemed sorry, he thought, and this frightened him more than anything.

"When you get to the station," the man said. "Yes."

"If you could give me," Trent said, "a few minutes—"

The man stood at the bathroom door, viciously alert, while Trent vomited. When he stood from the bowl, he felt better. He wiped the seat with a scrunch of paper. He dressed in the suit he had bought to meet Ray Cleave, and ignored the policeman's eyebrows. It would be important to look smart when he arrived at the station. It was the kind of thing Ray would do.

He had considered the suit lucky that day, though here, in the bedroom mirror, he looked shiny and sad.

"It was my mother, wasn't it?" he said.

The police officers exchanged a long, pleasureless look. He would have preferred a little sadism. It would have made it a whole lot easier to hate them.

"There'll be plenty of time to talk about that," the woman said, "when we get to the station."

The first number he tried was Ray Cleave's office. The woman who answered asked him how she could help, but as soon as Trent started to explain the situation, she informed him that he had the wrong number and hung up the phone. He tried Susan next, who was not at home; who was, Trent later discovered, confined to her own interview room, a hundred miles away, refusing to comment.

The policewoman stood beside him, a fold deepening between her eyes.

"Anyone else?" she said.

His mother arrived faster than he had thought possible. He glimpsed her, sitting in the waiting room, on his way to meet his lawyer. There was an overnight bag packed on her lap. He couldn't bear to think about what would be inside it. To imagine her trying to press it into a police officer's arms. Fresh underwear, a towel. Miniature toiletries, gathered over the years from a range of four star hotels. She did not know, any more than he did, how this thing worked.

His lawyer was not Ray's lawyer—not the compact, clever American he had seen standing beside Ray on television—but some bag-eyed man, next in line. Things might go better, the solicitor said, if he was willing to cooperate. If there were other, grander enterprises he could discuss. Anything about these conspiracy theorists—this movement, then—more generally.

No, Trent said. That was OK.

"From what I understand, Mr. Casey," the solicitor said, "it was Ray Cleave's office that offered you up."

Trent tried to tame his face, his body. If he had maintained his composure at Tim's dinner table, he could do so now.

"Ray Cleave was facing criminal charges, Trent. Harassment. Incitement. Those crimes, they're difficult to prove. But theft? Vandalism? They're slam dunks. Put away a few of the foot soldiers and keep the generals clean. The police hawk you out in public, while this Cleave fellow—"

"There's nothing I can give you," Trent said, "on Ray Cleave."

"Your fellow offender, then. Susan Purcell. Was she the instigator? Did she pressure you, perhaps, into taking the camera? She was the one to project this image, yes? At the inquest? She was a ringleader, of sorts. That's what it sounds like to me."

Trent found he was smiling. It was the kind of smile that could go either way, to laughter or tears. And he really didn't know, just yet, how it was going to go. They had done it, hadn't they? They had got to the truth, and this was what it looked like. It looked like a table bolted to linoleum. It looked like his mother, woken by an unknown number, hugging a bag of luxuries that she truly believed he could receive. It looked like claggy coffee, served in rimmed plastic cups. It looked like they had been right, but not nearly right enough.

"We were just as bad," Trent said, "as each other."

"I have to say, Mr. Casey. You're not helping yourself."

"That's OK," Trent said. "I'll be pleading guilty. If that's all right with you."

"It's no skin off my nose," the solicitor said, although he touched the bridge of his glasses, as if to check.

YEAR TWO

MARTY

The rubbish was collected by an association of bowling club members, bending tired beige knees to the streets. After the glass was swept, and the vandals charged, and 338 percent of the GoFundMe target for full repair of Main Street achieved, Stonesmere readied itself for summer.

Tourists drove tentatively into town, as if they suspected the shooter may be lurking, just out of sight. But no: the cobbled streets were still pretty and old. The lake was still beautiful, in its particular, bleak way. The shops were still pleasant enough. And it was kind, wasn't it, to visit somewhere that had suffered like Stonesmere. They were doing us a favor. If they happened to take a detour to the school—to crane through the gates, closed for the summer holidays, and speculate how it all went down—they were usually disappointed. It was an ordinary enough building. There were summer camps held within the hall, and the noise of children soared from the open doors, out across the car park.

I knew well enough that it would be my last summer in town. I wasn't ashamed by what they had seen of my body. Breasts, wrists, ribs, hips: it was nothing much. They had watched me summer after summer at the lakeside, swimming out two hundred meters, then three; returning to incredulous faces and a frightened lifeguard pacing the shore. But they had seen my face, caught in the space between his shoulder and hair. The dumb love of it.

There were some things that would never be forgiven.

When I couldn't sleep, I would run my favorite routes, the long hill out to the Sprawl or the sleepy curves of Lake View. One night, I found myself passing the house where Rowan had lived. I climbed from the bike and looked through the smeared little windows. I had this idea that we could talk, Helen and me. She would invite me in. I would thank her. She would take me to her chest and hold me like an infant. But I couldn't bring myself to do it. It wasn't like she would have answered the door, anyway.

Anoushka told us about Trent Casey's arrest. She sat at our kitchen table with his photograph face down on the table, as if this was the picture that would do the damage. She apologized, profusely, for the ambush at the inquest. A case of identity fraud, she said, which the police would be sure to add to his charges.

"It would seem," Anoushka said, "that Stonesmere was his obsession."

"It's not an obsession," my dad said. "It's a sickness. These people. They're unwell."

"Who does he live with?" I said.

"He lives alone," Anoushka said, and my dad gave a noise that said: Like you needed to ask.

"Come on, then," I said. I took the photograph from the table. Trent Casey looked back at me. I don't know what I expected. Horns, fangs. He was a little older than I was. He looked just like anybody else.

"This is the guy," I said, "who tried to dig up my mother's body?"

"It is," Anoushka said.

"They spend all of their time online," my dad said. "Don't they?

That's how they meet the others. They're online, or they're masked. And then you see them—like this."

He gestured to the photograph, and a slop of tea landed on Casey's forehead.

"He had a significant online presence," Anoushka said. "Yes."

My dad nodded, satisfied. "In real life," he said, "they're nothing."

"I'm happy to let you know," Anoushka said, "that he's pleading guilty."

"What?" I said. "Why?"

"Look at him," my dad said. "He wouldn't have the fight."

"He hasn't cared to elaborate," Anoushka said. "But this is a good thing, Marty. Whatever the reasons. It saves you—"

It saved me from any more interviews. But Anoushka, trained in delicacy, said: "Any more stress."

"How did they find him?" I asked.

"Find him?"

"How did they know it was him?"

"The other truthers," Anoushka said. "His co-conspirators, so to speak. They turned him in. By all accounts, he wasn't particularly careful. He told quite a few people what he'd done."

"These people," my dad said. "They don't even have loyalty to one another."

"Can I keep it?" I said. "The photo?"

Before she left us for good, Anoushka asked for five minutes of my time. We sat together on the front step, looking down the garden to Crag Brow. I turned my face to the sun. I sought out small, pleasant things. A warm afternoon or a walk around the lake. When they were over, I would feel undeserving, as if I should long have removed myself from their pleasure.

"Where do you go now, then?" I said. "Some other miserable family?"

"So to speak. But I'll go home first. I'll spend some time with my own."

I had never thought that Anoushka's life extended beyond Crag Brow. But there she was: returning home, welcomed into a fold of children. My face turned hot, thinking what she could say of us.

"Listen," she said. "Marty. What you said, at the inquest. It was very brave. It was a very brave, honest thing to do. But I can't help but think you should be talking to somebody. About Rowan. About everything. Is that something you would try? I'm sure it could be arranged, if you would like."

"I have my dad," I said.

"Your father, Marty—"

I had my usual defenses at the ready, a whole artillery, turned against everybody from my mother to Leah. But that day, I couldn't bring myself to do it. And I knew, as soon as the moment had passed, that I would probably never defend my dad again.

"He does love me, though," I said, and Anoushka said: "Of course he does."

We sat there a few minutes longer. If I changed my mind, I was to call her. "You must look after yourself," she said. She put her hand on my shoulder. I guessed that was about as close as she was allowed to get, being a professional and all—and Anoushka was nothing if not a professional—but before I could catch myself, I found I was holding it, clinging on for dear life, pressing her fingers to my bones.

YEAR TWO

TRENT

The judge concluded he was a low flight risk. He had neither the resources nor the contacts, the judge said, to leave the country. Trent waited to smile until he left the courtroom.

Neither the resources nor the contacts.

Awaiting sentencing, he was still quite sure Ray Cleave's people would contact him. There were days he was hesitant to look away from his phone, in case he missed the call. Tim had the grace to be away for business—away, Trent suspected, to avoid having to look at him—and Trent spent most of his time in his room, imagining how the phone call would go. You've sacrificed so much, Ray would say, in the name of the truth. Ray would have an explanation for why he had missed the Truth Rally, a sick parent or a deserving subject.

What can we do for you? Ray would say. A lawyer? Oh, have three.

They said *what?* Ray would say. That we gave you up? Trent. These people, they would say anything.

His phone did not ring. As the weeks passed, he began to accept that it never would. Ray had abandoned the Truth Rally. For legal reasons, he would no longer talk about Stonesmere on his radio show. ("Wise," Aidan said.) The blog posts on Stonesmere were quietly removed, and the comments along with them.

Trent received notification that his ownership of the Stonesmere Exposer domain would soon expire. He did not renew it.

The only person he heard from was Susan. She was preparing for her trial, she said. She would be representing herself. Just you wait! She had already uncovered some very interesting information about the judge. He read the message once, twice, and the more he read it, the funnier it got.

Only his mother came to the sentencing, and so there was nobody to look at when the judge mispronounced *GIFs*, or when he described Reddit as a chat room. He was well accustomed to loneliness, but it would have been nice. A single glance of humor.

The judge described Trent's theft of Martha Ward's belongings as an early affront in the campaign against Stonesmere. He described the damage of the graveyard at St. Oswald's as an abomination. The computer records presented in evidence attested to the fact that Trent Casey was a delusional individual, driven to criminality by a conspiracy that was misguided, at best, and sadistic, at worst. Trent Casey was sentenced to twelve years of imprisonment. He did the maths, as his solicitor had advised. Six years, then. Maybe seven. In the gallery, a few people cheered.

YEAR TWO

MARTY

didn't attend Trent Casey's sentencing, but I saw sketches of him in the dock. He looked cartoonishly timid. He wore a terrible suit. I overheard Katie Malone in the supermarket, announcing with great authority that prison wouldn't be easy for a man like Casey. Not a man that slight. That young. Katie Malone: Stonesmere's resident expert on prison relations.

That left Ray Cleave. Cleave settled the defamation suit for an undisclosed sum, which everyone in town knew to be enough money for Stonesmere Primary School never to need another bake sale. Cleave stood at the porch of some country mansion and issued an apology. The Stonesmere Massacre was not a hoax. His radio show would not mention the atrocity again. But he, Ray, was not going anywhere. Oh, no. He would continue to tell the stories they feared.

My dad called me down for the evening news, as if I hadn't been watching the whole sorry statement on my laptop. He nodded to the television, glass in his hand, and he raised his arms as if he had just scored a magnificent last-minute try.

"Stonesmere won," he said. "We won. Didn't we?"

I was working on ruining fewer days. "We did," I said. I gave him something between a high five and a hug. He returned his arms, mercifully, to the sofa. We sat there awhile, my dad texting, me watching a segment about a new addition to the local alpaca farm.

"There's a little gathering," my dad said, "down at the lake."

He nodded to his phone.

"A spontaneous kind of thing," he said. "A celebration."

I let him go, bundled into the cold with his fleece and a hip flask, and I followed him ten minutes later. I didn't want to speak to anybody, but I wanted to see them. I wanted a little proximity to victory. From Main Street I could already hear it, music and laughter, snippets of conversation slipping up the alleys. There was the hot crackle of a fire, and flames in the lake.

And everybody—everybody had come. The Boaters had offered their terrace, but people in coats spilled from the doors, out toward the water. They held cigarettes and glasses. Children darted from huddle to huddle. I saw Samuel Malone, sheltered between parents, telling a story that Leah was pretending to enjoy. I saw my dad's back, close to the fire pit, and I was surprised to find he was alone. I saw Father Wicker, trying to cajole people into prayer. The air hummed happily with news: next week's bonfire, and a tender to repair the damage done to the town hall, and how chilly it was for October. There had been a time when all I'd have wanted was to be in the heart of it. For people to open their circles and welcome me in. I hadn't even needed to want it. It was just how things were. But it was nice to stand there on the outskirts, with my hands in my pockets and nobody to entertain. It was the place where my mother had lived; the place, my mother said, where you found all the best conversations.

The fire was wobbling. It was time to go. I cut back up the alley at the side of the Boaters, the site of Larkin's fabled punch. There was a figure on the ground, settled between the restaurant bins. Larkin: as if they had built a statue to his defiance. He sat among the smells of bottle dregs and chips, his hands dangling from his knees.

I rested my body against the cold stone of the alley and sank down to the cobbles beside him.

"I'm so sorry," I said.

"Don't be."

"But really—"

"It wasn't that I didn't see the evidence," Larkin said. "I did. All the speculation online. But there was always just enough doubt, wasn't there? The CCTV, say. It could have been anybody. That was what I told myself. And that was what I told the rest of the force, too."

He was turning to me. I braced myself. But Larkin's face was still gentle. I didn't know if I was relieved or disappointed. I had been craving so long for somebody to hit me the way Rowan had done, to hit me just as I deserved. But it seemed like everybody just felt sorry for me, instead.

"I was always expecting them to call me back in," I said. "To push me a little harder. About the gun. About just how well I knew him."

Larkin held up his hands.

"If you want something to be true," he said, "badly enough—"

I knew it. There had been days when I had woken up sure I was in the audience. I sat beside my mother, begrudgingly attentive, and watched the children gambol onto the stage. I knew the dust motes, the heat, the stick of the chair. I knew my mother, mouthing every line. I knew how glad she was that I'd come along, that after all the dull rebellion, I still showed up to see her do her thing. I knew Kit's hand, small and hot in mine. I knew that I hadn't kept up the lie just because Stonesmere needed it, but because I needed it, too.

"Do you know what I found out," Larkin said, "as part of the claim? There's a whole body of these truthers—a whole school of thought— where they simply don't believe it could have happened. They say, no- body would do that. That kind of evil, it doesn't exist. That world! Their world. Right there. That's where I want to live."

"If you find it," I said, "let me know."

"I don't hold out much hope, Marty. But I'll be on the lookout."

"You're leaving?"

"For a little while. I've never lived anywhere else. It seemed about the right time. To . . ."

"To?"

"To move on."

He gave me a long, sly look. For Larkin, there would be no moving on, only the endless trudge through it.

"I'm going to climb," he said. "It's something I used to do, long be- fore they were around. I suppose now—there's nothing stopping me. I never made it farther than Europe, in the past. But this time—something bigger. I'm going to take my time. Nepal, maybe. By the spring."

"The big ones."

"The big ones, indeed."

"And when do you go?"

"I'll need to get training," he said. "I'm driving down to France on Monday. Catch the end of the season. Start off small."

There were more silhouettes on Main Street, hurrying to warm houses. At the lake, the music was louder. And Larkin was preparing to leave. He climbed to his feet and looked down at me.

"I'm glad you found me, actually," he said. "There was something I wanted to say to you. About Kit. I should have told you before. But there were times—it wasn't easy to speak about him. It still isn't easy, to be honest. Anyway. Kit. In that last year at school—your mum of- fered him a lot of kindness. There were the performances, sure. I mean,

Kit, of all people, up there onstage. And happy about it! Happy! But there were so many smaller things. That whole year—she gave him all his best moments. I won't forget that. Really. I think about it all the time. I hope you get a chance to think of her now, too."

I was arranging my voice, trying to think of something sufficient to say, when he said: "Well. Goodbye, then, Marty."

"It isn't goodbye, really," I said. "Is it? If you're coming back."

"Of course," he said. "Of course it isn't."

And he was leaving then, zipping his coat to his neck. He raised a hand just before he disappeared around the corner, and although I waved back, he didn't turn to see it. I knew, already, that Larkin's cottage was for sale. I had seen the photographs online. Every room looked the same, emptied and newly painted. There was photoshopped sunshine at the windows. It was a turnkey home, the listing said, and ready for family living.

The next summer, Larkin went missing on Kanchenjunga. There were quite a few reports in the press, items that read a lot like obituaries, testaments to how he had fought the conspiracy theorists and won. By that time, I lived in the city. I spent whole nights reading up on the mountain, everything from Larkin's route to strangers' blogs to guides on the best gear. I read it all.

Each report said the same thing: that Larkin was alone and insufficiently prepared. But I knew the man from the Stonesmere Mountain Rescue Team, who had lectured class after class on mountain safety. I knew better.

YEARS THREE
TO EIGHT

TRENT

He wrote letters for cigarettes, and he gave the cigarettes to the men who asked for them, and for the cigarettes he lived in a precarious peace, which was less peace than abject boredom.

He was in the cell for twenty-two and a half hours a day. He had not expected the landscape of prison to be quite so small. The cell included a minute television and a shelf with space for three books. He had inherited a fan the size of his palm, which he conserved beneath his bed until June, when he realized the thing was broken. The sink was a thimble, and when he washed his hands, water drenched the floor. His socks were always damp. He entertained himself with small games, the relics of a childhood spent mostly alone. He guessed offenses. He ascribed the prison decor its proper titles. The cell was painted in Sunday Gloaming. The corridors were Scrub Green. Over the winter, his skin turned Embalming White and flaked from his body.

The day he was led in, the officer saw him glance between the walls. He lifted a curtain aside and found only the toilet, bare and foul.

"What were you expecting?" the officer said.

"Are there computers?" he said. "Communal ones?"

"Communal ones," the officer said, and laughed.

"There's one or two," the officer said, "in Education. If you want to do a course."

The courses he had read about were in basic numeracy and literacy. Trent didn't imagine he would want to do a course.

"Who the fuck will you be, then," the officer said, "without the internet?"

But he was becoming somebody, stubbornly and surely. In the third year, he applied to teach literacy. Had never felt smaller, standing at the front of that classroom, trying to keep the shake from his hands. There were days when he was lampooned, when people called him a madman, a necro. Fucked any corpses recently, Casey? But other days: other days, they listened well enough. The textbooks were battered, damaged; for new books he had to speak to the right officer, who had to catch the right senior officer, who had to submit a request to the board. The board requested further details, of course, and Trent was granted paper to make his case. They wanted a case: fine, fuck them, he had the time. He spent a week refining his arguments, and the books arrived three months later.

There were other days when he was sure he would not survive the hour. He woke gasping in the night, convinced the air supply was cut and diminishing. The Stonesmere families, they had paid a prison officer. They had the money, now. They had the sympathies. He saw the room becoming smaller and closer. He would suffocate. Who would miss him? He did not call for help. He held his mouth to the corridor hatch and passed the worst of it there, sucking against the metal.

The only person to visit him was his mother. The first time she came, he refused to see her. The anger was long gone by then, but it was replaced

by something that made it harder to walk through the doors. The way
she had looked, sitting in that police station, the bag on her lap—

Or on the day of his sentencing, when they had only five accompanied minutes before he was sent down. When he asked if Tim would pick
her up, and she said: No, Trent. I don't think we'll be seeing Tim again—

And there she was, driving a ninety-minute trip on a Sunday in December, and driving right back again.

The second time, the very next week, he came ashamed down the
corridor. Even amid the bustle of a visiting Sunday, he saw her right away,
small and gray in the plastic chair. She looked—strangely, awfully—as
if she belonged there.

He sat down, and for a long while they looked at each other, each
waiting for the other to speak. One of the toggles on her coat was missing, lost in the material. She wore no makeup, and her hair was getting
longer.

"I'm sorry," he said, just as she said: "Hello."

They talked in their own ancient language, beneath the words that
were said. Yes, the prison food was revolting, and there was never any
choice; and for him, who had always been such a fussy eater. No, she
had moved from Tim's house. She was in a little cottage now, close to
the beach. It wasn't much. There were two bedrooms, at least. And she
would make it nice. She had upped her hours. She had joined a choir
for military wives. They weren't very good, no. She liked the events,
but when all was said and done, they were actually pretty awful.

All the while, he watched her. The changing lines of her face, new
or forgotten. He hoped she saw all he was trying to say.

And then, one day, she came looking different. She held a newspaper in her hands, ruffled by security and bunched back together. It was
the local *Observer*. She handed him the paper. Between each page, she
gave him an encouraging nod.

The story was printed across pages 14 to 15. "The Dead Sea." Edited, sure, but right there, in print. His mother gave a great burst of a laugh. When the room turned, she corked her hand back over her mouth.

"How?" he said, laughing too.

"I went into the office—"

"Oh, God."

"—and I told them about your work."

A few days later, he started a campaign to create the *Daily Jail*.

In the evening hours, his body unfurled. The relief of another day passed. The proximity of sleep. This particular night, he was installed in the back of Community, close to the pool tables, looking at the television. He looked at the television in prison the same way he did everything else: with his eyes passive and unfixed, so nobody could accuse him of staring at them.

And then, there: Ray! Ray Cleave, right there on the screen. He blinked his eyes into focus. Ray stood behind a kind of podium, hung with red, white, blue. There was another man, besuited, at his side, and it was this man who was speaking. The sound on the television was off, and Trent didn't want to make the request, but he stood from his chair and moved closer. He was smiling, in spite of himself. It had always been the case, hadn't it? That Ray would be fine. He wore a navy blue suit, beautifully fitted: a better suit than he had worn at the Never Surrender. When the man finished speaking, Ray smiled broadly, and Trent found he was shaking his head. Found he was clapping along with the crowd on the television. His clap was slow, sardonic. He knew that smile. Had seen it so many times, without ever appreciating what it meant.

Well. Now he knew.

This man, this speaker: Ray Cleave didn't believe a word he had said.

YEARS THREE
TO EIGHT

MARTY

The day before I left Stonesmere, a student hairdresser severed my ponytail for free. She cut it neat to the shoulders with wide, anxious eyes. "You're OK?" she said, once it was done, and I said, Yes, thank you, it was just what I asked for. And, to her credit, it was.

I didn't let my dad drive me to the city. I filled my mother's old backpack and a series of plastic bags, overspill additions, slung around my wrists. I took a late train, the first one after rush hour, thinking that the darkness may help, that it would be less painful this way. Bats fluttered under the railway bridge. The mountains watched, impassive. From the train came a last few commuters, two girls in sports kit, early weekenders with backpacks and maps. I was the only person to leave.

Approaching London, buildings closed around the compartment. I stood outside the station, watching the taxi lights, the loom of skyscrapers, restaurants full of strangers. The underbelly of the sky was orange. Somebody stumbled into my shoulder and kept on walking. I stood there for five minutes, then ten, and although nobody else trod on anything, I still had the sense that I wasn't really there, like I could scream or collapse and the most I would get would be a glance. After a while, I hauled up my bags and wiped my nose on my sleeve and found the right bus for my hostel.

I first passed the bar on a walk to the river. There was a handwritten sign in the window, warning of antisocial shifts. It was surrounded by offices, a squat doorway with a bagel counter at the threshold. It was the kind of place people came after karaoke, when there was nowhere else to go. When I interviewed for the role, the manager looked slowly down my CV. His eyes stuck on the first line, and he gave a small, unpleasant smile.

"Head girl," he said, and I nodded.

"We don't get many of those," he said. He set the paper down, and the ink sank into the previous night's spillage.

"And what," he said, "do you think you have to offer?"

I shifted on the leather stool.

"I get along with people," I said. "I mean. People like me."

"You pour them drinks," he said. "You give them a smile."

He shook my hand. His fingers were bottle-cold and crept for the wrist. I guessed I was employed.

"They'll like anyone well enough," he said.

I wasn't as bad at my job as either the manager or I had expected. A resident barman walked me through the cocktail list, talked about little flourishes, a sense of performance, the things a customer might remember. He mentored me for three weeks straight, right up until the night he offered to wait for me at the end of my shift, when I told him, dully, that it would never happen. After that, he left me to my own devices.

I didn't look for friends or lovers. If there were days when I wanted to ask Leah to visit, to invite her to the bar and make her a Ramos Gin Fizz, I always imagined the expression on her face when she saw where I lived, and stopped myself in time.

I lived on the fifth floor of a new build, in a neighborhood people asked me how to spell. There was little else I could afford. Three new trees separated my block from the next. After that, there was only concrete, glass, wire. The sky rotated from a banal summer blue to winter fog. It was tolerable enough. There were good seasons, I suppose, but good only in that they reminded me of somewhere else. The color of a particular tree along Roman Road; the reflection of this building or that, caught in a weekday walk along the canals, when the rest of the city seemed to be at work.

Every day, I thought of Trent Casey. I knew him well enough by then. I knew that he had been here before. In some strange way, I liked to think that we suffered together. I didn't have many people to speak to in those days, and every now and then I would catch myself at the kitchen drawer, holding the paring knife, talking as if he sat with me, across the table.

YEAR EIGHT

TRENT

On the day of his release, his mother waited at the prison gates. He had always imagined leaving by himself with a kind of valiant loneliness, but he had to admit it was nice to see her, standing beyond the wire. She waved, though she was the only person there. She had brought along a balloon in the shape of a 7.

"I wonder if anyone else ever bought it," he said, "for this occasion."

On the drive home, he couldn't stop looking at the horizon. He blinked happily against the colors of the countryside. "It isn't much, you know," his mother said. She had been warning him of this for years. He had asked her, many times, to describe the cottage. Tell me everything, from the moment you come to the front door. And on bad days, he would lie in his cell and travel there: he would step into the narrow hallway, hang his coat on the banister, and take a right turn. The rug beneath his feet. The snug, firelit lounge.

She turned onto the street. "This one," he said, as they passed the front door. "Right?" And she nodded, a little proud but careful not to show it.

The town had changed in the time he had been away. There were caricatures he recognized from Bermondsey, bearded men in ironic T-shirts. Interchangeable women, each pushing the same buggy. He wrote sketches about them, brief and caustic. And there were good things, too. A gallery had opened on the seafront. The leisure center had been refurbished. The town paper was having an unusual revival, petitioning long reads from journalists across the country. A decent website, too. He must have walked past the office fifty times before he went in, and when he did, a small, furious woman was sitting in the middle of the room, impatient, as if she had been waiting for Trent all along. In his arms, he carried four years' worth of the *Daily Jail*, which had come out once a quarter. Each edition featured cartoons, satirical canteen reviews, and The Outsider, a dispatch from somebody recently released.

"I'm Trent Casey," he said. "I wrote 'The Dead Sea.'"

"'The Dead Sea,'" she said. She was nodding. "You know how to write, Casey, but my God, you use a lot of words."

His first assignment was the theft of the pirate statue from outside Smugglers World. Everybody had to start somewhere.

In the second week out, he visited London. He found the Chinese restaurant busier than he had ever seen it. He hovered at the PLEASE WAIT TO BE SEATED sign, suspecting the owner might have forgotten who he was. She was not on duty, the waiter said, but he would try to persuade her to say hello. She came crowing from the kitchen with her arms open, and every diner turned in his direction.

"You!" she said. "We thought you had died."

She beckoned him between the tables, knocking edges and handbags, and he apologized his way after her. She left him in the cold of the courtyard and emerged with steaming spring rolls and a pot of tea. They sat on crates reserved for smoking staff, with plates on their laps.

"You're very gaunt," the owner said. "You look very unwell."

"Oh," he said. "Thank you."

"Eat up," she said.

He was thinking of the things Ray had said. Things that had sounded fair, when they were delivered with Ray's passion; when they were accompanied by Aidan's acquiescence. Ray, on a half-hour monologue about identikit takeouts littering the streets of London. Ray, freewheeling on the links between MSG and stomach cancer.

"Have things been good," he asked, "with you?"

"Business?" the owner said. "Yes. You've seen the flats, right? The new ones? They're building hundreds a month. The kids moving in, they're younger than you. They're hungover every Sunday and dragging themselves through the doors."

"Good," Trent said. "I'm glad to hear it."

"We're on Deliveroo," she said. "So you may still be able to order."

There was a strange rustling from behind the bins, and he turned, expecting a fox. Instead, there was a small, ragged cat. She was in bad shape, with a furless tail and sores on her belly. But she had retained her old, skeptical expression.

"Our little friend," the owner said. She snapped a spring roll and dropped half on the concrete. Zombie hunched over the scraps and started to eat. She didn't turn to Trent until she was finished, and when she did, she looked displeased. Like: What took you so long?

"This cat," Trent said. "This cat. I know her."

"We like her," the owner said. "She wrestles with the rats."

"She used to live upstairs," Trent said. "With me."

"A pet?" the owner said. She clapped her hands. "Anita wouldn't be pleased."

"No. She wasn't."

"She's been waiting, then," the owner said. "Hasn't she? She's been waiting for you to return."

In the courtyard, there was a flurry of small kindnesses, phone calls and visitors, well into the afternoon. By dusk, Trent had obtained a crate of outdated cat food, a bag of litter, a collar, a frozen half of duck, and a carrying case intended for a large dog. Leaving London, he set Zombie on the train seat beside him. She looked at him as if he was still the same person who had woken in the night to lift her from the garbage, a person capable of good things. Good servitude, at the very least. Through the twilight, he watched the people of the city moving in their flats, like so many small televisions. They cooked and ate, they spoke silently across dinner tables, they lay in stupors, holding controllers. He saw a man removing a suit jacket, with children gathered at his feet. He saw dogs on balconies, contorted bicycles, tiny, desperate gardens. The sun fell in the glass of the Shard.

Each week, he attended a writing class at the library in the Old Town, surrounded by retirees. He spoke little, but he enjoyed their conversations. He heard of their children's disappointing spouses, and the best cashier at Morrisons, and an extensive legal dispute over a prizewinning rosebush. He worked on his own copy for The Outsider. Zombie woke him each morning at dawn, with escalating acts of violence. And if there were days when he opened his eyes heavy with the banality of this life, he made himself get out of bed, down the stairs, and to the cupboard where he kept her food.

YEAR EIGHT

MARTY

Trent Casey's mother kept a cottage one block back from the beach. After Stonesmere, I went there right away, as soon as I arrived in the town. My hostel was on the seafront, wooden beds set along high, bare walls, but I left my car on their street. In the glove box I kept the paring knife. Each time I had used it—and I'd used it for some years, now—I had indulged a new, careful fantasy. Ears, tongue, eyes.

The cottage was a small clapboard building, squeezed between grander houses. It was painted a proud powder blue. Wind chimes hung above the door. A scrawny black cat stared from the windows. There were flower boxes along the ledges, shriveling into autumn. I touched the soil, the petals. I traced a finger for the cat to chase. I wiped the windowpanes and looked into their life.

He had been out for a few weeks when I arrived, and I watched him for two weeks more. There was a kind of pleasure to it, I guess. I had expected him housebound, timid, but he was out every day. He took fierce walks along the beach, his head pressed forward into the wind.

Twice he left the house with a folder of documents, and dithered out-side a concrete office block in the center of the town. He looked thin and tired, but when he sat down to dinner, there was a kind of exuber-ance in the way he lifted the cutlery, drank from his glass. I wasn't sure if prison had shrunk him or made him bigger.

I counted along to the house that shared his fence, and apologized my way inside. A lost football, I said, and peered into his garden. Somebody had just brushed the leaves. His mother was at the kitchen hob, danc-ing stupidly. I saw myself on Crag Brow in the light of a long window, licking my fingers, touching my skin. These mundane, daily things, made mortifying by scrutiny.

No ball, I said. Thanks, though.

His mother worked long hours. She left the house in a tired trench coat and returned ten hours later, when the road was quiet and dark. Each night, he turned on the hallway lights so she could find her keys. It was such a small, good thing. When I first saw it, I hoped it was a co-incidence. But he did it the next night, and the night after that; and sit-ting in the car, turning the knife in my hand, I wished I had never noticed it at all.

YEAR EIGHT

TRENT

I t was after his third writing class, returning from the library on a Tuesday afternoon, that he found Martha Ward waiting for him.

She sat on the front step, unmoving. She had a strange, sad smile on her face. He stopped dead on the pavement. She had been watching him come. She wore a rucksack and a formless jacket. Zombie sat beside her, a casual traitor.

He had never tried to find her. He had never written to her or asked how she was. The prison had offered him some miserable initiative to invite her for a visit, and he had laughed in the officer's face. It was its own kind of penance. Martha Ward, who had once occupied each of his waking hours. When he wished to suffer, he read again what she had said at the inquest.

He still woke most nights to the shame of it; to the shock of all that Rowan Sullivan had been.

And here she was.

He stepped closer.

He didn't know the woman on the steps. She was weary and still.

She was nothing like the girl in the interviews. She was nothing like the girl who had run toward the hall. The wind moved above them, unsettling the gulls. His mother's wind chimes rattled at the door, a sound he knew so well that he believed it the noise of the wind itself.

"Hello, then," she said.

He made the last few steps and sat down at her side.

"Hello," he said.

One of her fists was closed, and hidden in the fingers of the other. OK. OK, then. There was a funny side, he guessed. Seven years of glancing from trouble. He knew how an atmosphere could plummet; he knew when to leave a room. He had seen a man lose an eye to a plastic toothbrush. The wind caught Martha's hair, and it skimmed his arm. He watched the side of her face, but she stared straight ahead, out to the empty road.

"Welcome home," she said.

"How did you find me?"

"It's not like it's hard, these days. You should know."

"I suppose I do."

"How did it feel," she said, "to be right?"

He found that he was laughing, then. There had been so many months when it was all he had wanted. He would have traded time, organs. And he had done. Hadn't he? He had traded almost everything he had. Now, perhaps, he would trade all that was left.

She turned, baffled. He was shaking his head.

"That isn't quite how I think of it," he said.

"I read your statement," she said. "I finally read it. I read that you knew him."

"Rowan?"

"Yes. Rowan."

Why not tell the truth? He looked to her face. The photographs, the videos. He had believed that he knew her, and knew her well. But here there were smells, shampoo and sweat, the fake pine of a hired car. Un-filmed, her voice was quiet and flat.

"I did," he said. "A long time ago. He was kind to me, I think. That's how I remember it, anyway. My dad had just died, and we were in this strange new town, and I hated everything. But Rowan—well. I loved him, to be honest."

"I thought that, too," she said. "I thought that for such a long time."

She opened her mouth, as if she might tell him more, and closed it again. He realized that she was crying. She had been older than he had been when she met Rowan, but she had still been a child. He remembered, often, how she had looked in that very first interview. How young, and how scared. They had both been children, and when you were a child it was easy to mistake almost anything for love.

He reached for her. He could hear the sound of her breath in his ear, and within his arms was the warmth of her, warmth and damp from wher-ever she had walked. He had not been so close to somebody for many years. It occurred to him that she could still kill him, if she wished.

Would he fight? He wasn't sure. He knew that must be why she had come here.

He knew, after all, what she had been through; and she in turn knew him.

There was nobody else in the world, really, who knew him better.

YEAR EIGHT

MARTY

expected him to call the police, or else turn and run. I was braced for
fists. And instead, here we were, sitting outside the bright little house.
I had spent years imagining how it would go, but never this. The cottage, the steps. Seagulls veering in the breeze. Bony wind chimes rattling at the door. And Trent Casey beside me.

He looked about as tired as I was.

My hands were crushed close to his chest, and I could feel the rise
and fall of his skin, just there. Thinking about my mother's grave, and
what was left of my dad—thinking about Casey at the funeral, ran-
sacking my medals, toys, childhood—I clutched the knife so hard the
blade split my palm. I held a fistful of blood and closed my eyes.

I didn't know whether I was there to apologize or kill him.

I was thinking about this one line from his statement. He had been
asked to explain his connection to Stonesmere, I guess, and he'd said
something like: My mother and I struggled to settle in the town, but
Rowan Sullivan welcomed us in. I'd smiled, the first time I read it. Rowan,
welcoming. I knew just how kind he could be; and how much kinder, if

you were twelve or thirteen, in search of another father. He would welcome you warmly and wait for you to boil.

But what I thought, now, was that I wished I could have shown Trent Stonesmere myself. I had this stupid idea that we might have been friends, him and Leah and me. I had to admit—taking all the evidence into account—that he'd have made a pretty decent deer stalker. I would introduce Leah as my closest friend. We would hike together up to Old Man's Edge, boots stirring the bees. We would hunt for fairies along Crag Brow. We would brave our way through the woods to St. Oswald's, and I would show him the otters, the home of the lake gods, the place where my parents and I swam in the summertime. I doubled my grip on the knife. That he could have said it—

That there was any world in which she hadn't existed.

Trent's whole body was still. He just sat there, waiting for whatever I decided to do next.

I hadn't thought about those summers for years. Had thought about my mother very little, when it came down to it. Her death, sure, her grave; but not the stuff of her. The habits and expressions, the disappointments and quiet hopes. The stuff that makes up a person. I looked at Trent, and from the pain in his face, I had the crazy idea I could tell him those things, and he would listen.

DAY ONE

AVA

I n the greenroom, she hurried the children behind a costume rail. She rested a chair beneath the door handle and gave them a reassuring kind of nod. Among lost property and props, she gathered them into her arms. They smelled of their homes, their bedrooms and baths. They smelled, too, of her classroom; or perhaps, over the months, her classroom had started to smell of them.

"We need to be quiet," she said. "Quiet, now."

"Like in heads down, thumbs up?"

"Even quieter," she said. "Even quieter than that."

"Will we get to finish the play?"

"I don't know. I hope so."

They huddled to the wall, waiting.

"Were we brave?" Kit said.

"Yes," she said. She found his hand and took it. "Of course! Of course you were."

There was a noise outside the door. Alicia shook in her arms. She believed she could feel the girl's heart beating beneath her palm.

"Just a few more minutes," she said.

"Did someone call the police?" Alicia said.

There was another noise, closer now.

"Maybe that's them," she said. And maybe it was. She smiled at Alicia, and the exertion of it felt impossible, insurmountable, until it was on her face. It would be nice to have another adult, she thought. It would be nice to share the effort. She would have liked somebody to say: You're doing a good job.

The door lurched, and the chair fell away.

"It's OK," she said.

She spread her arms around them. She stretched every muscle in her body, trying to make herself bigger. She tried not to think of their frailty, here behind the costumes. Of what would happen next.

The door was opening.

Instead, she thought of Justin and Marty. Marty, who was not in the hall. The gift—the gift of that. Marty was elsewhere, making her mistakes, muddling on. You will be fine, Ava thought, fine and loved, and in the darkness, she began to cry.

Marty's life, a book Ava would not finish.

She said: "Don't look."

She closed her eyes.

There had been a summer when Marty was nine or ten, when Justin declared, in the middle of the night, that he was not going to work another weekend until September. Fuck it, he whispered. Fuck it.

Those—those were weekends.

On Friday afternoons, she would will that clock down like she was some kind of superhero. Like she could make it move. By four p.m., they were cycling out to St. Oswald's, where the church teetered into the water. In an old rucksack, Justin packed crisps and wine and plastic cups, and they implored Marty to pedal faster, so the wine would still be cold when they arrived. Ava lay on a towel, the grass warm beneath

her back, a book in her hands. If she squinted, she could see the splash-
ing of them above her pages, and pride shifted in her stomach. My husband. My daughter. Happiness seized her from the page. She stepped
into the shallows, staggering on the peaty bed, and let the water engulf
her legs. "Come on," Marty called, and Justin shouted: "Slowpoke." Low
sun scattered over the ripples cast by her body. She ducked beneath
the surface and swam deep to where the water chilled, blackened,
moving slick, easy, expecting to touch a leg or a toe. When she emerged,
they would be before her, close enough to kiss. Any moment—any
moment now.

ACKNOWLEDGMENTS

The support behind *Girl A* changed my life, and means the world to me. Thank you to the readers, bloggers, book clubs, retailers, booksellers, librarians, and journalists who held the book in their hearts and spread the word.

To Juliet Mushens: you've made the most fantastical dreams come true. You're a life force, a brilliant friend, the very best in the business. Thank you to Jenny Bent, my great champion across the pond. Thank you, too, to the Mushens Entertainment family: Liza DeBlock, Rachel Neely, Kiya Evans, and Catriona Fida.

Thank you to my editors, Julia Wisdom at HarperFiction and Laura Tisdel at Viking. Your care, cleverness, and insight have made this book all it is. A huge thank-you, too, to Phoebe Morgan, who worked on this book for so long, with such grace and skill. How I'll miss you.

There are so many brilliant people behind every novel! Thank you to my incredible publishing teams, and particularly to Claire Ward, Fliss Denham, Abbie Salter, Sarah O'Shea, Lizz Burrell, Kim Young, and Jenn Houghton.

Thank you to my international publishers and co-agents, who work every day to share stories across the world.

Many things happened during the writing of this novel, some wonderful, some glum. My friends and family have been there all along. A special thank-you to Paul Smith, James Kemp, Jessie Burton, Ella Therrien, Lauren Garvey, Claire Fellows, Sophie and Jim Roberts, Fiona McKenzie, Rosy Cheetham-West, the Trinick family, Lisa Erlandsson, Rachel Edmunds, Gigi Woolstencroft, Sarah Rodin, Anna Abraham, Kate and Lesley Gleave, Elizabeth and Paul Edwards, the Parker-Pickards, Marina Wood, Rachel Kerr, Matthew Williamson, and Ruth Steer. Your company and humor made every day brighter.

To my parents: you've supported me through everything, the good and bad. Thank you for your boundless love, and for always moving *Girl A* onto a more prominent shelf.

And to Woody, Rich, and Josh: without you, this would all be so joyless. I love you.